POOR LITTLE RICH GIRLS

POOR LITTLE RICH GIRLS

Moss Murray

Book Guild Publishing
Sussex, England

First published in Great Britain in 2011 by
The Book Guild Ltd
Pavilion View
19 New Road
Brighton, BN1 1UF

Typesetting in Baskerville by
Keyboard Services, Luton, Bedfordshire

Printed and bound in Great Britain by
CPI Antony Rowe

A catalogue record for this book is available from
The British Library

ISBN 978 1 84624 536 7

1

The newly-created Dame Penny Welling was determined to look like a duchess as she sought to persuade the British government to invest millions of pounds in the British tourism industry, which they regarded as unimportant, instead of a major export earner. She had long ago learned that making a striking first impression could be all important, and the way she could afford to dress as a multi-millionairess made it easy for her to look eye-catching. She had become used to the looks of envy and admiration that her couture clothes, magnificent diamonds and expensive furs aroused in other women. She did not always understand that much of their fury was because they were in their forties, fifties and sixties and she was just twenty-five, and also an attractive and sensual young lady with an hour-glass figure. Her obvious wealth made her a magnet for men of all ages, but she knew how to ward off the Lotharios.

She exemplified the irrepressible desire of every woman for beauty and the chance to be extravagant. She could turn from warm to cold in an instant, flirt one minute and reject with iciness the next. All that mattered to her was being in control, and getting her own way. She accepted that she was a bitch, and that almost any man would adore sharing her bed. But few did. She was happily married to a man twice her age. Her full and provocative lips were mostly for his mouth only, except when she deliberately locked her dark, shining eyes onto a man and made him tremble with excitement, little realising that all she intended was to find out whether he might be helpful to her latest business ambition. Mostly she was pitiless. All that mattered was being the winner. Her relentless pursuit of money and wealth was confirmed by the empress-size solitaire diamonds that blazed on each hand. One was a thirty-five carat square cut which had been bought for her at Van Cleef and Arpels in Monte Carlo by a millionaire financier as her engagement ring. Sadly they never married as he died in a night-time car crash

1

on the Corniche three days before their wedding. She had inherited more than $35 million from his estate. The second ring was a present from her husband who had inherited it from his American heiress wife who also died in a car crash, but in England where they lived. It was pear-shaped and weighed thirty carats. Both gems were insured for large sums, but were probably worth more.

Even after several years of living in a world of great wealth and success she still regarded the two gems as her lucky charms. She was not only expert at making money on a grand scale from property developments, but had pocketed millions from leaked investment opportunities. She insisted she never gambled, except on certainties. Her collection of banking friends and others with inside knowledge simply made it easy. One of these coups began when Penny received a phone call from an American banker alerting her that a small oil company in eastern Europe had struck a new rich field which would send its shares soaring skyward when an announcement was made. He urged her to empower him to invest £1million for her. She agreed. Six days later her £1million investment was sold for just under £2million. That was the world in which Dame Penny moved. With part of her massive gain she bought two Renoirs at London auctions. Although she never publicised the fact, Dame Penny was also generous with her donations to charities, and her cheques were often for four, sometimes five figure sums. In the mid-1960s these were vast sums of money.

However, her wealth and generosity were balanced by her steel-sharpened tongue with which she whipped any woman who earned her displeasure or a man she was determined to humble. If someone had to be destroyed before she could be victorious that, to her, was what happened to losers in a commercial war. To her they were expendable, like front line infantrymen. Nor did she believe in runners-up.

Now her target was to persuade the Prime Minister and his advisers from the Treasury of the importance of backing the British tourist industry which had elected her to lead them in a campaign to encourage more international tourists to Britain, and the British to take their holidays at home. She had spent an entire fortnight at daily meetings with Sir Robert Flint, the Home Office's representative on the committee which had been

2

set up by the Prime Minister to advise on the future of the tourist industry, and where she was now both vice-chairman and its public spokeswoman. She had earned a reputation for being a woman with power, determination, and immense ability. The Prime Minister had decided to woo her and her talents while encouraging her and her wealthy husband to donate some of their joint millions to keeping him in power. Both had agreed to make substantial contributions, but Penny had demanded a near cast-iron assurance that their contribution, plus the time she was prepared to devote to the country's tourist industry, would be publicly recognised and rewarded. Her attitude was that while cheques from herself and her husband totalling £50,000 hardly made a dent in their bank balances, there were few men or women who could match such donations. Confidentially she made it known where it mattered that she would not be satisfied with public praise for her work and achievements; only deeds would be acceptable. If the PM thought her brains might be worth more than her money, he needed to realise they would not come cheap. She wanted to be a Dame.

He and Penny were both aware that one of the biggest problems facing the tourist industry was that many hoteliers, both large and small, were doing well in the postwar era as families began to stretch their legs and take their first holidays for more than two decades whether at home or overseas. As owners of hotels, or boarding houses, they saw little reason for changing the ways that were earning them high profits. They were unenthusiastic about what might happen if that Welling woman had her way. But Penny had not risen from the bottom to the very top to be thwarted by four or five business fuddy-duddies, as she thought of them. One journalist had described her as someone who 'has moved from a semi into outer space. She is a modern Venus who enjoys acting like an Amazon'.

It was accepted that sooner rather than later she would have to receive the title of Dame which she had demanded, and the Queen was happy to recognise her talents in her Birthday Honours List. Numerous men of power learned that once they fell under her spell they were as helpless as sailors who heard the call of the sirens. Now she and her companions on the tourism committee were at the House of Commons for their meeting with the Prime Minister and members of the Treasury in the small boardroom that was part of the PM's suite of offices. With her were Sir William Hackett who, in name only, was the chairman of the committee, and Reginald Houndsditch, MP, the PM's representative on the committee and Sir Robert Flint, a top civil servant. The four of them were driven to the Commons in her Rolls. The policeman on duty had been alerted of their arrival and directed her limousine to a reserved parking space. His salute was to Penny rather than her companions, and no wonder when she possessed all the attractions of youth, plus beauty and the kind of wealth that could afford a sable coat.

It was still hanging loosely around her shoulders as she stood up to speak after the Prime Minister had introduced her as probably the most successful businesswoman in Britain, adding, 'We could not have a more impressive ambassador for the country's tourism industry. Gentlemen, Dame Penny Welling.'

She began, as she had warned her colleagues she intended, with shock tactics: 'In a nutshell, gentlemen, the British tourism industry is heading for bankruptcy. It has its head in the sand and is being outmanoeuvred by its continental rivals. Thanks to massive financial assistance from other governments, their competitors are surging ahead with modernisation, training programmes and an understanding that he who dares wins. They are winning and we are stagnating because they understand tourism can be a major source of export incomes, and we do not.'

She recalled that on several occasions during her official visits overseas she had been asked why Britain was so good at winning wars and so poor at winning the peace. 'On the first occasion, I hesitated longer than is normally my habit before explaining that we are slow starters, but successful sprinters when we see the winning post. I only wish that were true of the British tourist industry which may give the impression of being successful, but in truth is facing a parlous future. It needs an injection of public money totalling many millions of pounds which should reflect a determination to face the future. Nothing less will have any lasting impact.'

She suggested that any government money should only match whatever sums individual companies were prepared to invest in their own survival, whether they were one or five star properties. In some cases the government might be matching several million

pounds and in others only a few thousand. All had their part
to play. She sat down with a pre-agreed peroration: 'One last
word, Prime Minister. I realise that as a businesswoman who
has not been unsuccessful, I am used to making quick decisions
that are not always possible for you or your colleagues. Nevertheless
time is vital. So much needs to be encouraged, and quickly,
otherwise it may be too late for us to catch up with our European
and worldwide competitors. Several small nations are already
expecting their own government's investments in tourism to see
them become one of the top three industries for export earnings.
Please, sir, make your motto – "massive assistance in the quickest
possible time".'

Dame Penny sat down not to applause but a compliment from
the Prime Minister who told her: 'I am sure my Treasury
colleagues will have been impressed by the vigorous word picture
you have drawn and presented to us. It would be unwise of me
to anticipate the advice which the government will receive, but
I shall encourage them to be as generous as possible, but that
is more a wish than a promise of what might be forthcoming.
I can make no forecasts, but I like to think that help could
soon be at hand. But you may have to be more patient than,
so my informants tell me, is the pace at which you speed towards
your own commercial goals.'

It was left to the member of parliament, Reginald Houndsditch,
to sum up and urge the members of the Treasury to realise
how fortunate the tourism industry was to have the near constant
services of Dame Penny. 'But she is a very impatient lady and
can become intolerant of other people's slowness compared with
her own sense of urgency. I have learned to respect her ability,
and agility to move from one topic to another without a moment's
hesitation. For this reason alone I urge the Treasury to make
their decisions as rapidly as possible. Speed is essential, and so
is generous government assistance. Much of the tourist industry
is teetering towards a crisis and needs to be thrown a lifeline
which will enable people like Dame Penny to encourage hoteliers
and others to grab the lifeline that hopefully will be extended
to them. And, finally, thank you Penny for your dynamism. You
may not always be the easiest of ladies to work with, but they
don't come any better.' There was a hear, hear from Sir William
Hackett, the committee's chairman.

While Penny politicised and travelled throughout Britain and around the world as Britain's recognised, though unofficial, ambassador for tourism, she was also grooming her protegée, twenty-year-old Marianne Wilkinson, to take over the running of her growing property empire, Penny Pincher Properties. Marianne was overseeing rebuilding more than fifty bombed out properties in London into a series of one-room flatlets for some of the tens of thousands who were crying out for a roof over their heads at a time when demand far outweighed supply. Result? Women like Marianne and her boss could demand and obtain weekly rentals that their tenants could only just afford providing they cut down on food and utilities. On average each property now consisted of fifteen flatlets and a total of more than seven hundred which brought in an annual income of more than three hundred and fifty thousand pounds at a time when few shop girls or typists were earning much more than twelve pounds a week. Such was the demand, if one tenant failed to pay their weekly rent there were three more waiting to pay a higher rental in order to move in.

At the same time Dame Penny and her youthful and ruthless assistant were snapping up several stately homes and country estates from hard-up aristocrats who could no longer afford the upkeep of historic homes that had been in their families for centuries. Once planning permission was obtained, Marianne supervised their conversions into large luxurious apartments which were quickly snapped up by the new rich who were cashing in on the hundred and one shortages that still persisted. With commission on sales plus a salary of £25,000 plus expenses and her own car, she was reckoned to be one of the highest paid women in the capital. Architects, surveyors and ordinary workers learned to fear her verbal explosions because there was no appeal against anything she decreed; out of hearing she had been described as having 'the venom of a viper'. Victims were humbled and finally submitted to her onslaught for failing to measure up to the high standards she set.

To give Marianne added authority whether meeting senior executives or lowly paid staff, Dame Penny presented her with one of her cast-off, but expensive mink coats. This, together with the way she could now afford to dress, ensured that women she employed, although twice her age, were forced to treat her with respect, and fear. She insisted on being addressed as Miss Marianne.

Slowly the signs of a wind of change began to blow as memories of the recent conflict with Nazi Germany and Japan were being despatched to the waste bins of history. After a forecast of at least three million unemployed, the total now seemed to be steadying around the two-and-a-half million mark. A new generation was starting to flap its wings, but those on the lower rungs continued to find life a struggle. However, Marianne was finding it increasingly easy to persuade families who were growing wealthier by the hour to spend tens of thousands of pounds on a four-bedroom apartment that had once been the vast ballroom of an eighteenth-century stately home where kings and queen had often stayed. Surrounding the previous mansions were acres of grounds that were open to all the new owners of the luxurious conversions. Although her work involved working nearly a seven-day week travelling in her own new car to half a dozen reconstruction sites, it also meant that her salary was now above £30,000 a year, plus commissions from every luxury apartment she sold. She averaged a fourteen-hour day, but without a man in her life she was able to devote every hour to Penny Pincher Properties. In turn, Dame Penny could spend her time justifying her damehood, while her partner in the business, the fabulously wealthy Rachel Simon, spent much of her time speaking to one of her stockbrokers deciding what to buy or sell, or playing with one of her constant stream of toy boys on whom she spent thousands of pounds making sure they dressed to a standard she regarded as the norm for someone whose mother had been part of one the families known as the Gnomes of Zurich. On her death she had willed her entire fortune to her only daughter, Rachel, who once told a Fleet Street columnist that 'no matter how much I spend I am always wealthier at the end of the day than I was when it started thanks to worldwide investments'. Marianne accepted that she was unlikely ever to reach such heights as either of her bosses, but her bank account already showed a credit balance of almost six figures and she still lived by herself in a two-bedroom apartment in Knightsbridge. Known as the ice princess, she did not forget that royalty did not mix with commoners.

The more stately homes she bought and converted the more she mixed with hard-up members of the aristocracy. Her ruthless ultimatums did not make her acceptable into their society, but it did mean more money in her bank. She had long ago ceased to worry about the aristocratic families who were being forced to sell their centuries-old homes because they found it impossible to adjust to changing times, and had forgotten that even the deepest wells could run dry. They fought her for as long as they could not because they thought they could win, but just to show this snotty-nosed upstart that breeding was more important than money. Finally, however, they were forced to bow to her threats which led to the young twenty-eight-year-old viscount who had inherited and gambled away the family estate and other treasures being forced to raise the white flag. Their Leicestershire property passed to Penny Pincher Properties for less than half what they had originally asked. She had broken his, and their, resistance by issuing an ultimatum that unless her final offer was accepted within the next hour, it would be reduced by one thousand pounds for each subsequent minute. Knowing the millions at her disposal had sapped all resistance she then insisted that the magnificent library with its 20,000 books be included in the sale, but she would increase her offer by a further one thousand pounds. Set in thirty acres of grounds, Marianne described the Grade II listed building in her promotional publicity as 'an historic castle that has been transformed into apartments of such distinction that new owners consider themselves aristocrats without a title. Many of its walls are four feet thick.' Once the contract was signed, but subject to planning permission, she called a meeting of the architects and builders and gave them her instructions as to how she wanted the building to be converted, yet preserved. No one queried her orders and she headed for the local country house hotel where she had been staying. She decided to have dinner in her room, watch television, and head back to London in the morning. She phoned her office in London and talked to her own PA, Anne Bradley, a woman in her forties who had decided that retirement did not suit her and knew that whenever Marianne was away she would be in charge of the office, and was to rule the other three girls so that they were left in no doubt that slovenliness of any kind, whether in their work, their manners or their appearance, would not be tolerated. When Mrs Bradley told her boss that all was quiet, Marianne responded, 'It won't be once I get back in the office tomorrow morning. I have a mass of work for you all.'

She had already showered and was in her silk pyjamas and wrapped inside the hotel's bath robe when her phone rang and reception informed her that a gentleman from the castle was downstairs and wanted to see her. Thinking it was one of the architects she had him sent up to her room. To her surprise it was the the young aristocrat who until a couple of hours earlier had been the owner of the property she had purchased on behalf of her two millionairess partners.

Marianne had already rejected his invitation for dinner to show, as he had put it, there were no hard feelings. Knowing his reputation as a bully and womaniser she was certain that his appearance in front of her was going to be a problem that she was far from certain she could solve. The look on her face was a mix of horror, surprise and disbelief as he pushed into her bedroom, and slammed the door shut. Using the voice he always used when talking to servants he shouted, 'I am not in the habit of having my advances refused, or having my face slapped. You may have succeeded in winning a financial victory, but when it is my body against yours there is no contest. I intend to enjoy your nubile body which has excited me since we met. You have two choices; either I rape you, or we make love. After you have satisfied me we shall go our separate ways, but you will never forget the man who conquered you.'

He began to undress, and for the first time in her young life Marianne was physically afraid. 'Let us talk and enjoy our time together,' she suggested, smiling for the first time. 'I am beginning to have second thoughts about you. You are a man who likes to assert himself as men should do whether in or out of bed. That is something I admire. You can be certain there will be no need to rape me. I intend to enjoy our encounter and so, I hope, will you. Strong men usually have the gentlest touch. So let us open your champagne, find out more about one another and then enjoy what pleases us both. It is going to be much better than spending the evening alone. Perhaps you will stay and have dinner with me and, who knows, enjoy our pleasures for a second time.'

While he was congratulating himself on the ease with which

he had humbled the bitch who had bullied him into surrender, insulted his mother and taken unfair advantage of the loss of the fortune he had gambled away. Marianne's mind was working overtime to find a way to humiliate this pompous pauper who still regarded her as occupying a position in society far beneath his own. Somehow she had to find a way to deny him the pleasure of her body.

She untied the towelling belt of her robe so that he could stare at her nakedness which he was hungry to humiliate and punish with a weapon – his manhood – which could either inflict damage or be nursed into providing the ultimate delight. He was convinced his physical strength was making the bitch submissive because she sensed she would be forced to make an abject apology for her earlier rudeness to him and his mother. He intended to slap her face harder than she had slapped his earlier in the day.

He was already savouring the pleasures of vengeance and retaliation. He wanted to feel her excitement as he first toyed with her before thrusting himself inside her with the savagery of a man forcing a whore to suffer physically for the financial disaster this bitch, who was now at his mercy, had inflicted upon him. He wanted to hear her scream with pain as he pushed deeper and deeper into her delicate anus and made sure she could see the smile of revenge on his face.

But Marianne's scheming mind decided that her only slight chance was to present herself as a willing supplicant and, perhaps, encourage over-confidence and carelessness.

'Would you mind if we smoked a cigarette while drinking the champagne?' he decided rather than asked. 'By that time we shall be on the same sexual wavelength.'

She admitted, 'I never thought I would feel the urge to stoke up your fires, but mine are equally ablaze and ready to receive you and satisfy your natural manly cravings.'

Her tormentor showed his strength by using his powerful hands to draw the champagne cork out of its bottle. She apologised that she could not offer him champagne flutes, but as hers was a double bedroom she knew there were two toothbrush glasses in the bathroom. At least, she joked, they were not plastic. She was also aware that there was a phone in the bathroom. Once inside, she locked the door, phoned reception

10

and said there was an intruder in her bedroom and she needed two male members of staff to come up immediately while she dialled 999.

'You bitch,' he shouted while banging on the locked bathroom door in his frustration of being denied the pleasure of treating her like a common whore as he intended. His fury only increased as for the second time in a single day he had been out-manoeuvred by a girl who was nothing more than a rich bitch. As soon as she heard members of the hotel staff enter the bedroom she reappeared and quickly covered her body in the towelling robe and ordered them to keep him locked in a windowless room until the police arrived. 'You need to be taught a lesson,' she mocked. 'In future you will know better than to challenge a modern Amazon. Now you will pay the price with public humiliation in the courts, and the likelihood of a prison sentence.'

However, she was not to enjoy that satisfaction. Although she gave evidence against him, the local magistrates were friends of his family and, while finding him guilty, accepted his defence that she had agreed to his request for sex, but had then changed her mind. He was let off with a caution and fined £100 which he could ill afford.

The day after the incident Marianne drove back to her office in the City where she immediately began dictating a series of letters alternately to the two shorthand typists so that each could check her notes while she dictated the next letter to her colleague. She quickly learned that neither had shorthand speeds that enabled them to keep up with her. Forced to accept that she had no alternative but to work with the tools available, she slowed her rate of speaking. What should have occupied no more than twenty minutes took more than an hour before she decided to dictate the rest of her letters to Mrs Bradley, including those to her two senior partners reporting on the progress made and others to the firm's architects and solicitors, all with the proviso that nothing would be finalised until the local council had authorised the conversions. When all the letters she had dictated to her two young typists were presented for signature full of errors and needing to be retyped, they were warned: 'Neither of you leaves here this evening until I am satisfied with the letters you both type.' Mrs Bradley could hear the explosion when it erupted and was not surprised when she was called into her boss's office and Marianne immediately began dictating the first drafts for the two brochures that would require writing, designing and printing in advance of the final agreements.

It was past eight before she allowed the typists to go home.

2

Dame Penny decided to spend three days learning why the Lake District was such a jewel in Britain's tourism crown. And whether the facilities it offered matched the beauties that nature had bequeathed. As she wanted to be unrecognised, she booked into a country house hotel close to Lake Windermere and signed the visitor's book, Penny Pincher. It was out of season, but the weather stayed beautiful, and she quickly learned to enjoy wearing heavy walking shoes and the long sheepskin coat she bought locally. She only wore one diamond ring and this became a plain gold band as she revolved the gem out of sight. Its true beauty was only on view at dinner in the restaurant. She hoped to remain inconspicuous. She told the receptionist that she would like to see as much of the area as possible during her three days' stay, and could she recommend a car hire driver who knew the area and would also be pleasant company?

In his thousand-pound Rover saloon which had earned its keep several times over throughout every high season in the Lake District, and for much of the rest of the year, Joe Stelling drove Penny round Lake Windermere as well as Grasmere, Kendal, plus the challenging Scafell. They shared lunches in a couple of the best pubs he knew, and where the local brew was tasty without being too potent and she ordered a half-pint for herself and a lemonade for him. He had an abundance of tales about the raw beauty of Flamborough Head and his revelation that the area possessed the most northerly outcrop of chalk in Britain. He helped her stagger to the top of a couple of 1,000 feet climbs where she was rewarded with a feeling of freedom only found in such sanctuaries of peace. She discovered ancient villages with strange-sounding names as well as village greens dotted with old market crosses. She was delighted to hear about a clock that announced 'Time is Short; Eternity is Long', and decided to reveal its existence at her next committee meeting as an example of what they should be promoting.

However, she disappointed her driver when she admitted that she thought Stamford Bridge was a football ground in London rather than, as he explained, the scene of a decisive victory in the nation's history when King Harold defeated the Norse invaders and ended the Viking hold on Britain. But she laughed while drinking her half-pint one lunchtime when told of a flat race which was not only famous for being possibly the oldest in the country, but also the weirdest because the prize for coming in first was often less than for the horse that finished second. He explained that the first prize was set, while the second was determined by the number of horses entered.

Each evening she returned to her four-star-plus hotel where after a half-hour soak in the bath, she enjoyed a half bottle of champagne in her suite that helped transform her back to being the Dame Penny she preferred. At dinner each evening she wore a different gown, much to the consternation of other guests who sat down in jumpers or twin sets. Although she enjoyed her half-pints at lunch, they did not compare with the half-bottles of fine clarets the hotel had to offer. During her last dinner the waitress who served her admitted that she never stopped admiring her diamond ring which was bigger than any she had ever seen. Penny did not reveal that it weighed thirty carats as she was convinced that it would mean nothing to her admirer who back in the kitchen described it to the head chef as 'bigger than a robin's egg'. Later she could not resist asking, 'Are you a princess?'

'Something like that,' Penny whispered, and left her a five pound note after breakfast on the day of her departure.

Her final surprise came when Joe, her driver, was on the last mile before arriving at the rail station and she was nearly jolted out of her seat, not because the car had gone over a pothole, but when he told her, 'I know who you are, madam. It took me a whole day to place you and suddenly over supper I saw your picture in a magazine and pointed you out to my wife as the lady I was driving. May I get a porter to take a photograph of you getting out of my car with me holding open the door?'

'Of course, Joe, if you think it will help your business, as you have helped mine.' And for the first time since arriving in the Lake District she was wearing her fur coat.

Back in London she had a meeting with Sir Robert Flint,

head of the government department responsible for tourism in his office in Whitehall and brought him up to date with her thoughts about the slow Treasury response to her plea for money for British tourism. In reply he quipped, 'Nothing ever happens quickly in a government department.' All he really wanted to do was look at her. Each time they met, her physical effect upon him increased. He was yearning to touch her, yet his long civil service training demanded he showed restraint. He knew it could be disastrous for his career if she showed any displeasure at his approach, and problematical if she flashed a green signal. She seemed to regard him as someone who might never be admitted into her rarefied world, but now tantalised him with her hypnotic perfume while he wondered whether he could ever break free from his civil service cage. Once when he had suggested a change of emphasis in part of one of her speeches, her reaction had been to lean across and squeeze his hand and tell him 'that is brilliant. I don't know what I would do without you.' Yet he remained convinced that to her he was nothing more than a pawn on the chessboard she had been given by the Prime Minister, although Penny herself believed partners in a marriage who always remained faithful were as rare as needles in a haystack.

She was now travelling thousands of miles not only throughout Britain but around the world selling what her country had to offer, while constantly gaining an insight into what was happening in other countries that were also seeking to sell their tourist attractions. Mostly their standards of service and hospitality were better, their streets cleaner, their hotels refurbished and modernised, and they had large sums of government money to spend. The results were powerful magnets that attracted many more tourists than were being wooed by Britain's memorable history, historic sites, pageantry and its Royal Family. Everywhere business was picking up as people started to spend again, but although profits were rising there was too little sign of economic investment, and almost none at all by British hotels except a few in the five-star category. Few hoteliers were looking into their crystal balls. If they did they would see only dark clouds. Sadly they were hypnotised and revelling in the constant ringing of their tills which they were convinced would last forever.

When she authorised a survey of more than fifteen hundred

overseas visitors and their thoughts on Britain as they departed to return to their own countries, more than fifty per cent complained of poor service, dirty streets, unfriendly taxi drivers and, worst of all, out-of-date hotel facilities. It was this report that had encouraged her to suggest to the Prime Minister and his Treasury advisers that every hotel, irrespective of size or location, should be offered tax subsidies which would be the equivalent of a fifty per cent government contribution to whatever sums they were prepared to spend on refurbishing and modernising their internal and external facilities, including staff training and vastly-improved cuisine. Three days later she was forced to remember an expression she had used when she had been speaking to him in his chambers at the House of Commons that 'a smile can be worth ten thousand pounds in repeat foreign business'.

She had hailed a taxi, said good morning to the driver only to have her politeness ignored. Seated in the back she gave him the address to which she wanted to be taken, but received no reply. When she asked whether he did not speak to his passengers there had been still no reply. Finally, she had asked whether he expected a tip, and as she was wearing one of her expensive coats she was convinced he knew he could be onto a good thing. When they arrived, she paid her fare, but did not offer a tip, and informed him, 'I am the government's overseas ambassador for tourism. I shall be reporting you to Scotland Yard, not for your bad driving, but your bad manners.'

And she did.

Shortly afterwards when she was preparing for her visit to Germany her husband decided not to accompany her. He explained he tired easily, but believed a few days' rest, and being looked after by Sarah, their long time maid and housekeeper, would see him restored to his old liveliness. Penny promised to telephone him each evening, while she set about encouraging more Germans to visit Britain, while also finding out why Germany was doing so much better than Britain on the postwar road to recovery. As Penny put it to her husband: 'I want to get more German bums on seats on aircraft heading for this country.'

To Sir Robert Flint she insisted her schedule should include two nights in Berlin and two in Munich where she wanted private dinners with the general managers of the hotels where they would be staying, and also that their party should include Kimberley, a secretary in his department who by now she regarded as her own secretary-cum-maid. She knew that because of her near ambassadorial status he was unlikely to challenge her request. Kimberley was thrilled to learn that once again she would be travelling with Dame Penny and Sir Robert, although he hardly noticed her except to give orders. He tolerated her presence, while Dame Penny introduced her to a world she never knew existed. Back in her office the tales she told about working for a multi-millionairess gave her a feeling of superiority over her colleagues whose work was always routine. What Kimberley did not appreciate was that Penny simply found her useful.

As soon as they arrived at their deluxe hotel in the heart of the western section of the former German capital, Penny instructed Kimberley to collect any messages and bring them to her suite where she could unpack her suitcase and press the suits she was planning to wear while in Berlin. She knew Kimberley relished being able to feel the touch of silk and the warmth of furs which until then had been unknown to her. She also warned during the first time they travelled together: 'Look after me as I expect to be looked after and you could travel the world, but let me down even once and it will be goodbye.' From then onwards Kimberley knew how tenuous her new life was.

Among the messages was a note from Herr Julius Rheinhardt, confirming their dinner that evening and suggesting they meet in the main bar at eight o'clock. A second from Munich confirmed her suite reservation and also that the owner of the hotel was looking forward to greeting her. A third acknowledged a press interview at the Berlin hotel at ten the following morning.

The three of them lunched in the hotel's coffee shop and Sir Robert reminded her that at two o'clock a car was coming from the British embassy to take them on a tour of the city. The first shock for Penny as they were driven through west Berlin was the number of streets and buildings that had been destroyed by Allied bombings and heavy Russian artillery as the Red Army tore the heart out of German resistance before systematically pulverising whole districts until they were unrecognisable. East Berlin had suffered an even worse onslaught, but in the west there were more than just signs that universities, academies, research institutions and many world-renowned German museums were all rising from the rubble. For example, the number of hotel beds had passed the 20,000 mark, and was still rising. The city was planning its own film festival and an international motor show as well as building an International Congress Centre that promised to be the most modern in the world. They spent half an hour in the KaDeWe department store on Wittenbergplatz, mostly in the gourmet department on the sixth floor where Dame Penny bought three sealed tins of Russian Beluga caviar, two large sizes and one smaller for Kimberley. Back at their hotel Kimberley was dismissed to her room and told to wait until Dame Penny sent for her, while Sir Robert, who was to escort her to dinner was asked to restrict himself to polite diplomatic conversation while she probed for answers from the hotel manager to questions she intended to ask. 'Call for me in my suite at eight o'clock,' she instructed.

Ten minutes later Kimberley was in her suite having been forced to abandon the tussle she had been having with herself in deciding whether she should open her caviar now or wait until she returned home. Her present had cost more than she earned in a month. She was to told to 'run my bath, but not too hot, and while I am soaking, put an iron over my bright purple evening gown with the halter neckline, and get out a bra and the pair of shoes that is an exact match to the dress. Have a brush and comb ready for my hair, but don't touch my crocodile vanity case with my jewellery and money. I'll decide which gems to wear after you have gone to have supper.' Half an hour later Kimberley was still pressing the dinner gown Penny was confident would excite the juices of her German host, probably Sir Robert, too. Kimberley, who was now on her fifth trip with Penny, apologised for still ironing her dress but it was so delicate and beautiful she dared not allow the iron to be too hot. She could not resist adding: 'You are going to look irresistible tonight, madame.'

Penny ignored Kimberley's flattery and told her to get herself some supper and buy a half bottle of wine which she would pay for.

Once Kimberley had curtsied and departed, Penny opened her crocodile vanity case and spent the next twenty minutes deciding which jewellery to wear that would dazzle her host into understanding the power she wielded. For different reasons she had never allowed Kimberley to see the jewels she carried with her, only what she wore. The temptation might prove too much for a young girl who was forced to spend every penny she earned. The gap between them was not so much unbridgeable, but unthinkable. Instead, she would have to be content with a gift of fifty pounds when they headed for home.

Dame Penny and Sir Robert found their host waiting for them at a reserved table in the far corner of the large bar where they could talk with little interruption except from the constant attention of the waiters. At first Herr Rheinhardt appeared determined to show his guests that the British and Germans had much in common, and began talking about the weather, and agreed that in Germany it was just as unreliable as in their country. However, speaking for himself, he found the weather a boring subject because there was nothing they could do to change it. Most Germans preferred to spend their time making decisions on matters over which they had some control.

Penny countered: 'The weather is never regarded as boring in Britain. To us it is the easy way to break down barriers, and create a subject on which everyone will have an opinion, but seldom a disagreement. Rain or shine are topics that make everyone feel equal.'

The manager, sensing that he was going to have a very interesting evening with this quite beautiful young English lady, was already resenting her insistence upon being accompanied by an escort. He challenged her: 'Surely you are not suggesting we are all equal. Take for example yourself. You are not only one of the most attractive ladies I am ever likely to host at this hotel, but if I have done my homework correctly, you are the perfect example that some women, how shall I put it, are more equal than most others. If you were a German you would be regarded as a reborn goddess.'

'Or perhaps a siren.'

Penny, who had deliberately asked to be seated next to her host, with Sir Robert placed opposite, moved a fraction closer and mocked her host. 'I am happy to accept your compliments, but I refuse to be silenced. Tell me about German men and women.' And she touched and gently squeezed his hand as encouragement.

19

He realised she would be a formidable opponent under any circumstances and explained: 'Even today German women are brought up to accept that, while having the freedom to live their own lives and seek any career they choose, men remain dominant. Households are controlled by the wife, but in everything else she is ruled by her husband. German men are brought up to demand obedience.'

She suggested, while still touching his hand: 'You make them sound like army officers, while women are regarded as infantrymen who are there to be ordered. Yet in some ways it is the same in Britain. Or, more correctly, was until recently. During the war more than one million women moved into our factories or undertook work on the land, as they took the place of those who were called up for military service. The sparks that kept the home fires burning during the war became a blaze in the post war years. Woman wanted a fairer share of the opportunities, and I suppose I am one of the best examples of those who demanded more than just equality with men. I believe that many men are grossly inferior to females in equivalent positions, present company, of course, excepted. Sir Robert is a man I have admired and respected from the moment we met, not least because he did not treat me differently because I was a woman, but accepted me as his professional equal. And I like to think, Herr Rheinhardt, that is how I shall be regarded by you before the evening is over.' Unseen by Sir Robert, she squeezed his hand a little tighter.

'That is already my opinion,' he told her as he dared touch her diamond ring that was larger than his own oversized thumb nail. But would she ever submit to him? And turning to Penny he asked why it was that there were so few women hotel managers, or head waiters.

Penny countered: 'I might just as well ask why there has never been a woman Chancellor in Germany, or a woman Prime Minister in Britain. But I am prepared to wager a considerable sum of money that within the next two decades, one of these high offices will be occupied by a member of my sex. Women like myself are merely the vanguard of an international resurgence of the feminine gender. And to show you how much women are enjoying this resurgence of power, I would now request that we order dinner.' She accepted that their host should be allowed the privilege of ordering for the three of them. They began with a white fish caught that morning in a nearby lake. It was followed by wild boar that was another of the chef's specialities, and ended with a memorable *crepe suzette* prepared at the table and fired not with brandy, but a fine cognac. 'I appreciate that madame is used to the very finest of everything,' claimed their host.

Penny was equally aware that he was becoming more hopeful by the minute and rubbed in her great wealth by suggesting, 'If you can afford the best, why not have it? I have never understood the commandment "Thou shall not covet". How would we ever make progress if we did not desire something we did not possess? Envy can be the spur that inspires success. I can be vicious, callous, and quite merciless to anyone who stands in my way. Perhaps I have some German blood in my veins. I also have weapons that assist me in getting my own way. Isn't that right, Sir Robert?'

With his undoubted diplomatic skills he replied, 'Madame is a lady who automatically commands respect.'

Yet again she secretly joined hands with her German host as she encouraged him from hopefulness to expectation. She was toying with him. As she touched him she could feel the arousal of his natural desires. It was hard to guess whether she wanted to tighten the silken noose she now had round his neck or was content to be the Englishwoman who was triumphing over an arrogant one-time foe. Certanly he appeared unaware of the trap she had set.

She admitted: 'I have been admiring the Germans and Germany for more than two years. They have obviously found the key to open the door to full postwar economic recovery despite the devastation she suffered as defeat became inevitable. What has been your secret?'

With that question the noose was tightened as he foolishly imagined his English guest was begging a German to reveal how his nation almost always achieved its goal, whether to ensure recovery from the past, or when marching forward to a new supremacy. He wondered whether, if he told even half their story, she would please him later in the evening. His arrogance made him quite unaware that the lady who was holding his hand was an experienced trapper of men, just as others were experts in trapping the foxes, mink and sables she loved to wear. Or put another way the British were subtle manipulaters while the Germans preferred an onslaught.

He withdrew his hand because he liked to have both free to emphasise in a loud voice his argument. 'Germany's post-war secret is our national characteristic. We like to be, as you put it, top dogs. Like the knights of old we believe in our destiny. When Hitler was voted into power with promises he did not keep, people quickly discovered they had no choice but to obey. I remember being in a room when an SS officer took out his pistol and pressed its cold steel against the neck of a man who had dared criticise Hitler. He pulled the trigger, and no one interfered. The nations of Europe, too, quickly concluded that it was impossible, to argue with Hitler's tanks and dive bombers.

'When the war ended we suddenly found ourselves, if not free, with a freedom we had not known since the morning Hitler seized power. We accepted that the past, like indelible ink, cannot be erased, but it can be ignored and forgotten. What mattered was the future. Workers accepted that if they wanted bread plus salami for their families they would need to work long hours as their contribution to national recovery, and rebuilding what war had destroyed. They were no longer cannon fodder, but part of a peacetime army of reconstruction.' He suddenly realised that he was almost shouting and apologised. He asked, 'Have I answered your question, Frau Welling?' In his flow of nationalistic fervour he had forgotten her title.

Dame Penny decided he had said enough, and she had learned all he could teach her.

She rose, held out her hand for Herr Rheinhardt to kiss and asked Sir Robert, to escort her to her suite As a parting shot, she told her host, 'The British secret is that whether we are working-class or aristocrats, we are all citizens of what Shakespeare called a Sceptred Isle. It really is that simple. And when eventually we allow a woman to rule us, everyone, including the Germans, will be in for a surprise.'

In the lift it was Sir Robert who was responding to her squeeze and it was his confidence that was growing into anticipation, until she decided she had won sufficient victories for one night, and declined when he asked whether he might come into her suite. 'Not tonight, Robert. I am feeling exhausted as a result of my duel with the German. Just keep hoping your day, or night, will yet come. Good night.'

She knew she would have tantalised him and made him dance to her tune like a puppet who was utterly dependent upon which way she pulled the strings. Almost since their first meeting he had been under her spell like an animal in a circus ring. She could have him whenever she wanted. Before she closed the door of her suite she kissed him on his cheek and told him, 'There could be other opportunities during our travels together, but no promises.'

Next morning Sir Robert awoke feeling not disappointed, but as though he had been given a glimpse of what heaven might be like, while Penny opened her eyes refreshed after an uninterrupted night. When Kimberley arrived to find out whether there was anything she could do to be helpful she told Penny that she had dreamed she was a servant of Queen Cleopatra of Egypt and attended her when she bathed in ass's milk. She explained: 'I had been reading a book in which the queen insisted upon sleeping on layers of tiger and cheetah skins that had been specially slaughtered for her pleasure and comfort. She never ate a mouthful of food until it had been tasted and swallowed by a captured slave.'

Penny interrupted: 'The worst I can do is to have you sacked, while Cleopatra would have had you whipped for the slightest offence. To her you would have been worth less than the animals she had slaughtered. My only power is to torment people like yourself. Do I torment you?'

She was scared to reply. Whatever she said would be wrong. Yes, would be like saying she lived in fear of Dame Penny, and if she replied that she didn't she was likely to assert that it was time she started. Instead she bit hard on her lower lips until she plucked up the courage to admit, 'It is such a pleasure being with you.'

'In that case you can run my bath while I finish my breakfast. Then press the gown I wore last night. It is lying on the floor somewhere. After that pack my large suitcase for our flight to Munich this evening. I shall wear my blue pin-striped suit.'

Her interview with *Die Welt* presented no problems. She spent half the time expressing her admiration for the new postwar Germany, and the other to extolling the historic sights that abounded throughout Britain and fascinated every overseas visitor who arrived. Much of the time she was thinking ahead and wondering how different Munich would be, and what surprises it would hold. The first came when their flight was delayed for almost two hours. This meant it was past nine in the evening before they checked into their Bavarian hotel. The receptionist made them welcome and asked them to wait a few moments as the duty manager had left instructions that he was to be informed. In less than a minute Penny and her party were welcomed by a tall Adonis wearing a carefully pressed morning suit and clicking his heels. Penny held out her gloved hand which he shook, but did not kiss. He offered to show them to their accommodation which, in Penny's case, was the presidential suite, while her colleagues had been allocated two luxury double bedrooms. To Penny he explained, 'We have arranged for a butler and personal maid to be available throughout your stay.' The presidential suite consisted of an entrance hall, lounge, study, conference or dining-room, mini gym and two bedrooms, the largest with a wide four-poster bed which she suggested was 'perfect for any president, plus his or her consort'. He smiled at her quip, said nothing, but wondered whether Sir Robert, whose own double room was on the floor below, and next to Kimberley's, filled that role for the Dame who acted more like a princess than a titled lady; imperious, yet gracious.

Penny told Sir Robert and Kimberley to settle into their own rooms and then meet in her suite before going for a delayed dinner in the hotel restaurant. And to the duty manager she explained: 'I am starving. The food on the plane was inedible even after we had been kept waiting for two hours before take-off.' In reply he asked whether she would like a light snack sent up to her suite immediately, and he would reserve a table for three in the main restaurant in half an hour. Penny accepted both suggestions except that the table in the restaurant would be needed in forty-five minutes. The manager was now aware their guest was a lady who was used to giving, or changing, orders.

3

It was less than ten minutes later when there was a knock on her door and a maid appeared and asked whether she could unpack madame's suitcases. A few minutes later a waiter arrived with a trolley which he quickly converted into a small table on which he laid out a plateful of smoked salmon with two halves of lemon both covered with gauze so that Penny's hand need not come into direct contact with the juice, plus a side plate of thinly sliced buttered brown bread and half a bottle of champagne which he opened and poured. As soon as she had finished the smoked salmon she went into her bedroom where all her clothes had now been hung up inside two wardrobes whose sliding doors were blessed with two full length mirrors. She told the maid she would wear her short black dress for dinner and she should lay out fresh underwear, a pair of open-backed black shoes and a pair of sheer stockings. While her orders were being carried out, Penny decided on the jewellery to wear to complement and provide relief for the darkness of her dress that was fringed with fine Brussels lace. She graced her neck with a twin row of perfectly-matched pearls.

Speaking in English with hardly a trace of an accent, the maid admitted to Penny that 'it is seldom that I am privileged to serve a lady who makes the clothes; rather than the clothes making the lady. You make simplicity look sumptuous, madame.' With a white fur jacket round her shoulders she was a portrait of wealth and elegance. The maid was told to bring her breakfast at eight the following morning.

When Sir Robert arrived he immediately asked, 'Does Kimberley have to join us for dinner? Why can't we have a twosome?'

Penny snapped back, 'Don't be such a snob! It would be the height of bad manners to ignore her. As far as I am concerned we are a threesome, until I change my mind.'

Dinner proved a torture for all three. Sir Robert was afraid to speak his thoughts in front of a typist.

25

Penny was already awake when a waiter arrived with her breakfast, and shortly after there was another knock and her maid entered and at once noticed Penny was still wearing the jewellery she had worn for dinner, and at once decided that was what she would do if she was ever so blessed. Penny told her to press the black dress she had worn for dinner and then arrange for the suite to be cleaned in readiness for her press interviews. She should also press the Balenciaga dinner gown she proposed to wear in the evening. While waiting for the first journalist she read some clippings Sir Robert's office had prepared about Munich. She learned that Thomas Mann had once described the city as 'resplendent with festive squares, white colonnades, classic monuments, baroque churches and leaping fountains, plus an air of secret exultation'.

Another magazine revealed that her hotel was a place to eavesdrop, while the place to listen was in its bar where the in-crowd congregated, and the people who felt important were sometimes taught how unimportant they were. The report concluded: 'if you are in, you're inside this report'. Penny smiled as she read: 'Munich, a sexy city which is due, perhaps, to its invigorating climate or, maybe, because the city is mean. People bitch with personal pleasure about one another. In addition, Munich has more than its fair share of gorgeous women and sought-after bachelors.'

Penny realised Sir Robert was likely to be given his marching orders if only half of what she was reading was true. As though her thoughts had been read there was a knock at her door and she shouted to her maid to see who it was. It was a bell boy carrying a sealed letter on a silver tray which was from the owner of the hotel officially welcoming her and suggesting they should meet in the bar for a glass of champagne at seven before dining together. What she did not know was there should have been a second invitation to a party being hosted by BMW at the Nyphenburger Schlosspark, a chateau in its own extensive grounds. Dress would be formal. It had been cancelled by the head of Munich Society who was to be the hostess, and for two reasons. She had also invited the Count von Rugerstein, Bavaria's most eligible bachelor, who she intended to pair with Dame Penny. It could be the match of the season with vast wealth on both sides. Then it all went awry. First she learned that the English lady would be accompanied by her own escort and, second, the count apologised but had to decline because he was already committed to being in London for meetings with some of his business associates. The fact that Dame Penny was already wed had not entered into the hostess's calculations. Penny rang for Kimberley and dictated her reply to the owner, accepting on behalf of Sir Robert and herself.

Sharp at ten the maid answered the telephone and informed Penny that the first journalist had arrived. As expected the interviewer was accompanied by a photographer who spent the next half hour interrupting the interview as he requested more shots of Penny in different poses. The intrusions annoyed Penny, but she kept silent as they did not seem to worry the journalist who went on asking questions. After an hour she apologised and explained that another journalist had arrived. While she fixed her make-up she told the maid to order another bottle of champagne.

Journalist number two also had a photographer with him, but this time it was a woman who as soon as she saw Penny's fur jacket wanted to photograph her wearing it. She asked whether Penny had any other furs as nothing expressed a lady's standing more than her furs. Penny told her she had brought a mink coat with her and called for the maid to bring it to her. The photographer's verdict was that although she had illustrated several collections of fine furs, she had never seen a coat to compare with Penny's. She told the interviewer, 'It is not your lucky day. Dame Penny is wearing some of the finest furs I have ever photographed. I shall tell the editor the feature deserves a full page and I shall need three quarters of the space for my pictures. You can have the rest.' When she asked whether Penny minded showing off her perfect legs, the reply was, 'Why not? They were God-given.'

That afternon they toured Munich which revealed itself as a major metropolis, crowded with people who worked hard, enjoyed life and believed the quality of their beer was without equal. Their chauffeur stopped at the city's most famous beer hall and joined them while his three passengers were brought standard Stein sized mugs each filled to the brim with a thick white froth. While Penny and Kimberley sipped their beers Sir Robert was quickly onto his second Stein and had Penny wondering whether he was about to lose his unblemished reputation. Penny ordered the chauffeur to drive them back to their hotel. In the lobby she reminded Sir Robert that they were invited for drinks and dinner with the hotel's owner at seven He should have a rest.

An hour later when the maid let herself into the presidential suite without first knocking Penny was beginning to lose her temper at the lack of respect everyone was showing her. It began that morning when the photographer had wanted to take pictures of her in the most unusual poses which she had refused and in the afternoon Sir Robert had drunk too much and wanted to paw her in front of Kimberley and the chauffeur. Manners had been thrown to the wind in Munich. Was everyone beginning to think they were the equal of everyone else? Was the freedom they had fought for already being abused and replaced with laxity? Fortunately, the maid was sufficiently experienced to know that rich, wealthy women were demanding and intolerant, and those who served them had to accept that they came from a life where money bought everything including submissiveness and people like herself had no alternative but to accept that the chasm that lay between must not be crossed.

It was more than an hour before Penny regained her composure and decided that, thanks to the attentiveness of her maid, she had achieved the elegance she demanded for dinner with the owner of the hotel. She would never apologise to a servant, but instead asked, 'Should I wear one or two diamond rings for my meeting with your boss?' Her answer was to explain that it was not for her to tell her ladyship what to wear, but if she ever had the chance to be in her place she would wear a diamond ring on each hand. Dame Penny followed her advice because it was what she had already resolved; she had completely recovered her composure.

In the bar the owner was waiting for her and Sir Robert, with the obvious tact of a lady who was the latest in a family line of successful hoteliers that had begun with her great-grandfather. Their hostess was dressed neatly in a black silk suit that in no way challenged the reputation of her guest for display. She kissed Penny on her cheek, and Sir Robert took her outstretched hand. 'I saw you on television half an hour ago,' she told Penny, 'and the publishers of our leading daily newspaper sent me an advanced proof of an article about you they are publishing in tomorrow's paper. I shall see that a copy is sent to all three in your party in the morning However, an article is not quite the right way to describe what is being published. Almost two thirds of the page is taken up with photographs of yourself. You look like an empress. And you still do.'

She paused: 'May I call you Penny?'

Although not tall, the hotel owner carried herself with feminine dignity and wore little jewellery other than a family heirloom that was a brooch worn on the lapel of her neatly tailored suit. Formalities over, she signalled to one of the waiters who immediately responded by bringing a bottle of champagne to their table. Dolores smiled and joked that, 'Because one of my spies informs me that your favourite champagne is vintage Bollinger, I must apologise because the half-bottle that was delivered to your suite after your arrival was not what you would have preferred. I hope we shall be forgiven.'

Penny gave the Bollinger that was now offered her seal of approval and added: 'I could not have been made more welcome, first by your duty manager and then by the maid you allocated to me. She is a gem who understands how to care for every garment however delicate. I also asked her advice regarding the jewels I should wear this evening. She showed good taste.'

Dolores joked: 'I hope she did not forget her position. You are quite obviously a lady who makes her own decisions ... and very successfully.'

Penny accepted the compliment, but was not ashamed to admit that she had not been born with a golden spoon in her mouth, not even a silver one. However, by sheer hard work, good ideas, a little luck and some good advice she had clawed her way to the top. What about her hostess?

'I was born to be a hotelier like my father and his father and grandfather. It is in our blood. I love the work. It means I am able to meet fascinating and interesting people like yourself, Penny, and of course, Sir Robert who must forgive us if we two women enjoy a friendly gossip,' which they did until it was time to move to the reserved table in the main restaurant. Each dish they were served was a Bavarian speciality, and each met with Penny's approval. She had expected the food to be heavy, but instead each course had the light touch of a master chef. As they ate Sir Robert was encouraged to join the conversation and regaled them with tales of the many political and industrial celebrities he had met and served. Their hostess suggested he should write a book when he retired, and if he mentioned her hotel she would personally order 500 copies providing the publishers would agree to type the section about Bavaria in bold type so that she could justify sending copies to all their regular clients. Penny interjected, 'I shall expect a signed copy.'

After they had moved back into the bar for a final night cap, Dolores insisted that they should both join her for Bavarian elevenses tomorrow morning which were very different from the British much lighter mid-morning break. 'Ours,' she explained, 'are more rural, at any rate in origin. Everything comes warm and fresh from the kitchen. They are nearer to a Bavarian version of Spanish tapas and can go on forever, and are quite different. I promise you will enjoy every mouthful, especially our pretzels and rolls, as well as the sausages and other fried dishes that are prepared individually for every guest. Enjoy the rest of your evening.'

Again Sir Robert insisted upon escorting Penny back to her suite, but again had to be content with a good night kiss and that she was looking forward to seeing him again in the hotel's keller. She added, 'I enjoyed the stories you told at dinner. You really should write a book and you can write anything you like about me so long as you describe my clothes correctly. I could not want a more delightful companion for my travels.' She added a second kiss.

While this was taking place in Munich, a complementary event was taking place in London. As Marianne was to put it later, 'Call it fate; call it a coincidence; or better still think of it as my good luck. After all money is a magnet that has always attracted me, not least because of the power it provides. Whether you like it or not it is as true now as it was in ancient times that the majority have to defer to the powerful. And that is what I now possess. Perhaps it was due to the lucky sovereign I always carry in my handbag. Who knows?'

At the same time as Dame Penny was having dinner in Munich, and might have been going to a party being hosted by BMW where she would have been introduced to Count von Rugerstein, who was well known as Bavaria's most eligible and wealthy bachelor, the count was in London being introduced to Dame Penny's junior partner at Penny Pincher Properties, the equally attractive Marianne Wilkinson. They were at a reception being hosted by one of the count's British associates. Was it luck, good fortune or just an amazing coincidence? As Marianne put it later, 'Who knows?'

Nor did it matter to the count. For him it was love at first sight. And that was all that finally mattered. Marianne, too, reacted positively when she was introduced to the ramrod figure of the German count who bore down on her like the commander of a panzer division about to capture a helpless young lady whose heart began fluttering the moment she saw him. He was majestic, manhood personified. Although it was not her first introduction to immense wealth, the others had both been mega-rich ladies. The difference was like comparing the Arctic with the Antarctic. He whisked her away and took two glasses of champagne off the tray a waiter was carrying. 'Tell me about yourself,' he asked as they sat down together, 'and why are you here, although I believe we were fated to meet.' Although a girl just out of her teens, while he had passed his thirtieth birthday, she was already fully developed, attractive, tall and with expressive eyes. Everything about her was fascinating to the count.

In answer to his direct question, she told him, and blushed as she did so, that 'some people think I am the highest paid businesswoman in the City of London; I am not sure whether it is true, but I can confirm that compared with some of the other guests here tonight I am little more than a pauper. I would guess from the attention people pay to what you have been saying that you are quite certainly one of them. My main work during the past year has been buying historic homes and country estates whose owners can no longer afford their upkeep. Then I convert them into luxury apartments and sell them to a new generation of millionaire businessmen who have everything except a title. I am paid a good salary, but my commissions from my sales now mean that I have a reasonable bank balance.' She was not boasting, but seeking to convince him that she was not a gold-digger now that she sensed his interest.

Almost by way of confirmation of what she was thinking, he took hold of her hand and said: 'As well as being a very wealthy bachelor, I have for the last year been a target for many women

31

who heard that I was looking for a new countess since my mother died. Several of them slept with me, but I was quickly aware that beyond satisfying my normal manly needs their main interest was not me, but my wealth. None were invited a second time. When I flew to London the last thing I had on my mind was finding the next countess. But I would now like to take home the lady who could fill that role.'

'But you know nothing about me,' teased Marianne.

'But I do. From the moment I set eyes upon you and asked about you and who you were it became obvious that I was talking to the future Countess von Rugerstein. Until now I have never met anyone worthy of assuming the title carried with such distinction by my late mother. Quite simply, I have now. As a businessman I need to make quick decisions. But none of them have been as important as the one I have made this evening. Now my task is to persuade you that I am worthy of being your husband. And why am I so certain we were made for one another? One of the men I was talking with before we were introduced, used an expression which convinced me you were the lady I was seeking. They said that in business you were known as the ice-maiden. A German countess has to be just that although no one would dare use such an expression. When we are married you will not only be one of the wealthiest women in Germany, but you will live in a castle and be served by an indoor staff of more than thirty, all of whom will either bow or curtsy whenever they see or leave your presence. Because of your age you will be treated as a princess who must be obeyed. When you arrive I would like you to occupy my mother's suite of four rooms where you will be looked after by your own team of four maids. My own rooms are across the corridor where you will be welcome at any time of the day or night. The castle is also the headquarters from which I control my business interests. I hope you might like to share some of the responsibilties.'

Hearing all this, she suddenly withdrew her hand and there was a smile of expectancy as she asked: 'Are you asking me to marry you, count, and become your countess?' If he was, she knew it would be hard to refuse, even though she had only known him for a couple of hours. But time did not matter; only people were important. If her life was about to be transformed, it was only something she had always dreamed of. She was already trying to work out how far below a countess a Dame might be. She was even wondering whether Penny would be expected to curtsy to her.

The count's answer saved her further worry or speculation. 'I am not going to ask you to marry me in London. That is something I shall only do once you have seen and accepted not only me, but your future home and everything else that will become yours because you will be my countess. I have some meetings all day tomorrow, and will fly home in my own private aircraft a day later. Please come with me. Then it will be the time for me to propose. One question I would like to ask. Do you speak German?'

'My mother is French, but she married an Englishman and I was born here. As a result I speak perfect French and English, and reasonable German which would improve if I ever came to live in your country.'

'*Wunderbar.* May I have the privilege of escorting you home, Miss Wilkinson? But if you answer, yes, you will forever be my Marianne.'

They left together, and the taxi took them to her new flat in Knightsbridge where she accepted his invitation to dine with him the following evening when she would let him know whether she would fly with him to Munich the next day. They hugged one another and she whispered, 'I think I am falling in love.'

He answered: 'I already have.'

She spent all the following day clearing up any loose ends, and briefing her deputy to look after everything as she had to fly to Munich the following day and thought she would be away for possibly three, perhaps four, days. She would telephone. At dinner she said yes to the count's invitation and before midday she was in the air and alone with him in his own private plane with a pilot and second pilot who also acted as a steward. She was now calling him Wilhelm and dreaming of a new life where she would never again have to worry whether she could afford whatever it was she wanted. For most of the three hour flight they kissed and cuddled and when the deputy steward saw them wrapped in each other's arms it was she, not the count, who told him not to interrupt them. To the count it was further confirmation that she had been born to be a countess.

The longer she remained in the count's arms the more she became convinced that she was already a German countess. No longer need she feel inferior to both Penny and Rachel Simon, but their equal, perhaps their superior. After all, neither of them had such a title. Soon she would have the dignity she had always yearned for, as well as the indignities she could inflict upon her tiny secretarial staff or those architects and builders who had to accept every instruction this 'ice-maiden' gave. Soon her life would be turned upside-down, and in a country where anyone with the title of countess was regarded almost like royalty. Best of all, however, she would match fur for fur, and jewel for jewel, with almost anything her former two bosses had delighted in inflicting upon her ... and everyone else. For Marianne Wilkinson it would be all-change time.

Everyone at the airport seemed to know him and twenty minutes after landing they were in his stretch Mercedes and heading for Rugerstein castle. The rear of the limousine was cut off from the chauffeur through a smoked window which allowed them to see him, but they were in their own exclusive world, and could communicate with him by phone. As a result the castle was alerted that the count – and a female companion – would be home in ten minutes. There were six members of staff waiting to greet them, and each of them in turn either bowed or curtsied to them both. The count saw that two of the welcoming group were members of the team of maids who had looked after his mother. He instructed them to 'take madame's cases to the former countess's suite and wait for her there, and obey any orders she gives'. He spoke briefly to the head butler and cook and gave them instructions. Then he took Marianne's arm, kissed her and welcomed her to her new home so that all the staff could hear what he said and did.

As she looked around the magnicent hall which alone was ten times the size of her apartment she began to take in what the count had told her during their flight and how his family had made millions during the recent war making guns and tanks for the German army, while now those same machines had been converted to produce and satisfy the growing demand for refrigerators and washing machines by the thousand every month. He probably employed as many workers as BMW, but was tired of living alone with no one to spoil.

His staff was already sensing that the lady on his arm was not some temporary fad, but almost certainly the lady who sometime soon could be the next Countess von Rugerstein and châtelaine of the family castle. As for the next countess, she was overwhelmed by the size and height of everything. As her eyes travelled upwards they rested on a stained glass cupola through which a fading winter afternoon's light was still magical. One entire oak wall was covered from floor to ceiling with muskets and weapons of every kind with two suits of historic armour standing upright on the oak floor. Like many before her, Marianne found herself thinking how small the men, even the warriors, had been in bygone centuries.

'Every piece was original, madame,' the head butler assured her before the count rejoined her and arm in arm escorted her up the wide carpeted staircase to the first floor where the two maids who had welcomed her now gave her another deep curtsy before the count ordered them to wait in the corridor until the future countess called them to unpack her cases and put away her clothes. At last they were truly alone and he found it impossible not to take her in his arms and squeeze her with a passion she had never before experienced. He told her that her suite had previously been occupied by the late countess who died a year ago, and that no one had occupied it until today, although it was swept, cleaned and polished every morning by the team of four maids whose sole task from now onwards was to obey her every order or capricious whim. The aroma of fresh furniture polish filled the air. The dark orange velvet curtains were drawn and obliterated the growing darkness outside and replaced it with the warmth provided by the lights that had been switched on throughout her suite, plus several gas fires. To Marianne there was a feeling of warmth, well-being and an aristocratic elegance that breathed wealth and good taste Although the late countess had been nearly seventy when she died, Marianne sensed she had lived her life as her position demanded, and her family's fortune allowed. Every item of furniture and each picture that hung from the walls was perfectly placed to draw the eyes of anyone she entertained in her suite. Wherever Marianne's eyes rested there was something to command her attention.

Already she was hoping, wishing, and silently praying, that

this was where she would spend the rest of her life surrounded by luxuries and whatever else she was entitled to possess as one of the youngest and wealthiest German countesses. All the three walk-in wardrobes were crowded with suits and coats, dinner gowns and ball gowns for every occasion. All had been pressed as the late countess demanded, and many seemed never to have been worn. The spacious drawing room accommodated two large settees and half a dozen armchairs that were almost certainly Chippendale, and covered with a strawberry and cream striped rich satin, while on the walls were portraits of earlier counts and countesses, but all were dominated by a lifesize painting of the late countess wearing a lavish ball gown of golden silk and many of the famous family jewels that reminded her of the diamonds and other gems that always graced the fingers and wrists, ears and necks, of both Dame Penny and the heiress Rachel Simon. But she had never seen either of them wearing a diamond tiara that crowned the head of the late countess or a three row necklace of darkest black pearls There was even a diamond and ruby brooch that had been designed as the Rugerstein insignia, while on her fingers was a ruby as large as the gobstoppers Marianne remembered buying when she was a schoolgirl, plus two blazing diamond rings. From her ears diamonds fell like stalactites. In a corner of the bedroom, which itself was as large as the lounge, Marianne recognised what was almost certainly a Louis XV chest of drawers with a pink marble top. It might be a perfect copy, but its latest admirer was convinced that it was original and near priceless. She had gained knowledge from some of the furniture she had seen and had identified when walking through the numerous historic homes she had purchased for Penny Pincher Properties. The canopied double bed, in which the present count had been born, had sheets of finest pink silk, and covering the whole bed was the fur of a white arctic polar bear. Above the pillows the Rugerstein emblem was embroidered onto the same dark orange velvet that had greeted Marianne as she entered the suite. The bathroom was all pink marble while in an adjoining private sitting room a fire had already been lit. There was a small desk where the late countess had written her personal letters as well as a throne-like upright chair on which the Rugerstein emblem had been engraved and where she probably sat when receiving visitors. No one was ever allowed to forget the status of a German countess, positions that survived through the years of Hitler provided they did not seek to oppose the Nazis. Many senior ranked members of the then ruling party were proud to boast of their friendship with members of the nation's aristocracy. Like all the others, the Rugersteins quickly learned that their only choice was to accept the new laws or suffer the consequences. They never joined the Nazi party, and never met Hitler, but they contributed money to any cause requested and in return received vast orders for tanks and armoured vehicles. In a word, they prospered and were among the six wealthiest families in Germany during the war. Within three months of the war ending their factories were once more producing washing machines and refrigerators. They were never investigated by any of the Allied nations and high ranking officers in the occupying forces were frequently entertained by the former count and countess in the Rugerstein castle. Factory output increased month by month and by the mid-1950s these near essential household items were coming off the production line in each of their four factories at a rate that soared past pre-war figures. They, and millions more, hardly gave a thought to the former army corporal who had promised so much and left behind nothing but misery. Perhaps Hitler did believe he was the Napoleon of the twentieth century, but sadly for him, and Germany, he made the same mistakes.

The more Marianne saw the count the more her confidence in the future grew, as her blood seemed to bubble round her heart. Surely, if she was the first lady to occupy his mother's suite despite so many flirtations, it had to mean that he was convinced she would become the next countess who would maintain the family's name and reputation where it had been for centuries. Her thoughts were interrupted by a knock on the door and the arrival of two footmen carrying solid silver trays with her tea. One tray was heavy with a silver teapot, hot water jug, sugar bowl and milk jug. The other carried a selection of perfectly cut finger sandwiches, a plate of the creamiest pastries and an uncut rich fruit cake. They laid a table, poured her tea into a gold rimmed, hand painted Limoges cup before offering her the sandwiches. She took two and then dismissed them with the single word *danke* as she tried to remember her German, which was passable, even good, but could certainly be improved. She nibbled the sandwiches and this set her worrying about what to wear that evening. She had bought several dresses, but nothing compared with the collection of couture garments that were hanging in the late countess's closets. Only her mink coat was suitable for the surroundings in which she now found herself. The clothes she had packed were fine, but hardly compared with couture design and workmanship. And now she was staying in a castle whose impregnability had never been breached during several centuries. Was it possible that she was fated to be the first foreigner to conquer it, and rule over all who lived within its historic walls and elsewhere throughout Bavaria? Although she had achieved a considerable degree of success, what was happening to her now could only be described as going from darkness into light. A miracle was happening and she was at its centre. Or, perhaps, there really were fairies and one of them had touched her shoulder in the same way that the Queen of England touched chosen men on the shoulder and changed their position in society. Being what could be described as one of the chosen few was not frightening, but immensely satisfying and uplifting. From being a successful nobody she was going to be envied by millions of less fortunate women. And she was determined to enjoy her good fortune. Many of the richest men and women in the world had inherited their vast wealth. Now it seemed she was about to become one of them. It was a delightful feeling.

For almost two hours she lay on top of the white polar bear bedcover enjoying its arctic softness while admiring the carved ceiling with its Wagnerian musical notes. She wondered whether she should have the bearskin made into a pure white coat that would be ideal for a German winter. Equally quickly she discarded the idea. As a countess, more than anything else, she would need a new mink coat that would challenge anything in Penny's wardrobe. Yet the more she linked the past with the present, the more she began to realise that Penny had seldom done anything unless it benefited Dame Penny. Her interest in Marianne Wilkinson was because her success would give Penny more freedom to enjoy her wealth and the power it had given her in the world of politics. When she had encouraged Marianne to develop her negotiating skills it was in the hope that it would give Penny more time to devote to her government responsibilities. Even the mink coat she had passed to Marianne was not because she was being generous, but because she knew that wearing such a coat would give her the appearance of a successful businesswoman, and that would be helpful to Penny Pincher Properties.

As Marianne lay surrounded by luxury in her own castle suite, she decided that to Penny she had always been little more than a puppet who had to dance to whichever strings were pulled. Marianne was now dreaming of being queen of the castle. She recalled how Penny had told her, 'As a partner you can be as arrogant as you think fit, and don't hesitate to tread on anyone who dares challenge your authority.' Marianne was of course aware that all young women dreamed dreams, but the difference was that hers seemed about to come true. She was convinced that she could present herself as a 'catch' worthy of becoming a countess. She wanted him to be captivated by the light in her eyes, the arch of her eyebrows, the bloom of her lips, and the joy of her body.

It would soon be time for two of the four personal maids she had been allocated to come and help her prepare for the evening and, possibly, night with the count. Two of them answered her call within minutes and were ordered to run her bath to medium heat. Their names were Matilda and Marlene. Matilda prepared her bath while Marlene helped her choose between one of the several evening gowns that had been part of the collection of the late countess. It fitted and she was told she looked like a reincarnation. Matilda dried her body and powdered it with Halston talc before spraying a Chanel perfume round her neck and ears so that she felt she had the aroma of a goddess, or at least a countess. She glowed with a radiance that was like the beginning of a spring day and encouraged her belief that the prologue would soon end and the curtain rise on the first act of a drama in which she would star as a young woman who had all the graces necessary to carry off a German title that had been respected for several centuries. All she needed was the applause from a single pair of hands. The maids, who were convinced that they were serving the future countess, told her that her figure was almost identical with that of the late countess, but she would look even more beautiful in the clothes that were waiting to be hers; many of them had never been worn because their late mistress often ordered three or four of the same suits or dresses, but in different colours. Her suits were all of finest merino wool and the dresses were of pure silk or velvet. Marlene revealed that the jewels that decorated the countess's slim figure were the talk and envy of every woman in Bavaria. The way they now fussed around her encouraged Marianne to believe that her dream might be answered. She deliberately took time finishing her dressing because she believed the count would expect to be kept waiting, even by a countess in waiting.

It was five minutes before the time she had indicated she would be ready to meet her host that she dismissed the maids, but not before alerting them to be on call should she need them later that night. She descended the wide staircase to the main hall where the head butler was waiting to escort her into the castle library. 'Good evening madame,' he greeted her and bowed. 'If I may say so, you look a picture of elegance. The count is waiting for you. Please to follow me.' They walked along a dark wood panelled corridor hung with more paintings of earlier counts and countesses and their children, a walk which seemed longer than it was because of the butler's insistence upon introducing her to the many previous generations of Rugersteins. He was proud to be part of such a family, and this forthcoming addition would bring a youthful beauty and elegance that outmatched anyone in the portraits she was now seeing for the first time. There was even a grace in the way she carried herself and walked. But all Marianne could think of was the joy of having the count's arms around her neck as he poured kisses onto her lips. The butler also expressed the hope she had been happy in the accommodation the count had insisted she should occupy. 'It is very pleasant,' she answered, determined not to admit she had been overwhelmed by its size and lavishness.

After a gentle tap on the high double doors the butler stood aside and allowed Marianne to step into the library with himself behind her, as was his place, behind someone he was convinced would be his mistress for many years to come. 'Count, here is your honoured guest.' He clicked his heels and bowed to them both. The count rose from behind a magnificent mahogany carved desk at which a couple of centuries earlier the grand duke of a tiny east European provincial state that was being annexed by the all-powerful ruler of the Austro-Hungarian empire would have been sitting. When that empire ceased to exist at the end of the First World War the desk had been acquired by the count's grandfather, although no one knew quite how, or perhaps it was simply that no one was telling.

When the butler withdrew, Marianne Wilkinson was at last alone with Count von Rugerstein in his own castle. 'Welcome, Marianne,' he kissed her hand. 'I hope you are happy in your suite.'

His touch convinced her that dreams could come true. But still she could only hope. He held the high cards, and he alone would decide the future for them both. For the time being she could only pray that a new day would dawn from an evening sky. How could she know that in the eyes of the count she already seemed like a goddess? He was bewitched. Even touching her hand was a visceral delight such as he had never known. It was as though his good fairy had waved her wand and expunged all his previous conquests. 'You are quite lovely, and have the bearing of an aristocrat that I have been seeking for so long,' he admitted, while she sought to let him know without saying a word that she reciprocated his emotions, but dared not reveal them until she was certain this was what he wanted to hear. For the moment he had to be content with the curves of her body, her small waist and full hips, attractive ankles and almost military style shoulders that her dinner dress helped display. As she devoured the look in the count's eye she remembered that one of the men who had had been attracted to her in recent months had told her she had an hourglass figure. She wondered whether this was to be her hour, and whether the count believed in the hand of fate that was bringing them ever closer.

As their hands touched she gave him the gentlest of sqeezes because she believed he was beginning to treat her like a countess. It was a wonderful feeling.

But instead of uttering words she was longing to hear, he apologised for being such a poor host. 'Normally my butler pours me my evening drink, but tonight I told him I wanted to be left alone with my guest. Your loveliness has made me

41

forget my manners. Let us drink our first toast in Rugerstein castle, and my wish that it will not be our last.' That was nice to hear, but was it sufficient?

He walked across to a long sideboard that was twin to one that Marianne had admired in her own suite. This, too, was crowded with cut glasses for every occasion, and her host slowly filled two champagne flutes and carried them back to where Marianne was staring at another full-sized painting of his mother. The count handed Marianne her glass, and encouraged her to sit down beside him on a small settee where he proposed a toast to 'the English lady who would like to become a countess'. Was he deliberately teasing her? Perhaps she should tease him back. She looked into his eyes, moved inches closer which was what she was convinced he desired, and admitted, 'I am happy to share your toast, although the wording is not quite right. I do not want to become a countess, but I would be happy to be called the Countess von Rugerstein. But let me enjoy the moment and the toast, nonetheless.'

'Perhaps this will make the moment last longer,' and he kissed her gently on her cheek. 'None of those who in the last few months have sat here drinking champagne has ever occupied my mother's suite, nor been as beautiful, nor had your elegance and none your inbred, aristocratic refinement. You, if you will allow me to say so, are in my eyes near perfection. All you lack are the jewels to emphasise your beauty. And that is a situation I can easily remedy.'

She again returned his touch, and insisted upon telling him that with the exception of her few God-given gifts, she had many faults, although she was smiling when she admitted, 'I have a temper when people annoy me, and can enjoy belittling those who are inferior to me in the business status I achieved in Britain. I think mostly of myself.'

'These are not faults, but the virtues of a true countess. You might have been describing my mother. She had most of the faults you claim as your own. I won't say she enjoyed belittling people, but she never hesitated to reduce anyone near to tears who forgot to pay her respect. Her maids adored and feared her. Those who helped her prepare and dress for dinner had to stand and watch her decide which pieces of jewellery to wear, many of which were worth far more than they earned in several years. It was her way of continually reminding them of what you call their inferior position compared to her own. I can visualise you acting in the same way, dearest Marianne.'

'As your countess, my maids would quickly become acquainted with my temper. They would need to learn to curtsy when entering my presence and before leaving. But just as they have duties, so I would always dress, from breakfast through to dinnertime in a way that pleases you and befits my position as châtelaine of your castle. I nearly wore one of the Balenciaga or Worth gowns which I saw in your mother's closets, but chose something simpler and less elegant because I am still just your guest.'

The count smiled with contentment as he told Marianne, 'I fully understand. But it does not matter. You still look elegant.'

Marianne admitted she was now beginning to understand 'why so many of the ladies you took to bed failed the test they were secretly undergoing as you watched their reactions to the irresistible collection of jewels your mother wore for her portrait. Most would be overwhelmed. Fortunately for me I have spent the last four years surrounded by two of the wealthiest women in Britain who are just not interested or concerned that ninety-nine per cent of women have to go through life without ever owning a single fur however cheap, or the tiniest diamond. They never buy a pair of shoes, but three or four pairs of the same style. One of them told me after making me the third partner in their business that I must never become interested in a man unless I knew my engagement ring would weigh at least ten or twelve carats.'

The count smiled, kissed her again and became increasingly determined to woo and win this gorgeous girl who had entered his life, as though on a broomstick. She was magical. He asked, 'If you could choose, Marianne, just one piece of jewellery that my mother was wearing for her portrait, which would it be?'

'I told you I was selfish and now you are forcing me to show just how true that description was. I would like to be seen wearing everything she was wearing, but if I am allowed only one item it has to be the red ring, which I assume was a ruby, but cannot believe any ruby could be so large. But for tonight I would be content with a single diamond brooch to bring some sparkle to my dress.' The count stood up and, realising that both their glasses were empty, went to refill them and then asked Marianne to follow him. He wanted to show her something she was entitled to see, and hoped she would not mind coming upstairs to his own bedroom, 'even before we have had dinner together.' Seeing her look of surprise, he assured her: 'My sincere wish is that you will be happy to return to my bedroom after dinner, and then not leave until well past tomorrow's dawn. For now I simply want you to see something that has never been seen by anyone except my mother and father and myself.'

The butler was waiting as they left the library and at once took their champagne flutes, placed them on a silver tray and followed them upstairs. The count told him to inform the chef they would be ready to eat in forty minutes. Taking Marianne's arm he guided her into his suite that was opposite her own. Like everything else in the castle it was immense as befitted a bastion that had never raised the white flag of surrender, and was now the headquarters of a modern powerhouse, from where the count kept an eye on his significant business and industrial interests, international investments and the rentals he received each month from the half-dozen extensive farms the Rugerstein's owned. He regarded such monthly rentals as his pocket money. He also owned two entire Bavarian villages which together totalled more than one hundred cottages as well as all the shops, village hall and the church grounds. His suite which he was now showing to Marianne was a mix of antiques plus brief touches of modernity like an electric typewriter, but the several timepieces could all have been in museums rather than on display in a private collection in a glass-fronted cabinet that included pieces of Sevres and Meissen including the famous monkey orchestra. Marianne could well understand the confusion that must have gone through the minds of the young frauleins who were being inspected. They might have been dizzy as he described piece after piece to them. Their remarks, if there were any, would have given him an insight into their backgrounds and suitability The fact that he was still a bachelor suggested that few had impressed, any more than his servants whom he expected to know the true magnificence of what they were not even allowed to dust.

Now at thirty-two he was convinced he had at last found the lady on whom he would happily lavish his wealth and his life.

He was determined to persuade Marianne to become his countess, a title that would at once elevate her to a position from which she could have whatever she wanted. The fact that they had only recently met was unimportant. All that mattered was that his search was over. She might be a young woman who did not own a single gem, but it was going to be his pleasure to weigh her down with jewels worth a ransom. He intended to woo her with luxuries she had never dreamed of. Although his body was pleading for her and his lips wanted nothing more than to be allowed to embrace hers, he knew his passion had to be controlled. This was not a flirtation, but the beginning of his final romance. He clutched her hand possessively and again felt the bareness of her fingers as he whispered that her jet black hair reminded him of his mother's three row necklace of perfectly matched black pearls which he intended to place around her swan-like neck. His eyes were pleading with her to return his love, and finally as he was stroking her hand and wrist she whispered, 'I am falling in love with you, too, Wilhelm.' In response he pleaded with her, 'Please forget any tales you have heard about me. They were yesterday. That was an adolescent Count von Rugerstein. The person who is holding your hand knows that he has found his heart's desire. Now I want to show you how much you mean to me.'

He led her into a tiny room without windows whose steel walls were hidden behind thick damask wallpaper, while facing them were two metre high solid steel doors. 'Behind them,' he explained, 'is what in England you would call an Aladdin's Cave, although in Germany it has been nicknamed the Riches of Rugerstein. You are about to become the only living person with the exception of myself who has seen what lies beyond. I am now going to enter a complicated code which I shall reveal to you once you are my bride.' She could hear locks engaging before the door swung silently open to reveal scores of files and numerous black crocodile jewel cases. The count took the largest off its shelf, pressed in another secret code and Marianne found herself gazing at a collection of jewels that lay on white satin cushions and reflected the strong lights that had come on as the steel doors opened. 'Oh my god' was all she could say as he whispered: 'This, and so much more will soon be yours, my darling. Until last year everything in all these boxes, except one, belonged to my mother. Downstairs you admired the ruby ring that she wore for her portrait.' He picked up another matching crocodile box, opened it to reveal the ruby ring which now glowed with the intensity of flowing blood. He told her, 'I would like you to wear it tonight.' And he placed it on the second finger of her left hand. At once she knew for certain what it meant. She wondered what could come next, to match its magnificence. It was a square-cut solitaire diamond ring that to Marianne seemed as large as the gem Penny always wore. It was placed on her right hand, and was followed by a brooch designed round a single twenty carat pear-shaped diamond. 'These are the first of my personal presents to you, my darling.' He could no longer hide his feelings and hugged her in a loving embrace. Her youthful magnetism had him trapped, while she was beginning to understand for the first time the power of her own sexuality. It had opened the door to untold riches. As a final gesture of his love he placed his mother's three row necklace of matching rare black pearls round her delicate neck. 'For me, darling, it is a gesture from my mother that she approves of the next Countess von Rugerstein. When we are married you can wear them whenever you like. The necklace will belong to you.'

Although he had not formally asked her to marry him, she knew that once they were wed he would be like a toy for her to enjoy; golden putty in her hands. Now she smiled, looked into his eyes and told him: 'I shall make you very happy tonight, and always, Wilhelm. I shall be a countess to make you proud. But please be sure it is me you want to marry. Then I shall accept not with gratitude, but with my love for a very generous and loving gentleman. Already I am wearing jewels that are like forbidden fruit to everyone except the next Countess von Rugerstein. Do I have your permission to regard my suite and everything in it as my own? But even when I am there you must go on treasuring every memory of your dear mother.' What followed was an indication of the strong personality that had first been recognised by Dame Penny as Marianne insisted that all members of his staff should be informed of her new position and that she was no longer just another guest.

His reaction was to tell her: 'Every word you utter, darling, only makes me more certain that you are the girl I want to love and be with for the rest of my life. Whatever you want you shall have,' he assured her. He kissed her and was happy that already she exuded the confidence and authority of a German countess. It was now he who followed her as she walked down the wide staircase. The butler escorted them to the small family dining-room that, when needed, could seat twenty-four, but now had to be content with just the two of them. Noticing that she was now wearing the late countess's black pearls as well as two of her rings, one on each hand, he knew that within a short while she would be taking her place in Bavarian society. He was not surprised when the count confirmed the news.

The waiters filled their fluted champagne glasses and the count proposed a toast that confirmed the butler's thoughts, and allowed the waiters to be privy to what had been decided. He looked at Marianne and toasted 'the lady who will soon become the next Countess von Rugerstein'.

4

Their first meal together had begun with a warming home made winter vegetable soup and was followed by a side of English roast beef as a salute to Marianne who everyone now knew was to be the next countess. At the last minute the castle chef had created what could only be regarded as an engagement cake.

The count admitted that the moment she walked into his library a few hours earlier he had instantly known he was looking at the next Countess von Rugerstein. After they had been served coffee and schnapps the count suddenly clapped his hands and ordered his butler and the rest of the waiters and maids who had been fussing around them, and smiling at the young lady they all now knew would soon become their new mistress, to leave them. His only instruction was, 'Leave the schnapps.'

What followed was a complete surprise. The count rose from his throne-like chair and walked half way up the large but otherwise empty salon and stopped at a long seventeenth century cabinet, where he pressed a switch. A moment later the salon was flooded with the music of the Blue Danube waltz and he invited his bride to be to join him for their first dance. She happily accepted because what she wanted was to put her arms round his neck and draw him close to her so that she could feel his love. He was enthralled both by her touch and the lightness with which she moved across the highly polished dance floor to the music of Strauss. Although she had consumed a considerable amount of champagne and wine, all of them fine vintages, she did not feel even a little tipsy, and floated over the floor as only an idyllically happy lady could. After one final twirl he suggested it time for the main event of the evening. In response, she challenged to race him up the stairs, but he insisted upon carrying her to his suite in full view of the butler and the two maids who had helped Marianne dress earlier in the evening. The count laid her gently on his bed, kissed her

again and poured each of them another flute of champagne.
The wine showed its breeding by encouraging them to link their
two bodies into one, forcing Marianne to jovially ask: 'What
happens if we want a second bottle?'

'We ring for the butler and either he, or one of his underlings,
will bring it to us. There are always several bottles kept at the
proper temperature so that when either of us wants to enjoy
the finesse of vintage champagne, it is ready and waiting to
provide my countess with what she desires ... although I hope
her preference will always be myself.'

'Even if it is two o'clock in the morning?'

'Darling, as my countess-in-waiting you have staff waiting to
serve you whatever the hour. From now onwards whenever you
pass through the gates of our estate you will be entering your
own private kingdom. Here you can do no wrong. Your title
may be countess, but I am looking forward to seeing you dressed
like a young princess. Tomorrow morning I will take you to the
premier furrier in Munich which by the way, I own, but which
I intend to bequeath to you once we are married. Any profits
it makes will be yours alone. I want you to wear only the finest
furs and be admired and bowed to and respected wherever you
go. In a very short time you will be recognised as the wealthy
Countess von Rugerstein. After you have bought yourself a new
fur coat and matching jacket I shall take you to the best boutique
in the city where I shall leave you to spend the next two hours
buying whatever you need for your trousseau. I shall leave
instructions that everything you choose is to be charged to my
personal credit card. After that my bride to be and her count
will have lunch together. But now I would like you to feed me
with your love which will bind us together.'

What followed were moments of bliss and delight for them both.
As she walked towards him and revealed herself for the first time,
she was more than simply beautiful; she walked like an empress.
Her every movement had a grace and rhythm that created an aura
of nobility. With her smile she flirted with him as though challenging
him to be worthy of her. All her childhood dreams of regal
privileges were coming true. She decided she would never take
off the huge ruby ring that now graced her engagement finger,
nor the square-cut diamond that blazed from her other hand. They
were symbols of the immense authority that was within her grasp

The world she had always yearned for was to be hers. Even now she found herself looking down on her lover, rather than up to a count. She sensed how easy it was going to be to condescend to allow him the pleasures of her body, or deny them until he begged like a baby to be given his feed. He was going to be the suppliant, not Marianne. She would not be the châtelaine of his castle, but its ruler. No matter how long members of staff had served the Rugerstein family they would from now onwards obey the whims of a countess who might be half their age.

For now her breasts were filled with love and her dancer-like legs were curling themselves around the count's limbs with a possessiveness from which there was no escape unless she released him. He was completely infatuated by her liquid, emerald-green eyes, her high cheekbones and her desirable lips that made him quiver like a slave before a goddess. As their two bodies touched it was like the final bars of a rapturous symphony. For the first time the count found himself anxious to please the woman he was with, rather than use her to satisfy his personal needs. His bed had become an altar of fulfilment which Marianne had created. She would be a countess who always had her own way ... even with him.

As he entered her again she whispered, 'Wilhelm, wearing your mother's ruby ring assures me that I am a countess worthy of the name Rugerstein.'

He found delight in sinking his head deep into her forest of thick, soft hair as he felt every part of her delicate body, as it touched him. Soon her photographs would begin appearing ever more frequently in newspapers and magazines as columnists and women's editors relished publishing stories highlighting her beauty, fabulous clothes and jewels.

As they lay exhausted, he said she could keep all the jewels he had given her, and wear them whenever she liked. Later that morning he came to her suite and explained that although they were not yet man and wife, 'in my eyes you are the Countess von Rugerstein. When my mother bore that title she had an unlimited spending allowance. She thought nothing of going to Paris twice a year, or it might be London or New York, where she seldom spent less than fifty thousand dollars replenishing her wardrobe, Now that is your privilege, but with one exception; it will always be my privilege to give you presents of jewellery.'

Marianne's response was to joke: 'Until now I thought you only went to heaven when you died. I am there already. I shall be your personal Angel.'

From the day of their first shopping expedition she decided that, as his Angel she was entitled to be extravagant, and this was encouraged by his frequent gifts of jewellery which began at their first breakfast when she was given a pair of five carat diamond earrings that sparkled like searchlights under the two chandeliers above their breakfast table. As a result of all his gifts she asked whether she could have her own baby crocodile jewel case with its own secret lock to protect his generosity. He brought it to her later that day after rearranging the boxes in his safe.

At that breakfast she had her first clash with a member of staff when one of the two waitresses seemed more interested in her jewels than serving them breakfast.

'What is your name?' she snapped.

'Suzy, madame.'

'Don't ever dare call me madame again. I am now your countess and will always be addressed by the family title.'

'I am so sorry, countess. I did not know.'

'And stop staring at my jewellery. I am wearing what belongs to a countess, and to please the count. They are not for your eyes. Now stop annoying me, and begin serving our breakfast.'

Marianne knew her outburst would quickly spread through the castle, and doubted whether anyone would dare show her any disrespect in future. She joked to Wilhelm: 'With your three rows of jet black pearls round my neck I felt I had the authority to warn the maid of her behaviour.'

The count took hold of her hand and in a voice that was loud enough for the maids to hear told her: 'You were absolutely right. Since the death of my mother who had complete control of whatever happened in the castle and its grounds while I took care of our business interests, discipline has declined. From now onwards I shall expect you to take whatever steps you think necessary to let everyone know that your orders must be obeyed without question.' Turning towards the two maids who immediately curtsied, he warned: 'I hope you both heard what I just told the countess. Make sure every other member of her staff understands that she is now in complete control of everything that happens here. Nothing is to be done without her permission. Now bring us the rest of our breakfast and more coffee.'

'Yes count.' And both curtsied first to him and then Marianne.

He waited until the maids were back in the room before confirming: 'Now the size of the ruby ring you are wearing on your engagement finger will always be the equivalent of your crown. I don't think you will ever see its like.'

Two of her personal maids, Alice and Angelina, were waiting in her suite and each gave her a deep curtsy. News that she was to be known as countess had spread rapidly. 'How do you like my new jewellery?' she asked. 'They suit you to perfection, countess,' replied Alice who had lightly pressed the yellow silk suit the count had asked the countess to wear when they went shopping. Angelina helped her choose her accessories. She could have worn a matching pair of yellow shoes, but decided that black was a more impressive contrast. Before leaving she instructed them both to spend the time she was away cleaning and polishing everything in the suite and then to press as many of the outfits that now belonged to her. She wanted all four maids to be on duty when she came back in the afternoon as she intended to explain their future duties.

'Yes, countess,' they echoed.

Remembering that as a countess she should always wear a hat when away from the castle, Angelina was told to show her where the late countess kept her *chapeaux*. All the shelves of the largest of the two empress-size, walk-in wardrobes were given over to a collection of hats for every occasion from mink for luncheon parties to lavishly decorated wide-brimmed hats that were the required headdress at the races, as well as half a dozen straw hats each decorated with ribbon to match the collection of silk suits. She wore the boater that was the perfect match for her suit.

Where did the countess keep her furs, she enquired? On the other side of the empress-size wardrobe for hats, was a two-doored closet. When Alice opened one of them she was met by a draught of cool-refrigerated air that had kept the collection which varied from mink to fox as well as a sable wrap. Marianne was excited by the blackness of the skins of a three quarter mink coat which had been worked in the round instead of the traditional vertical style. She slipped it on and shivered, but liked what she saw in the full length mirror, and told Angelina to hang it over a radiator while she decided at which jaunty angle to wear her boater. As she was assisted into the warmed coat, Alice told her 'You look magnificent countess.' Her compliment was ignored; not so the welcome from the count: 'Furs suit you, darling. You look more eye-catching than ever. My mother believed that mink and diamonds went together.' Marianne promised it would be her rule, too.

The same chauffeur who had met them on arrival at the airport was at the wheel of the stretch Mercedes which drove them into Munich. Their first stop was at the fur salon that the count owned, but would belong to the countess after her wedding. The furrier, Max Springeld, was waiting to welcome them and bowed, while his two female sales assistants curtsied. They were shown into chairs in the private showroom reserved for VIP clients where coffee was immediately served. Marianne explained that she was only interested in their darkest ankle length mink coats and a long matching jacket. They should not waste her time showing her anything else. A few minutes later the two assistants wheeled in a rail containing their four longest coats and two jackets. They paraded each in front of her and then helped her into the two coats that attracted her most. The furrier recognised the three-quarter-length she had been wearing as he had made it for the late countess a couple of years before her death. It had been made from the finest and darkest skins. Marianne said she would take the ankle length coat and longest jacket, although they were not exactly what she wanted. Herr Springeld spent the next ten minutes noting down the exact measurements of a new almost floor length coat and the jacket he was to make for her. Only blackglama pelts were to be used. She again put on the ankle-length coat she had chosen and ordered the senior sales lady to take the jacket and the coat she had been wearing out to their car.

Before leaving she let the furrier know, 'I am a very demanding lady. In the City of London I was not only successful, but had a reputation for being ruthless in my business dealings. As a result I made a great deal of money, but as the Countess von Rugerstein I shall be far wealthier, and more demanding. When I am ready we shall have a meeting, Herr Springeld, and you will be given instructions concerning the future running of the salon which I shall own after my wedding. I am interested in increasing the profits. Finally, give priority to my two orders as I shall expect to try them both on within two weeks and for both to be ready a week later.'

Back in the limousine she told the count: 'I was disappointed. I shall make many changes. How many will depend on how good the coat and jacket he is making to my specific measurements are. That will tell me whether he is worthy of being furrier for the Countess von Rugerstein.' Anyone who heard what she was saying would either have admired her obvious belief in herself, or accused her of bigotry. Certainly the words error or mistakes were not in her dictionary. To Marianne her new title was the equivalent of the epaulettes of a general or field-marshall.

She was wearing her new ankle-length coat when she entered the boutique which the count considered the best and most expensive salon in Munich. He introduced her as the new Countess von Rugerstein and explained to the owner and manageress that he would be back in two hours and would then arrange payment for everything his wife had purchased. Quietly, he alerted her that the countess had been a highly-paid businesswoman in England and was used to getting her own way in all her business transactions. 'Look after her and she could be a very valuable customer.' The owner assured him she would personally attend to the countess.

She introduced herself to Marianne and ordered her senior vendeuse to serve the countess. Marianne told her: 'As the new Countess von Rugerstein I want to buy as much of my trousseau in Munich, but not my couture clothes or my shoes which I shall mostly buy in Paris. First, I need silk underwear which will excite the count, plus a selection of finest cashmere and merino wool knitwear, dozens of pairs of stockings, plus slippers and an exciting leather car coat when I decide to drive my Mercedes. Also a dozen pairs of trousers for day or evening wear, plus silk, wool and cotton skirts and blouses, and I am sure much else. The count expects me to be the best dressed lady in Munich. Succeed in helping me to achieve that status and I could be your most loyal customer. People could flock here if they knew I bought my clothes in your salon. I purchased this mink coat this morning. Its price was in five figures.' She was determined to impress the owner of the salon with her purchasing power.

The owner was almost on first name terms with Marianne by the end of the first hour of showing and selecting, and she impressed Marianne with her understanding of what she was seeking. She now had two vendeuses scampering up and down ladders to bring down packs and boxes for her inspection. Most she rejected and had them taken back to their high hideaways. She learned that they were all part of the salon's 'Royal Collection' because each item was priced beyond the reach of many clients, although three or four items were on display as baits. Marianne bit back: 'I am not royal, but I liked to be treated with the same respect.'

By now Frau Wolf, the owner, realised that it would not be easy to establish a close relationship with the countess. She could only think of half a dozen ladies in Bavaria who had the buying capacity of this English-born German countess. Seeing her senior vendeuse was beginning to wilt by the number of times she had been forced to climb ladders, she suggested a break for coffee. Marianne agreed and the two of them disappeared into the privacy of Frau Wolf's office. The vendeuses were told to begin packing and itemising the items the countess had selected. Marianne appreciated the business approach which insisted that the needs of a customer took priority over any discomfort of her staff. Marianne joked that she had always made it a rule, although it was not quite true, that for as long as she could remember she had always refused to iron her own clothes or sew on a single button, and now she had four maids whose duties were to do such chores so that there would never be a single item that had not been pressed before she wore it.

Frau Wolf was used to the whims and capriciousness of her wealthy customers, but admitted while they sipped their coffee that she was finding it hard to take her eyes off the lavishness and quality of the countess's coat. She could not remember a single customer wearing a coat as eye-catching. 'May I ask how much it would cost?'

The words were hardly out of her mouth before she knew she had made a mistake. 'You may not,' the countess spat at her. 'Only customers are entitled to ask such a question. But I will tell you that you could not afford it. Even at half-price it would still be out of reach.'

Unknown to Frau Wolf, the businesswoman in Marianne was moving into gear. 'Do you have any furs, Frau Wolf?' she asked.

'I have a mink jacket, but your handbag would have cost more that I paid for it.'

Marianne's reaction was to realise that Frau Wolf might own the salon, but as a businesswoman she was not in the same league as herself. She would take full advantage of the difference. She fired her first salvo and explained, 'I never pay what I am asked. I have been known to force shopkeepers to accept only a little more than half what they had originally asked. I could easily arrange for you to receive a discount of at least twenty per cent from my furrier. In return that is the kind of discount I shall expect to receive today.'

'I shall be honest with you countess. Because I think there is a good chance that you will become my best customer, I was planning to offer you a ten per cent reduction. But because of your generosity to me I will make an exception and deduct fifteen per cent off your final total.'

'Because I am in a good mood this morning, I shall accept your deduction, but don't expect me always to be so generous. Now let us get back to something which gives me a great deal of pleasure; spending money on myself.' Back in the main salon all her purchases had been packed or put in the special carrier bags, and the two vendeuses were waiting for their next task. Marianne told Frau Wolf to 'tell me the worst, and don't forget my fifteen per cent discount. By the way, do you sell handbags?'

'Yes, I do, but it is only a small selection, and all are the latest designs and made from softest leather while three or four are baby crocodile.' She stopped preparing Marianne's account and ordered the younger of the two vendeuses to bring out the entire collection of handbags. There were twenty in all and each was packed in its own lavishly designed box beneath several layers of soft silk wrapping paper. 'Open them all,' she instructed, 'so that the countess can decide whether any match her excellent taste.'

With little hesitation Marianne set on one side two crocodile clutch bags, a Princess Grace-style handbag in softest black baby crocodile, and went on, 'In addition I want you to order me a second Princess Grace handbag in white crocodile. I will pay for all four handbags now, but I demand a twenty per cent discount on these extra purchases.'

'Please countess. Don't bleed me.'

56

'Oh, but I shall. That is how I made my own fortune. I began buying up a score or more of bombed-out London homes which no one wanted. Each cost me only a few hundred pounds, but years later when I started to sell them I was paid tens of thousands of pounds for each property. And in between I converted the buildings into one-room flatlets when there was a post-war shortage of homes in bombed-out London. People were prepared to pay whatever I demanded just for a roof over their heads. Five years later I was a millionaire. Now I have still more to spend. That is why you have no alternative but to grant me this extra twenty per cent discount. And don't argue with me, Frau Wolf.'

'Please countess. I cannot afford to give anyone a discount of twenty per cent.'

'Frau Wolf. You do not have any alternative. I am either given my extra discount, or I cancel everything I have ordered.'

Frau Wolf accepted defeat. 'The total, including your extra twenty per cent discount is thirty-one thousand seven hundred and thirty-five dollars.'

'Make it a round thirty thousand dollars and the count will pay you at once with his unlimited platinum credit card. If you refuse, I shall simply tell him I did not see anything here I wanted or liked.'

Frau Wolf felt like a whipped dog. She called her senior vendeuse and told her to type out a new invoice for the countess for $30,000, and address it to The Countess von Rugerstein, Rugerstein Castle, Munich.'

'May I still have my twenty-five per cent discount off my next fur, please countess?'

'I'll see.'

As she walked back into the salon Marianne noticed the young sales assistant was putting a Burberry raincoat on display in the window. 'Why didn't you show it to me?' she asked

The owner hearing her complaint explained that the Burberry had only arrived the day before and it was only opened that morning, and, as it was lined with dark mink, she had not had an opportunity to price it.

'Show it to me and let me know the special price to me, and don't try to cheat me.' Marianne warned. If she liked it she would buy the raincoat. The owner helped her put it on. Her verdict was. 'I don't suppose I shall wear it very often, but I like it. Pack it up with my other purchases with my usual twenty per cent discount.'

The owner first had to convert the invoice price from sterling into marks and then marks into dollars for the countess. The price for the Burberry including the expensive mink lining was twelve thousand dollars, 'But to you, countess, it is only nine thousand dollars. I cannot afford to lose your custom even though you may never enter my salon again. Enjoy your purchases, although I doubt if there will be many occasions when you will walk in the rain and need your Burberry.' Secretly she was content because, knowing how the countess would always haggle whatever the asking price, she had already added one thousand dollars to the price any other customer would pay for the hidden delights of owning a mink-lined raincoat. Now she could afford to order an immediate replacement.

When the count arrived to take his bride to lunch, he paid the sum demanded and congratulated his wife on having had a successful morning's shopping.

He took her to lunch at one of Munich's several men-only clubs, but where women were allowed as guests until four in the afternoon. All the staff in the restaurant were women in their late teens and early twenties, and all sexually stimulating, including the manageress and sommelier. Marianne guessed they were employed more for their attractions than their more mundane capabilities. The count admitted she could be right, but he only came to the club occasionally and always for lunch, and usually with a male business associate. Meanwhile, the eyes of all the female staff were magnetically drawn to the vision of youthful beauty that was not only clinging to the arm of the Count von Rugerstein, but was wrapped in a coat that they could only describe as erotic. Marianne soaked up the admiration, but knew the true words were jealousy and envy, perhaps hatred and malevolence. She added to their misery by wrapping the coat tightly round every inch of her body from her neck to her ankles in a way that created a portrait of voluptuousness that was like a pedestal that put her far beyond their reach. While they could not identify the three row necklace of black pearls, her diamond and ruby ring, and her solitaire diamond earrings simply confirmed that they could never enter what would soon be her castle. The one-time richest bachelor in Bavaria was *verboten*, from now onwards.

The future countess ignored them, except when she snapped at one of them: 'Can't you see my wine glass is empty.' The unfortunate waitress was brought face to face with the truth that her life would always be one of submission; at lunch time when she took orders, while in the evenings she and the rest of them served up their bodies.

Marianne nestled into Wilhelm's arms and described them as part of life's failures who will spend their lives obeying orders, never giving them. 'I don't think a man can fully understand what it means to a lady who is placed on a balcony from which she will always look down on all other women who have no alternative but to be subservient to her. To me these women are nothing more than cogs in the wheels they help turn to provide the wealth that men and women like ourselves have created. They are powerless in the face of our millions.'

Next she regaled him with how she had used their wealth to force Frau Wolf to give her a fifteen per cent discount on all her purchases, plus an extra five per cent on the final items of the four expensive handbags plus a mink lined Burberry raincoat. 'In all, your business-minded countess saved you almost twelve thousand dollars against what ordinary customers would pay.'

Later she whispered: 'To some people I shall snarl like an angry tiger, but with you I will always purr like a kitten ... providing my fur is mink.'

When he did not ask what else she had bought, she described what she had chosen as 'everything every woman wants, but few can afford'. All the woollens were either cashmere or finest merino wool, scores of pairs of sheer stockings, silk scarves in a dozen different designs, a dozen pairs of soft leather gloves, silk blouses, a few silk handkerchiefs. 'By the way, I have fallen in love with my new coat. I want to keep it.'

Instead of saying yes, as she had expected, he teased: 'You don't understand that there is hardly a German woman who does not have to beg on her knees, or offer her husband an extra ration of sex, just to obtain his permission to spend a few extra marks on some trinket that has caught her eye. However, you are not one of them. You are marrying a man who is worth hundreds of million of marks, or tens of millions in dollars. Buy yourself four new mink coats if that is what you want, and it will not even make a mark on the vast wealth you are inheriting. I want you to become famous for your diamonds, emeralds and black pearls Tonight your gift will be your first diamond bracelet from Cartier. I hope you will wear it at dinner.' More than ever she knew she was a lady who was being assiduously spoiled.

Back at the castle she had all four of her maids working until past eight seeing to her personal needs before dinner as well as unpacking the fifteen packages that confirmed her purchases at the boutique, and deciding where they should be put. It was a task they would not complete for another twenty-four hours. She forbade them to stop even when the count came into her suite and presented her with her Cartier diamond bracelet, and her own baby crocodile jewel case. Later she went into her sitting room to phone her parents and tell them what had happened to their daughter during the last few days. As she phoned home three of her maids carried on with the unpacking and putting away while Alice manicured her nails and toe nails before painting on a light, almost colourless shine.

Her mother answered the phone. 'It's Marianne, mother. I have some exciting news for you. Please sit down before I go on.' She paused for a few seconds before continuing. 'I have accepted an invitation to become the bride of Germany's most eligible bachelor. He lives in a castle surrounded by nearly thirty servants, and where I have been since my arrival. I have four personal maids and one of them is manicuring my nails while I am speaking to you. My future husband is a count which means that your daughter will soon be the Countess von Rugerstein, one of the richest women in Europe. He owns a business empire worth hundreds of millions of dollars and employs more than five thousand workers. As a wedding present he is passing the ownership of the most expensive furrier in Munich to me.' She described the day's spending spree adding that when she left the castle she had the choice of a chauffeur driven stretch Mercedes or a Rolls Royce.

In a voice that was little more than a whisper because her mouth was suddenly as dry as a desert, her mother told her: 'I can't believe what I am hearing. When am I going to meet my future son-in-law? Will I have to curtsy to him, and you?'

'That is what all the staff at the castle have to do whenever they see me, but you will be excused. I cannot wait to show you my engagement ring. It is a huge single stone ruby and blood-red. I never take it off, and on my other hand is an equally large square-cut diamond.' She decided not to mention the black pearl necklace because her mother would not know the immense value of what she was describing. Already she could hear her mother either sobbing with joy, or with equal disbelief at what she had been told.

Marianne had to repeat her unbelievable story to her father, adding that they would try to fly to London, probably within the next week, and she would let them know.

To celebrate clearing the first hurdle of explaining her new status to her parents and friends like Penny and Rachel Simon, she wore not only her new Cartier bracelet at dinner with her usual two rings, but also another of her gifts, this time a single row diamond necklace. To the count he was only following what his mother had taught him, that the way to a girl's heart was with diamonds. Marianne's eyes lit up wider with each jewel she received, and she never ceased to wear them as a way both to please him, but also to confirm the position she held as the next Countess von Rugersten. But even he was surprised at the ease with which she had cleared the leap from yesterday to today. Playing the part of a countess fitted her perfectly and was already acknowledged by all who served her. He agreed that they should delay any official announcement of their engagement until after he had met her parents, while she sensed that with each passing day, her control over the count was increasing. While she never denied him his night's ration of unadulterated sex she sometime forced him to await her pleasure before he was permitted to enter what was now his second home. She liked to watch his eyes bursting with desire for full possession of her tantalising nakedness. One evening when they lay exhausted after a double dose of her personally provided stimulation, she chided him that he was like a salmon who was compulsively drawn to its own spawning ground. The next day she suggested she had become his Achilles heel; the more he was allowed to possess her the more she became like a drug he could not do without. It was done with such feminine finesse that long before they were married he found it impossible to deny her anything. The staff now asked for her approval and permission in all matters affecting the running of the castle and the estate.

Whenever they arrived back at the castle, whatever the hour, they were always greeted by a butler and at least one of her maids who would curtsy and await any orders her mistress might give. Within a few weeks every member of staff was aware that the new couness intended to rule like an empress. Her four personal maids quickly learned that she would always leave her clothes on the floor for them to pick up and press or wash, and had been ordered to turn up the temperature of the closet where her furs were kept to prevent them being too cold when she put them on.

She confirmed that their sole duty was to obey every order she gave. She would not endure disobedience. Nor did she expect to see a fleck of dust on any piece of furniture or picture frame, or fluff on the carpets in her suite. At least one of them was to be on duty throughout each twenty-four hours, and preferably two. Not a word they heard was ever to be repeated. She appointed Alice as her senior personal maid with responsibility for seeing that all her orders were carried out.

A few days later the count told her he had some business meetings in London and thought they should use this opportunity for him to meet her parents. His secretary booked them a suite at Claridges for three nights with the option of a fourth, plus a double room for her parents for two nights. He suggested that on the first night they would dine in the hotel as a family foursome, and the next evening host a larger dinner party for her friends. Cables were sent.

Even before she flew to London she was looking forward to being an admired member of Bavarian society, but knew that her lively business mind would never be satisfied with running just the family estate and the fur salon she would own. Just like many married couples she and the count often had similar thoughts and ideas at the same time. He had also been thinking about the changes in his own life now that he had found the countess he needed. He recalled how his mother, then the countess, telling him when he was fourteen and was taking his first fencing lessons, that he had reached an age when he must end his friendships with their servants. From then now onwards the only contact he should have with them was to give orders. That was how it had always been since. And his new countess accepted her new status as though it was what she had always expected. In truth it was simply that she had always been able to adapt. From almost the first moment she had started work she was surrounded by two women of great wealth.

Now he wondered how long it might be before Marianne with her flair for business would want to share control of the family's vast commercial interests. She was a proven businesswoman who knew how to exercise control. Perhaps it would be sensible to first give her authority over the scores of farms the Rugersteins owned throughout Bavaria and other parts of Germany. As he had not increased their rentals for at least ten years, she would enjoy announcing a high, but justifiable rise. He knew she would not tolerate any tenant who objected to whatever increase she decided. But would that be enough to satisfy her appetite? She had recently hinted that together they would make an invincible business partnership, but before then she wanted to enjoy planning her wedding that would be the start of a happiness such as neither of them had known before. Together they drafted the wording and style of the wedding invitations having agreed to be married at a civil ceremony at City Hall.

While they sat talking he told her there was something else she needed to know. Nowadays there were a growing number of women with the title of countess, who had lost their fortunes. Because of their breeding they would automatically treat her with the respect that was her due while secretly envying her youth, her beauty and her wealth which she enjoyed displaying.

'Wilhelm, I am a very female female. Although I promise to sleep with only one man, I like being admired by other men, but even more being envied by women who cannot compete with the clothes and jewels I wear, which will now include your pauper countesses. They once looked down on other people, perhaps still do, but I shall look down on them. By the way, why don't we get married tomorrow. It will save you a lot of money, which you can then spend on me,' she joked.

To Marianne's surprise he told her he would like to delay their big day, not because he was having second thoughts, but due to the need to delay the ceremony for a few weeks after the official announcement in newspapers, and a press release for the German media confirming that he had asked a strikingly beautiful English lady to become his countess. He went on: 'This will be followed by a photo call and requests for interviews, especially from the German press. There are the invitations to be printed and the guest lists to be agreed for both the ceremony and later in the day a dinner at the castle. This could be anything from fifty to one hundred. The truth is that after we have made our announcement every one will want to meet you. You will not only be in the public eye, but a member of the German aristocracy ... and beautiful. You will be a celebrity.'

She took his hand, and looking at him with the love she felt, assured him: 'I shall be so happy being the Countess von Rugerstein.'

All her love, thoughts and plans were now directed towards her own future and her husband's happiness. That evening the count wore a dinner jacket as she requested, while she wore another of the many dinner gowns she had inherited, or had fought for herself. Jewels sparkled as they now always did. She joked: 'I fear my mother will remain in a state of shock until I give her the mink coat I wore when I travelled to Munich. She always admired it. Now it will be hers.

'And what about our honeymoon?' she asked with a smile of anticipation on her pouting lips.

'Stop being impatient, young lady. All is arranged and will be revealed in exactly twenty-eight days' time.' Marianne said nothing. She knew there would be plenty of opportunities for her to peck away into forcing the count to reveal his secret. How could she know what to take with her if she did not know where they were going, or how?

The days before their wedding flew with hurricane speed, but nothing was allowed to interfere with their nightly moments of delight. They even found time on a couple of afternoons to enjoy a matinée performance while their servants carried on with the spade work of preparing and checking all the announcements and invitations, plus double checking the addresses of every envelope. To the count and countess those daylight moments in each other's arms were their version of sex-filled siestas. Once satisfied they spent the rest of the afternoon working out table plans. The count insisted that miniature German and British flags should be placed on every table.

Before they flew to London the count's butler and his personal private secretary, Frau Heide von Welterstein, an aristocrat in her own right, were given permission to act on their behalf in respect of the wedding plans while they were away. Frau Heide who had worked for the count for several years, and often travelled with him on business trips, had spent many evenings in her bedroom dreaming that one day he might remember her pedigree and ask her to become his countess. Now she knew that would never happen. Except for her birthright, she was the proverbial also-ran. While the future countess was beautiful, she was no more than good looking; the next Countess von Rugerstein possessed a first class business brain, while she was simply a good secretary. Now it was always Marianne, Marianne and Marianne. No one, and least of all herself, meant anything to him any more. In addition, Marianne seemed as hard, and perhaps as cold as the marble in her bathroom, a fact that made it essential for Heide to keep under control her own Prussian upbringing. Finally, the future countess possessed an air of justifiable superiority. Heide told the count: 'You have found the perfect future countess. She will do honour to your name and, hopefully, help perpetuate it.' The Count made her blush as he asked: 'Providing the countess agrees, would you bless our marriage by being her maid of honour?' When told of the suggestion, Marianne was happy to agree because there was no one in her own family to carry out such a duty. Frau von Welterstein might also be the friend she would need during the coming weeks and months. Together they planned the allocations of rooms and suites at the castle for special and family guests while making bookings for many to stay at the Bayerischerhof and other deluxe hotels in Munich. Marianne insisted that her own parents should stay in her suite, and the butler was instructed to give them his personal attention throughout their stay. She would move into the count's suite.

Still higher priority was given to choosing Marianne's wedding dress, and what she should take with her when she headed off on her honeymoon. She again rebuked the count, 'How can I know what to take away with me if you won't tell me where we are going? I want to remember those weeks for the rest of my life, and I want you to be proud of me wherever we go.' Faced with her logic and his desire to please her, he succumbed and revealed that one of his personal friends, a multi-billionaire Greek shipping magnate and his wife, had offered them their ocean-going yacht for a two week cruise around the Greek islands as their wedding present. 'What a wonderful way to start my life as the Countess von Rugerstein,' was Marianne's reaction. 'I shall write them a short, but very sincere, personal thank-you on behalf of us both.'

Earlier they had agreed that after their London visit she would fly to Paris with Frau von Welterstein as her chaperone and seek wedding and honeymoon outfits. As each day passed she walked with the natural grace of a countess and the aloofness of a German titled lady. Her voice was warm and loving when talking to the count who in different ways told her she looked ravishing, but it was cold and impersonal so as to confirm the distance that separated them, when she talked to staff. Many of the former countess's gowns had been altered to show off the perfection of her shoulders, even to hint at the potential seductiveness of her almost invisible breasts. And if that was not another way to confirm the loftiness of her position, there were few evenings when her neck was not encircled by a diamond necklace as she and the count dined together in the castle. No wonder the count was continually declaring, 'You look more ravishing each time I see you, darling.' She kissed him and they drank champagne. Mostly they slept in the count's suite, but one of her maids was always on call to help her prepare for bed whether she rang at midnight, 2 am or never.

When they flew to London aboard the count's private aircraft, Marianne took two large suitcases with sufficient clothes to allow her to change twice into different outfits each day. The count made do with a single large suitcase. She wore her new mink coat and carried her old coat, which would soon belong to her mother. Soon it would be her turn to be envied. Her own new fur jacket had been packed. Their departure was delayed half an hour, but they were only fifteen minutes behind the expected checked in time at Claridges. The count signed the hotel register, Count and Countess von Rugerstein, and Marianne checked the number of her parents' room and was informed it was only a few doors away from their own suite on the second floor. Would the countess like a maid to help her unpack? The receptionist's offer was accepted. While her clothes were being put away, Marianne walked the few paces to her parents' double room, her mother's fur coat over her own arm, and still wearing her own coat.

When the door opened there was a split-second look of non-recognition in her mother's eyes. Was it really her daughter? A new hairstyle made her look more mature and confident. Marianne slipped out of her own coat so that her mother would not feel like a poor relation when comparing the mink coat she was given with what Marianne had been wearing. Marianne was content to let her perfectly tailored silk suit do the talking for her new wardrobe. Slowly her mother began to come out of her trance and realise her daughter was now a countess with wealth that was beyond her comprehension. Marianne admitted: 'I know I have changed, but I still love you and dad more than anyone except my husband-to-be. Neither of you shall ever want for anything again.' Next moment all three were in each other's arms. They were still family.

After half an hour she told them it was time for them all to get changed for dinner. Yes,it was fine for her father to wear a suit, collar and tie, but suggested her mother should wear her new mink coat over her shoulders plus the nicest suit or dress she had brought with her. 'See you in our suite at eight-thirty.'

The count clicked his heels and kissed the hand of his future mother-in-law. 'It is a pleasure for me to meet the parents of the lady I am going to marry and make as happy as she has made me.' He handed Mr Wilkinson a box of fifty Havana Corona cigars and requested he should let his daughter know when he needed a replacement supply. They drank a toast to the next Countess von Rugerstein before Marianne joined the celebration wearing only the minimum of diamonds a countess would be expected to wear at Claridges, and her dress was the simplest of the three dinner gowns she had brought to London. The count took her mother's arm and escorted her into the restaurant, while Marianne linked arms with her dad. Marianne wore her mink jacket while her mother looked puzzled when the maitre d' asked whether he could take her coat. Marianne intervened and explained, 'my mother feels the cold,' and the tension was eased, As the courses were served the conversation was largely between the count and countess with her parents contributing a polite 'yes' or 'I entirely agree.' Her mother was inwardly pleased that her daughter was the more expensively-dressed lady, but never conjured up sufficient confidence to ask Marianne to identity her ruby engagement ring or the monster diamond on her other hand. Not even a fine claret or cognac was able to coax her parents out of their cocoon.

Next morning Marianne took her mother shopping in the couture department at Harrods where the arrival of two ladies in expensive fur coats was sufficient to command immediate attention. She presented the count's special gold card which indicated unlimited credit and spent the next two hours being shown what the manageress thought might suit an English-born German countess. Eventually she selected three that might be suitable to take on her honeymoon cruise, and also bought a Chanel suit for her mother, who had to be stopped by her daughter from expressing her horror when she heard the price. Marianne suggested she should wear her Chanel suit that evening at dinner when there would be eight around the table, and she would be the only lady who was not a millionairess.

Following the previous evening's problems the count was concerned that his in-laws would again feel uncomfortable when surrounded by so much obvious wealth and three women who would be seeking to outshine each other. He decided the only – partial – solution was to seat himself next to his mum-in-law and Rachel's escort, whoever he might be, on her other side. It would protect her from the worst of the waspish tongues of Dame Penny and Rachel Simon whose Swiss banking millions probably dwarfed the lot of them, at any rate individually. All he could do was keep his fingers crossed. However, to ensure that no one would outshine his countess he had secretly brought with him to London a tiara with forty-two diamonds that had been given to his great grandfather by Bismarck, but he did not know who had been robbed before it was passed to his family. He was, however, a little happier when he opened the door of their suite and found himself looking at a transformed mother-in-law wearing an obvious Chanel suit, but also with a new hairstyle that had been created for her that afternoon in the hairdressing salon at nearby Selfridges. As Marianne put it, 'she looked exactly like everyone expects an elegant French lady to look.'

The first of their guests were Dame Penny and her husband Colonel Welling. Marianne performed the introductions to the count and her parents and Penny politely sniped that Marianne looked more like a duchess than the countess she was soon to become. Marianne's riposte was to thank her guest, and former boss, that she had worn one of her two sable coats as it might give the count ideas, and 'if not I shall give them to him.'

She was interrupted by the arrival of Rachel and her escort who Marianne recognised as one of her former toy boys who had obviously been reinstated, if only to carry her rare full-length chinchilla cloak which had probably cost as much as Penny's sables. For a second time he was handcuffed to her millions which had seen her listed in the latest Vogue register as among the world's ten wealthiest women, despite almost never being mentioned in the gossip columns, except when she was seen in the front row of the four most famous couturiers when they showed their twice yearly collections in Paris.

After Rachel Simon had been welcomed by the count who admitted he had been looking forward to meeting her, she quipped, 'And what is your verdict?'

'Magnificent. You are a lady who dominates any gathering she graces.'

'Be careful, count. You have not yet married the lovely Marianne, and if you continue to flatter me I might begin to lay down a challenge for your attention, and I am notorious for always getting what I want. Ask Freddie Fitzpatrick who was my lover-boy many months ago until I suspected he regarded me as a soft touch. Overnight he ceased to enjoy my millions. He was brought back into favour when I had no one else to torment and I received your invitation. Yet even when we are in bed I can sense his fear of me. I doubt his stay will last as long as last time, but he helps pass the time.'

The rancour, quibbling and needling continued throughout dinner and while cigars were being smoked and cognac drunk. Marianne's father had spent the meal sitting between the friendly barbs Penny and Rachel fired at one another across him as though they did not realise he was there. Finally Rachel relented and asked, 'What line of business are you in Mr

69

Wilkinson?' When he explained he was the regional manager of an insurance company she asked for his business card as she might be able to pass business his way. Sadly he had to tell her that he did not have one with him. She immediately lost interest in him.

Finally, Marianne rose to her feet and prepared a toast: 'To those who will be the favourite guests at our wedding. See you all in Munich in a few weeks time. The invitations go out next week. Just one more matter before I wish you all good night; none of you is allowed to refuse our invitation. I want to be surrounded by my parents and my best friends on what will be the happiest day of my life.'

Next day after her parents had left for home, they flew back to Munich where they were greeted on the tarmac by a pack of journalists and photographers from every major newspaper in Germany, plus half a dozen international news agencies who had been informed of their engagement. The count and countess answered questions, gave brief interviews and allowed the flashes from a dozen or more cameras to give the impression that there was a storm of lightning, but without thunder or rain. As well as the future countess's own striking beauty, all the media were fascinated by the size of her ruby engagement ring. It was more newsworthy than her equally large diamond ring and was photographed almost as often as the couple themselves. The count explained that it was a family heirloom that had been given to one of his ancestors by an India maharajah. It was insured for more than $1,000,000, although to buy today it would cost three times as much, but this fact he did not reveal. Before he brought the press-call to a close he confirmed the date of their wedding and its location, and then forced their way to his stretch Mercedes.

That evening the countess, as everyone now regarded her, was about to ring Max, her furrier, when Alice informed her that he had phoned and would like to deliver her new furs the following morning. 'Ring him and tell him I expect him here at ten o'clock.' There was a brittleness in her voice caused mostly by her failure to convince her mother that although she would soon be a countess and a very wealthy lady, nothing would change between them. Her mother's final words were also a verdict that could be a prediction of the family's future:

'You will change, darling. You are entering a world in which we will not be part.'

Having had a restless night thinking of those parting words, she was in an irascible and cantankerous mood next morning which meant that anyone she was with could expect a snarl or waspish reaction to anything they said or did. Her duty maids were the first to be on the receiving end of her prickliness because her breakfast coffee was not hot and the rolls neither crisp nor fresh. They sensed it would not be long before the furrier received a lashing. In this mood she seemed contemptuous of anyone else's misery.

At first she relished the extravagance of the finished look and feel of the long, lavish and luxurious mink coat she had designed and Max Springeld had interpreted as she wanted. The deep collar rippled to the rhythm of her slow walk as she paraded in front of the furrier and two of her maids. When she drew the deep collar over her shoulders it enveloped her neck and achieved the provocation she intended now that she was days away from being the youngest German countess. The long jacket and two matching hats had been created out of the second bundle of pelts she had ordered because she knew a single bundle would be insufficient for the lavishness of her ankle-length coat. Her intention was to wear the most expensive and darkest mink coat ever made from the costliest Canadian pelts that were only available from a single North American fur farm. Marianne knew she would never see anyone wearing a coat or jacket to compare with the richness of the light weight female pelts that were darker than a moonless night. She was so pleased with his expertise that she had trusted him to make another loose-fitting jacket, but this time in pure white mink with a dark collar. 'I want it ready before I go on my honeymoon,' she had commanded.

'Where will you be going, countess?' he asked feeling proud of yet another order from the lady who would soon be the owner of his salon. It surely indicated that she appreciated his skills as an international furrier. Instead, he had re-aroused her acerbity that someone in his position should dare ask her such a personal question. She walked over to where he was sitting making notes of her new instructions. 'Stand up when I talk to you,' she shouted. 'I am not prepared to tolerate your insolence.

71

I shall let you know when I return whether you are to be dismissed or punished in some other way for your rudeness. Now get out and start work on my jacket at once. You have my measurements. Just make sure it is delivered before I go away.' Her two maids were scared by this outburst and wondered what fate awaited them if something harmless could ignite a new burst of anger. Instead, the grandeur of her new furs acted like a tranquiliser and she asked: 'Do you like my new coat, Alice?' At once her maid knew the eruption had burned itself out, and answered: 'I have never seen a coat to compare with it, countess, and doubt if I ever shall.'

Two days later she and Frau Welterstein flew to Paris where they were met by a limousine sent by the hotel where they were booked for three nights. To pass the time during the flight Marianne asked Heide to 'tell me about yourself'. Heide revealed that she and her mother had succeeded in fleeing from Nazi Germany to neutral Sweden leaving behind her father and brother. They never saw either again. Her father had led an unsuccessful attempt to assassinate Hitler, but been betrayed by one of his own aides, and arrested by the Gestapo and tortured.

She had returned to Germany after the war and was lucky enough to find a clerical job in one of the count's companies. Her loyalty was appreciated and after three years she was promoted to be his personal secretary. She added: 'Now I hope we shall be friends. You have only to ask and I shall do anything within my powers to assist you.'

Marianne smiled, but explained: 'I don't think friendship will be easy, once I am the countess, perhaps impossible. Already, even before my wedding, I have insisted that everyone of our staff understands my superior status and treats me with the respect that is my due. My maids know that from now onwards they have only one duty which is to look after my needs throughout every twenty-four hours All the staff at Rugerstein castle know they must always bow or curtsy when they see me. I am not prepared to make an exception in your case. I speak reasonable German and when I speak to you in your native tongue that is how you are to answer. If in English you will reply in English. Is that clear?'

'Yes, countess.' Heide raised the white flag of surrender. She knew there was no alternative but to let the countess know that she would always have her complete loyalty and respect.

At their hotel Marianne had been allocated a one-bedroom suite on the second floor facing the grounds, and Heide a back single room two floors up. She was told to go to her room, unpack and dress for dinner. 'Then come back here and we'll open this bottle of champagne with which the hotel has welcomed me.' In the lift after dinner she confided to Heide that she would miss the count in her bed that night, and was assured, 'Not nearly as much as he will be missing you, countess. I look forward to serving you both.' There was both a fear and humbleness in her voice and Marianne knew her victory over the Prussian was now absolute. And to show how wide the gap was between them there was no 'good night', simply an instruction to meet her in the hotel lobby at ten the following morning.

The need for this division was emphasised when they arrived at the salon of Christian Dior where the countess was expected As soon as a vendeuse stepped forward to greet them Heide told her, 'This is Countess von Rugerstein from Bavaria. She requires a wedding dress for herself. What, if anything, have you to show her?'

The senior sales lady stared at Marianne's voluptuous fur coat and realised that, although young, she was obviously very wealthy, probably one of the *nouveau riche* in the increasingly prosperous Germany. 'What size is the countess?' she asked Heide, only to hear Marianne intervene in a waspish voice that almost reduced Heide to tears: 'I think I am the best person to answer your question.' And turning to Heide she exploded in German, 'Be silent from now onwards or I shall send you home in disgrace.'

Marianne took off her coat and told Heide to look after it. Immediately, the sales lady assured her, 'Now that I have seen the countess's figure, I think I have a creation that will fit you perfectly. We made it for an Italian opera star, but a few days before she was due to be married, she took an overdose of pills. The dress has never been worn. Would the countess allow me to show it to her?' She disappeared and both Marianne and Heide were left seated in armchairs that were meant to relax customers into moods of contentment. There was iciness in her voice as Marianne warned her companion, 'Don't ever do that to me again, Heide. You remembered your curtsy this morning, but obviously not your manners No one speaks for me unless I give them permission.'

Heide knew that for the second time in two days she had committed a serious *faux pas* even though she had only wanted to be helpful. She knew it was the fault of her Prussian upbringing and her inbred desire to control. When the vendeuse returned accompanied by a much younger member of staff carrying a wedding gown over her arms, plus bundles of needles, pins and reels of white cotton, Marianne followed them into a large fitting room where the wall paper and the chairs were all in matching pale blue satin. Heide wisely did not follow.

The close-fitting gown that Marianne put on was made of a heavy satin with an imprinted design of raised roses. It had obviously been made for a star who was used to the spotlight. The vendeuse explained that when the singer had been asked for a fitting she replied she was too busy rehearsing a new role. They never saw her again. Now she truly believed the gown had been meant to bless the day when the countess was married.

Marianne looked at herself through three full-length mirrors placed strategically so that she could see the gown from every vantage angle. She approved what she saw. The flow of the pattern was controlled from a halter neckline which fell onto her slim waist before exploding in an avalanche of material that ended in a two metre train. 'I like it. It is what I had hoped to find in Paris. Now I need a white silk suit that I can wear under a black mink jacket if it turns cool on my honeymoon, as well as two outfits, one to wear ashore and the other for dinner on board a private yacht.' She spent two hours before making her decisions, and Heide was left wondering what was happening, and what might happen next. The tension only ended when the vendeuse appeared and said the countess was asking for her. Heide was informed that Dior would deliver the wedding gown and several other purchases to their hotel that afternoon; all Heide had to do was arrange the payment through the count's gold, unlimited credit card.

As they walked silently back to the hotel Heide feared that being part of life with the von Rugersteins might be coming to an end. As though reading her fears, Marianne bitched. 'I have made a decision. From now onwards you will be employed as my personal secretary and companion. I shall inform the count and he will accept my decision. The only change is that in future you will carry out my orders, not the count's. I am not asking you to approve the change. That is how it will be. All I need is your extension on the castle switchboard so that I can call you whenever I need you. Let us celebrate with lunch at Fouquets and then go sightseeing.' After enjoying in near silence a freshly prepared *omelette aux fines herbes*, the restaurant ordered them a taxi to take them on a two hour drive of some of the highlights in the French capital. Back in their hotel she cancelled their bookings for a third night and flew back to Munich the following morning with five separate Dior exclusive packages. For their last night in Paris the concierge was asked to book them a table for two in the best bistro in town which turned out to be in the Bois de Boulogne. To the complete surprise of Heide the countess suggested that she might like to wear the mink jacket she had brought with her to Paris, adding, 'I have forgiven, but not forgotten your *faux pas*, but tonight you need not dress like my poor relation.' But despite her generosity, Marianne continued to treat Heide as her servant. Heide sensing this was how it would always be, found herself dutifully walking a step behind the countess, unless they were talking together.

At Munich airport her coat immediately put her in the spotlight and she was identified as the future countess when she stepped into the 'Something to declare' section of customs. Her extravagant fur coat was a giveaway, as she intended. Heide trailed behind the countess carrying her jacket but not daring to wear it or say a word. The head of customs also recognised the future Countess von Rugerstein whom, his wife had told him, would soon be one of tomorrow's leaders of Munich society. He addressed her as countess and when she told him she had been to Paris to buy the dress she would wear at her wedding, she pouted her lips at him, and he wilted under her capricious whim to treat him as an equal, and waved her through. 'I shall not forget your kindness. What is your name?' And she ordered Heide to write it down together with his home address.

Back in the castle all arrangements for the wedding were being finalised, while her four maids were waiting to welcome her home and unpack her packages. Marianne dictated half a dozen letters for Heide to type including a draft of a short but obviously sincere letter to Christiana and Ulysses Stephanopolous on whose yacht she and the count were to spend their honeymoon, plus a short note to the inspector of customs at the airport who also received a bottle of champagne to share with his wife or girlfriend. He could be a very useful ally in the future. She told Heide she would 'top and tail' both letters and she could sign the rest. The drawbridge on any close relationship between herself and Heide was now permanently raised. But for each of her maids she had bought a small bottle of Chanel perfume at the airport.

As well as a letter from her mother thanking her for everything during the time they had spent together in London, there was a short note from Frau Wolf at the boutique thanking her for her custom and assuring her of her personal attention whenever she visited the boutique in the future, as well as a brief and humble letter from Herr Springeld, her furrier, apologising for his intrusion into the privacy of her honeymoon and promising to remember his position whenever they met in the future. He hoped she would accept his apology. Finally there was a brief handwritten note from the count: 'Welcome home, countess. Champagne will be waiting for you in my suite at seven-thirty, and much else, including Little Wilhelm. Dress – informal.'

As she followed Alice who had been ordered to clear out most of the late countess's furs to make way for her own growing collection, she noticed four mink skins that had been linked together for wearing round the neck of the late countess when the weather was too warm for full furs, but she still wished to look impressive. Alice was told to take them to Frau Heide and tell her they were to be sent to the head of customs together with the champagne. As a postscript to the thank-you note she added, 'The furs are from my personal collection.' She was determined to encourage most-favoured-countess treatment whenever she passed through customs at Munich airport. He would also be put on her Christmas card and present list. Suddenly she had second thoughts. To her the four skins of mink she was gifting to the wife of the head of customs were only fit to be thrown away. Alice was told to bring back all the furs she put aside for returning to her furrier. The mink skins were sent to the furrier, but a simple mink bolero was sent in their place to the head of customs.

Wilhelm's request for informality that evening made Marianne smile, and was immediately ignored. On the contrary she took

76

extra care to look irresistibly sexy in a slim pink satin dress which was short enough to draw attention to the elegance of her race-horse legs. Wherever his eyes wandered they revealed Rugerstein diamonds to which she added a meal time of kisses as she later fell on top of his naked body. In his uncontrollable response to her closeness, he accidentally tore her dress and one of her diamond earrings fell to the floor. She told him his cuddle might cost him several thousand marks to replace the dress he may have ruined. She was annoyed at his roughness and as punishment she deliberately refused him entry while continuing to excite Little Wilhelm until he threatened to pour his love over the silk sheets instead of where he finally gave her the happiest of thrills she desired.

Once again he reminded her she could have anything she wanted, and soon she would not even have to ask. In reply she told him that she had told Heide that she was to regard herself as solely working for herself as her personal secretary and companion. 'She was of considerable help in Paris and I knew you would not mind as you cannot refuse me anything I need. She will also help me improve my German.' In answer he simply asked her to 'treat Heide kindly...' She assured him: 'You can safely leave it to me to treat her as she deserves.' She told Heide: 'The count has agreed that from now onwards you are mine.'

As the day of their wedding drew ever nearer and her presents became ever more frequent, the countess now began to think of her diamonds as the equivalent of the rows of ribbons on the uniform of a general. She might be only twenty-one, but the count already acknowleged that his countess would be more than just the châtelaine of his castle. She would be its ruler. She was beginning to dominate his life, too.

5

The wedding in the town hall, and the reception and dinner that followed at the castle all went without a hitch. Heide gave her own Prussian hauteur to the role of maid of honour as well as supervising all that happened, including the demands of the media. Their best stories came when they talked to the VIP guests and asked them to value the jewels worn by the bride. Dame Penny Welling guestimated that the diamonds, emeralds, black pearls and ruby she would be wearing at dinner were from the Rugerstein collection and could be valued at sums that varied between fifteen and twenty-five million dollars. Christiana, who gave permission to be quoted, told the press that the count and countess would be honeymooning on her own private ocean-going yacht, and she was looking forward to meeting the new countess and comparing 'the two Aladdin's caves of jewels they both owned.' It was her way of seeking to out-dazzle the bride.

The media labelled the guests who were seated at tables on either side of the top table as a *ménage a six* millionairesses, and their husbands and escorts, who bickered and gossiped among themselves about how much the ball gowns they were wearing had cost, while one news gatherer quoted a waiter called Josef who revealed he had overheard a conversation between Ulysses Stephanopolous and Count von Rugerstein during which the figure of ten million dollars was mentioned in respect of a business deal. There wasn't an iota of truth in any of these reports but they ensured spicy breakfast reading around the globe from a world where money and extravagance was the norm in the closed circle of the mega-rich. Marianne, Countess von Rugerstein, was now part of the closest of all closed-shops.

The new countess found time to talk to the eighty or more guests who were seated at the guest tables that fanned out in a semi circle from both ends of the top table. They were mostly

78

business associates of her husband, her family and close personal friends. And a dozen members of Munich society whom she was meeting for the first time. Marianne's attempt to show how reasonably good her German was turned into a failure by the insistence of all the German guests, in deference to the English born bride, to speak her language. Attempts to practice speaking to them in German were in vain as everyone insisted upon talking to her in English. The band played on until 1 am when she and the count finally fell into each other's arms and danced the last waltz.

They flew off the next morning with Christiana and Ulysses Stephanopolous and their daughter, Stephanie, who was seventeen and nearing the end of her three years at an expensive finishing school close to Lausanne in Switzerland. The five of them travelled in the Greek family's specially designed and luxuriously furnished Boeing 747 from Munich to Athens. Throughout the flight the Greek hosts and the newly-weds sat together at a solid oak table for four in the front of the aircraft which had been battened down in case of bumpy weather. It was the centrepiece of a lavishly furnished but elongated lounge-cum-dining-room. Three stewardesses hovered close to where the owners and their guests were sitting so that the slightest nod or raising of an eyebrow from Madame Christiana met with an immediate response. She deliberately sat with her back to the flight deck so she could keep an eye on the whole of the lounge area and its staff who were under instructions to remain standing and on duty throughout the flight. Their young, bewitchingly beautiful, but spoiled daughter, Stephanie, who would become a millionairess the day she reached her eighteenth birthday in less than a year's time could not sit with her parents because none of the chairs or other pieces of furniture were moveable. Used to doing whatever she wanted, Stephanie ignored the law of the air that only members of the crew were allowed on the flight deck while the plane was airborne, and spent the entire time after take-off on the flight deck flirting with the deputy captain and distracting him from his other duties. Her governess, who was employed solely to provide companionship for the young lady dared not follow her. Nor did she know that Stephanie was already looking forward to personally sacking her the moment she inherited the massive first instalment of her inheritance, a day on which she would also be elected a full member of the board of directors of Stephanopolous International, the family's empire which was recognised as the largest privately-owned global corporation.

After everyone had been served plates of thinly sliced smoked salmon with half sections of lemon wrapped in sealed cloth sachets to avoid soiling their fingers, Christiana suggested to Marianne that it was time to show her the bedroom which was for the sole use of herself and Ulysses. It was the same size as the lounge and together occupied nearly seventy per cent of the total cabin space. The rest was for a kitchen and crew quarters which occupied the minimum space demanded under air regulations. The bedroom walls were covered with pale pink silk wallpaper, with the largest windows air safety allowed. The bed was six feet wide and like all the furniture clamped to the floor to prevent any movement caused by turbulence. Marianne described it as elegant and feminine, but asked her hostess who was more than twice her age, 'Don't you sometimes feel that a lady in your position is entitled to more room than you have allocated yourself?'

'Don't think I worried about the size of the staff quarters,' she was assured. 'I am entirely indifferent to their comfort. They are employed and on board for one purpose only, and that is to look after myself and my family. For the rest of the time they are maids at our family estate outside Athens. They can seldom get away from me, poor souls.'

Marianne, being half French, thought the French word, *insouciant,* which had been adopted into English, was the only word that expressed Christiana's indifference to everyone she employed. The countess was prepared to admit that as far as possible she, too, had no contact with the staff employed at their castle except her own personal maids. Provided the rest of their servants carried out the work for which they were paid they had nothing to fear. Her own next priority would be to emphasise her own equality with this mega-millionairess despite the Greek's vast fortune which almost certainly dwarfed not only the Rugersteins' wealth, but if the rumours were correct every other family in the globe except perhaps the Vanderbilts and the Aga Khan, and Rachel Simon. She was already wondering if there might be a price to pay for their so-called wedding present. Like Rachel, it seemed that Christiana regarded everyone as her inferior. For the moment she left it at telling her hostess that, 'as soon as I accepted Wilhelm's plea to become his countess, I had everyone curtsy to me as soon as our engagement was known. I intend to be very insouciant.'

When the aircraft landed they were waved through Immigration and Customs and said their *au revoir*s to one another as their luggage was sorted and put into the appropriate Rolls of the two which had been sent to meet them. One headed for the Stephanopolous family's estate, the other for Pireaus where the honeymooners were saluted and piped aboard the *Christiana* which had been renamed after being given to its owner on her wedding day by her husband Ulysses Stephanopolous. Captain Gustavesen escorted them to the owner's suite which occupied half the area of the main deck. Marianne quickly undressed and slipped into one of the three bikinis she had bought in Paris and headed onto their private deck and the heat of the afternoon sun. When the captain saw she had no head covering he decided to disobey the normal rule that no one should approach the owner's private deck unless called, or there was an emergency. He took with him a selection of sun hats that were permanently on board for the benefit to the owner's guests, including a Panama with an extra wide brim for ladies with its silk band embossed with a series of hearts in all the colours of the rainbow. He excused his intrusion by explaining that when he noticed the countess was hatless in the still strong overhead sun, he felt it was his duty to come and suggest she should cover her head. 'The Grecian sun can be very fierce,' he explained. They both thanked him for his thoughtfulness. But before he departed Marianne asked him to send a maid to her. Within a couple of minutes the well trained Olga arrived and curtsied, as she always did to every guest. She was tall, well endowed, but all was spoiled by a pair of atrocious legs that looked as though they could have been stolen from a new born elephant. Marianne deliberately kept her standing so that she would understand from the outset that for the next fourteen days she would be serving a countess, and carry out all her orders.

Finally she was told, 'Go to our suite and unpack my cases and hang everything in the wardrobes. Iron anything that has become creased. Come back at seven this evening and run my bath, and help me dress. By the way, never enter our suite without knocking and receiving permission to enter.' When Olga had left she told the count, 'As you did not feed me last night, for which you are forgiven, I shall expect a double helping this evening.'

When they returned to their suite they found a note from the captain informing them that, if convenient, dinner would be served in the dining-room on the lower deck at 8.30 pm. They would sail at seven that evening and they were welcome on the bridge to watch the Greek capital and its Parthenon gradually slip away from sight. Marianne joked that the count had the choice of bidding farewell to an ancient beauty or being welcomed by a modern one. In answer he clutched her breasts which pleased Marianne, but also helped confirm her belief that in due course it would be the count who belonged to her, not vice versa. Perhaps she might prove to be his, and little Wilhelm's, Achilles heel. But now all she wanted was to suck his manhood as though it were a toffee apple She planned to torment him until he accepted that her body was hers, not his. Finally he would learn that it was not only their staff who had to obey her. Perhaps it would be like a game of tennis in which she served the aces and produced ground strokes that were penetrating and accurate until, just as he was showing signs of exhaustion she presented him with an easy lob to smash and win the point and think of himself as a fine player. The final arbiter would be the extra power and strength that her youth gave her.

That night as they lay locked and in each other's arms exhausted and happy, the count knew he could deny her nothing. He was trapped, yet it was only forty-eight hours since she became his countess, and already she had only to snap her proverbial fingers and he would come running. Marianne was aware that his needs would always be greater than her own. She would never accept the roles of a dutiful German frau. She could be as hard as any of her diamonds. He knew that, inevitably, she would exercise increasing control in his businesses, but achieved a measure of consolation in the English saying that two heads were better than one.

Marianne, however, was in no hurry, and was content to wait and plan before she pounced. Such thoughts had hardened after Christiana Stephanopolous had hinted to her during the flight that men could be like putty in the hands of a stronger woman. And when she had added that despite the vast Rugerstein group of factories, plus its printing works and magazines and the farms and villages that they owned, they were very small fry when compared with the worldwide interests of the Stephanopolous family that were valued at five hundred million dollars. At the time Marianne had wondered why she was being told so much when they hardly knew one another. For the first time she asked herself whether, perhaps, with her business background she might be able to have a foot in both camps.

What Marianne could not possibly know was that Christiana, as a far more powerful and astute businesswoman, had carried out her own research when she learned that the future countess had been successful in the City of London. She doubted, however, whether her earnings could be anywhere near her own annual bonus from Stephanopolous International of two million dollars. Not for nothing was Christiana on the quayside when her yacht docked at the family owned island which stretched for several kilometres in all directions. Like everything the Stephanopolous family touched, it had been turned into a money-making enterprise which she ruled as its empress. The family had bought the island during the war, when Greece was under Nazi occupation, for just ten thousand dollars. Today it had a price tag, although it was not for sale, of fifteen million dollars, and such offers had been made and refused.

What first caught Marianne's feminine eye as she waved to her hostess from her bird's eye perch outside the bridge, was the shawl that was draped around Christiana's shoulders. It fell down to below her waist, but was like nothing Marianne had seen before. As they threw their arms round each other her hands touched the woven blood red silk shawl with its yards of pure golden thread that had been woven into a unique pattern and had been given as a present from an Indian maharani. 'And how is my new best friend?' Christiana asked. Marianne responded by admitting that although she and the count and herself were having a wonderful cruise, it was still good to feel firm earth under their feet.

Welcomes completed, Christiana clapped her hands and two elderly peasant women hurried forward and were ordered to carry the luggage of the count and countess to the villa half a mile distant on the high point of the island from where every inch of land could be observed. Marianne was told, as she pointed towards the two women whose faces were lined by both age and the sun, 'Don't worry about them. They spend most of their time gossiping. It is time they did some manual work. And if you have anything that needs altering or mending they are wonderful needlewomen. They will work through the night if I tell them it needs to be finished by early morning. They are brilliant knitters and each has a contract to produce one finished garment every day, except Sunday. They are paid thirty-five dollars a week, and think of themselves as millionaires. I sell their exclusively-designed jumpers and sweaters for between three and five hunded hundred dollars in boutiques at our three luxury hotels in the centre of Athens and on the coast a few kilometres from the capital. How's that for profiteering? Every drop of virgin olive oil that is produced and bottled on the island belongs to us and together with the sea-salted wheat that is turned into rare and expensive loaves of bread, plus all the lamb from the hundreds of sheep that are bred on the island, are delivered to supermarkets in Athens. Whatever I do has to make a profit, and the bigger the better.' As they drove past the two women who were dragging their cases up to the villa Christiana explained that there was little crime, but any wrong-doing was punished with a heavy fine that simply put the miscreant further into the family's debt. The money was deducted from their wage until the debt was paid off. All food was free to every family, but only after they had produced the target of food that was required for selling in Athens and elsewhere in Greece.

'Between you and me,' Christiana joked and looking at Marianne in all seriousness, 'I have a magic wand and it is made of gold and dollars. Shall I cast a spell over you and become your protector?'

'I am sure I shall be the better and wiser for having you by my side, and as my friend,' replied Marianne.

'I shall protect you, Marianane. After dinner while the men smoke their cigars, why don't we disappear and talk about you and me? The entire first floor of the villa is mine, although I share a bedroom suite with my husband. He also has a second bedroom to which he is despatched when he displeases me, which is mostly when I discover that his eyes have been roving again. Most Greek men are tantalised by a pretty face and a curvaceous body which can turn them into predators for a night and often tomorrow night, too. Withholding my own body, however, is the weapon that quickly brings him to heel. He learned this lesson during the first year of our marriage. Nowadays a single night away is the most he can endure. And it is becoming more costly the older I am.'

Marianne rather enjoyed knowing that it had taken Christiana a year to achieve dominance over her husband, and she had achieved that goal in less than a month. Did she have so much to learn?

Christiana sensed that this stripling might need taming as well as training, but for the moment she was content to tell her, 'I shall protect you, Marianne, and make you even richer than you already are. But my real target is your husband, or more accurately his business. During the last three years I have doubled the size of our orders for the lightweight cotton cloths he produces at his Dusseldorf factory which convert in China into cheap dresses for the South American market and, increasingly eastern Europe. What costs us a few dollars to buy and make we sell for thirty dollars. As a result in Dusseldorf your husband is now entirely dependent upon my largesse. He also does a great deal of large scale printing for us. One day I shall withdraw my support, or maybe you will do it for me, and then I shall appoint you to take control in his empire. How's that for female dominance and astuteness?'

Lunch was served out of doors on a wide terrace that stretched the entire length of the villa which overlooked the unrippled blueness of a contented sea that stretched to infinity. The terrace floor was pink marble with the chairs upholstered in matching pink satin. Every inch of everything had a female touch and there was no doubt in Marianne's mind whose touch it was, but she wondered how many times her tongue had lashed the workmen until they finally did the work exactly as she had demanded and with most of their profit disappearing into Grecian thin air. The building where the staff lived had a corrugated iron roof which absorbed the heat of the daytime sun, yet turned the early morning cold into a near icebox and made sleep near impossible when it rained. For the family and guests the villa offered six double bedrooms and two suites, a dining-room, kitchen and two toilets. The sleeping quarters housed a staff of eight. But nothing was ever permitted to disturb Christiana, Ulysses, their daughter Stephanie, or their guests who demanded breakfast, lunch or dinner at any time they decided.

That afternoon the count and countess made love in their suite that had its own secluded terrace with the same pink marble floor they had looked at during lunch, while inside a large Aubusson rug half covered the highly polished wood floor.

They even toyed with the idea of having a cheek-to-cheek dance, but preferred lying together. When the count suggested, 'The sea air and sun bring out the best in all of us,' Marianne promised that 'even if we are one day forced to sleep in an igloo, I shall never be an ice maiden.'

At dinner their hostess was the last to appear, but both men agreed silently that it was a treat worth waiting for. What there was of her dress had the elegance of simplicity and looked as though it had been spun out of silver thread. It never touched her knees and only just disturbed the view of her full breasts. She had a figure to excite any man privileged to see it, and if they did they were soon putty in her hands. They might end up wealthier than when they met, but her profits inevitably dwarfed theirs.

Tonight, however, her target was Marianne, and her deliberate table plan at the long oak table put her and the countess at one end and Ulysses and the count at the other, and almost out of hearing. Her diamonds that were around her neck, dropping from her ears, and around her arms and fingers made her look like a Cartier heiress. She explained, 'The countess and I have much to talk about, and you two business geniuses will have plenty to plan, but I insist the end result must be sufficient to allow your wives to go on a spending spree.' Turning to Marianne, she insisted: 'That is the real purpose of husbands.' Such a remark found Marianne understanding that being an immensely wealthy lady, which now included herself, encouraged ruthlessness and intolerance. Was it simply their excessive affluence and the obvious power and authority it gave, or was there something more? Perhaps it was because extravagance was a powerful aphrodisiac, and considerably more potent than nagging which was the only weapon poorer women had when seeking their own way with their husbands. For their insolence they could often be given a beating. But with wealth you could belittle your husband and deny him the consequences of his meanness or foolishness. If it was a manservant he could be whipped by their tongues until he shrivelled with fear of what might happen next. As for maids they were so insignificant that it was demeaning to even sack them, and you simply passed the task to your housekeeper or someone else. There was much to be said for great wealth. As Christiana indicated again, she had the power to pass the count considerably more business than he had already received, or she could turn off the tap and as a result make him more vulnerable to any take-over approach she might make, The Stephanopolous family were on a golden pedestal, and that needed to be recognised even by their friends.

In an attempt to put herself on a near equal level with her hostess Marianne asked with a playful look in her eyes, how wonderful it must be to be able to snap your fingers and have some handsome young man, or even someone older, think that their life was about to change, only to find themselves trapped inside an electrified fence from which there is no escape unless she turned off the current. 'I know an English lady whose fortune might be comparable with your own, but certainly not her figure or her looks, and almost certainly not her corporate power, yet you can both be as cold as your diamonds, or raise an eyebrow suggestively, or pout your lips and any man will rush to please you. The English heiress treats her prisoners as toys to be thrown into the trash bin when they no longer amuse or satisfy her.'

Christiana ignored what Marianne had said, but told her: 'You have just convinced me that you are a very observant and intelligent young lady who could be a worthy foe because you would be prepared to stand up to me, which is very rare. Let me be straightforward with you. I intend to make you one of my close business allies. And the longer it takes the worse it usually is for whoever I am targeting.'

Marianne recognised a gauntlet was being thrown down, and it might be a risk too far, too soon, to pick up. At the same time she remembered that only a few months ago she had given an aristocratic family just one hour to accept her offer for their stately home or it would be reduced by one thousand pounds for every minute they delayed. They bowed to her threat, and the pressure of the millions that were at her disposal. It had given her pleasure to watch their humiliation.

Now Marianne found herself on the receiving end and could only admire Christiana's cold-blooded confidence, yet she was fearful that the price to be paid for being 'part of her team' might be too high. While she was not without power herself, any battle would be like her rifles attempting to challenge Christiana's tanks. Once she was opposed she would become like an Amazon determined upon destruction.

Marianne was becoming convinced it would make more sense to be on Christiana's side than against her. She decided to walk a tight rope and for the moment, keep her eyes focused on her hostess, while seeking to look after the best interests of the Countess von Rugerstein wherever they might lie.

The two of them adjourned upstairs to her suite of rooms that occupied the entire first floor of the villa, leaving their husbands with their cigars. Christiana stepped out of all her clothes and, like every other wealthy lady left them to be picked up by someone else. Now she was only wearing her diamonds. Marianne was also naked but decided to cover herself with one of the bathrobes that were hanging in a closet in the all-pink marble bathroom. To prove she was not ashamed of her body she selected a diaphanous robe that hid nothing and could not be more tantalising. She recognised that if either of them presented themselves in front of a man who was their target they would be irresistible, but only until they had gained what they wanted.

'Thanks, Marianne, for confirming something I have known ever since I first met you at your wedding. You are not only very beautiful, you have a brain, too. No wonder the count was attracted to you at first sight. Knowing what I was told at your wedding by your former boss, I intend to take advantage of your brain and business acumen.'

Marianne changed the subject and began to answer the question Christiana had first asked, as it was getting late. She revealed that she was half English and half French on her mother's side, while her father worked as a departmental manager for a large insurance company. He earned an average wage, but even at twenty her salary dwarfed what he brought home, and she was wearing a mink coat, and so enjoyed the envious looks of women who were obviously wondering how one so young could afford such an eye-catching and expensive coat.

Her hostess cut her short by announcing, 'I prefer sables.' Marianne accepted she had lost another battle which Christiana rammed home by warning there could only be one empress in her world. Her next words were meant to have the effect of a rapier being plunged into a defeated opponent. 'Don't try to oppose me, Marianne. I am thinking of making you my deputy.' And she gave her guest a royal box view of the monster square-cut single stone diamond ring which almost hid one of her thumbnails. 'Furs take second place when you can wear jewels like this. Nevertheless I am starting to feel cold. She walked out of the room and returned wearing a sable jacket. 'I keep one of these in each of my homes in case the weather turns chilly. Be prepared, is my motto.'

Marianne realised she was being outclassed, and surrendered: 'Life is full of surprises. If six months ago I had found myself in the same room as yourself, and you had been wearing your sables, I would not have merited a second glance from you or anyone else.'

Christiana dismissed such a comment: 'I am not interested in the past. Once you agree to what I shall offer you, Wilhelm will both be amply rewarded with new orders. Our accounts department has been instructed that all new contracts will be signed by me, but my husband remains responsible for signing and presenting our annual report as president of Stephanopolous International. I intend to allocate you some shares so that you will be among the future decision makers of our corporation. No one outside the family has ever held a single share. You don't have to say yes. I have made the decision for you, and I never change my mind.'

Marianne was not sure whether to be frightened or honoured at being offered entry into the inner circle of a privately-owned global gold mine. However, she insisted, 'I must be allowed to inform my husband of the generosity of your offer and the influence it will give me. I can assure you that I shall never seek to outshine you, not least because it will be near impossible, but I must be allowed to enjoy my own femininity and dress in any way that pleases me and the count. I, too, like to be admired and envied.'

Christiana's response was to kiss Marianne on her forehead. 'I think we both understand one another. You have just begun a climb towards the heights of global business decision-making. I shall inform you of all new business I pass to your husband so that you can make him understand that it was you who had made it possible. I have plans for you which I shall reveal when I am ready. Soon changes in the allocation of shares could see me in a position to obtain complete control of the family corporation. When that happens you will be the third most influential businesswoman, perhaps in the world, after myself and my daughter, Stephanie. Men hate to be bossed by women, but our directors know they have no alternative. And to make sure they never forget, I always wear an array of diamonds at our board meetings as a reminder of what I can afford, while they are aware they will never be able to buy such gems for their own wives. I may not be a nice person, but international business is not about being nice, but being successful. People get hurt, and I make sure it is never me. Now I will show you something that I wear when I really want to impress someone. Believe me, Marianne, it is better to have me on your side, and under my terms, than to try to oppose me.'

She walked across to the far wall and an unseen switch revealed a wall safe from which she extracted a sensuous, eye-catching necklace made from eighteen identical square-cut, purest green emeralds each oblong cut and the size of a postage stamp that Sothebys had valued at sixty thousand dollars each. She took the necklace off its bed and carefully placed it around Marianne's neck and whispered: 'Now you know what it means to be one of my closest friends, and what separates a mega-wealthy woman from someone who is just very rich.' Marianne's business brain was working overtime and guessed that the necklace she was momentarily allowed to imagine was hers, was probably worth more than one million dollars. She guessed, and rightly, that she would never wear it again. However, unlike almost everyone else who might see the emeralds, her own three row necklace of matching black pearls was equally valuable. However, the emeralds had one big advantage. Most people would recognise and yearn to own them, while black pearls were so rare that ninety-nine per cent of those who saw her wearing them might think they were some kind of junk. She doubted if one per cent of any group who saw them would have any idea of their unique rarity.

Christiana went on, 'A few months after that purchase which was the price Ulysses paid for a return to my bed, I decided that in addition to our sponsorship of a business school at the leading Athens university, it was time to show the Greek people that the Stephanopolous family was prepared to use its vast wealth to establish the Stephanopolous Foundation whose aim would be to help underprivileged children whose parents were living below the poverty line both in Greece and elsewhere. I would be its president. When I told my husband he said he would think about the idea. While he thought, I again denied him what he wanted as much as money. Unfortunately for him, he has the sexual appetite of a rabid dog. This time his starvation lasted five days before he surrendered and crept into my bed and told me his solicitors were drawing up the necessary documents announcing the formation of the Foundation, with an initial donation of five million dollars from himself. However, he had to be taught that when I wanted something I was not prepared to be kept waiting. I informed him that during the five days he had kept me waiting the amount I now needed had risen to six million dollars, and it was not to be a donation from him, but from the Stephanopolous family. He had the figure and wording changed next morning. We slept together that night.

'Since then we have raised and been able to distribute many millions of dollars in both Greece and several poor countries in Africa, as a result of twisting the arms of many other millionaire families in Greece, as well as our suppliers. Why don't you establish a branch of the Foundation in Germany?' Others will do all the day-to-day work while you use your brains and your title to attract donations and let the media know of the charitable work now being undertaken by the new Countess von Rugerstein. As a fairy godmother you will bring new glory to the family name, and once a year you could throw a party at your castle and invite one hundred deprived German children. I would attend and make a substantial donation which others would be encouraged, or perhaps forced, to follow. I can be very persuasive, as you know. Wilhelm's is not the only business in Germany with whom we place orders. I would help your new work by writing to all our other suppliers. If they did not respond with an acceptable contribution they would receive a note that I was surprised at the small amount of their donation to the German branch of my Foundation. It would send shivers through their boardrooms. I doubt whether any of them would not take my hint. If I should be proved wrong, whichever of the companies ignored me would be sent a cable from one of my junior executives informing them that due to a change in economic conditions all outstanding orders were being cancelled. Through the grapevine everyone in Germany and other countries where we have business interests will learn that when I ask for help for my Foundation I expected to receive a contribution of not less than fifty thousand dollars.'

Marianne was at once aware that Christiana could use the same tactics against the count if he did not co-operate. She asked: 'How much would you contribute towards the funding of the new Foundation in Germany? And how much would you expect the count and myself to provide?'

Christiana ignored the first question and explained that Germany would be the first country outside Greece to have its own Stephanopolous Foundation solely devoted to providing aid for deprived German children. 'At a guess I would expect the von Rugersteins to contribute a minimum of two million dollars. With the count's many close and wealthy business associates, and still more rich social friends, it will be hard for anyone to refuse making a sizeable donation, especially when they know how much the von Rugersteins are donating. Your personal reputation and prestige will soar overnight, but you should first hint to Wilhelm that Christiana would feel slighted if he did not agree to provide the initial funding.'

Once Marianne was back in their suite the count expressed annoyance at being denied the pleasure of his wife's company for a whole evening, and with something approaching an uncanny sixth sense, asked, 'What has she been planning?' Marianne decided it was time for half-truths. She told him about the sensational piece of jewellery their hostess had allowed her to wear, but avoided describing her other boasts. Instead, she concentrated upon Christiana's wish to found the first overseas branch of her Foundation for deprived children in Germany with Marianne as its first president. She added in a whisper: 'She would expect you to donate two million dollars to set up the Foundation with headquarters in Munich. We would then seek contributions from your many wealthy German business and social friends. The foundation has already raised million of dollars which have been used to help underprivileged children in Africa as well as Greece. However, all the money we raise would be used solely to alleviate the plight of underprivileged children in Germany. Christiana's view is that once your German friends know that you are putting up two million dollars to establish the branch, they will find it hard not to make large contributions themselves. In return for your agreement she will personally make sure that further, worthwhile orders are placed with your companies. She will, I know, feel slighted if you do not agree to her request.'

Hearing this the count told Marianne that strong rumours were circulating among the international business community that Christiana was moving ever closer to taking control of Stephanopolous International. 'The story is that she demonstrated her new impregnability at a recent board meeting after one of the non-executive members voted against a motion she had moved. She immediately told him to remember that only two people were indispensable, herself and her husband. The following morning he received a memo informing him that she had decided to reduce the numbers of non-shareholders on the board, and his services would no longer be required. He obtained permission to come to her office where he gave an abject apology. In reply Christiana told him she would accept his grovelling, but she would not reinstate him onto the board.'

Marianne's reaction was to tell her husband: 'I have known her only a short while, but I can believe every word of that story. Which is why I believe it will always be better to be on her side, than against her.' She also told the count that Christiana had indicated she wanted the Countess von Rugerstein to assume a senior managerial position within Stephanopolous International. 'She has been talking to Penny or Rachel about my business ability and successes.'

The following morning the two elderly peasant women who

had been ordered by Christiana to carry their heavy cases from the yacht, now took them back to the quayside. But the count and countess had to depart without an opportunity to say a farewell or thank you to their hosts.

Aboard the yacht most days were spent at sea although land was seldom out of sight. On board Marianne wrote a handwritten letter to, 'Dear Christiana and Ulysses, we cannot begin to thank you enough for your kindness and generosity in allowing us the sole use of your magnificent floating home for our honeymoon. Everything has been perfect thanks to your well-trained crew, plus the obvious trouble that Christiana has taken to guarantee that whatever we have wanted has been immediately provided. We feel like royalty. In addition, the weather has been perfect, the sea calm and we have often danced on deck. Our sincere wish is that soon you will find the time to spend a week in our castle where Wilhelm will be able to show all three of us the many attractions throughout both Munchen and Bavaria. Our very warmest greetings – Marianne and Wilhelm. – PS We both like your suggestion for a German Stephanopolous Foundation.'

To their surprise, Christiana's white Rolls was waiting for them on the quayside as the yacht slowly eased its way into port at the end of their honeymoon cruise. On deck, although the sun was blazing from a cloudless sky the temperature had dropped several degrees and seemed to be hovering only a little above freezing. Despite the plunge both the count and countess were gloveless as they held hands and looked over the side as they felt the slightest jar as the yacht touched its moorings. There was no sign of their host or hostess and they assumed Christiana had simply sent her limousine to take them to the airport. Such thoughts were quickly dashed. As soon as the gangway was in place the uniformed chauffeur got out of his seat and opened the rear door of the Rolls. And Christiana was there to greet them, wearing another of her frighteningly expensive coats. As they disembarked she told them she had cancelled their flight, 'And you are staying with us in Athens for a couple of nights, or longer if you can spare the time.' Her chauffeur was told to, 'Get their luggage off the yacht and put the cases in the boot.'

As the limousine joined the slow moving traffic out of Pireaus she told them to watch how other cars sensibly gave way to a Rolls because the cost of any repairs would be frightening for those who could only afford a run-around, even though its upkeep to her was little more than petty cash when compared with what it cost to service their yacht and their 747 aircraft, 'although much can be lost via corporation expenses'.

When they arrived at Christiana's mansion home Marianne was pleased to note that the count's castle was more than twice as large. The welcome that Christiana had arranged for them meant passing through a double line of fourteen servants who either bowed or curtsied, but whether to their mistress or a count and countess, Marianne never fathomed. Above them in the entrance hall was a canopy of marble supported by four Corinthian marble columns pieced together from several broken parts of original columns from an ancient temple. The head butler led the welcome while Marianne admired the estimated seven metre-high ceiling made from cypress wood which grew in a forest on the estate. The floor was more pink marble strewn with Turkish rugs. So much marble had seemed ostentatious on the island, but here in the Greek capital its cooling effect was only a modern continuation of the homes of the wealthiest families three millennia ago when Greece was the most civilised country in the west with both slaves and a democracy. Nothing seemed pretentious, not even the massive marble carved fireplace that had once been in the palace home of a courtier at Versailles in the sixteenth century which had literally been given away during the French Revoluion. Long lengths of double thickness damask framed every window while from the ceiling hung three matching Venetian chandeliers, each burning a dozen electric candles. The highlight for Marianne was a mahogany cabinet filled with a 240-piece Limoges dinner service that she learned had belonged to Frederick the Great. Christiana could not resist sarcastically suggesting, 'Shouldn't it be in your castle in Germany. Wilhelm?'

Although the countess did not appreciate her hostess's smug mockery, her verdict was to kiss Christiana and tell her, 'Everything you have done is exactly how I would have furnished your magnificent mansion home if I had the wealth to create what is as much a palace as a family home. It is not only ruthlessness that we have in common.'

Young though Marianne was, Christiana was more than ever convinced she had the making of someone she would need by her side when she began her final drive to push the family's global empire forward to new positions of influence, prestige and profitability.

Marianne thought their suite expressed the cool refinement of France, although she learned later that Christiana had obtained copies of photographs of the original suites at the London Ritz and instructed a Greek interior designer to copy them. Everything was of classical proportions and typically Louis Seize. Because Christiana shared the same dislike as the managers of the Ritz for free-standing wardrobes which collected dust, all hanging space was built with curved doors that stretched to the ceiling. Marianne was particularly intrigued by a pair of silver-plated tongs that had originally been used by maids to stretch the fingers of a lady's fine elbow-length kid gloves before she went out for the evening.

When there was a knock at the door, the count knew it must be a member of staff as their hostess would certainly have walked in without knocking. It was a young uniformed maid who curtsied and said her name was Lucille and she had been sent by Madame Stephanopolous to carry out any instructions given by the countess. Marianne told her to come back after 1 pm when the suite would be unoccupied and then unpack her two suitcases and hang all her clothes in the wardrobes. She was then to return at 6 pm that evening to help her prepare for dinner. 'Yes, countess,' Lucille acknowledged and showed the strict training she had received by adding, 'I shall wait in the corridor until you and the count leave for your lunch with Madame, and then unpack your suitcases. I shall return sharp at six this evening as commanded.' Lucille curtsied again before leaving.

Marianne next dialled the number of the Rugerstein castle and asked for Heide to come to the phone. 'It is the countess who is calling,' she told whoever answered. The next voice she recognised was her secretary, 'How nice to hear from you, countess. I hope you are having a wonderful honeymoon. How can I help?'

'Listen carefully and make a note of all I am about to tell you. Find the largest of the count's suitcases and pack it with my new mink coat, plus two of my evening gowns, one of which should be frilly and the other simply elegant, and then make sure to add matching shoes and other matching accessories. My maids will help you. But before doing any of this, book yourself on the next plane from Munich to Athens with a return flight later tonight. Then phone me at the number I shall give you in a moment and confirm your arrival time in Athens. When you leave customs there will be someone waiting for you carrying a sign marked "Countess von Rugerstein". Hand them the suitcase and fly home on the next available flight. That's all. *Auf wiedersehn*, and be quick.'

To the count she explained, 'Christiana may give me orders as the Vice-President of her Stephanopolous empire, but she cannot tell me is how to dress.'

For lunch Marianne had not troubled to change, but their hostess was now wearing a body-hugging silk Scottish tartan suit with a Mary Quant style mini skirt that demanded attention. The plaid design could not be identified with any Scottish clan, but the stitching was perfection and unseen while the complicated pattern fitted like a finished jigsaw. It was eye-catching. And so it should be, thought Marianne, considering the stratospheric price it would have cost. It was tailoring at its finest, and made its wearer appear almost kittenish now that her razor sharp claws were sheathed. And being a very female female herself, Marianne knew that the suit was merely the overture to what Christiana would dazzle them with at dinner. Much as she felt a compliment would be justified she remained silent and Christiana told the butler to pour the champagne and then insisted that Marianne should sit next to her at lunch with the count opposite, 'So that you can look at us both, but I shall not ask you pick between the two of us,' she teased. 'I may be a great believer in democracy, but in business I don't tolerate defeats.'

'How do you like my suit, Marianne?'

'It is stunning, fits you like a glove, and I wish it were mine. But being mercenary, I would settle for the emerald ring you are wearing.'

'It is an exact match to the necklace I showed you at the villa, and I plan to wear it at dinner.'

Marianne and her husband remained surprised that Christiana had never mentioned her charitable Foundation which they had agreed to establish in Germany. The count decided it was typical of her. Once her wishes had been agreed, the subject became of secondary importance. Instead she happily agreed to send a car and chauffeur to meet Heide at the airport. While they ate their Lancashire hot pot, prepared by her chef in honour of her English-born guest, she told them about the two couples who would be joining them for dinner. One man would only be there as the escort of a very beautiful and successful theatrical diva, but it was quite the opposite with the other couple where the wife was the dowdiest woman she ever invited to dine, but her husband was an important Athenian journalist who had learned that no one buttered bread like herself. Veronica, the diva, was glamorous and an actress now in demand for stage and film parts in both Italy and America. She had been discovered by Christiana five years earlier playing in some trivial town in northern Greece in a poorly directed version of Shakespeare's Macbeth. She went on, 'I was only there because I was in the area on a duty visit for my Foundation and had nothing better to do that evening. Veronica's performance brought out all the true cunning and viciousness of Lady Macbeth. I was taken backstage to meet her and later introduced her to an agent and an Italian producer. She has never looked back. Now she has a home on Malibu Beach in California and an apartment in Rome. I know she will be bringing a companion with her tonight, but he will be of no importance. Her beaux come and go with the speed of a Ferrari. She has already divorced two husbands and she is only twenty-six or that is what she admits to and will probably remain for the next few years. Both had to pay handsomely for the privilege of having been married to her, in one case for less than a year. However, she remains scared of me. When I call, she comes running. It is the same with the journalist; I pay him half as much again as he earns on his newspaper, but he knows my tap can be turned off if he does not provide the publicity I seek. As a result of his obedience he can now afford the dinner jacket I have told him to wear this evening. I hope you will, too, Wilhelm.'

Sharp at six Lucille arrived to run Marianne's bath and help her dress, and so did the outfits that Heide had brought from Munich. Tactfully the count disappeared into their sitting room while Marianne went through the feminine ritual of deciding which gown to wear. Eventually she chose her silver satin sheath-like dinner gown whose elegance would be reflected beneath the lights of the dining-room. What she did not know was that Lucille immediately told Christiana's maid what the countess was planning to wear, and she at once instructed the butler to turn down the lighting where she would receive her guests. But nothing could stop Marianne's silver sheath dress plunging to the floor while highlighting every curve of her body.

When the count and countess left their suite the butler escorted them into the reception salon where Christiana was waiting with Ulysses. The count as usual looked immaculate in his Savile Row dinner jacket and silk bow he had tied himself. Marianne's gown was femininely eye-catching but was hardly likely to win a second glance when in competition with Christiana's own dress that had the allure of sheets of gold that draped themselves over one shoulder before hugging a half-revealed breast, and ended with layers of golden silk that had originally been woven for an ultra-expensive Indian sari. It rippled like waves seeking the shore as her legs moved rhythmically forward with a gloved hand extended for the count to kiss. But there were no signs of her emeralds. Upon learning what Marianne would be wearing, she decided to blaze with diamonds including a hundred-gem choker that had been worn by the last Czarina of Romanov Russia before the communist revolution in 1917.

As the two couples embraced she whispered to Marianne, 'Your jacket is magnificent and you wear it as though you had been wrapped in mink all your life.'

'Thanks for the compliment, but I had to wait until a year ago.'

Christiana confided: 'I had a three year start on you.'

Christiana broke off their conversation as she noticed her butler escorting the first of her other guests. She held out her hand to be kissed by Peter Stathopoulou, a journalist of around fifty with an international reputation for his coverage of Greece and the Balkans for several western daily and Sunday newspapers. Deep furrows on his face were signs of the pressures of working for daily newspapers with their constant demands and deadlines. Yet he was still a handsome man whose eyes suggested he would be happier touching more than his hostess's hand, but was well aware that was a privilege she would never permit. He had to

99

be content with whatever largesse she passed his way for the publicity she demanded for herself and her corporation in newspapers including *The Times* and *Sunday Times*, the *New York Times*, *Le Monde* and the *Corriere della Sera* for which he was Athens correspondent.

His extremely unfeminine wife was wearing a long grey woollen dress that had the immediate effect of encouraging everyone to ignore her, and Christiana to signal to her butler to change the place cards so that his drab wife sat next to Veronica's escort, with her own husband on her other side. Both were only there because they were the companions of a man and woman who were useful to Christiana from time to time. Meanwhile, Peter was taken to one side and told he would have a story that would make the evening both profitable as well as enjoyable. He was to take shorthand notes of what Veronica, who would be sitting next to him, had to say. She was Veronica Lang, the Oscar-nominated Hollywood film star. There was an insistence in her voice that demanded he ask, 'Have I ever failed you?'

'You would not like it if you did.'

At that moment the final two guests arrived and were introduced as 'Veronica, my protégée who has so much talent she is contantly in demand in Hollywood, New York and Europe. Recently she was nominated for an Oscar.' There was just a touch of a smile as Veronica turned to each of the other guests. Like both Christiana and Marianne, she was strikingly attractive, beautifully gowned, in her mid-twenties with full breasts, long sleek legs plus auburn hair that tonight was combed back in a bun which helped define her fine, almost aristocratic, high cheek bones. Her lips were born for seduction. She introduced her escort as Philip Winterbotham. Christiana nodded in his direction and decided that, despite his well-cut evening clothes he, too, could be ignored as no more than another in Veronica's long line of disposable chattels. They lasted as long as they accepted her humiliation and never walked by her side unless invited. Already he was a forgotten man now she was talking to Christiana.

Because of the comparative intimacy of the salon where they were dining nobody could avoid noticing, even if they did not recognise, the Savonnerie carpet that covered the floor, or the silk wallpaper and matching satin curtains. A single Venetian chandelier hung above the table that could happily have hosted twice tonight's eightsome. At each place for the ladies there was a single fresh orchid.

Yet despite the time and trouble that had been taken by Christiana and her staff only Peter, the journalist, would regard the dinner as a success, despite each guest having their own waiter or waitress standing permanently behind each chair, ready to serve their allotted guest. Marianne sat next to Ulysses who was doubly disappointed because he was not to be sitting next to Veronica and instead had to put up with the journalist's wife. He satisfied his cupidity by allowing his left hand to stray onto Marianne's knee while not taking his eye off Veronica. She meanwhile had to accept being interviewed while eating dinner but fortunately she had become expert in supplying journalists with what they needed to hear. Christiana watched with amusement the disappointment on her husband's face while she made her own personal amusement by tormenting the beau who was Veronica's escort and was more interesting than she expected. She even suggested he might feign feeling ill and she would ask her husband to escort Veronica back to her hotel in Athens, and he could stay with her. However, the more she thought about the idea, the more she realised that all the advantages would be with Veronica. Turning back to Mr Winterbotham, she ordered him to forget what she had just suggested adding, 'And when I order someone to do something they obey. Is that perfectly clear? It had better be. I can be very cruel.' He indicated that Veronica had told him that she was both a very generous lady, but would be the most vindictive opponent. He assured her he had already forgotten everything she had said. Her reply was a withering whisper. 'Don't ever think of trifling with Christiana Stephanopolous.' And she held his hand as compensation.

Before dinner ended Christiana rose to her feet and told the table that she had some interesting news which in one way or another would interest everyone. 'The recently wedded Countess Marianne von Rugerstein has agreed to become the president of the first overseas branch of my Stephanopolous Foundation in Germany, while the count will become its first patron. In addition, Veronica Lang, the international star who has recently been nominated for a Hollywood Oscar, is here this evening because she has agreed to use her influence in the world of films and entertainment to raise donations for the Foundation.

'I have emphasised that I am not interested in sums of less than fifty thousand dollars and she told me she did not expect that would be a problem. She could think of at least six stars and producers in Hollywood who were paid several million dollars for each film, who should welome having their names among the patrons of the Foundation. I am sure she will become one of the patrons, too.'

It was not until after dinner that Ulysses had his first opportunity to begin his secret wooing of Veronica now that Christiana was nowhere to be seen. She had stayed behind in the dining-room to give the journalist further background information for his stories. While the cat was away Veronica ignored her own escort and devoted her attention to where the wealth was. She let the multi-millonaire Greek shipping and property tycoon know that she would welcome his attention, but not tonight. She slipped him a card with her ex-directory phone number in Rome. Veronica knew her problem was not trapping her prey, but keeping it secret from Christiana. She decided the risk was worth taking. Like everyone else she had no idea just how many millions of dollars he was worth, but it had to be multi. His empire was privately owned by himself and his family and they had their fingers in shipping, oil, armaments, aircraft, shoes, hotels, properties, textiles and clothing as well as owning a half dozen farms ... plus in his case, women. He could buy and spoil almost any woman he fancied. But Christiana always made sure that when it came to being spoiled no one came within touching distance of her own claims upon his wealth, generosity and foolishness. After her twentieth birthday, which almost coincided with their third wedding anniversary, both of which he forgot, she had him followed and within a week the detective agency reported that he was visiting a lady in an apartment three blocks from the Stephanopolous headquarters which the corporation owned. Because Christiana was pregnant with their first and only daughter, Stephanie, she had refused to consider either a separation or a divorce. Instead she demanded that for her own future security, and that of her child, he had to transfer twenty per cent of shares in Stephanopolous International to her, plus a seat on the main board, plus opening a fifty million dollar trust fund for their daughter with the first payment of ten million dollars being paid when she reached her eighteenth birthday, and the last when she was twenty-five. The alternative was for her to sue him for a divorce in the United States where they had a home as well as vast business interests for one hundred million dollars, and half his total assets. He agreed to her demands after long legal meetings with his lawyers on both sides of the Atlantic. He continued to live with Christiana as man and wife. Six months after Stephanie was born the trust was established. Ulysses however worried whether his daughter would be able to withstand her mother's overwhelming ambitions, and might be stampeded into joining some kind of takeover bid which might see her mother sitting in the presidential chair. He fought to avoid such a situation by abandoning sleeping around and, as a result, was invited back into the marital bed. However to stay there he was forced to give into her demands for increased percentages from the annual bonus pool which was based upon each year's profits, plus a greater say in the running of the family business. Her demands for new pieces of expensive jewellery increased and were mostly satisfied. He found it near impossible to resist the fascination of her young body, and she pandered to him with such assurances as, 'But, darling, you will always remain the president of Stephanopolous International. My only ambition is to be your Vice-President.' Her aim was power, not titles As the years passed this was what she won nibble by nibble until she knew what was within her grasp for passing on to her daughter who she was grooming for the future role of the presidency.

Only a little of all this was known to Veronica, or anyone else, but Christiana deliberately told her sufficient about her growing power and immense wealth in a gentle attempt to warn her off any idea of seeking to trap her husband.

Before the eightsome dinner party ended, Christiana took Marianne and the count aside and showed them a press release she had prepared and just given to the journalist, Peter Stathopoulou, which would be published the day after tomorrow in the leading Athens daily. He would also send it to other newspapers in Europe and North America for which he acted as Greek correspondent. It announced all she had told her guests at the dinner table, but added that it was the tenth anniversary of the founding of the Stephanopolous Foundation for under-privileged children throughout the world. It ended: 'Since its founding the Foundation has distributed more than ten million dollars not only in Greece, but to some of the poorest countries in Africa including Uganda and Buganda who sent pleas for aid.' Madame Stephanopolous's press release revealed: It was these requests that made her realise that there were countries in every part of the world where families were in desperate need of aid which their own governments were unable to provide. 'I remain dedicated to seeking to give every child the chance to develop their potential,' said the founder of the Foundation.

Reading the release the count realised that once again their hostess had them over a barrel and in less than forty-eight hours newspapers in Germany would carry the story. He decided that it would be best to confirm to Christiana that both he and Marianne were glad to have her confidence, and were sure it would lead to new orders from her global empire. Christiana smiled, kissed them both, and knew they were now firmly in her web.

Next she walked over to Veronica and gave her a copy of the press release, adding, 'You owe me many favours so you must not let me down. Keep me informed of the support you are able to win for my Foundation.' The actress simply smiled, but said nothing. She was worried. She knew she could not refuse what had been decided for her, but secretly it made her more determined to entice Ulysses into her bed, and then into her life. Was it possible to have her cake, and eat it, she wondered? Ulysses had only released her hand when Christiana reappeared and his suggestion for a stroll in the grounds had to be abandoned.

Veronica had to be content with a promise of a phone call to fix a meeting in Rome. The big risk was that since her Oscar nomination, whatever she did, wherever she went, who ever she saw, became fuel for the gossip columnists and the growing papparazzi. This meant that before she gave Ulysses what he wanted, he would have to give her what she had dreamed of possessing ever since winning her first highly paid Hollywood contract ... a full length sable coat, the final symbol of stardom.

Christiana knew nothing of this desire. It was more than

twenty years ago after she had married one of the richest men in the world, and two years later that she become eligible to be a member of an unrecorded women-only club made up of the one thousand who could afford to wear sables; the majority of them were American millionairesses, plus a smattering in Russia, western Europe and in the south of South America. The thought that her protegée, who would still be earning a pittance in rep in northern Greece if she had not provided an exit strategy, might become a member would have not only filled her with abhorrence, but her claws would have been out. Sadly there was no application form for her to veto.

6

The following morning Christiana drove to the corporation's headquarters where she wanted to show Marianne the building where she would shortly become one of the shareholders. By the time the Rolls pulled up outside the main entrance she had explained that Stephanopolous International had nearly one hundred offices, plants, warehouses and factories with a staff level of close to three thousand men and women. A couple of minutes before they arrived the chauffeur sent a signal that Madame Stephanopolous was on her way. As the car pulled to a halt two uniformed commissionaires rushed to open the doors for the two sumptuously-furred ladies, and saluted. One of them rushed ahead to make sure that one of the two lifts that went only to the top three floors where only directors and the corporate accounts department had offices was waiting for them. In addition to the two boardooms, here Christiana had her own three-room apartment with a view towards the Acropolis. But first she took Marianne to her own two-room office suite and introduced her to Maggie, her own private secretary, who occupied the outer of two rooms which was large enough for two desks and several armchairs for guests or executives who had been summoned to the Vice-President's office. The desks were occupied by Mr Charles Watson who had the title of her PA, while Maggie was her personal private secretary. 'This is the Baroness von Rugerstein whose name you have heard before, and who will shortly be joining the board of directors with powers only less authoritative than myself, my husband and, soon, my daughter, Stephanie.

'Now I am taking the countess to my private apartment where I do not wish to be disturbed unless I ring for one of you.'

Upstairs they threw their coats on to the double bed and Christiana mixed them both an ouzo, a Greek aniseed flavoured drink which becomes cloudy when diluted with water.

She told Marianne, 'I shall find you an office for yourself and a secretary on one of the three top floors for when you are in Athens for board meetings or discussions with myself regarding work I wish you to undertake for the corporation. I shall also arrange for a special key to be cut for you to use the two reserved lifts, and also this apartment whenever I am away. That is how close I want us to be. Meanwhile, I want you to meet a Mr Robert McDonald who has been one of our successful branch managers in Romania where we are achieving unexpectedly high profits from the sales of our textiles and cheap clothing. I sent him a replacement two months ago and now I have recalled him to Athens to take up a new assignment about which he knows nothing. Nor does anyone else. However, from now onwards you will be privy to my secret.

'As you may or may not know, Ulysses and I live together as man and wife in name only. It is for the sake of the corporation. We have not slept together for a long time, Mr McDonald is an attractive man as well as a good businessman, I am thinking of appointing him my aide so that we can spend more time together, if you get my meaning?'

'I understand his purpose, and as your aide-de-camp he must spend most his time in your company whatever the time of day or night.' Marianne appreciated that Christiana had the conceit of a prima donna who recognised that she was indispensable and everyone else was expendable.

Christiana picked up one of several phones on her desk. 'Maggie, there is a Mr McDonald in reception and waiting to see me. Fetch him and bring him up to my apartment.'

While they were alone it was time for Marianne to find out her own position. 'Christiana, I may be a countess, a status which in England is bestowed upon the wife of an earl, but I am also a businesswoman who is looking forward to working more closely with you than anyone else except your personal family. What am I worth to you?'

'That is a reasonable and sensible question. When I have finished, for the moment with Mr McDonald, I shall arrange for the director's kitchen to send up a luncheon for the two of us, and then I shall share with you as much as I know at the present moment. Be patient.'

There was a gentle but firm knock on the door of her

apartment and in came Robert McDonald followed by her secretary who was immediately dismissed.

'Sit down Mr McDonald. Would you like a drink?'

'Thank you, Madame Stephanopolous, but I prefer not to drink on an empty stomach.'

'As you please, but remember for future reference that I do not like to drink alone.'

She deliberately hesitated. She was suddenly not sure whether he was the right person for what she had in mind. But went on, 'I deliberately brought you home from Romania because I thought you were becoming too comfortable. I never like those I place in responsible positions to feel too secure. They get lax. Would that be a fair description of yourself?'

This time it was his turn to hesitate. He did not want to contradict her, and decided to try diplomacy. 'I concede that such a thought could apply to several of your deputies, but as far as I was concerned I was never satisfied with whatever successes I achieved. I was always aware that I reported only to you, and as a result, never stopped seeking higher profits for yourself and the Stephanopolous corporation.'

She wanted to say 'well put', but decided to utter what meant the same, but was put differently. 'Have you ever thought of working more closely with me?'

'It is not only girls who dream dreams, madame. I, too, have prayed for the impossible.'

She rose from her chair and her eyes penetrated like a knife. It could have been an empress looking at a slave. She was determined from the outset to make him understand that the gap between them would never be bridged but might be linked. He was not another Marianne. She had talent, was a natural born leader who could be given almost any task and would see it through to a successful conclusion. He, however, had a body she could use and, perhaps, a mind that she would test. She was carnivorous. If his body pleased her she would devour him and he would be as helpless as a wildebeest when the claws of a lioness were sinking deeper into its back. If his more commercial attributes continued to satisfy they might become closer, but she would look down on him like all her other servants. He had always known throughout the many years he had spent working his way up the hard-to-climb Stephanopolous ladder, the immense power she wielded, but now he was about to experience it at first hand. 'I have decided to appoint you my personal aide. You will carry out whatever orders I give at whatever time of the day or night I give them. You will seldom work less than a twelve-hour day, and never less than six days a week, sometimes seven. And for three months you will be on trial. You will continue to receive your present salary which is considerably below the five hundred dollars the corporation pays me for every minute I work, but it emphasises the difference in worth the corporation puts on the two of us. You will have no time for anyone else, or any other interests other than me.'

'That has always been my ambition, Madame Stephanopolous. You are a gloriously beautiful and attractive woman who I have always worshipped.'

He attempted to get to his feet, but stopped halfway as her voice, suddenly sounded more like a sergeant-major reprimanding a private than the woman he worshipped. 'You will need to remember that I give the orders; you obey them.' Her eyes were assessing him as meat she might enjoy. 'You may go now, but report to my outer office at nine tomorrow morning. You will sit in my office and learn everything that goes on when you are helping to run a five hundred million dollar empire. Your first task as my aide is to go back to my office suite and tell Charles Watson, my PA, to come up immediately with his notebook.

As he left her apartment he knew he had been given a sentence which she had the power to commute. An impossibly wide stretch of water lay between them, but he had to believe that the vision on the far bank was beckoning him to swim faster and stronger; he could not believe she wanted him to drown. On the contrary all she wanted was to have him around to satisfy her whims.

When he left them she turned to Marianne and confirmed that 'in business it is not always possible to tell the whole truth.' She explained, 'If his work impresses me, and even if it doesn't, he will have a second opportunity to perform in my bed. Like a good poker player, the royal flush I hold means his life is likely to be full of surprises, but all of them will always be to my advantage. Although I mostly appear to be a witch, I can occasionally play the role of the good fairy. We shall see. I am not sure.'

'Which brings me back to you, Marianne. With you, I am sure. You are fated to spend much of your life close to the centre of what is, almost certainly, the world's largest and most powerful privately-owned corporate empire. I aim to win control, but with my husband remaining president. Your task will be to help me achieve my goal. You will be well rewarded and, in addition, when I am ready to pounce, which will not be until your husband is much more dependent upon our orders than he is at present, you will be appointed president of his empire, with power to appoint him as your deputy. Slowly everything will be absorbed into the Stephanopolous cauldron which is always simmering, but ready to burst into life whenever the order is given. My immediate aim is a private valuation of at least six hunded million dollars. Once two other wealthy English women dominated your life; soon they will be replaced by two Greek women, myself and my daughter. After us and Ulysses you will be the fourth most powerful person controlling the Stephanopolous empire. Any orders you give will be obeyed just as mine are. Because you have my complete confidence, you will be like a deputy Supremo, and will receive the fourth largest bonus paid to a director which I estimate is likely to be not far short of half a million dollars after your first full year with the corporation.'

7

Marianne spent the first several months after returning to her castle home from her honeymoon setting up the Stephanopolous Foundation in Germany. She and the count decided that the von Rugerstein castle should be the temporary headquarters of the new organisation so that Marianne could be constantly available to run the charity as well as being châtelaine of her new home and staff. One of the count's senior company secretaries was deputed to be in charge of all office administration for the Foundation under direct orders from the countess. This did not satisfy her requirements, and she annexed two typists who were informed that until further notice they would also be working full-time for the Foundation. She had special notepaper and other documents printed using the artwork supplied from Athens including the three words at the top of each first page 'The Stephanopolous Foundation' followed by 'in aid of deprived children'. Then came the castle address and in strong bold type 'German President: Countess Marianne von Rugerstein'. Only at the bottom of the page was there a line announcing: 'Founder: Madame Christiana Stephanopolous'.

The count accepted the loss of three of his staff, and opened two bank accounts on behalf of the Foundation, one for out-of-pocket running expenses and the second for the receipt of all donations and any charitable requests that were accepted. It was arranged that either he or the countess could sign cheques on each account on behalf of the Foundation. He insisted that the cheques which he signed to provide funds for the German branch were clearly entered in the accounts as 'loan without interest'.

He was surprised how easy it became to raise large amounts of money once he and the countess informed the chief executives of more than a dozen major German companies that Count and Countess von Rugerstein had themselves presented two million dollars to the Foundation. While no one sought to match their contribution, several accepted an invitation to become official sponsors of the charity with personal or company donations of quarter of a million dollars, and so did a couple of his wealthiest friends. Others accepted the challenge to ensure that Germany outstripped the success achieved by the Greek founder and donated sums varying from fifty thousand dollars to two hunded thousand dollars. The count in his personal letters reminded recipients that before her marriage his wife had been one of the highest paid businesswomen in the City of London. Clever wording ensured that the letters struck both a charitable as well as a nationalistic chord.

At the end of three months the main bank account was in credit to a total of more than three and a half million dollars, in addition to the Rugerstein's two million dollars, and earning a high rate of interest. In addition, several of the donors indicated that they would be happy to make an annual contribution in return for being listed as one of the 'major donors'. It could be tax deductible.

At dinner one evening Marianne told her husband how much she was enjoying working for the Foundation and seeing it grow month on month in size, prestige and recognition. It was now time for her to reveal how, when they had been in Athens, Christiana had told her how much she admired her obvious business brain and achievements, and wanted her to become more involved with the Stephanopolous corporation. That morning a letter had arrived from Greece confirming her appointment as the third female member of the board of Stehanopolous International with an allocation of three voting shares, each of which had an estimated worth of five million dollars. The letter also confirmed that she would receive the fourth largest annual bonus paid to directors with voting rights which would vary from year to year depending upon annual profits announcd at the private AGM.

She felt it was now time for her to become a director of the growing Rugerstein business empire, and informed her husband, 'I want to let my beauty please you and my brain help you.' It was also a challenge. 'I think my name should appear on your notepaper and all company documents as a director. The reprinting will not cost us anything as you already own a publishing company and a printing giant which is one of the

112

largest in Germany with contracts from BMW, Siemens, Mercedes and Deutsche Bank as well as Stephanopolous International. Surely I am not asking too much?' She chose the moment to remember how Penny had taught her always to look businessmen and women in the eye when talking to them, and show she was their equal, or superior. And any successful modern wife was entitled to regard herself as the equal of her husband. After all she was a countess, a status with far more merit in Germany than Britain. She pouted her lips in order to tantalise him into agreeing to what she was asking, while hoping it would not become an issue. If the offer of her body was not sufficient to win what she wanted, then perhaps its denial would show Wilhelm that she possessed a weapon that would always win her whatever she first requested, but was always prepared to demand. For the moment her weapon was sheathed, as was the information that her job in the City of London was still open.

She need not have worried. The count responded to what she had been telling him by explaining, 'Ever since we married, I have been thinking along similar lines to what you are suggesting. Your German is good, and certainly adequate. Of course I agree that you should join the board of the Rugerstein business interests.' He knew his wife had an almost natural ability to climb every business mountain that faced her.

Hearing his words she rose and sat on his lap. Her lips became not only desirable, but irresistible as she made it known that, 'When I take my place on your main board, and any individual companies my aim will be to make a major contribution towards further expansion and increased profits, including your fashion and textile interests, the Munich furrier and all our wholly-owned farms and other properties.'

When one of the castle's staff knocked and entered the dining-room to ask whether they were ready to choose their dessert, the countess who was still on the count's knee, shouted at him to 'Get out! The count and I are in conference.' Her seductive perfume wafted over him and the count was now aware that not only could he never refuse her anything, but in so many ways she was his equal, and in some his superior. What a wise decision he had made when he had asked her to become his countess. At the same time, however, he was like a cracked vessel that would never be quite the same again.

With the new strings to her bow, and with the approval of the count, she decided to organise a ball at the castle to raise further funds for their Stephanopolous Foundation. Although tickets were priced at five hundred dollars and only available to selected guests, all two hundred were snapped up within a week. Her name on any announcement had immense pulling power in Bavaria and, increasingly, across Germany. Veronica Lang, the star who by now had won her first Oscar as well as her sable coat which Ulysses had bought for her before he was allowed to go to bed with her, had made a kind of peace with Christiana by assuring her that it had only been the mildest of flings and meant absolutely nothing to her, and, to show her support for the Foundation, agreed to present the raffle prizes at the ball. Fortunately, the ball was taking place in July and she did not have to decide whether or not to wear her new coat which might have forced Christiana to renounce any peace that had been agreed between them. For the moment Veronica decided it was best to keep her sables under wraps from such a powerful woman. It was not as though it was Veronica's only fur.

The raffle prizes, thanks to the influence of both the Rugersteins and Christiana, were exceptional in their value and eye-catching appeal, and included a new BMW, two Business Class return tickets to any destination in either north or south America courtesy of Lufthansa, a case of vintage Lafitte, and a score of only slightly less valuable prizes such as Gucci luggage, Chanel perfume, hampers from Fortnum & Mason, a weekend at Le Crillon Hotel in Paris and a journey aboard the *Simplon Orient Express*. At almost the last minute an auction was organised for a white mink jacket designed by Maximillian of New York, recognised by all who knew the value of fine furs, as the world's leading furrier. He had his arm twisted by Rachel Simon, one of his best international clients, who together with Dame Penny and her husband, had agreed to fly over for the ball. She brought the jacket with her. Maximillian made only one condition, that it had to be withdrawn unless bidding reached at least ten thousand dollars. Rachel assured him that at that price she would buy it herself.

As well as her guests from London, Christiana and Ulysses, with their daughter Stephanie, flew to Munich from Athens for two or three nights at the Rugerstein castle in their own private eight seater aircraft.

The bidding for the Maximillian fur, which followed after all the one thousand raffle tickets had been bought for two hundred dollars each, started at the reserve price and with an audience consisting of some of the wealthiest men and women in Europe quickly soared to twenty-five thousand dollars. At this point, although the money raised was going to charity, most of the women started to drop out of the bidding, and at twenty-eight thousand dollars began urging their husbands to do the same. When Ulysses bid thirty thousand he had only one competitor, Rachel Simon who was still staking a claim to the Maximillan fur jacket. Yet again Rachel raised a diamond encrusted hand to announce, thirty one thousand. Ulysses signalled thirty two. Rachel had never in her life been challenged with such persistent determination. She could not understand why Ulysses was so insistent when his wife already possessed at least as many costly furs as Rachel herself. Her jewelled hand shot up once again and bid thirty-three thousand dollars. It was then that Ulysses delivered his knockout blow: 'Forty thousand dollars'. Rachel stayed seated and silent, and annoyed.

To the surprise of everyone it was not Christiana who stepped forward to collect the snow white prize, but their daughter, Stephanie. To everyone's amazement the seventeen-year-old walked up to Veronica Lang with a dignity and confidence that confirmed she had been brought up surrounded by the kind of luxury most families would never even know existed. It was almost as though she regarded her prize as just another mink jacket; and not even a full-length coat. In fact, she was thinking of the sensation it would cause at her Swiss finishing school, but for now she was content to put it on and stroke the fur that had the softness of a heavy fall of snow as it was caught under a spotlight in the Rugerstein ballroom. Having inherited more than a little of her mother's bitchiness she was hoping it might prove more eye-catching than at parents' day at the college the previous October when Christiana arrived wearing her ankle-length Russian sable coat while every other mum wore only either mink or fox. Now it was Stephanie's poise and elegance that won polite applause from the men who were having their first close up of this tantalising young beauty, and a less enthusiastic clap from the ladies who were secretly furious that one of their own daughters might have been wearing the mink jacket if the bidding had not soared to what it would cost to buy the sable coat that some of them had seen Christiana wearing at parents' day. None of those who applauded Stephanie, or sat with their arms folded in annoyance, knew that in a few months' time when she was eighteen she would overnight become a multi-millionairess thanks to the massive trust fund that had been set up by her parents, and also take her place on the board of Stephanopolous International as well as becoming Director of Personnel which meant she would have direct control over the lives of considerably more than two thousand men and women they employed in sixteen countries.

Back in their suite at the castle her mother, who had spent every year of her daughter's life making sure that her own ruthless business genes had developed inside her daughter's heart and mind, was now preparing her for 'the next big step in your life when you join your father and myself and begin to govern our vast corporate business You must never get involved in the private lives or problems of those we employ. You provide them with jobs and it's their task to help produce our profits. They are expendable; we are not.' All very interesting, but Stephanie had heard it too many times. All she now wanted as a young, very wealthy seventeen-year-old, was to preen herself in front of a full-length mirror and admire the luxury of her new possession.

Her mother, however, denied her that pleasure as it was only 2 am and they could both have a lie in bed in the morning, and she wanted to recount a recent visit she had made to one of their many overseas factories a few miles from Shanghai. There several hundred female workers, whose ages varied from twelve to eighty, had a quota to produce six cotton dresses during every twelve-hour shift for which they were paid one dollar for each dress. As a result each month the factory exported something like forty thousand dresses, which were sold for at least ten dollars at outlets throughout China, Eastern Europe and South America. 'Even after paying wages and commissions to local Chinese Communist Party officials that single factory contributed more than four million dollars in annual profits to Stephanopolus International.' She concluded, 'A member of the local communist party told me there was little or no absenteeism because if they did not work they weren't paid. We have built the factory and they supply the workforce which is forbidden to strike.'

Seeing that Stephanie was tired she stopped talking business, but added, 'As you will one day be the president of our family business it is important that from your first day at headquarters you start learning everything about the corporation you will one day rule. And remember that from the outset it will be your responsibility, under my direction, to make sure that everyone earns their wages whether at headquarters and in all our offices, plants, factories and warehouses in twenty-six countries. How do we do so? Every month our accounts department checks the production and sales figures which are sent to head office from around the world. If figures fall for two consecutive months your father and I decide whether and where cuts in staff need to be made. That is one reason why we never become involved in the lives of any of our employees. In the best interests of the corporation a certain number have to be sacked which means that those who remain have to work harder to make sure that profits meet the targets we set. Within six months I intend to pass to you the supervision of the reports that accounts send us after they are supposed to have checked figures that we have to re-check. It is a good rule in a business as large as ours, never to trust anyone. Now go to bed. I have arranged for us to have a private meeting at noon tomorrow with the countess who is a very reliable and efficient young woman. I have appointed her to the board, but when you arrive for work you will be her superior.'

For once Marianne did not sleep with the count that night, and Matilda, the oldest of her four maids, was waiting in her own suite to assist her preparation for her delayed night's rest. She checked that a fresh pair of soft silk pyjamas had been laid out on her bed before sitting down in front of her antique dressing table with its silver-framed mirror and silver handles on every drawer that had to be polished each morning, and where Matilda spent the next ten minutes brushing and combing her thick head of black hair until it glowed with freshness. Before she was dismissed she had to arrange for breakfast to be brought to her at 10.30 am when she would shower and decide what to wear for her meeting with the two Stephanopolous ladies who would both shortly be among the most powerful businesswomen in the world. She was still wondering what the meeting would be about when she finally fell asleep.

When she was awakened with her breakfast her first thoughts were about Stephanie. She had obviously been pampered and spoiled, and because of her great wealth was unlikely to gain many close friends, only hangers-on. Her several governesses had all been told at interviews with Christiana that her daughter had to be addressed as 'Miss Stephanie', and treated with respect. Marianne sensed that she had grown up to be as hard and aloof as her mother, and doubted whether she realised, or cared, that the price her father had paid for her fur jacket was more than double, perhaps quadruple, what most men and women earned in, perhaps, two years. Her apparent aloofness to all around her as she strode up to collect her fur had shown a confidence that few seventeen-year-olds possessed. But perhaps this was to be expected when you knew that by the time you were twenty-five your personal fortune might have moved towards the hundred million dollar mark. Living in a vast mansion surrounded by servants who curtsied even when they were twice her age, was all she would ever know. Could there possibly be a softer side to her nature?

8

For her meeting with Christiana, Marianne wore her favourite Chanel suit of Cambridge blue that never failed to emphasise her position as a lady of considerable wealth and importance, certainly in Germany. Alice had been told she had two guests arriving at noon and to make sure everything throughout the suite was immaculate with not a speck of dust anywhere. And to bring up a fresh bottle of champagne and three spotlessly clean fluted glasses.

Christiana arrived punctually at noon accompanied by her daughter. Both looked as though they had come straight from Balenciaga in Paris. The mother wore a waistcoat styled jacket with a matching flared ankle length wool skirt and shoes that had been dyed to match the dusky green merino wool. She was obviously dressed for what would be a business meeting, while Stephanie breathed youthful elegance in a superbly cut silk dress that highlighted every curve of her fully developed young body that must already be inviting admiring eyes, although getting close to her was not yet an option for any man however eligible. Marianne sensed that those fully developed rounded breasts were yearning to be fondled, although the jewellery she wore at the ball seemed to suggest an untouchability. Last night's display of diamonds had been replaced by a large single stone diamond ring. Marianne contented herself with telling them both that they looked sensational and joked that she was considering changing what she was wearing to provide something more in keeping with the standard her guests had set. Mother and daughter sat next to one another while Marianne nestled into her favourite heavily upholstered armchair. She admitted to Stephanie: 'I had hoped to see you wearing your white mink jacket. What a way to begin what I am sure will one day be a wonderful collection.'

'I went to sleep wearing it last night,' Stephanie admitted, 'but mother insisted that my Dior dress and this jewellery was

119

sufficient to show that I have learned good taste thanks to her meticulous upbringing.' Marianne could not help noticing the glint in the eyes of this near eighteen-year-old that seemed to be trying to express an independence rather than gratitude towards her teacher. She was yearning for the time when she could let her wealth do the talking; just as her mother did. It was obvious to anyone who met her that she was a very formidable young lady. All the extra studying in both economics and business management which she had undertaken at her finishing school rather than play hockey or tennis might soon be paying dividends for herself as well as Stephanopolous International. It was only months before she would leave school for the last time.

As though reading her daughter's thoughts Christiana intervened: 'That's enough of your own pomposity. Now keep quiet while I explain to Marianne what we have in mind for her.' At that moment there was a knock at the door and as soon as they were given permission, two of Marianne's duty maids, suitably uniformed in spotless starched aprons and tiny caps that denoted their status in the castle's hierarchy, entered carrying two silver trays, with three delicate gold-rimmed coffee cups with matching saucers and plates, and a cafetière of freshly ground coffee, plus cream and sweet biscuits, while the second bore the weight of an opened bottle of champagne swimming in a filled bucket of ice, plus three fluted glasses. They were told their mistress would do the pouring and they were not to be disturbed.

'You have come a very long way since we first met,' Christiana told Marianne. 'I believe the three of us could make a very formidable triumvirate in the world of global business, but on behalf of Stephanie and myself, I have to draw attention to certain situations. Although we shall share in the annual profits, I shall remain in control of the organisation with Stephanie as my immediate deputy, so her status will always be superior to your own, and to everyone else in the corporation except her father. The two of you will soon be on the main board where I now sit as vice-president. Later I plan to recruit two or three of the most successful businesswomen in the world to join as executive directors of what will become the first female dominated board of any global corporation. Although a threesome, Stephanie and I will always be able to out vote any opposition. My aim is dominance. If anything should happen to me, Stephanie will automatically inherit all my shares. However, such a situation is unlikely in the near future as I am only just into my forties. But if it does, the family will remain in overwhelming control. And until his death, or he becomes incapacitated, or when I decide otherwise, my husband will wield the powers of the president. Stephanie will gradually assume greater authority under my supervision. We could be an invincible threesome, or just a twosome.'

Marianne found it hard to believe that Christiana was seriously planning, with her daughter, to take control away from Ulysses, a task that might, perhaps, be made easier because, despite its immense size, it was not a public company, but a gigantic and global corporation whose shares were all owned privately by members of the Stephanopolous family, and whose assets had recently been guestimated at several hundred million dollars. During the last decade it had largely been Christiana who had spread its wings beyond its shipping interests and into oil, office and residential construction, luxury hotels, whole villages and agricultural land, plus textiles, fashion and the manufacture of sensibly-priced shoes for the mass high street markets that existed in every continent. Recently Christiana had hinted that the next phase of expansion was likely to be into armaments and aviation.

Christiana went on, 'Already I take most of the decisions that have led to our continuing expansion and higher annual profits. My husband may still be president, but in reality he has become my rubber stamp. He does whatever I tell him. And I allow him to have his little romps. If he wants to buy his gold diggers expensive clothes and jewels that is his privilege, but he must never bring them home. If that happened the explosion that followed would catapult him out of his present position of power. But there will be no divorce. When he dies I want either myself or Stephanie to inherit most of his own vast wealth as well as his holdings in the corporation.'

Marianne could hardly believe all she was hearing, or that everything had the apparent co-operation of his daughter. Put simply a family revolution was being planned which, if successful, would have worldwide repercussions and almost certainly lead to powerful rivals bidding for parts of the empire, although it was doubtful if anyone had the resources to make an outright bid. Nevertheless the business world would know that the first cracks had appeared in the Stephanopolous dominance. Marianne was forced to ask, 'What is unclear is why you need me. You are already internationally the most powerful businesswoman, and by your side will be Stephanie with ever increasing, authority over everyone.'

'The answer is that I want your brains and your obvious business ability, and am prepared to pay a high price to obtain it.'

'What is the price? And what is the catch?'

'There is no catch. And once you have given us your written agreement to become part of the team you will be allocated three shares which are currently valued at around five million dollars each. By my calculation that makes your holding worth fifteen million dollars. That is how much confidence I have in you. But Stephanie and I will always make the final decisions. Yet the three of us will be responsible for all expansion and growth once my daughter reaches eighteen and receives the first payout from her large trust fund which when it matures when she is twenty-five will have paid her instalments totalling far more than fifty million dollars, but will probably then be worth nearer double that sum. She will also be elected to the board of directors, and Director of Personnel. You will both then be members of the board, and I shall expect your constant support.

'Finally, I must make it absolutely clear, that with the substantial holding I am offering you, the time could come when you might have to decide the future of your own husband's business empire which, as you know, I have long wanted to take under the Stephanopolous umbrella but only when I decide the moment is right, which is not yet. What are your reactions, Marianne?'

'I am in a mild state of shock. I cannot believe what I am hearing.' Nor was she convinced that she had heard the full story, probably only what Christiana was prepared to tell. Nevertheless, she was being offered an immense reward. But how close was she to penetrating the mind of this multi-millionairess who was a dragon in super-expensive clothes. She was certainly duplicitous, which meant that with Christiana lies could become truths. All her targets had to be achieved and a bullseye scored, whatever the price or cost to others including, so it seemed, her husband.

Christiana had been described in one newspaper as having 'the legs of a Derby winner'. If the writer had known her better he would have suggested that she moved with the speed of a cheetah, so fast her victims did not even realise they were under threat before they were gobbled up. After one lightning coup she had been asked why two hundred workers had been made redundant if the company was so valuable. She answered, 'If I had not moved quickly the entire workforce would have been without a job. Now one hundred and fifty are still at work.'

She was also prepared to use her breasts as a weapon if it became necessary. They were as firm today as when Ulysses first touched them. It was these sensuous and physical advantages that made senior executives with whom she was negotiating little more than bars of soap in her hands as she rubbed away their resistance. It had been while she was still in her final teens that she realised she could use the nightly attractions of her body to tie up her husband with softest lengths of silk so that he had to carry out whatever she asked, until at last little was done within the corporation without her authority. As vice-president of Stephanopolous International she remained in the background, allowing Ulysses to take the glory when he announced the regular increases in their annual profits; she preferred to beaver away largely unseen, but not unknown to those who needed to know. At headquarters everyone had learned several years ago never to cross swords, or words, with Madame Stephanopolous. Dismissals could be instant and a couple of announcements that someone had been sacked for refusing to obey an order she gave had instant effect upon everyone else.

Nevertheless, offstage a new script was in the process of being written by a new star standing in the wings. The next prima donna was called Stephanie, although it might take several years before she took centre stage. When the time was right for a new heroine, the old guard would bow and applaud a much younger, but equally ruthless, leader who was not only interested in growth and profits, but glory and fame as well.

Marianne was sensing that all might not be quite as Christiana was explaining. An occasional smile in her direction from Stephanie, plus her equally revealing frowns at something her mother was saying, made the countess wonder whether she and the younger of the two women visitors might have more in common than Christiana believed. Only a few years separated their ages and that could soon count for nothing.

Marianne found herself thinking of what might happen if the daughter, despite all her persistent years of grooming, took it into her head to throw all her shares into her father's pot leaving her mother with no alternative but to capitulate. The problem facing Marianne was that the more she studied Christiana, the more she saw a mirror image of herself. They were out of a similar mould and had risen from nowhere. Money, power, success, unlimited authority were the goals that drove them both. Each would be happy to have it written on their tombstone, 'there are two kinds of woman, those who are feared and those who are afraid'. Marianne knew that when, and if, the time came she would happily allow the Stephanopolous empire to buy all the count's business interests, providing she was put in control. What she did not know was that Christiana had become acquisitive and intolerant within a few days of her marriage to the multi-millionaire Greek tycoon. His signature on their marriage certificate transformed her from being nothing more than an attractive teenage Australian girl with the genes of a Greek, into a wife who possessed the riches of a modern Queen of Sheba. An hour before they wed a monster single stone diamond ring had been placed on her engagement finger. Some years later she had it valued at two hundred and fifty thousand dollars which was more than her father would earn in several years.

Now having assured Marianne there were no catches to what she was proposing, Christiana got up from her daughter's side, walked round the marble coffee table and stood looking down at her future business colleague. 'You will continue to live in your castle in Germany and head up the Stephanopolous Foundation branch in Germany. But you will be required to attend board meetings in Athens, usually once a month. At these meetings everyone has sight of the profitability of every section of our company that are spread around the world. Any decisions that have to be taken will be on resolutions moved by the president and seconded by the vice-president, or vice versa.

124

'Now to Stephanie. Soon she will be eighteen. On the day she joins the corporation I would like you to help her settle in and ensure that everyone pays her the respect due to a Stephanopolous. Will you do that?'

'Willingly, providing Stephanie agrees.'

Stephanie now stood up and playing with her over-large diamond ring, told Marianne, 'I'm not sure. I will make up my mind when I take over as Director of Personnel. I must make it clear that whatever my decision I shall always be your superior while you work for Stephanopolous International.' Stephanie seemed anxious to emphasise her future authority and went on: 'Marianne, whether you like it or not, you will have to get used to the idea that I shall control the purse strings, in co-operation with my mother. Do as I tell you, as everyone else will quickly learn to accept if they intend to remain with the Stephanopolous corporation, and we shall get on. As my mother has told you we want your brains and your ability, You will have authority over ninety-five, perhaps ninety-nine, per cent of our staff, but not over the three who control everyone including yourself. I think you are sufficiently intelligent to realise that you really have no alternative, but to accept. Failure could spell ruin for yourself as well as the count. At my finishing school we are taught to accept the luxuries that life has provided for us, and let the rest enjoy the simpler necessities they can afford.' Marianne, too, now stood up. 'Despite Stephanie's aggressiveness, or should I say her honesty, it is not easy to reject your financial offer. However, I must discuss it with my husband.'

'We require your decision in writing within one week,' warned Christiana. 'And don't worry about your husband. He is a businessman and he will understand what he has to lose if you should reject what has been offered by Stephanie and myself. So far I have kept all my promises and his profits have soared. I am sure he is aware that I can flush him out from all this authority at any time I think the time is right. And don't forgot, in addition to your large shareholding you will also receive a share of the annual bonuses which are decided privately by Ulysses and myself and soon with help from Stephanie. It will be best to have us both on your side when we take decisions that could involve hundreds of thousands of dollars.'

Stephanie interrupted, 'Marianne, try to understand that in

a few years the difference in our ages will count for nothing. But one factor will not have changed. My family will still have immense economic power, and as time passes more and more of it will pass into my hands. I shall never hesitate to use it to shower favours on those who earn my respect. My mother and I both want Marianne, Countess von Rugerstein, to become a very powerful international business lady. Join us and at once you will be the fourth most powerful member of the Stephanopolous empire. Just one final question. Do you think you could work with me?'

Marianne hesitated, although she knew her reply had to be in the affirmative. Stephanie had the confidence of someone who was twenty-five, not seventeen. In some ways she was like a Grecian Joan of Arc who believed in a kind of God-given strength to win any battles she fought.

Marianne answered, 'Of course.'

That night the count agreed that, in the best interests of all, his wife should accept the offer that had been made, and that with Marianne sitting on the board she could help increase profits for the Stephanopolous empire, and also look after her own family's interests.

It was around ten the following morning and Marianne was back in her own suite and alone having bathed and breakfasted when there was a gentle tapping on the door. Thinking it might be Penny or Rachel she called out a welcoming 'come in'. To her complete surprise it was Stephanie. She was wearing her new mink jacket, but was without any lipstick or make up, and looked more like the schoolgirl she still was, rather than the multi-million dollar heiress she soon would be.

Marianne got up to greet her and give her a hug, but instead she found herself being embraced by a tearful Stephanie whose heart was pumping with emotion. A moment later she was in tears. Her sobs made Marianne worry at their cause. 'Oh my dear, what is the matter?' she asked. 'Sit down and tell me. And whatever you tell me will be our secret.'

She passed Stephanie a hanky to wipe her tears. As soon as she stopped crying, she whimpered, 'I am so ashamed of myself. Please forgive me. I did not mean a word of what I told you yesterday. I was only doing what my mother had rehearsed me to say, it was not the real me. But this is. I would like to think of you as my elder sister. Love me as I want to love you. I am so alone. Of course, I have everything a girl could possibly want, except love. Both my parents are so busy with their own affairs and running the family empire, that I seldom see them, even when I am home on holiday. I have a couple of girl friends in Athens but they are mostly away on their own holidays when I come home. Please accept the offer that was made to you. I want us to work together and be colleagues. Don't think of me as your boss, but as your sister. Will you?'

She held Stephanie's hand and whispered, 'From now onwards you are my younger sister. Hi, sis! But we may have to tell a few white lies, if we are to keep our secret, and keep you safe from too many bad influences. We'll carry out the instructions your mother gives, but we shall find time to have some fun, as well as being colleagues. But when we are with either of your parents we will let them see that we enjoy working together, but I will try to show that I never forget the power you have at your disposal, or the ocean-wide monetary gap that will one day lie between us. Any problems, we shall solve by discussing them together, and alone. And, by the way, you really look wonderful in your jacket. It lets everyone know, including me, that although you are still a young woman, you are also a very special and unique young lady. I may be a wealthy countess, and be even wealthier very soon, but I realise that once you start wearing couture clothes, fabulous furs and diamonds, it is going to be difficult for your elder sister to compete. You are about to become perhaps the world's richest heiress. Of course, there will be times when I feel envious. But all the time you will have my love.'

'Please don't forget that we are sisters. More than that, we shall be family.'

'Well, as your elder sister, I think you should go into my bathroom and wipe the smudges made by your tears. Use any of my toiletries. Then I think it is time you returned to your mum, but say nothing about what we have agreed. That is our secret. Just tell her you wanted me to see you in your jacket, and then add that your furs will always be finer than mine. She will think she has trained you well.'

As soon as Stephanie left, Marianne sought to resolve the puzzle of her own future now that Stephanie, as well as her mother, were seeking her support. Would she be a winner whichever way the dice fell, or would she be forced to decide soon which side to back? Christiana was certainly far older, more experienced and more ruthless than her daughter, but Stephanie had time on her side to develop her own ambitions and there were already indications of a near passionate enthusiasm for making money, and spending it. Perhaps she, and not Christiana, might in a few years make the first move to seize control of the family empire. If so, she would expect Marianne's full support. But was time all she needed? Would not cunning, and patience, prove more effective weapons? It was also reasonable to suppose that a youngster who had not reached her eighteenth birthday was going to need many years of senior business experience before she could seriously think of challenging her mother who already controlled a large slice of the family's half a billion dollar corporation. On the other hand, Stephanie was showing signs of being an exceptional young lady who had been groomed to handle great wealth as though it were no big deal. She had also been brought up to have her own way. The ten million dollars she would inherit on her eighteenth birthday meant she could ride over everyone, except her parents, and with a whip in her gloved hand. If Marianne was reading the signs correctly she would quickly insist upon being treated as an equal by both her parents.

People were already in fear of Christiana. Her daughter would expect similar respect, and from the beginning. Marianne could visualise how, during the first few days after her arrival at headquarters every female on their staff would be envious of the way she could change her eye-catching clothes every day, and before the end of her first week they would accept that she was a Stephanopolous and was to be feared as well as respected. Men who had become accustomed to taking orders from her mother who was a mature woman as well as being vice-president of the corporation, would see Stephanie more as a sexually exciting princess to be admired and wanted rather than respected. That would be a guaranteed way to feel the undoubted power and authority she possessed. From the outset everyone would have to learn that with Stephanie age did not matter. But her name did. Marianne guessed that it would be a comparatively short time before everyone, not only at headquarters, but throughout the family's empire would know that Stephanopolous International was now ruled by a threesome, father, mother and daughter.

What Marianne did not know was that for years Stephanie had sat at the family breakfast table and listened to her parents discussing plans that would earn the family more millions whether through new ventures, bonuses or buying out rival companies and then closing them down to reduce competition and move nearer to creating a near monopoly. Most families talked in terms of hundreds of dollars while her parents talked in millions. How could Stephanie be anyone but the young, formidable lady she had been born to be. She even walked with the casual stiff grace of a powerful woman who demanded humility and instant obedience.

The more she wondered, the more certain Marianne became that one day young Stephanie would challenge her mother's wish for supremacy, but first she would need to remember to be patient which was not a Stephanopolous virtue. Marianne was determined to use her influence to avoid the inevitable clash between the two generations breaking out too soon because of impetuousness on the part of Stephanie. Her task was to encourage youthful caution because there could only be one winner and only one battle. It would be a winner take all contest, but Marianne remembered that in boxing the strength and confidence of youth sometimes defeats experience. There was always a future champion in waiting. And where would that leave Marianne?

A week later the Countess von Rugerstein flew to Athens for her first board meeting, and stayed for three nights with Christiana and Ulysses at their palatial mansion home where she had ended her honeymoon. Only now she was aware that Christiana was at work on plans that would increase her control and reduce her husband close to impotence. As Christiana had put it, 'I believe in a *fait accompli*.'

On the first night of Marianne's stay she was told, 'I have three tasks for you, Marianne, which will probably occupy you for at least the next twelve months, probably longer. How quick and how successful you are will decide the level of your annual bonus. Now that you are part of my triumvirate, I have printed you one thousand gold embossed business cards that are similar to my own. They will let everyone know that you are a member of the board of Stephanopolous International, and have full authority to negotiate on our behalf. But, please, keep me informed so that I can confirm what you have agreed. First, there is a tiny company employing no more than fifty workers. It is owned by an English woman and manufactures a couple of vital parts that are essential for the efficient firepower of the latest British army tanks. No other army has this tool. I want to buy the company and use it as a launch pad for our entry into the armaments industry worldwide, and also to put a little pressure on the British government. Get it for me, Marianne.

'Second, my husband and I are both aware that the world is changing and every country is becoming more and more dependent upon oil. We already have large investments in the oil industry, but are also building a new fleet of tankers of between one and two hundred thousand tonnes, and one of almost three hundred thousand. They will all be part of our fleet before the end of next year. This means that many of our smaller tankers could become obsolete. For the last two years I have been keeping my eyes on the growing interest in containerisation. A dozen of our smaller tankers will be converted into container ships. By estimates I have received it will cost us ninety per cent less to convert a tanker than to build a new container ship. That means we shall be able to undercut our rivals. While our profits rise we shall also be building more container ships to add to our fleet and together with our strength in tankers we should become one of the top two or three companies carrying the world's trade. Where do you fit in? Start studying the industry, develop contacts with companies like P&O and Furness Withy as well as others in Germany and Japan. Your task will be to recommend whether we join them, or buy them, or go our own way.'

Christiana hesitated for a moment as though not sure what to say next, although such halts in her flow were seldom due to any concern for how it might be affecting her listener. She knew a pause sometimes frightened people into worrying what blow she might deliver next. Her icy aloofness could freeze the atmosphere before she fired a salvo which would create personal or corporate destruction. Only her daughter never had anything to fear when listening to her mother because she had inherited her parent's venom in her own genes.

Marianne took advantage of the short silence to ask, almost jokingly, 'and what else have you in mind for me?'

'You are quite right, there is more, but I was not hesitating for fear of burdening you with too much responsibility too soon. But you must earn the large six-figure annual bonus I am planning to pay you as my second closest business ally. For your information our annual profits are usually around forty million dollars, sometimes more, sometimes a little less. That mean we allocate seldom less than six million dollars in bonuses to those who have helped build our profits. Last year both Ulysses and I were each awarded a bonus of two and a half million dollars. Next year Stephanie will need to be included in the distribution. As a result, we shall reduce what we receive to two million dollars each, and Stephanie will be rewarded with one million dollars. That leaves one million dollars to be distributed outside the family, mostly to other directors and senior executives. My current intention, subject only to the results I expect you to achieve, is to award you, probably, half a million dollars. The rest will be divided between non-shareholders who have proved their continous loyalty. None of the bonuses are paid as salary. The rest of our profits are put to reserve. Now you have some idea of how I look after those I love and respect, and who do my bidding.'

She went on: 'Let's not worry for the moment about your third assignment. It is one that I know you will enjoy, but it does not have the priority of the other two, and can wait until I am ready to pounce. Your sharp eye for detail plus your charm, or viciousness, is going to earn us both a great deal of money. But please get close to Stephanie.'

Christiana was reminding Marianne of a human peacock who was never so happy as when she was displaying her plumage which in her case was her wealth and power. 'Back to you and the future. As far as worldwide trade and exports are concerned we already hold a dominant position through our fleet of tankers which will increase as we build more container ships.

'Nevertheless, I am convinced, there is another future to be won in the skies. But my target is not in the ever-growing size of passenger aircraft, but as global business flourishes and the rich get richer, the increasing number of businessmen and celebrities including sportsmen, stage, film and television stars, plus operatic tenors and divas, and heiresses like Stephanie, who will demand their own private planes to whisk them speedily in comfort and convenience to where they need to go. My intention is that an increasing percentage of these planes will be built by a new branch of the Stehanopolous empire. But my powerful magnet is also attracted to the airfields from which these planes fly – mostly in Europe and the United Kingdom. America is too big and already dominated by US companies. Outsiders are seldom welcomed, or succeed.

'Your third task, for the moment, is to keep your eye on the cream of this specialist section of aircraft and let me know when there are signs that someone could be enticed into the protection and advantages our net would provide. Your growing knowledge will by then have given you an insider's knowledge of how the Stephanopolous empire operates. Look out not only for a company that is showing signs of wobbling, but also for the best technical and creative brains. I am prepared to pay high salaries for their experience and their ideas. And they will be staying in the business they love and know.

'This might be one of those occasions when your beauty, your body, and brains, not to mention the way you dress, might help lure them into accepting what we offer. Tell them they will be working closely with you which is not a promise, simply a statement. Overall, I believe our expansion in the air will be largely centred in western Europe, the Middle East, Asia and possibly parts of South America where wages are low, but the rich are very rich with eyes that quickly fix on any attractive woman they think is worthy of their attention, and doubly so when they dress as though they are already worth millions. That, I think, is a fair description of Marianne, Countess von Rugerstein. A lady like yourself will know how to encourage one thing but only when she knows it is going to lead to something else. And always keep your eyes open for possible takeover opportunities. Keep in focus those regions and countries where wages are low, strikes banned and any machinery can be made to work round the clock. I am not interested in people, only profits. In the past when I have had to shut factories because of a change in economic circumstances which has meant dismissing hundreds of workers. I always assured their union bosses who control the lives of the workers, that their own perks are not in danger. The vast resources we have built up make us immune from the worst effects of worldwide downturns while others sink as a turbulent sea sweeps them into oblivion. That is when we strike. Workers will accept lower wages rather than lose their jobs. Although I have never bought a single loaf in my life, isn't there a saying that half a loaf is better than none? In life, Marianne, there have to be winners and losers, and you don't wear diamonds like mine by being a loser.'

But even Christiana understood the need for discretion. To satisfy her natural needs which an ageing Ulysses was not always able to satisfy, she owned a secret hideaway hidden away in the countryside a few miles from their estate. This was in addition to her apartment at headquarters and a much larger penthouse in a luxury block hardly more than four hundred metres from the corporation's offices which they also owned. She mostly used her secret hideaway when she wanted to get away from the telephone and think through new plans for her growing empire, and occasionally for her second-favourite pleasure after making money. It was mostly where she took her human toys. To her they existed to be discarded and forgotten once they had served her purpose and were no longer required. It was the least impressive of the three, but in many ways it was her favourite. Although a pub, its telephone was ex-directory and there was only one key to the two rooms she needed for her occasional nights out, and that was kept in a zipped pocket of whichever handbag she was carrying. The rooms were also reached from the bar and the wife of the couple who ran the pub on her behalf also kept the place clean. She was also a fine cook of good plain food who could make a boiled egg taste as though it had been Michelin-prepared, and laid by a swan. When Christiana was in residence, however, she would treat finest fillets of chateaubriand steaks plus well-cared-for bottles of Lafitte and Mouton Rothschild with the care they deserved.

In town when the flames of desire began raging inside her, the routine began with her white Rolls driving her to a mid-market bar where her chauffeur escorted her. She sat alone and spread her net. Dressed expensively with diamonds sparkling from her ears, wrists and fingers, heads inevitably turned in her direction as men were naturally fascinated that such an obviously wealthy and alluring woman should be in such a bar when she would be more at home in one of the expensive private clubs close to the royal palace. Did she want to attract one of them into her bed? Or was she waiting for someone? None dared risk finding out, especially as one or two of the younger drinkers recognised her from her photographs that frequently appeared in newspapers. Controlling men was something she did every day, and that was what she was about to do as her deep, dark, almost threatening, eyes began to rove. Once she identified her target, a nod of her head indicated that he was welcome to join her. Few refused a million-dollar invitation. In a voice that was unusually soft and hardly above a whisper she invited him to sit down and explained that she felt lonely and hoped she was not taking him away from his friends. Assured they were only people he periodically met in the bar after work, she would ask if he would like to keep her company, and without waiting for his reply ordered him an ouzo, and would ask, 'What shall I call you?' On the most recent evening he had replied 'Frederick' and when she queried 'Not Fred?', was informed he preferred Frederick. She was impressed. A moment later she enquired whether he knew who she was, and he admitted, 'Yes. From your photographs.'

'Do you like what you are seeing in person?'

'Only a blind man could not,' he told her, at last gathering just a little of his manliness in the presence of a lady whose reputation for ruthlessness in business he had read about. At once Christiana sensed his confidence growing and resolved to whip him back into his place. 'For your sake it is unwise to be too clever when you are with Christiana Stephanopolous. A word from me and you could lose your job wherever you work. But show me respect and you could quickly see yourself elevated far above those you have just left. Sitting here might be the equivalent of winning the lottery.'

'I meant no harm, madame.'

She could see that he was mesmerised by the size of the solitaire diamond on the hand which held her glass of ouzo and now took off her other glove to reveal an equally tantalising gem. Her hand wandered onto Frederick's knee. She watched his immediate reaction to what he was feeling, and queried, 'Would you like to see more of your hostess? My limousine and chauffeur are outside. Why don't we leave our drinks and adjourn to my apartment where we can share champagne, and much else? It is a ten minute drive away and from my enclosed balcony we can look down upon the Acropolis by moonlight. And you will hold my hand and feel my nakedness.' Then, as she always did, having aroused a man's expectations she deflated him by announcing: 'I have decided not to call you Frederick, but my toy boy. After all, that is what you are.'

'Whatever you desire, madame. I am enchanted by you, and also afraid.'

'Stay that way and all will be well. I have a very short fuse so do as you are told and we will enjoy one another.' Once in her penthouse apartment where she had been saluted by a uniformed security guard as she entered the ground floor lobby and a lift whisked them to the top floor where the touch of a concealed switch opened her front door and automatically switched on the lights to reveal a deep piled white carpet. She guided him to an intimate two seater settee while she disappeared into her bedroom before returning naked except for a near see-through silk robe. They sipped champagne and she asked whether he liked the fizz, and what he could now see. He answered: 'I would like to be able to afford champagne, but I would sacrifice everything to be allowed to touch you, madame.'

She was about to rebuke him for being flippant, almost insolent, but instead excited him still more by asking, 'Why let our glasses have all the fun of touching one another? Take off your clothes.' The next thing her toy boy remembered was her on top of him and her soft lips embracing his. As her seductive perfume worked its magic his hardness forced itself upon her and she ordered, 'Not so quick. Do as you are told. Let the moment last.' They were enjoying the comfort of her wide four-poster and he was trapped under her control. At first he thought she was rejecting him until he was told in a welcoming, yet condescending, voice that was she was ready. At first he entered her like a supplicant, but for the rest of their hour-long togetherness he felt like her lover who she wanted so badly. But it was not so. Once satisfied he was returned to the society where he came from. 'That is all. You can go,' he was informed.

When he asked when he could see her again it was with her mocking, imperious voice that she told him, 'Don't be silly. You have pleased me. Think of the past couple of hours as moments spent in heaven from which you are now being banished.' A satisfied Madame Stephanopolous was a different person from a hungry Christiana. She wrapped herself into the fur coat she had worn when they met and took hold of his hand. When he opened it he was he was three hundred dollars richer than when he had entered the bar. Once he had gone she phoned the porter and instructed him to tell her chauffeur she did not need him again tonight, but he should call for her at nine in the morning. She switched on the alarm and her latest toy boy was already a forgotten man.

On the final morning of Marianne's three-day stay with Christiana in her Athens mansion where she attended her first board meeting she entered the dining-room where breakfast was served, and was surprised to find the room empty except for a waiter with a spotless white apron that complemented his dark jacket and trousers. 'Where is everyone?' she asked, only to be told that Mr Stephanopolous had flown to Rome, he thought he had heard him say, and had left at seven o'clock, while Madame had not yet come down. Marianne ordered a breakfast of freshly squeezed orange juice following by bacon, eggs and tomatoes plus hot coffee and toast. As he prepared to leave the waiter handed her a copy of that morning's English language newspaper. While she waited for her juice she opened the front page and there in monster type was the headline, 'Billionaire in love with Oscar winner' and underneath a story of Ulysses's affair with Veronica Lang, plus photographs of them together in both Rome and New York, and a blow-up shot of the large diamond ring she was wearing 'which he is believed to have bought for her' according to the caption. The story ended with a comment from the billionaire that, 'We are just good friends'.

Marianne was shocked by what she was reading and wondered whether Christiana had any knowledge of the story. She did not have to wait long to find out as her hostess burst into the room in an obvious fury. At once she saw that Marianne had been reading the story. When the waiter arrived with Marianne's breakfast he was told to 'Get out. I am not in the mood for breakfast,' and Christiana poured herself a cup from Marianne's coffee jug.

'You've seen the paper?' she asked, more a statement than a question.

Marianne asked: 'Did you have any idea what was going on?'

'Yes and no. Greek men, especially when they are wealthy, have a history of not being able to keep their hands off an inviting pair of tits. After we were married I found out that the day before we met he had slept with America's top coloured model. It must have been a black day for her when I came along. Since then I have lost count of the number of affairs, both major and minor, he has had. I've had a few flings myself, and we have both paid off our lovers when necessary, but he has spent a small fortune on his women; mine have cost me a few pence by comparison.

'I can't remember the last time we slept together, so I guessed he must be sleeping around. As for me, the last time I went to visit Stephanie at her finishing school in Switzerland a month ago, we had dinner with her head mistress, plus the only male teacher, a twenty-four-year-old sports coach from America who made it a foursome. He offered to drive me back to my hotel and, of course, I invited him up to my suite where I first seduced him with caviar and champagne and, in return, he provided me with what I had been missing for far too long. It was almost a sleepless night but, somehow, he was able to get up and be back at the school before eight o'clock. I am thinking of visiting Stephanie more often.'

'Good for you,' was Marianne's comment, 'but what are you going to do about Ulysses?'

Christiana started to walk up and down the breakfast room, an activity that Marianne knew many senior businessmen and women adopted, perhaps because it helped them clear their minds, or more likely due to the feeling of superiority it engendered because they were on their feet and their listeners were sitting down as though in a classroom. Christiana told Marianne: 'In my own good time I shall take care of Ulysses. For the moment my mind is more occupied with how to see more of Harold, that's the name of my new find in Switzerland, who seems to have an abundance of his own brand of Swiss milk on tap. When term finishes he will be free, but so will Stephanie and she will come home to Athens for a month before we go sailing on my yacht. Dare I stay in Lausanne without going to visit my daughter, and instead have a long weekend of unbounded sex which I feel I deserve? It would be a spending spree for him.'

Telling Marianne about Switzerland brought Fred, the toy boy, back into her mind. She had only taken him to her bed because of the craving for the sex Harold had stimulated. She had needed a man and the toy boy she selected had momentarily satisfied her. But that was a few evenings ago and she no longer remembered what he looked like. But she did find herself wondering how much of her sexuality had been impregnated into her daughter's genes. Would they someday boomerang back on her? Stephanie was certainly showing signs of her mother's despotism and intolerance. And when she had children...?

For now, however, all that was in the future. What mattered now was Harold. Suddenly Marianne, who of course knew nothing of the recent escapade with Frederick came to the rescue. 'I may be able to help, and prove once and for all who is your best friend, and why I am your highest paid colleague.'

Hearing this Christiana sat down. 'If you can, I shall be forever grateful.'

'Why don't you phone Harold and ask when he could be free to fly to Athens at your expense for a long weekend from Friday until Monday? Then book him into a quiet airport hotel, not one of the luxury hotels where you are too well known to be seen with a younger man who could almost be your son. Indulge him and treat him like a pet poodle; after all that is what he will really be. Once you know his convenient dates, I shall telephone Stephanie and ask whether I could come and see her that same weekend. I am sure she will be delighted. And she need never know of our collusion.'

'Marianne, you are already worth every penny of the fifteen million dollars you are being paid via shares in Stephanopolous International. You can sell them through selected brokers at any time for more than five million dollars a share, but I would advise you not to.'

She got up and told Marianne, 'I'm going to phone Harold.

Thank you for answering my SOS, darling.' Her clouds were starting to disappear.

But the script was never written. When she tried to phone Harold the school told him he had been sacked for interfering with one of his pupils. But Marianne still went to see Stephanie, telling Christiana that she would seek to take on the role of her elder sister during her first weeks at headquarters and friendship could be the long term result. What she did not reveal was that such a bond of friendship already existed. Sometimes it was necessary to scheme against the schemer.

For Christiana what had happened to Harold meant she was left with a lost weekend. Finding another man would not be a problem, but hearing the kind of man she had nearly trapped in her golden web was a rogue left her temporarily feeling disgust at all men. But the mood could not last. There was always Robert McDonald whom she was planning to make her aide.

However, on the Sunday of her lost weekend her sharp, active brain remembered that the three university graduates at the family's academy who were annually shortlisted by the Director of Personnel as potential senior executives in some branch of the Stephanopolous empire, were due to be seen by her on Tuesday morning when she would make the final decisions about their future. She decided to see them on Monday now that she had nothing better to do. It had become an annual exercise on which she rarely wasted her time and usually delegated to one of the non-family directors to decide which, if any, of the year's chosen candidates fitted into the needs of the corporation. This year was different because her volatile mind had been wondering whether, despite what she had told Robert McDonald, she might discover that a younger man, perhaps like Harold, at any rate in age, had the credentials, and everything else to satisfy her by appointing him as her aide. After all, McDonald was just another member of staff who could be sent to wherever she decided, perhaps overseas where he would be out of sight and out of mind, yet always available; a kind of reserve.

She remembered glancing at the three files which had been sent to her with full biographical details and photographs. But it had been no more than a cursory look and she could not remember a single detail about any of them. Now her mood was different. She was looking for help in many different ways...

The fact that it was the weekend did not stop her telephoning the current Director of Personnel and ordering him to contact the three candidates and tell them that their interview would now be with the Vice-President on Monday afternoon instead of Tuesday morning. If this was inconvenient for any of them they were to be struck off the list and she would restrict her interview to whoever was available. He was to let her know on Monday morning who she would be seeing in the afternoon.

She drove herself to headquarters and ordered one of the two uniformed security men to park her car and walked briskly to the private lift that took her directly to her suite of offices on floors which were out of bounds to all except her husband and herself, plus visitors, other board directors and their staff. All had special keys that allowed them to travel to all floors including the top three. Reception quickly alerted her Australian-born secretary, that she was on her way up and, almost automatically, Maggie was standing ready to wish her a 'Good morning, madame' which was mostly ignored. Christiana threw her sable jacket onto a chair before picking up one of several phones on her desk and dialling the number of Fred Surplus, the Director of Personnel for the entire corporation. He answered brusquely, 'Yes?' but instantly changed his tone when he realised who was calling. 'Fred, this is Madame Stephanopolous. Which of the three university candidates are available for interview this afternoon?' He was able to inform her that he had contacted everyone and all were free to be interviewed by her that afternoon. She told him: 'The interviews will commence at two o'clock, with the second at two forty-five and the last at three-thirty. If this time-table is inconvenient for any of them cancel their interview.' What she did not tell him was that she had also decided that he would shortly be demoted and replaced by her daughter, Stephanie, who after her eighteenth birthday would join the corporation as a full board director, and take over his responsibilities as director of personnel. It would be up to the new director to decide his future.

For several years the Stephanopolous family, under the leadership of Christiana and her husband had provided millions of dollars to publicly sponsor the Stephanopolous Academy of Business Management at the university. Only students whose results during their combined course in Economics and Business Management had been sufficiently impressive could be sent forward for a final twelve month study course under a team of half a dozen highly qualified instructors. Now this year's ten were down to three who were automatically assured of an interview with one of the directors of Stephanopolous International. In addition, all three received the highly regarded Foundation Degree that confirmed their above-average skills after preparing an international management plan for a mythical corporation of their own creation. Under the watchful eye of their tutors they would have achieved excellent marks in such competencies as team building, leadership, employment law, managing financial resources, and the promotion of a product or service. Finally, they were given a project and it was their responsibility to manage and see it through to a conclusion. It was unusual if all three were not offered executive positions.

Christiana found time before the first interview to read through the three files that contained details of their family background, academic achievements and two photographs, one a head and shoulders, the other full length so that she would have an indication of how well they dressed. She was a stickler for presentation. Although she glanced through the pages of information she digested little. All she needed to know about them was how they behaved at the interview, and how they answered her probing, often personal and unexpected questions.

Her technique was mostly the same whenever she agreed to carry out the final interviews which was now every three or four years. Knowing they would be grilled in the rarely-visited office of the vice-president of the five hundred million dollar empire they hoped to join was enough to worry anyone, but the post was occupied by a lady who was both elegant and attractive, and with a reputation for being a ruthless businesswoman. Even worse, as they would quickly find out, almost all the questions she asked were unlike what they had expected, and certainly seemed to have little connection with the subjects that had won them marks of distinction at university. Usually she would keep them waiting in her outer office and then leave them standing when they were finally admitted. This gave her visitors time to be impressed by the lavish femininity of her office. Except for the small marble-topped boardroom table for six with its high backed ergonomically designed chairs that guaranteed everyone's full attention throughout a meeting, everywhere were sumptuous armchairs, a small matching sofa for two, and vases of fresh flowers. She sat at a desk which she had bought at an auction in London's Bond Street after she was given a written assurance that it was where Napoleon had sat before the battle of Waterloo. It was now on a raised platform that enabled Madame Stephanopolous to look down on all her visitors. Napoleon's chair had been re-upholstered to match the rest of the armchairs. The walls were hung with portraits of her husband and herself as well as photographs of some of the corporation's fleet of tankers and factories around the world.

Ten minutes before he was due, Maggie buzzed to say the first candidate had arrived and was told to bring him in. He was asked to sit down but ignored until it was precisely the time scheduled for his interview. Without warning, the vice-president put down the document she had been reading and demanded: 'Tell me about yourself, your family background, your achievement at university and your ambitions, and what you know about the Stephanopolous empire. You have ten minutes.' She clicked a stop watch. He was on a losing wicket from the start. First, he wore spectacles and she wondered what other unrevealed disabilities he might not have disclosed. After only twenty minutes she brought the interview to a close. 'Thank you. You will be hearing from us.' And on his file she scrawled, 'Good, but no better. Offer him a job in one of our overseas offices.'

Graduate number two impressed her more. He was well built, good-looking, had excellent qualifications, a clean-cut appearance, but spoke with too many pauses that seemed to suggest he might lack the confidence she regarded as essential, especially as she was hoping that one of them might have the qualifications to become her aide. She was looking for someone who was presentable, had confidence in himself and much else. The second student fell short of this peak, but he certainly had promise. Her written verdict on his file, read: 'A first-class brain. But lacks confidence. He is not a salesman, but should make a good administrator.'

She almost stood up when the third candidate was shown into her office. He was more than six feet tall with by far the most manly appearance of the three. His hair was neat as though it had been specially cut for the interview, and his suit was well pressed, if not well cut, while his tie was tied in a neat knot and his finger nails might have been manicured. In addition, he had excellent academic qualifications, although such advantages were beginning to be less important than he was. After he had lucidly told her his background and his ambitions she interrupted and asked, 'Would you be happy working for a woman?'

'I like to think I would get on equally well with both men and women, madame.'

'What if it were me who was your immediate boss?'

'I would regard myself as the luckiest and most privileged of men.'

He was impressing her. She understood his nervousness at what was, perhaps, the most important interview he would ever attend. She had already decided to appoint him as her aide, but was still determined to test him to the full and rose from Napoleon's chair and came and sat on the other side of her desk so that she was as close to him as was possible without their legs actually touching. Her crossed knees were only inches away from his own, and he had a front row view of her diamonds. Her intoxicating French perfume was wafting around him. 'How many women have you slept with, Byron?' His name was Byron Walters. He had a Greek mother, who had named him after Lord Byron, and an English father. Before he could answer, she went on, 'More important, do you currently have a girlfriend?'

'I have been going out for several months with a fellow student who is studying art at the university. Is that a problem?'

For a few moments she discarded her mask and became the imperious lady who dominated the lives of thousands, most of whom she would never meet. 'If I were to appoint you as my personal aide you would have no time to do anything but serve me twenty-four hours a day – that means day or night. Won't your girlfriend be jealous when she finds out how much time you are spending with someone who is regarded as the richest woman in Greece? And how would she react if I started to spoil you as I might? That will depend entirely on my whims and my mood, and on you. I can be very intolerant, but very generous, too.'

'She is not a problem. We have no serious relationship. We are just friends.'

143

She leaned forward and was now still closer to him. His files confirmed his age as twenty-three which meant he was sufficiently experienced to be seduced. Several of her toy boys had been in their early twenties, although mostly in their thirties. But Byron was different. He was sitting opposite her as possibly her first aide. All she needed to find out was whether he wanted her, as much as she was starting to want him. She allowed their knees to touch and watched with undisguised pleasure as he grew in size at her touch. 'Are you happy at the thought of spending so much of your time with the vice-president of this corporation? Before you answer let me tell you that to run an organisation the size of ours means I have to be ruthless and demand constant twenty-four-hour loyalty from the few who are part of my inner team. Could you spend your life working with such a woman, and obeying every order and command she gives? And if I asked you to sack someone, could you do it?'

He sealed his fate by answering, 'If my ambition is to become a senior executive at Stephanopolous International I shall have to be prepared to take decisions, and carry out orders that are for the ultimate benefit of the corporation.'

'You have just talked your way into being appointed my direct aide. Would you like to celebrate by kissing me?'

He eased himself out of his chair, and took her hand and kissed the ring that had mesmerised so many men, adding 'that is the wealthiest kiss I shall ever give a lady.'

'If you admire jewellery, you are going to have a feast during the coming weeks and months and, hopefully, long after that. Now I think we should return to our more normal positions while I dictate memos confirming your appointment.'

Back at her desk she called Maggie to come in with her notebook. Before dictating she introduced them to one another. 'Maggie is my personal secretary who has somehow managed to put up with me for many years. I think this is largely because we were both born in Australia. And this is Mr Byron Walters who has dual British and Greek passports because his father is British and his mother Greek. I have appointed him my personal aide. Look after him Maggie, show him the ropes and get the necessary keys cut for the lift and my apartment. You will call him Mr Walters or "Sir", but never Byron.'

The first memo was to her husband, Ulysses, which explained that she had decided that, because of her growing activities on behalf of the corporation, she needed an aide to make sure she never forgot anything, or anyone. Byron Walters was one of the three winners of this year's academy top prizes, and the best of the three she interviewed. She would bring Byron to meet him whenever convenient.

The next was to Mr Surplus, the current Director of Personnel. 'Thank you for arranging this afternoon's academy interviews. I am returning their individual files with my comments. I have appointed Mr Byron Walters as my personal aide with immediate effect. For the present he will share my office, etc.' Turning to Maggie, 'Arrange for a suitable desk to be delivered for Mr Walters, and ask Roberto to draft a suitable press release which should be on my desk first thing tomorrow morning. Tell him his file is with Mr Surplus.

'Finally send one to the Countess and say I hope she will meet him soon. I nearly forgot the most important, but this time a confirmation letter to Mr Walters.' Turning to Byron she suggested he should disappear for five minutes. 'There is a toilet on this floor.'

Maggie was told to send the normal corporation appointment letter with the three months' trial period and details of salary, which she scribbled on a notepad, but to make no reference to hours. 'I shall decide that. And send a copy to accounts. You will find his address in his file. And lastly book a table for two for twenty-thirty this evening at our Constitution Square hotel. Tell the Rolls to pick me up at the front entrance at twenty-fifteen.'

With Maggie back in her own office, she and Byron sat together on the two seater settee which she regarded as her reserved property and explained that in something like fifteen years she had only sat on it twice, once with her husband and again with her daughter. 'I hope you feel honoured. I do. I am determined that we shall get on, and to make sure we have the perfect start I have booked for us to have dinner together this evening at the hotel we own on Constitution Square. It is quite plush. Do you want to change and put on a suit? Where do you live?'

'During term-time I share with three other students on campus.

When it is not term-time I rent a bedroom in a house which is part rented to students who are provided with breakfast and dinner.'

When she asked how long it would take him to get to work each morning he answered: 'I imagine around forty minutes by bus, perhaps longer during the morning rush hour.'

She told him that was not satisfactory for the man who from now onwards would have no regular office hours any more than she did. She had to lean across him to pick up a nearby phone and, before dialling, told him, 'Your body feels very comfortable.' He did not know who she was calling but whoever it was she spoke to them in a voice that had authority. 'This is Madame Stephanopolous. I need to borrow one of our run-around cars for my new aide. Have one brought to the front door at once and wait for Mr Walters to come down. He will need it for the next few days until I make other arrangements.' To Byron she asked: 'I presume you drive?'

'Yes, but I do not have a car.'

'Mr Walters, there are going to be many changes in your life, as well as saying goodbye to your student friend.' And she kissed him on his lips. 'That's compensation.'

She told him he would find one of the corporation's many small cars which staff usually used for delivering urgent messages or whatever to any address in Athens or anywhere in Greece. 'Only directors could authorise a booking. You should drive home, pack all your clothes into a suitcase with your toiletries and then drive back here, park the car, but tell them you may need it later and then take the lift to the twelfth floor where I have my own private apartment. I shall be waiting for you.'

It was two and a half hours later at 7.30 pm before he gently tapped on the door of what he hoped was her apartment. When she asked what happened he explained that he had lost his way three times, twice going home and once coming back. He had never driven in Athens; until this evening he had always travelled by public transport.

'Count yourself lucky I did not ask you more questions before I gave you the job,' she joked. 'I think you deserve a drink. I have opened a bottle of champagne.'

Their wide-rimmed glasses seem to play a duet as they touched. 'Shall we do the same?' she suggested. And their lips met in harmony for the first time. Neither of them wanted the electrifying moment to end. She only called finish by explaining that she had booked their table for twenty-thirty, but it would still be ready whatever time they arrived. When he asked how they would get to the hotel she explained that her car and chauffeur were calling for them. She decided not to tell him she had her own Rolls Royce. She would keep the news as a surprise. And she wondered how long it would take him to fit in with her quite different lifestyle.

He had quickly changed from the blue blazer and matching trousers he had worn for his interview, and put on his only suit, but kept on his white shirt because the only other white shirt he possessed was at the laundry. However, he changed his tie and hoped she would not notice that it was still the same shirt. When he stepped out of the bathroom she was waiting for him in her bedroom. He gaped at her in disbelief. Now she truly looked like an empress. Her floor-length black dinner gown was the perfect background for her diamonds and the body that was dominating his thoughts and dreams. He wanted to kiss her, but sensed such a move was for her to decide. Instead he was told to get her sable jacket from the wardrobe, please. His next surprise after the soft feel of her fur was the arrival of her white Rolls Royce followed by a 'Good evening, sir' from the chauffeur which, ten minutes later, gave way to a near royal welcome when they arrived at the hotel. Uniformed doormen opened the car doors for each of them, and then it was a personal greeting from the hotel manager who had ordered one of the lifts to be labelled out of service so that it would be ready to take her to the rooftop restaurant without a moment's delay. There were more bows and curtsies before being escorted to her reserved table with its twinkling panoramic views of Athens at night.

Byron worried, what if she became so irresistible that he would not be able to reach and hold her hand without receiving permission. She sensed what he might be thinking, but in his new position it was important he learned to show restraint until she released him from his feelings. She was not deliberately making him suffer, simply treating him as her aide, and her servant. The longer they talked, the more she was convinced she had made a good choice. She flicked her hair in a way that let him know she liked his company which was far removed from her normal attitude towards staff. With him she was sure it would mean respect and a closeness.

At dinner it was she who held his hand as she tried to give him confidence for what lay ahead for him in the months to come. She whispered in his ear what his salary would be and that it would be confirmed in writing at the office in the morning. She told him that, despite what he was probably thinking in view of her great wealth, she was very lonely and hoped for his respect, obedience and affection. 'I want someone to look after me, and I have chosen you. You will spend a great deal of time helping me with my many business and company responsibilities, and also when it is time to relax. I hope you will be good to me. I am tired of pampering myself. I want to be spoiled as I think I deserve. I believe in starting as I intend to continue. Let's go back to my apartment now that we have finished dinner. I'll get the bill. We can have our cognac when we get home.'

In the back of the Rolls instead of holding hands on the leather cushioned back seat, she cuddled as close to him as the car permitted. Her heart was pumping like a horse that was racing towards the winning post. She was growing in confidence that she would never again have to degrade herself by picking up a stranger and taking him to one of her personal homes and give him money for satisfying her femininity. Her eyes never left Byron's and she found happiness in licking his lips. Her body was on fire. She had seldom felt more sensuous. To her Byron was like a gift waiting to be unwrapped.

Once in her apartment she asked him to pour them both a long cognac while she changed out of her evening gown which she let drop to the floor as though it was something she had bought at a bring and buy sale in a charity shop, instead of having cost her a four-figure sum. As soon as she was naked she threw herself into his arms and almost screamed her need to be as one with him. 'Bring the cognac into our bedroom where we can enjoy it while enjoying one another still more. Get undressed and don't worry about putting your clothes away. I pay maids to do that for me. I cannot wait a moment longer to feel your body lying on top of me while we both explore one another.' His touch had the gentleness of a gentleman as he moved his fingers over her loins and up to her nipples which hardened at his touch. Every nerve in her body was sending out signals that were so powerful she did not know how much longer she would be able to control herself. Byron whispered, 'I feel I am both your slave and your king at the same time.' And a moment later she felt his firm fingers fondling her clitoris so that all her passion burst into life at exactly the right moment as he exploded inside her and she responded with an orgasm that had her crying out her surrender to whatever he had to give her.

Her apartment at headquarters included crystal chandeliers from Murano, armchairs covered in her favourite pinkish salmon satin, two marble statues, one of a male and one a female goddess. There was a small balcony large enough for two cushioned chairs and a table for drinks or books and, because it was the highest building within a square mile, no one could overlook them or see them if they were naked.

Being with him was relaxing. He was not someone she was paying to be with her for a single night, but a man who gave her a new kind of security, someone who would be happy looking after her. She had so much pent up love to give him as well as the material gifts that would give him the confidence to feel he was worthy of her. She moved on top of him and fixed him with a near X-ray stare that would last if ever they were not together. She let him know that this apartment was one of three hideaways she had around Athens, although her main home was in a three hundred hectare estate fifteen minutes from the centre of the capital. 'I also own an ocean-going yacht on which we will one day enjoy a long weekend cruise around the Greek islands, one of which we own.

'Here is what I plan. You will sleep here with me tonight, and by tomorrow morning we will have discovered everything about one another, or at any rate about our two bodies. We shall get up early, say seven o'clock and be in my office before Maggie arrives. Then I will tell her to order the kitchen to send two hot breakfasts and hot coffee up to my office. During the morning we shall work, and you can get to grips with what is involved as my aide. You can go through my latest files, read through my office diary and gradually learn to become the best aide a lady could want. After lunch I am going to take you shopping.

You must have at least three more suits and a dinner jacket and trousers, plus white and grey slacks and shorts. I don't like men to wear the same shirt two days running, so we shall also buy a dozen white shirts, six in silk and six in sea island cotton, as well as at least a dozen pairs of sock and half a dozen pairs of shoes. And to complete the first of many shopping expeditions you will need a cashmere overcoat, a leather car coat, and a Burberry raincoat. We shall bring everything we buy back to my largest apartment which is a walk away from here, although someone in my position is not allowed to walk in a public street, but must always be driven to wherever I need to be. Too much money is like a chain, but I would not be without it. And from now onwards I must keep myself safe for you.'

They went back to bed. 'Until now I have had to lie here alone, sometimes to think about the running of our empire and how to make still larger profits, sometimes with a book, but always alone. Not any more. Now I shall be loved.' Just having him by her side and feeling his soft touch was like she believed it would have been to have sat for the great painter Botticelli who was renowned for looking after his models. But when he was inside her again she simply moaned her contentment. Lying with him was the difference between feeling sensuous with an aristocrat rather than a peasant ordered in from a field. She was reminded of a book by Voltaire in which he wrote about a French duchess in the years before the revolution who was in bed with her lover and enjoying the moment so much that she could not resist asking what the peasants did; only to be told, 'just like us'. Her reply was, 'It's too good for them.' Although Christiana had no wish to deny anyone the same delights that Byron was giving her, she nonetheless felt something of an affinity with what the duchess had expressed in her ignorance. And Byron was certainly no peasant.

Next morning they were both in their office before Maggie arrived, and busy preparing for the day ahead. The kitchen was instructed to send up *café complet* breakfasts for two with a hot black coffee, and a flask of coffee for Maggie. When she next came into their office she was weighed down with files which she placed on Byron's desk as his equivalent of a little light reading. She also handed him his lift keys and a key to Madame's apartment which had been cut during the night, and remembered

150

to call him 'Mr Walters'. She also informed him that she would type him a list of the senior executives and directors and their staff who worked on the top three executive floors, and was having printed a name badge so that people would quickly get to know his position within the corporation.

'These files should keep you occupied for the next two or three days,' Byron was told.

When Christiana was away from her office Maggie decided to alert Byron that, 'Madame is a woman of whims. She cannot praise you too highly one moment, and the next she can be like one of the Furies. I thought it best you were alerted.'

Byron said nothing. He was already aware that his only loyalty was to Madame Stephanopolous who wielded the kind of power that was only possessed by a lady who was second in command of one of the mightiest privately-owned conglomerates in the world. That was where his future lay. For the present Maggie could say what she liked, but once he felt himself secure, she would be warned never to criticise her boss to anyone, and certainly not to him.

At one o'clock Christiana stopped what work she had been doing throughout the morning and instructed Maggie to order two lunches for Mr Walters and herself. She checked on how much information he had digested from one of the files he had been reading and at two o'clock, as planned, they set off in the Rolls on their shopping expedition which lasted until six o'clock. Instead of returning to the office they headed for her penthouse apartment where the porter and her chauffeur were ordered to take the dozen or more boxes and parcels which contained Byron's new wardrobe up to her apartment. When they departed she poured him a large Scotch and herself an even larger vodka and tonic. 'I think we both need this,' she said with a smile. Their glasses played a different tune from the champagne flutes of yesterday, but did not stop her asking: 'Shall we dance?' She apologised that her own personal maid was on holiday or she would have ordered her to drive into town from their mansion and do the unpacking for him. Byron assured her he would put everything away in less than an hour if she would tell him which wardrobes could be his.

As they sipped their drinks he let her know that, having read through some of her personal files he was beginning to grasp just how great were her widespread responsibilities. He hoped that soon his increasing knowledge might prove helpful when he attended meeting and internal discussion groups with her. 'At least I know what an asset and investment you are to the business and how much new business you have developed.' Her response was to tell him, 'It is not my intention to keep you permanently as my aide, although I certainly intend to keep you for myself. I shall find a niche for you that matches your potential. There is almost no limit to where you could end up. All I want is the opportunity to reveal myself to you, and for you to meet the real me, as well as the public Christiana who can be ruthless, even vindictive. To some I snarl like a tiger, but with others I prefer to purr like a kitten.'

As she sipped her vodka she admitted it was only her occasional choice. Her favourite was champagne which the famous Madame Bollinger had insisted, was to be enjoyed when you're happy and when you are sad, when you are alone or in company, when you are not hungry and when you are. 'At the moment I am feeling hungry.' He knew what she meant and wanted.

As she refilled their glasses she told him she had decided that for the moment he should use this apartment as his temporary home until they decided where he should live permanently, providing it was close to headquarters. His home would be like her fourth hideaway.'

She kissed him passionately on his lips. She almost begged him to enter his other new home. Afterwards she asked him to 'Remember that I have an immensely wealthy husband who can buy me whatever I want. But I need you to spoil me in other ways now that he is no longer interested in the Madame Stephanopolous he married nearly twenty-five years ago. Thank you for making me feel wanted again.'

His arms drew her closer and his touch encouraged her to reveal whatever she wanted him to know. 'During the last couple of years I have had occasional nights with a few expendable men or I would have begun to wonder whether I had lost my femininity. Now I know I have not. I am exactly twice your age, but love knows no boundaries. Am I right?'

'I can only answer for myself. Yes I love you, but not only for your body, but for your generosity in so many different ways. My task is to give you all you want and deserve, while

152

somehow also earning your respect as a businessman. I know we shall never be more than we are now, but I am prepared to wait and enjoy being with you for as long as you want me. I cannot think of anything more delightful.'

She explained, 'My husband is more than twenty years older than I am and now feels that he has to prove to himself that he can still satisfy the desires of far younger girls, and with his millions he does not find it hard to prove to himself that he is still as virile as he was when we married. If his illusions please him, I have come to accept that it is easier for me to allow him his freedom. And you are making it easier with every hour that passes. Thank you Byron.'

He gathered her up and carried her onto her bed that was to be their home for the next few hours. He lay over her making little attempt at love, just happy in the knowledge that she was as content as he was happy, until he sensed his organ was reaching a climax that matched her own and she demanded his entry. Yet still he continued to nurse her until he knew her climax was ready to match his own, and they exploded in a double eruption. Their own physical symphony had again reached a crescendo of mutual harmony. Her ecstasy matched what she had experienced as a seventeen-year-old when a sensuous multi-millionaire was inside her for the first time and whispering, 'Now we belong to each other. Everything I have is yours. When you came aboard my yacht I thought of you as a beautiful princess. Now you are an empress who controls the lives of everyone around you. From now onwards nothing is too costly for the lady who is my wife.' Just as she had been much younger than her husband, now it was her lover who was so much younger than herself. Yet they matched perfectly. Now it would be her turn to shower him with whatever he needed in addition to her body, just as she had been showered with jewels that today amounted to a queen's ransom. She told him: 'My jewels are lovelier now that you have kissed them. When I wear them in future it will be as much for you as for myself. You are a wonderful lover. I think you have a job for life. I want nothing else from you except to make love to me and be by my side when I am making more millions for the corporation. Stay with me, and Everest could be yours.'

Until now it had always been in her nature to tantalise men

with tales of her immense wealth and the power she wielded. But with Byron it was also to win him for herself alone. They spent the night in each other's arms. She was at peace with herself and Byron dreamt of Aphrodite who now looked like Christiana. 'Love me again, darling,' she urged. 'When you are inside me I feel that together we can face the world. I have some potentially difficult negotiations to undertake this morning, but with you by my side I know we shall be successful.'

He answered: 'Having read your files I know that today you have to decide between two competing hotel groups which both want to be awarded the contract to manage one of your two five-star hotels in the centre of Athens. I have some thoughts you may find pertinent and helpful, but they can wait until we are back at the office. For the moment it is not the vice-president of the corporation that I want in my arms, but the most beautiful, generous and loving lady I know, or ever expect to know. As he satisfied her, he whispered: 'Do you know you slept with your diamonds on?'

'It was the safest place and, anyway, you were there to protect me.'

He said no more, but kissed her belly button as though it was the key to her heart. He gulped her perfume which remained as alluring as last night. And for no reason, she told him: 'I am so glad you don't smoke. It is such a filthy habit, especially cigarettes. But if you ever want an after dinner cigar I won't mind.'

As they drove back to headquarters she told him: 'Life's a gamble, and I am a winner because I have found you. I love you.' A few minutes later at just before eight o'clock she pulled up outside the main entrance to her headquarters where the two duty security men were in their shirt sleeves and without their uniform jackets and caps, but still recognised her car and opened the driver's doors. Usually both of them would have been reprimanded, but this morning her mood was that of a princess who had met her prince, and nothing would be allowed to spoil her belief that she was wanted again. She joked, 'It is time to get dressed,' and added: 'Tell my secretary when she arrives to buzz me in my penthouse apartment and I will give her instructions. And park my car.' As she and Byron stepped into the apartment where the central heating was just beginning to provide the warmth she needed, she suggested, 'As it is likely to be at least an hour before Maggie arrives, why don't we carry on doing what comes naturally to us both.' She fell into his arms and held him as though afraid he might disappear. He admitted: 'I think I am even happier than you are.'

'Bet, you're not.' And they settled for a draw.

'You think of yourself as my aide. That maybe your title, but to me you are the man I am beginning to want to be with forever. Show me that you feel the same.' They lay and loved until sharp on nine o'clock when the bedside telephone rang. It was Maggie asking for instructions. She was told to 'Make sure the small meeting room is ready for my first meeting at eleven. Put out notepads and glasses and soft drinks for six. Then wait in your office until I call you.' Next she showered while Byron shaved, brushed her hair and put on her make-up. Byron was quickly dressed in one of his new suits, tie and a white silk shirt. While she spent fifteen minutes deciding which of the three emergency suits that were in her wardrobe she should wear, he did some revision reading of her files, especially the one marked 'Hotels', in readiness for the eleven o'clock meeting. Christiana read the morning mail and dictated replies while she finished dressing. She had made it a rule ever since being appointed a full director of the board that each day's mail should be dealt with that day, and if any correspondence was left over, it had to be actioned before the next morning's letters, or cables, were dealt with. She was a stickler for keeping to her own rules and Maggie had no alternative.

One of the first memos she dictated was to the corporation's Director of Accounts and Finance and her voice rose so that her aide could hear what she was saying. 'In my previous memo in respect of the salary of Mr Byron Walters, there was a typing error. Please amend the first figure and increase it by one hundred per cent. Confirm that the necessary action has been taken.' To Maggie she added, 'Give this memo priority.' Maggie knew that she had typed the figure her boss had dictated, but there was no point in protesting. What intrigued her was how Mr Walters had found a way both to her heart and her generosity in such a short time. She had not had a salary rise for two years; but she also knew that no one would pay her more, or even as much.

Maggie was sent back to her office with instructions to tell the kitchen to send up hot black coffee for two to her apartment with rolls, jam and marmalade, and let her know when her guests had arrived and been served coffee. They were to be given the necessary documentation confirming the conditions for their appointment to manage one of the two luxury hotels which the group owned in the centre of Athens, but not the document with details of the Vougliameni resort hotel a few miles along the coast from Athens.

As the two of them held hands while eating their *café complet* Byron gazed at her with renewed admiration. Her navy blue suit with white silk piping down the front and on the sleeves and lapels was now highlighted by the diamonds she had worn last night, but her handbag had been changed for a Gucci blue crocodile clutch bag to a large blue crocodile bag that mixed with her suit. She looked glamorous, but businesslike.

The worldwide hotel group whose senior executives she was due to meet that afternoon, knew that the renewal period was to be for ten years rather than the present five. Their rivals who she was meeting shortly represented a smaller group with well-respected luxury properties in Paris, Brussels, Lisbon, Madrid, Istanbul, Barcelona, and several more in North and South America. Byron was attending the meeting as Madame Stephanopolous's aide with instructions to confirm, if necessary, anything she told her visitors. However, he wondered whether having read the notes of the previous meetings with the two contesting companies, she would welcome hearing some alternative views of his own. After Maggie had departed having been instructed to make sure there were chairs for Mr Walters and herself, he asked whether he had her permission to put forward a couple of suggestions that might be helpful before the meeting. He feared, however, that she would not like hearing that he did not agree with some of the points she insisted upon including in the final contract. Would he be taking a step too far, too soon? Yet, as she might be the first to admit, success sometimes involved taking risks.

'Why have you stopped?' she asked. There was interest in her voice. 'I want to hear what you have to say.'

'I am afraid.'

'Of me?'

'I know I am not your equal, nor ever will be, and realise that with a mere whim you could tell me not to interfere in matters about which I know very little, and have I forgotten who you are, and what I am. Yet I so want to show you that I can already be of real value to you, and that you made the right decision when you appointed me as your aide.'

'I promise I shall not sack you, darling. I want you, and need you. You belong to me. Please let me hear what you are thinking. I impose my views on most people, but you, believe me, are not most people. You are Byron, and you are special. Now speak up,' and to his surprise she squeezed his hand in encouragement. 'And that is an order,' she added to tease him.

'Thank you, darling. Now I know I mean more to you than just being your lover. I really am your aide. First, I think it could be unwise to suggest a new rental agreement in the form of an increase every year for the first five years. Whatever increase you decide should be for the entire five years, and renegotiated for the second five years. You will not lose any money, but it could taste better to both the two competing groups; more digestible, if you like. Second, I think you might find it wiser at least to think again about demanding a twenty per cent share of all profits earned by the management company. My concern is that this might prove a stumbling block, and be regarded as unreasonable.'

Christiana now told him to stop by putting up her hand. She was biting her lower lip before telling him: 'But I am unreasonable when I am wearing my business suit, and always aim to be demanding when I am negotiating on behalf of the family business. I know you are trying to be helpful, but I am quite convinced that both groups are so determined to win the contract, they will finally accept our profit sharing demand, simply because they would be losing far more if the contract went elsewhere. And don't forget I can always dangle in front of them a very tasty carrot; whichever of them wins the current contract could well be awarded the contract to manage our resort hotel at Vougliameni which comes up for renewal towards the end of this year. That, too, is making large profits, and I intend that we should have a worthwhile share of its success.

'Darling, try to understand that I may become a softie when I am in your arms, but I am as hard as steel when negotiating.

And prepared to bulldoze my way to my target. I have no intention of letting their shareholders grow rich at the expense of the Stephanopolous family. We own three hotel properties in and around Athens and all are gilt-edged and making increasing profits for those who manage them. I intend to demand a twenty per cent share of those profits in future, instead of the current fifteen per cent. I might however, finally accept eighteen per cent, just to please you. But if that is not acceptable, I shall simply walk away. They will agree my terms, believe me. They really have little alternative. You are working with a very aggressive lady who, since she began playing a major role in running the family corporation, has seen profits rise by between five and eight per cent each year. As a result I am currently paid an annual bonus of two million dollars and, in addition, I have already increased your own salary by one hundred per cent. And nothing you have said is going to make me change my mind. But I have also discovered that you are a thinker on behalf of the corporation. Your thoughts are always going to be worth hearing. Meanwhile, I intend to consider your suggestion regarding the way we should present our rental terms for the duration of the ten year contract, although I have no intention of revealing what the rental might be for the second five years. By that time I expect whoever receives our contract could be making such a level of profits that it will be impossible for them to reject almost any figure I demand.'

Byron knew the discussion was now closed as she rose and walked into her bedroom to check her make-up. It was almost as though intuitively she knew the phone was about to ring and that it would be Maggie letting her know her guests, four of them, had arrived and she had taken them to the meeting room and served coffee and biscuits and given them copies of the appropriate updated contractual terms they were required to read and sign. Christiana instructed her to tell her guests who had arrived fifteen minutes early, that she would join them as soon as she finished an earlier meeting. 'Serve them more coffee until I'm ready to bludgeon them into accepting my new terms.' She admitted to Byron that she was furious with her guests for arriving early and expecting her to be ready. Only he had that privilege.

'Now fetch my the mink coat that is in my wardrobe. Best

let them know from the outset that they are dealing with a super-successful businesswoman.'

She entered the boardroom accompanied by her aide, and Maggie who would take minutes of the meeting. She made no attempt at an apology for keeping them waiting, slipped off her coat and asked her secretary to refill everyone's coffee.

'Gentlemen,' she began, 'I thought it best to give you sufficient time to read and digest the latest financial statement in respect of one of the two five-star properties we own in the centre of Athens, and whose management contract will be awarded before the day is out. Your company is being given first refusal of my terms. You have indicated a willingness to take over the contract which in future will be for a period of ten years. The present management chain has already informed us of their willingness to agree the new terms, but I have delayed giving them our answer until we have had this meeting. I am due to meet them later today, but if you accept the terms which are before you, I may well decide to cancel that meeting. My personal view is that it is time for change.'

She spent the next ten minutes outlining the reasons for doubling the period of the contract and why this necessitated new and higher rentals, and why she was demanding a larger share of their profits. As a sop she added: 'If during any year there is not a profit, there will be no share out. But our hotels always make a profit. All the terms and conditions have been agreed by the board of Stephanopolous International. However, on the advice of my colleague, Mr Walters, who is sitting next to me, I am prepared to make a concession so that the rental figure for the first five years will be the same throughout the period, and be reviewed for the second five years. If, however, Stephanopolous International is not happy with the way the hotel if being managed and promoted, we reserve the right to cancel the contract after five years.

'Any questions? If not, I shall leave you to discuss among yourselves what I have indicated. I shall return with my colleague in thirty minutes to hear, I hope, that you are happy to accept the reasonable terms I have outlined. In that case you will be awarded the contract.' Maggie was ordered to serve them fresh coffee.

Back in her apartment she asked Byron, 'How do you assess the situation? Do you think I convinced them?'

He told her, 'I am not sufficiently expert to answer your question, but to judge by their faces I would hazard a guess that they will first seek concessions.'

'In other words, you don't think I did sufficiently well.'

'Heavens, no. I did not mean that at all.'

She knew that, but was finding it difficult to become used to someone having better ideas than herself.

'Pour us both a drink,' she commanded. 'I'll have a vodka with a splash of tonic. Have whatever you like.' He had no time because a moment later Maggie buzzed to say her guests were ready to meet with her again.

Back in the meeting room she simply asked: 'Are we to be allies and partners, or are we to go our separate ways.'

The spokesman for the hotel chain, Reginald A. Willoughby, an American whose card indicated he was Senior International Vice-President, stayed on his feet while his colleagues sat down. 'Let me say at the outset that we want to be your ally, Madame Stephanopolous, but we are unable to agree with some of your terms. It is not so much that we consider them excessive, more that we shall be moving into uncharted waters as this is our first enterprise in Greece.'

Christiana interrupted him: 'Mr Willoughby, all you need to know is that the Stephanopolous empire has been swimming very successfully in these waters for around forty years and as I tried to explain, your competitors in these negotiations have already agreed verbally their willingness to accept our new terms, especially as they, like yourselves, are being offered a ten year contract and have made good profits during the past four years and I have no doubt the final year will be just as satisfactory. You are not taking a risk, just missing an opportunity. Nevertheless, as I said earlier, I think it time for a change of partners. What I am about to say is not a promise, but I find it hard to believe that whoever wins this contract will not also be offered a five year management contract for another of our five-star hotels, a few miles along the coast at Vouliagmeni which is due for renewal within a few months. And, for your information I am responsible for all three of our luxury hotels. That is all I have to say.'

With a nod of her head to her aide and her secretary she indicated she was about to leave.

'Madame Stephanopolous,' said Mr Willoughby rising to his feet, 'you have just put our relationship with your organisation in a new light. Please allow me a little more time to discuss the new situation with my colleagues.'

'Mr Willoughby, my time is very valuable. Not for nothing is the organisation of which I am the only vice-president the largest privately owned corporation in the world with an earning sales target of one million dollars every week, but I must also make it clear that I am not saying that you will for certain be awarded the second contract, but if you don't win today, you will not be in the running tomorrow. I always try to look after my friends. You have one last chance to become associated with my empire. And just ten minutes in which to do so. When that time expires I shall simply accept that we have not reached an agreement, and I have wasted my time.'

For a second time that morning she and Byron went back to her apartment. 'Now what do you think, mastermind?' she enquired.

'They will accept thanks to your masterly negotiating skills. The fifty-fifty chance of winning a second contract is too tempting a bait for them to refuse. Thanks for allowing me to witness you in action.'

She admitted she had learned her tactics from her husband, but now believed she was the better strategist. 'I always keep something in reserve with which to force an adversary to change his mind on a new, very chewable, carrot. Women have more, and better, weapons than men, including our feminine wiles, while I have something still more powerful and effective. Millions and millions in almost any currency they wish to deal. And in this case the near certainty of making millions of dollars more from their new opportunity. I will bet you ten thousand to one in dollars that I shall win today. If I don't succeed, you win ten thousand dollars. If they do accept, I will give you ten thousand dollars to finish buying your new wardrobe. It will be my thank-you for helping us win.'

They hugged and kissed and were still in each other's arms, and yearning to stay there, when Maggie knocked on the door. There was a smile on her face. 'They have accepted, madame.'

She was told to go back to the meeting room with a bottle of champagne and six glasses and tell them that 'I hope to be able to join them, but I am on the telephone and there is a second international call waiting. Two other tasks. Telephone the other group and cancel this afternoon's meeting and tell them I shall be writing to them. Then tell our legal people to be in my office at ten tomorrow morning to finalise a new contract which I shall dictate to them.'

As she was closing the door of the apartment, the last words Maggie heard from her boss were, 'Now we can have our own private celebration.'

9

It was inevitable, and quite natural, for those who had only met Christiana Stephanopolous briefly or seen newspaper and magazine photographs of her smothered in diamonds and dressed in the most expensive clothes, to think of her as the spoiled wife of a Greek multi-millionaire shipping magnate and business tycoon. How right, or wrong, were such assessments? The truth was that she mostly worked a twelve hour-day as Vice-President of Stephanopolous International. As well as sponsoring the final year of training for a dozen students at their Business Academy, she had set up the Stephanopolous Foundation for deprived children worldwide. But it was her regular twelve-hour day for the multi-million dollar family empire with its global interests in shipping, tankers, construction, brewing, hotels, as well as its clothing and fashion factories and offices in China, Asia, South America and Eastern Europe, that occupied most of her time. No major decisions were taken without the authority of either herself or her husband, and mostly both of them.

Waiting to appear on stage was their only child, Stephanie, who had been groomed not only to be the future president of the corporation, but also to be one of the world's wealthiest poor little rich girls. Once she had celebrated her eighteenth birthday she would inherit a first instalment of ten million dollars from a trust fund that her parents had set up when she was born. Further proof of her riches were the eighteen perfectly matched diamonds that Cartier in Paris had selected each year on her birthday and were making into a necklace which only a very wealthy young lady would wear.

Her grooming by both her father and mother ensured that she would enter the corporation in an immediate position of power and responsibility as Director of Personnel which meant she had final control over far more than two thousand men and women around the world who worked for Stephanopolous International.

163

Her mother's only unspoken regret was that Stephanie had not been brought up and educated in Australia like herself, where she would have been injected with the national characteristic of always wanting to be a winner. She consoled herself by hoping she had injected some of her own ruthless genes into her offspring.

It was almost D-Day. In four months Stephanie Stephanopolous would begin inheriting her vast fortune and join Marianne, Countess von Rugerstein, as the third female member of the board of the family's global industrial empire, and become the third largest shareholder after her mother and father.

Ulysses Stephanopolous, who had inherited a vast shipping and tanker fleet from his own father, had expanded the business beyond anything his papa had ever visualised. It was also undeniable that the recent expansion had been made easier by the aptitude of his young Australian bride to anticipate trends and use the corporation's vast, and growing, resources to undercut rivals and force others into bankruptcy which in turn enabled them to win a dominant position in several of the industries where they operated internationally. Although Ulysses, now in his sixties, remained president it was his wife who, with her sagacity and uncanny ability to look ahead to future opportunities, now took more of the decisions. Soon their daughter would enter the fray as the corporation's next diva. Even though still a teenager her attitude was already empirical and she openly regarded most people with disdain. Long before she had control of her own fortune nothing had been denied her, and she accepted that luxuries were what she had been born to enjoy. Whether it was her mother's genes or not, she grew up to be contemptuous of most people. At her Swiss finishing school one of their teachers had told the pupils: 'You may not have quite the same powers as Cleopatra exerted over her subjects in ancient Egypt, but the fortunes that your families have accumulated will give you all a superiority over other men and women who will learn to accept that they have to carry out your orders.' Stephanie had not forgotten.

In the months that remained before her big day scores of temporary typing and administrative staff had been recruited to assist those at headquarters who had been seconded to help Christiana plan the gala celebration that would make her daughter's coming of age an event to be reported worldwide. Her parents had happily agreed to spend more than half a million dollars ensuring that she arrived into the world of finance and big business amid a blaze of diamonds and every other luxury a woman could desire. Already three members of Europe's depleted royal families had indicated they could attend, plus a president, two heads of state and scores of lesser dignitaries from countries where the name Stephanopolous exerted immense business and financial power.

Christiana planned to convert the ballroom at the better of the two five-star hotels the family owned in Athens into a replica of the Acropolis and alerted Marianne that she wanted her to undertake responsibility for all the arrangements for their royal guests and other international VIPs, adding: 'I need your razor-sharp mind to focus with me on whatever remains to be done. Maggie will devote most of her time to Stephanie's coming out, and I have given her permission to buy herself a ball gown and a dinner gown to wear during the celebrations, and charge them to expenses. As for public relations I plan to fly to New York to brief three of the largest international PR agencies of our plans and then decide which of their proposals I like best. I shall take Byron with me. Once I have decided, he will be in charge of all publicity in co-operation with the agency we retain. While I am away you will have sole responsibiity. But your own personal priority is to supervise the arrival and departure arrangements, and everything in between, for our VIP guests. I cannot afford any mistakes here, and there is no one I trust more than you.' To her Marianne was the equivalent of a piece of molten steel that had been moulded into a razor-sharp sword that forced everyone to wilt. She was like a ruthless general who would slice through any opposition to Christiana's targets whether the liquidation of another corporation, or her craving to own another Picasso. Marianne's title, her own fortune and her eye-catching femininity were simply additional fire power that few could withstand. Christiana told her: 'Marianne, I trust your judgment implicitly to take whatever decisions are needed to make Stephanie's coming out a worldwide success while I am away. Nevertheless, don't let that British armaments firm get away from our clutches.'

Christiana herself could think of little else except her daughter who to her was tomorrow's leader of the Stehanopolous clan. No one else mattered. When Byron dared suggest she might be a little young for too much authority her mother snapped back, 'I have still to decide whether her authority will extend to you.' Yet it had become obvious to Marianne when she was in Athens for board meetings and staying at the family mansion, that Christiana hardly went anywhere without her aide. It was also obvious that he had other duties beyond those he was paid to perform. Marianne's verdict was that if he kept Madame Stephanopolous content that was best for everyone, and not just himself. His arrival had already led to the dismissal of Robert McDonald from Christiana's private life and he had been despatched to South America as her deputy to oversee every aspect of their business interests, which were her responsibility in that continent. He was already sending her regular reports, but she never wrote back except to give him new orders. He was no longer part of her life.

It was after dinner at the family home where Marianne had dined with Christiana and Ulysses, but without Byron, that Christiana, for the first time, revealed to her husband that she and her aide had spent much time recently thinking ahead to the next ten years. She believed inflation would become rampant and that meant soaring overheads. 'And what,' she asked, 'are the most costly items on any company's balance sheet? Labour, wages and salaries. In Europe increases are currently rising by between two and four per cent annually. Such increases have to be passed on by way of higher prices. We need to find cheaper labour. My answer is in Indonesia, India, China, Singapore and perhaps the Middle East. Some, if not all, of our future tankers could be built, not in Europe, but in Asia which could cut our costs by almost half. Our aim should be to win more than fifty per cent of the tanker market as well as a similar percentage for container ships. I suggest we first alert managers in Europe of these new opportunities and select suitable candidates for three-year supervision stints overseas.

'Ulysses, you should also know that I have given Marianne the responsibility of buying on our behalf a medium-sized armaments firm in England that will shortly come onto the market. But I want us to strike before it does. It has been run by a woman for many years, but now she wants to retire.

166

Throughout the last war, and since, her company has been making vital parts for a succession of British army tanks. An English-born woman with a title should be the ideal person to negotiate the deal. The company has been making profits of several million pounds annually which means that the owner must be a comparatively wealthy woman and, probably, an astute business lady. My target is to increase the company's present level of profits by around forty per cent within two years. Marianne, twenty per cent of whatever profits are achieved will be yours. We already have an office in London and you can use it as your business base. This should avoid any regulatory problems with the British government. Their tanks will still be equipped by a British firm, and they should not then mind if we land some large export orders for the UK.'

'When would you like me to fly to London to make contact with the lady concerned?' Marianne asked.

'I think it might save time if you wrote on Stephanopolous International notepaper in a business style, but equally a woman-to-woman letter, outlining our intentions as well as our financial strength. Explain that you are planning to be in London shortly, and why don't the two of you have a tête-a-tête luncheon at Claridges, where I suggest you stay. She will be impressed, and doubly so if you use your title when signing the letter. After you have aroused her interest over lunch you should ask to be shown a copy of the financial statements for the last three years, after which we shall send her an official offer for her business. My guess is that the figures will show a decline in profits which could be your opportunity to apply some feminine pressure. But don't use the thumb screws too soon.'

Christiana stood up and began pacing the room. 'I want us to be recognised as a rising player in the worldwide armaments industry. However, I have no intention of staying solely in the business of making small parts for large tanks. Why not concentrate on small arms? This is a very cut-throat business, but contracts can be worth multi-millions in any currency. We must not forget to be generous to those who assist us to gain our objectives. And I am not only thinking about money being paid into a Swiss banking account. Businessmen throughout the world, and not only Arabs, have an appetite for pretty women, especially when they are away from home ... and with a title, too.' Although she gave a smile and a nod of her head, as though suggesting she was only joking, she certainly was not. To her, sex was a weapon. And never more so when millions of dollars were involved. Marianne decided that now was the time while they were with her husband to make it clear that, 'I might be prepared to give hints of being physically co-operative, but nothing of the kind will be delivered until a contract is signed, and probably not even then. My brains, but not my body, are for sale.'

Christiana fired back: 'Stop playing the innocent. You know as well as I do that when the stakes are high so is the price that may have to be paid.'

Marianne decided to back off, but not surrender. She retired to safer ground. 'So long as the wording is right, I have no worries. The decision must always be mine so don't let's fight when we have not yet entered the ring.'

The next day Marianne returned to Munich en route to London. Before leaving she had to make yet another excuse to the count for not being with him at the castle, explaining that her mission to London, if successful, could be worth around £200,000 to her, as she had been promised twenty per cent of all profits the arms firm made after it became part of Stephanopolous International. The figure could rise to half a million dollars if she proved to be as good a saleswoman as she intended. Once again he had no alternative but to accept her excuses, although he would have preferred to have her in bed beside him, and keeping a stern female eye on the staff which was now her responsibility. However, the anticipated rewards could not be ignored, Wasn't it Oscar Wilde who wrote, 'nothing succeeds like excess'?

Marianne was in London for a week staying at Claridges but using the corporation's London office as her base for further research into the worldwide armaments industry. She returned first to their castle and the count before heading to Athens to report on the progress made in her negotiations. Fortunately, she and Mrs Veronica Fox-Willams, the sole owner of Fox Armaments, had so much in common they had become good friends. She was a widow without children and was willing to sell her company for what she had called a fair price. It was her intention to use the money she received to enjoy a still more luxurious lifestyle of travel and pleasure, even though she already flew First wherever she went and was taken everywhere in a chauffeur-driven Bentley. No longer would she have to spend half her time at meetings and in negotiations with civil servants. She and Marianne had similar tastes, and even though she knew Claridges well, she was happy to be invited to have lunch as the guest of Marianne, Countess von Rugerstein in the hotel's restaurant where she was well known to the staff. They greeted her before they welcomed the countess who was her hostess. Both women found they had a mutual love for expensive clothes and jewellery. Marianne told her while they were both sipping their second Martinis, 'If you admire the clothes I wear, you should see how my boss dresses. More than anyone I have met she understands the allure of couture. Thanks to the count I can wear some very special jewellery that has been in his family for centuries, but I am not in Christiana's league. I can't recall ever seeing her without her two thirty-five carat diamonds, one on each hand. While you and I are content to wear mink coats, she prefers sable. She thinks nothing of spending two thousand dollars on a dress or suit from Dior or Chanel. And why shouldn't she? She works twice as hard as anyone she employs.'

'I'd like to meet her. She sounds like one of our tanks to which there is no response,' joked Mrs Fox-Williams.

'I'm sure that when you are ready to sign a contract passing responsibility of your company to Stephanopolous International, she will come to put her signature underneath yours. Next time I come to London, I am certain she will be with me. She is the boss and likes the glory. I prefer my title.'

At the board meeting in Athens, Marianne told her fellow directors after she had reported personally to Christiana: 'Not only is the owner willing to sell the business to us, but will almost certainly open many doors as well as introducing us to contacts and friends who are involved in the arms business. I have had three meetings with her, one at Claridges where I was the host, the second in her home in Belgravia, and the third in her office at her factory which is now located in Essex, a county that adjoins London. I think it fair to say that we have become friends. She has even stayed with my husband and myself at Rugerstein castle. She has assured me that it is not her intention to hold an auction and sell her company to the highest bidder. I have examined the company's accounts for the last three years and they vary between three and four million pounds annually after tax, and all from a single piece of classified equipment, for which they hold the patent, which when installed increases the fire power of British tanks by almost twenty per cent. Her asking price is thirty million pounds, and I have offered twenty-five with the consent of Madame Stephanopolous. Her sole client is the British government, but this is only because Mrs Fox-Williams of Fox Armaments has been content to make her profits with comparatively little hassle. She has, however, promised to pass to me correspondence with those countries that have expressed interest in her secret once she has passed ownership to Stephanopolous International. There are at least half a dozen potential clients in addition to the UK government. My own estimate is that within two years orders from just three of these countries could be worth four or five times what we are being asked to pay. And if we build a new, modern factory, as is Madame Stephanopolous's intention, we could plan to manufacture other armaments such as automatic weapons based upon the same secret equipment we shall be purchasing. These weapons will almost certainly be of interest to those factions which are engaged in hostilities, often with one another, in this unstable world. My own view is that our new factory should not be built in the United Kingdom, just in case any problems arise when the British government learns that it is not our only customer. I believe it will be wise to restrict our sales only to those who can be regarded as friendly towards Great Britain. Anything else might be a risk too far.'

She stopped and took a long sip of water. She continued:

'While Mrs Fox-Williams was staying with my husband and myself in Munich she admitted that although she had not had any formal dicussions with other would-be buyers, she knew that at least three were aware she was planning to sell her business. I suggest we need to proceed with the utmost speed now that we are the current favourite, as that position could change in an instant if we prevaricate for too long. I want to avoid an auction which could easily see the business sold for more than the present asking price. I have promised that I shall let her know our intentions within a few days of this meeting. May I have the authority to proceed?'

Christiana followed so that other members of the board would know which way the vote should go. 'I agree with the countess. It seems, if her estimate is correct, that we are unlikely to lose any money, even if we pay the full asking price. We may find ourselves owning a small gold mine. However, I am reluctant to break with corporate tradition. I move that we ask the countess to make a new offer of twenty-eight million dollars with a guarantee that the ageed purchase price will be transmitted within forty-eight hours of the contract being signed. If, however, our new offer is rejected she should be instructed to complete the purchase for whatever sum the lady concerned is prepared to accept. I move we instruct the countess to close the deal without delay. May I have a seconder?' The resolution was passed unanimously. The non-family members of the board were aware how foolish it would be to vote against the vice-president who was exercising ever-increasing control. The rest of the meeting dutifully consisted of recording acceptances to a series of financial and sales reports from various segments of the company's worldwide interests.

When the meeting concluded Christiana asked Marianne to follow her to her apartment where they opened a bottle of vintage champagne and she congratulated the newest member of the board on her lucid and successful presentation, adding: 'Try to conclude the negotiations during the next month and insist upon control passing to us within ninety days of the contract being signed. On second thoughts, why don't I come with you to London, then we can both sign the contracts as two directors of Stephanopolous International. We can do some shopping together, and it will be interesting to meet another successful businesswoman, albeit on a rather different rung of the ladder. I think that, at least in the beginning, we should keep the same name as now, but with you as the new Chairman and Chief Executive.'

Marianne interrupted: 'I had no idea I was to run the company. I was under the impression that my task was to negotiate the purchase and then it would be over to you.'

'That is still the position. You run the business but under me and I have final responsibility.'

'But I know nothing about the armament industry!'

'Neither do I. But we are both quick learners. Why do you think I chose you for a well-paid position on the board with growing responsibilities? That is another reason why I should come to London with you. We shall both need to pick the brains of Mrs, what's her name?'

'Mrs Fox-Williams.'

'Thank you. Now I have another expansion plan that I need to discuss with you.' She lifted her glass, 'To you Marianne. You have proved to be an even better businesswoman than I anticipated. As a result I am starting to wonder whether I should propose to your husband that Stephanopolous International would like to buy his entire business empire and appoint you both as joint presidents, or would you refer to be in sole charge, while letting him do all the hard work?'

If she expected Marianne to be shocked by such a suggestion, she was wrong. Instead, she simply asked Christiana to stop surprising her with such extreme and sudden ideas. 'For the moment I would prefer to leave things as they are. I have sufficient home-grown problems as it is, as a result of the time I give to your charitable Foundation, as well my continuous travelling as a director of Stephanopolous International. It is a good idea, but with your approval, let us keep it as it is ... for the moment.'

'You are a sly young bird, Marianne,' but what she was thinking was that if ever the count interfered with her best interests, she would happily crush him, by first cancelling all her orders. There could be only one outcome.

She refilled their glasses and changed the subject back to Stephanie's lavish coming out party and confirmed that one grand duchess would be bringing her personal maid, while a prince and princess will be arriving with valet, maid and security guard. She was happy to leave it to Marianne to make sure that all their requests were met. She added: 'I expect the final total could be more than twenty VIPs. Together we shall decide who stays where; some will be accommodated on our own estate and others will be allocated suites or other accommodation in our number one hotel in Athens.'

Marianne assured her that she had hired limousines, security guards and arranged exclusive tours of historic sites while a team of four middle-management executives, chosen by Maggie, had been briefed to be on duty throughout twenty-four hours to satisfy any requests the most important guests might make, including booking tables at some of Athens' most exclusive restaurants.

Christiana's response was to tell Marianne, 'I am so pleased you are not playing nursemaid yourself, but will be using some of my up-and-coming executives to prove that they can handle any kind of situation before it becomes a crisis. Let me know if any of them let you down.' Marianne could never get used to the manner in which Christiana delighted in dropping new bombshells, This time it was to warn her, 'When it is all over in less than three months I shall have a new task which should be ideal for your kill-or-be-killed temperament, which I admire.'

Now that everything was going according to plan for the gala celebrations, Christiana was thinking ahead. Once she and Marianne had agreed the London purchase of Fox Armaments for the full asking price, they would concentrate not only on the secret tank weapon for future profits, but develop a new high-powered automatic rifle that would appeal to governments, insurgents and revolutionary groups. She was convinced this was a market that could be worth millions.

She told Marianane: 'The world is entering a new era of local wars, uprisings and revolutions, Everywhere there are men who want to gain power and eliminate their rivals. Selling arms to them does not mean we agree with them. However, I intend to be a supplier of the weapons they need. Once we deliver what they are buying, forget about any possible use to which the weapons may be put. In some cases they may never be used. In others it may benefit the majority. Just remember that the more we sell, the happier I shall be when I authorise a minimum twenty per cent share of the profits of Fox Armaments to be paid to you.'

This all followed their visit to London for the signing of the contract. A copy had been sent to Mrs Fox-Williams in advance of their meeting which took place in the large lounge of the two-bedroom suite they had booked at Claridges. The owner of the arms firm was accompanied by her solicitor. It took little more than an hour for them to dot the i's, as Mrs Fox-Williams had already instructed her legal adviser that she intended to accept the package and the price. The meeting began at 10.30 and by noon all last minute changes had been initialled and the final contractual agreement signed by the former owner plus Christiana Stephanopolous as the Vic President of Stephanopolous International and Marianne, Countess von Rugerstein, the new Chairman of Fox Armaments. Over lunch Christiana told Mrs Fox-Williams about the gala celebration she was hosting in Athens on her daughter's eighteenth birthday, and she hoped Veronica, as she now called her guest, would accept an invitation to join several members of Europe's royalty who had already accepted. Then she dropped her bombshell and asked the former owner of Fox Armaments to stay on as a Vice Chairman and Consultant for twelve months. Christiana, with her acute business acumen, knew she would accept, which she did, but with the proviso that, 'I shall be happy to give Marianne whatever help I can, providing it does not interfere with my private and personal commitments. I am planning to travel a great deal and I have already purchased a villa on the isle of Antigua in the Caribbean. It has four bedrooms, a swimming pool and its own staff of two, plus acres of palms and bougainvillea, frangipani and jasmine, as well as cooling floor tiles and ocean breezes. Perhaps you will both come and visit.'

Now that all the documents had been signed Christiana could not resist having the last word: 'Being mega-rich is pure joy. I would recommend it to anyone.'

10

Normally Maggie had little contact with the rest of the staff because her own office was in the restricted top three floors of the skyscraper which was out of bounds to everyone except the handful who worked directly for the senior management. Now, however, with the extra authority given her by Madame Stephanopolous she found herself wandering through the lower floors and stopping by selected desks and ordering a typist to stop what she was doing and give priority to the letters, lists or instructions that needed typing. When one of the girls failed to recognise her and objected to the orders she was given, Maggie snapped, 'You either carry out these commands which come directly from Madame Stephanopolous, or you will be sacked and out of this building within the hour.' All other work was quickly put aside. Maggie relished her new powers and authority. For once she was the bully instead of the bullied and understood what a pleasure it was to look down on someone and see the look of fear in their eyes as she whipped them with her now commanding voice. She also remembered being reminded by her boss to get used to playing only the cards that life had dealt her. Now, for once, she held some aces.

Twenty-four hours before the gala ball Christiana and Ulysses sent their personal 747 to Charles de Gaulle airport in Paris to fly their royal and other VIP guests direct to Athens where a fleet of limousines was waiting to transfer them to where they would be staying. Marianne instructed her team at the airport that there were to be no hold-ups getting baggage off the aircraft plus porterage, or delays at immigration and customs. All limousines meeting the arrivals had a Stephanopolous sticker on their windscreens and priority parking space outside the VIP exit. Security teams, maids or valets were being accommodated wherever their royals or heads of state were staying, but would not travel from the airport with the VIPs, but in a separate coach.

Earlier, Byron had flown to New York with Madame Stephanopolous where she interviewed three possible consultancies, one of which was given the responsibility of handling all international press and public relations for the event at an agreed fee. Once she had made her choice she handed responsibility to Byron for all liaison with the chosen consultancy who quickly succeeded in selling special rights for reporting and photographing the gala event to three full colour magazines, one in the US, a second in Paris and a third in London. These included facilities to take shots of the eighteen-year-old who overnight would become a multi-millonairess, plus her mother, wearing the various gowns and other outfits they would be seen in during the celebrations ... as well as shots of other selected VIP guests. Each publication agreed to pay an agreed donation to the Stephanopolous Foundation in return for the exclusive publishing in their circulation area. So great was Christiana's influence that the Greek authorities agreed to close the area surrounding the Acropolis for an entire morning so that her VIP guests could visit one of the most historic and fascinating sites in the world without being jostled by tourists.

On the day before the Big Day the royal and VIP guests were invited to join a celebration luncheon for fifty at the family mansion. They had awakened to find a clear Grecian blue sky welcoming them together with tiny cloudlets scampering in clusters as though they were little boys playing hide and seek with one another. The only outsiders allowed entry to the estate were security, extra temporary staff serving or preparing the reception and luncheon, plus photographers and writers from the three publications which had been given exclusive facilities. Each of them had agreed to syndicate their reports and photos to selected newspapers in order to recoup at least part of their high donations to the family foundation. One of the most sought after photos was of the birthday girl wearing the extravagant couture outfits at different times throughout the two days. She relished the attention, but never forgot who she was and how little was her regard for the photographers who she regarded as pests. 'That's all I have time for,' was her exit line. And she meant it.

As the William Hickey column in the *Daily Express*, which had the second largest daily net circulation in the world, wrote:

'Tomorrow the newest of all the world's poor little rich girls comes of age. She will take centre stage at a gathering of several hundred guests who have been invited to celebrate her eighteenth birthday at her family's 300 acre estate on the outskirts of Athens. Guests include half a dozen reigning, or deposed, European kings and queens, plus a couple of grand duchesses.

'Sometime before she goes to bed tomorrow night Stephanie Stephanopolous, the golden girl and heiress to her family's vast shipping, banking and industrial empire, will have inherited a fortune of nearly ten million pounds, a sum that will dwarf the wealth of most who have been invited to help her celebrate her coming of age. Her parents are reported to be spending half a million pounds on making it an occasion to remember. The ballroom of the hotel which, of course, is owned by the Stephanopolous dynasty, and where the gala dinner and ball takes place, has been converted to resemble that glory of Greece's past, the Acropolis. Here they will be welcomed by the eighteen-year-old blazing with some of the family's vast collection of finest diamonds. According to one of my Greek spies, she will wear three different outfits before her day is done. At lunch it will be a simple Chanel suit followed by a Dior dinner gown before she changes into a Ballenciaga ball gown in which to dance her way into her multi-million pound inheritance to which it is whispered her parents have added tens of million of pounds in shares in the family's multi-million dollar company that is still a privately owned corporation with worldwide interests. My City colleagues tell me it is valued at more than five hundred million dollars. No one has yet added a guess at the value of the jewellery the new heiress and her Australian born mother will wear ... or whether her father's latest conquest, the actress and Hollywood star, Veronica Lane, will be among the guests.'

The sting, as with any worthwhile gossip column story, was in the tail.

The photo that proved most in demand from the score that were syndicated was taken by one of the photographers with the UK magazine that was one of the three with exclusive rights. The shot that fascinated many picture editors was of Stephanie in the Balanciaga gown she wore at the ball with the caption: 'She was a blaze of diamonds estimated by those in the know to be worth at least twenty million pounds, some from the

177

family collection, some that were birthday presents as well as the Cartier thirty-six carat diamond necklace which was one of her parent's many gifts to their daughter. Value £300,000.'

11

During the months when she was helping plan the event that received worldwide media coverage, Marianne had succeeded in turning herself into a contortionist who spent two or three days each week in London staying at Claridges, getting to know every detail of Fox Armaments that was now part of Stephanopolous International while holding meetings with its senior executives, before flying back to Athens to make sure all her instructions had been carried out. She still found time to spend a least two days each week carrying out her duties as châtelaine of the Rugerstein castle and also satisfying the needs of her husband.

At the offices of Fox Armaments she was mostly accompanied during the first few weeks by the former owner who kept reminding her former colleagues that they now had a new boss who, like herself, expected their complete loyalty. Out of Marianne's earshot she also let them know that it would be unwise to let her youth deceive them, adding, 'She has one of the sharpest minds I have ever encountered. For the moment, she might not know much about the armament industry, but that is what we must teach her. Before six months have passed, I assure you she will be in complete control. And you had all better let her know you are on her side. She may appear to be the nicest of women, but she will be merciless to anyone who does not pull their full weight.'

When it was Marianne's turn to talk to the three senior executives who from the outset she thought of as the gang of three because they all seemed capable of standing in for each other, so wide was their individual knowledge of every aspect of the company's business, she was determined to become the fourth member of the team, and its leader. She told them, 'My aim is to expand the business internationally. I am an impatient person who is prepared to work long hours to attain my objectives. I shall expect you to follow my example. I shall occupy the office that was previously used by Mrs Fox-Williams, and the

179

door will always be open. The greater the company's success, the greater will be the rewards for us all. This is not just a promise, it is also a challenge.'

Soon the three learned to accept that their new boss had a mind of her own, as well as having the immense resources of the Stephanopolous empire behind whatever she decided. She was always accompanied at client meetings, whether at home or overseas, by one of the three, and word quickly spread among government civil servants and potential overseas customers that Fox Armaments no longer produced just a single item of vital equipment for modern tanks, but also a revolutionary and efficient automatic hand-held weapon that was digitally controlled. After little more than six months, the English-born German countess was in complete control of the company and exercised full powers over everything that took place. She might still leave the technicalities to her deputies, as she now regarded them, but all the final decisions were taken by herself. At the end of her first full year with her finger on the trigger, the company reported a thirty-five per cent increase in profits to a level never seen before. As a result she received a six figure dollar bonus of $250,000 and each of the gang of three sums equivalent to ten per cent of their salaries.

To celebrate Christmas, and to make him realise that all her many absences from his arms had been worthwhile, she bought the count a fur-lined cashmere overcoat. She told him it was her way of showing how much she missed him while away on her travels to meet those overseas government officials who were responsible for arms purchases, especially the new light weight, automatic rifles that the company was now producing at its new factory in Bavaria only a few kilometres from their castle. To her colleagues she was regarded as a beautiful whiz kid who knew how to coax large orders out of Middle Eastern and Asian governments by reducing the price for every order for their automatic rifles above five thousand. Although many expected to be allowed to feel her body as an additional reward for their orders, all had to be content with a kiss and a reminder, 'I am a married woman.' Anyone who felt cheated was quickly made to realise that the lady they were doing business with was as hard as the lightweight steel of the arms she was selling; and as cold, and was prepared to walk away from even the largest order if they expected more than she was prepared to give. Nor did she hesitate to remind them that her price per weapon became lower the larger their order. The end product was highlighted when one of her new customers admitted, 'Doing business with you, countess, is always a pleasure, but always full of hope.' Her reply was a smile that made her look still more ravishing. As the level of orders for the new automatic weapon headed past the magical one million mark all production became concentrated in Germany, and the British plant became solely responsible for producing the secret piece of tank equipment which was now more in demand than ever since it became available to friendly overseas governments as well as the British.

There were, however, looks of dismay on the faces of her colleagues when she announced the changes, and told them it made life easier for her to have the profit-making factory in Bavaria that was only a few miles from her castle home. She smoothed some of their worries by promoting Harold Wilkins, the most senior and experienced of the three, to the position of Managing Director UK, while she became the president and chief executive of the company that was now winning worldwide orders. She did not tell them that sometime soon the name would be changed to Stephanopolous Armaments, a decision that had been taken by Christiana as she began to appreciate the high level of sales Marianne was achieving almost single-handed, although increasingly with additional backing and encouragement from the newest member of the board, Stephanie Stephanopolous. Marianne finally smoothed any lingering concerns in the minds of her British colleagues by assuring them that their annual bonuses would be based upon the profits made from the production and sales at both plants.

Whenever she flew out of the UK she was accompanied by Harold Wilkins, who she regarded as her back-up on technical matters, although a few weeks earlier she had threatened to sack him, through no fault of his own. She had been invited to dinner at his semi-detached house close to Richmond Park. His wife, June, was more than twice Marianne's age and had been brought up to believe in age before beauty. She made the mistake of seeking to tell Marianne what she should do and in the middle of dinner finally took a step too far. Her guest put down her napkin and exploded. 'Mrs Wilkins, you either stop telling me what I should, or should not, do, or I shall be forced to sack your husband. My own wealth and title makes me a very much stronger lady than yourself, and I possess a hundred times more power than your husband thanks to the hundreds of millions of Stephanopolous money that will back whatever decisions I take. I think the best thing I can do is to thank you both for your invitation and ask your husband to get my coat and see me to my car.' She never referred to the incident again, and nor did Mr Wilkins.

On a business trip to the Middle East they were brought face to face with the fragility of both their lives; they had been welcomed as VIPs and escorted from the airport to their hotel in a bullet-proof limousine with an armed guard sitting beside the chauffeur. They were constantly assured that their safety was of paramount importance, and alerted that a few months earlier a group of extremists had snatched a visiting Swiss businessman who they held in chains for five weeks before leaving his decapitated body outside the hotel where he had been staying. A western woman, like herself, would be an even more highly prized prisoner who could be abused in any way they fancied. Forcing a white woman to have sex with them would give them added status within their own community. Hearing this Marianne reacted by telling her hosts she would obey any safety precautions they offered her. These included a posse of four armed men who accompanied her wherever she went until she was safely back inside her own private suite, and two of them were continuously on duty outside her locked door.

Negotiating with a businesswoman was a new experience for many of the ministers and government officials responsible for the purchase of the arms she flew thousands of miles to sell. Her body was also very desirable. But having Harold Wilkins with her was like possessing an extra security guard. She baited her targets with ever more attractive prices for her automatic weapon. Finally, she agreed to reduce her initial price by fifteen per cent for an order of twenty-five thousand quick firing rifles. At this point she requested Harold to leave the office where the negotiations were nearing a conclusion. She decided that he might be upset if he knew about any additional concessions she might feel it necessary to make.

A few minutes after he had left her, she heard gunfire. She and the minister both dived behind the desk in his office. They quickly realised his office was not the target and that the shooting was on a higher floor. Later they learned that the target had been her suite where both guards, having heard guns being fired, decided to leave their positions and move a short distance away so that they could see any intruders coming from the staircase on the third floor. They waited until two armed men stopped outside the suite of the countess. Before the men had a chance to smash the lock they opened fire and killed the two terrorists. And again they waited because they knew that Marianne was not in her suite. Shortly afterwards two more gunmen appeared and, without being asked any questions, were immediately despatched. Although the authorities believed the countess had been the target of the attackers, the official press release said there had been an attempt on the life of the minister who at the time was in business discussions with a representative of Stephanopolous International. Marianne's name was not revealed. Two hours later both she and Mr Wilkins were taken to the airport in a heavily-guarded VIP car waiting to board the early morning flight to Munich. It had been a kidnap attempt and somehow the kidnappers knew which suite Marianne was occupying. The attempt on the life of a senior minister made a few lines in international newspapers around the world, but if a countess and representatives of the Stephanopolous family had been the target there would be headlines. On the flight home Marianne suggested to her colleague that he should say nothing about the incident to his wife or anyone else. It would only upset her, and would serve no useful purpose. As far as the count and Christiana were concerned all they knew was that there had been attempt on a minister's life in the hotel where she was staying, and she had heard shots, but she was never in any danger. However, although it did not stop her travelling the world selling arms and ammunition, and much else, she seldom returned to the Middle East. A few years later it became unnecessary as Stephanie was in the final stages of being prepared to take over the presidency of Stephanopolous International, but that is a tale still to be told. There was even a happy ending to the Middle Eastern episode. Three months after her return to Europe a letter addressed to Countess von

Rugerstein arrived at the Bavarian factory of what was now called Stephanopolous Armaments confirming an order for twenty-five thousand automatic weapons at the agreed price less a fifteen per cent discount.

12

When Stephanie reached her last day at finishing school, her mother asked Marianne to fly to Geneva and escort her daughter back to Athens. She could use the corporation's short haul aircraft. That would avoid the inconvenience of joining the inevitable long queues at customs and immigration, and take advantage of the VIP facilities at Athens airport. Christiana was waiting to greet her daughter when she arrived, but was surprised when, after the initial kisses and hugs, the first question Stephanie asked was, 'When can I start work?' After an unusual moment's hesitation, Christiana answered, 'Have a couple of days' rest before the exhausting time we shall all have at your birthday celebrations, and then we can fix the date for your arrival as the corporation's newest director.'

Marianne told Christiana she had been asked the same question during the flight, and had told Stephanie that, if she wanted, she could sit in her office and listen in to whatever was happening. Christiana retorted, 'She could also sit with me in my office.'

With a cuteness that surprised her mother, Stephanie solved the problem by saying that she thought it would be best if she accepted Marianne's offer because her mother was so much busier than everyone else, and she would only be a nuisance by asking too many questions, whereas it would not matter how much she inconvenienced Marianne who could not answer back. This said, she gave a knowing wink to Marianne as a reminder that she was still her elder sister. Christiana sensed that a lot of people were going to have a hard time when her daughter joined the corporation. She was obviously determined to enjoy her privileges which to her were simply entitlements.

It was D-Day minus two before Stephanie's coming of age ball, and Marianne and her husband were occupying the large bedroom she always had in the family home when she was in Athens for board meetings. Now it had the extra advantage that she would be on the spot to sort out any problems that arose, especially from the VIPs. At the private luncheon in the ballroom at the family residence, and the gala ball at their hotel in the centre of Athens, a host or hostess were seated as hosts or hostesses at every table. They included Christiana and Ulysses at the top table, the Count and Countess von Rugerstein, Byron, even Maggie and, if needed, any of Marianne's self-appointed junior executives. At the opening luncheon Marianne hosted a table that included a grand duke and duchess, a prime minister and his wife, and two youthful members of the Greek royal family. She wore a long brocade gold and black jacket with a deep collar that left her neck free to show off von Rugerstein's three row black pearl necklace. The grand duchess hoped she had not caused too many problems, while knowing that she had, and always did.

Next day at the reception and dinner all the finest gifts that Stephanie had been given were on display, and guarded by two uniformed security guards. The array included a twelve-place setting of solid silver cutlery in its own mahogany cabinet, a freshly made copy of the Monkey Orchestra from Meissen, a full-length mink coat from a Canadian business associate of her mother, plus a copy of Marianne's long dark mink jacket from the count and countess. There was also a large ruby brooch, diamond bracelets plus her own diamond necklace, as well as a square-cut ring from Christiana's collection, and a Limoges china dinner service. It was more like a trousseau than a birthday.

The reception was followed by the gala dinner in the hotel's ballroom. It was one the few occasions when Christiana Stephanopolous knew her jewels would face severe competition from the dozen or more mega-rich guests each determined to outshine everyone else. To her surprise the most eye-catching collection of gems was worn by the eighteen-year-old Indian princess who had been Stephanie's closest friend at their finishing school where they had both completed their final term. Now her life would be that of a princess with all the privileges of being the daughter of one of the wealthiest maharajahs while accepting whoever her parents chose as her husband. Tonight she was wearing a softest silk sari embroidered with uncountable yards of golden thread which draped round her fully developed body that no man would be allowed to touch, except her husband. Her picture of fully developed femininity was completed by jewels withdrawn from the mammoth family vault many the size of small pebbles. Her sari was supported by a deepest green emerald brooch. Everywhere she was followed by a uniformed Indian ceremonial guard. She was also accompanied by two family maids.

Stephanie, in contrast, could choose the man she wanted to marry, and it was assumed that Christiana and Ulysses would automatically approve her choice. For the moment, however, she was only interested in being wed to the family business. That night diamonds fell from her ears like stalactites, her diamond necklace embraced her pearly neck, and her new square-cut diamond ring, a birthday present from her mother, blazed from one hand and a pear-shaped diamond ring, which she would have to return to her parent after the ball, decorated the other.

Yet it was still Christiana who outshone every one of her guests. As she put it to Marianne a few days later, 'I out-bitched them all.' Her floor-length ball gown was composed of a low-cut sable embroidered neckline, from which dripped masses of heavily embroidered white satin that grew wider as it fell until it was greeted by another border of sable at the hemline. She wore the family's largest tiara and around her neck was the hundred-plus diamond collar that had been worn by the last Czarina of Russia. Stephanie, as the evening's golden girl, wore a golden sheath dress of fine firm satin that clung to every curve of her youthful body.

As Stephanie and her parent finally appeared, Chistiana and Ulysses moved forward first and took their places at the top table. Finally the birthday girl was given a standing ovation from the guests who acknowledged her elegance, beauty and polished refinement as she walked to her place in the centre of the top table.

Marianne could not resist moving away from the table she was hosting and going to where Stephanie was sitting and whispered that she looked 'like the princess in waiting before assuming the title of empress'. In return Stephanie asked her to 'Watch over me tonight, and for always, sis.'

13

Three days later, she drove to the family headquarters and took up her new position as a director of Stephanopolous International, as its new International Director of Personnel. She was accompanied by her mother and both wore long, costly fur coats. Alerted by downstairs reception, Dolores, the secretary she had inherited from the previous director, stood and curtsied as she entered her office for the first time. It was a similar homage that had been shown a few moments earlier by twenty-five (or was it more?) typists and clerks who worked in the open plan outer office of Personnel. One of the typists found herself whispering to a colleague, 'Look at the way she can afford to dress, and she is only eighteen.'

Stephanie's first instruction was to tell her secretary to help her out of the mink coat that was to be her first duty each morning and hang it in her private closet. She was following her mother's advice to 'Begin as you intend to go on'.

Later that morning, Christiana dictated a memo 'To all who work at headquarters. My daughter, Stephanie Stephanopolous, has now taken up her position as the new head of personnel. She is to be addressed at all times as Madame Stephanopolous or Mlle Stephanopolous, and paid the respect due to her as a director of Stephanopolous International.'

Stephanie told her secretary to sit down and she would shortly begin giving her dictation. Dolores already recognised that her new boss was determined to establish her position within the corporation from day one. The blue silk suit she was wearing must have cost at least three times what she earned in a month, and she was well paid, while her large diamond ring could only be worn by someone who was worth millions. And it was matched by multi-carat diamond studded earrings. She was a young lady who had been born to power. There was a note of sarcasm in her voice as she suggested: 'When you have finished admiring my jewellery, shall we get on?'

'Sorry, madame.'

It was only a few hours before everyone at headquarters understood that the curtain had risen on a new era. The star was Stephanie who was at the centre of headquarters' gossip. Women could only envy her, while men were forced to realise that she was untouchable; like forbidden fruit. She was feline with claws she was prepared to use to savage the first sign of familiarity, lack of respect, disobedience or inefficiency.

'Take down this memo,' she told Dolores. 'To Mr Surplus, and deliver it to him personally as soon as I have approved it and signed the top copy. "Dear Mr Surplus, I am pleased you had the good sense to move out of your office which is now to be for the sole use of myself as the new Director of Personnel. From today you are to make yourself available to me whenever I need your experience. Dolores will now work solely for myself. You have my permission to recruit one of the typists in the main pool for your own work. Please ensure that everyone in the outer office is aware that I expect them to stand up whenever any member of the board enters this floor, and to address them as either sir or madam, and in my case, Mlle Stephanopolous. This order is to come into force immediately. Failure to obey will lead first to a reprimand and if repeated, dismissal. I shall shortly decide whether there is any future for you at Stephanopolous International, (signed) Stephanie Stephanopolous, International Director of Personnel."

'You seem a reasonably sensible girl, Dolores. How would you rate Mr Surplus? Or is his name his future?'

'He was easy to work with, madame. He made few demands. And most people liked him. He seemed to regard us all as his equals.'

'I think you have just opened the exit door for him; signed his death warrant as far as this corporation is concerned. Don't ever think of yourself as my equal. I am being paid one hundred times more than your own salary. Any future increases to your own wage packet will depend upon letting me know you are both efficient and always recognise my position by standing up or curtsying whenever I arrive or leave. Now let's get on.' She dictated two general memorandums, one making sure that everyone who worked at headquarters was aware that she expected them to be ready to begin work at nine each morning which was no longer to be regarded as the time they could arrive at headquarters. No one was to leave their desks until five o'clock, or until they had finished whatever work they were carrying out. The second announced a no smoking rule, plus a warning that men were to wear a jacket and tie at all times unless she rescinded the order for that day, while women were forbidden to wear trousers at work, and skirts should be below knee length.

Three mornings later she received a note signed by three typists in her own department asking her permission to wear shorter skirts whenever the temperature was above 28°C. She immediately instructed Dolores to tell the three typists that Mlle Stephanopolous wanted to see them in her office at once, although she ignored them as they stood meekly in front of her desk, not knowing what to do with themselves, while she continued reading the many documents that now began appearing on her desk. It was a full ten minutes before she snapped, 'Which of you was the instigator of your offensive note?'

'I was,' said the oldest and tallest of the trio whose voice was so dry with fear that she was barely audible.

'In which case I shall give you the privilege of being the first to tear up this copy of your offensive note. You have one minute to carry out my order and to apologise in a way that assures me you now recognise my position as a director of this corporation. The alternative is dismissal. The time starts now. Your silence will mean the dismissal not only of yourself, but also your two colleagues.'

'I apologise, Madame Stephanopolous. I made a mistake. I am so sorry if I offended you. That was never my intention.' And she tore up the offending note.

Hearing this one of the other girls said, 'I would like to apologise, too, Madame Stephanopolous. It was foolish. How can we be allowed to challenge an order that someone like yourself issues?'

The third apology automatically followed.

Stephanie turned to the leader and told her, 'I am impressed by your courage in risking dismissal. What is your name?'

'Helena Konstantinidis, madame.'

'Yours is the first name to be put on my list of possible talent for future promotion. It may not be in the too far distant future when you could have men and women under you who have to obey your orders, just as you have to obey mine. But don't risk another mistake.'

An hour later as she walked through her department everyone stood up. She took the lift to the ground floor and then the private lift to the tenth floor where her mother had her office. 'Maggie,' she asked, 'is my mother in?'

'No, Stephanie. She is upstairs in her apartment.'

Mlle Stephanopolous sat on top of the desk where her mother's secretary worked. 'Maggie, let us get one thing perfectly clear, Now that I am a board director working full-time for Stephanopolous International, you will from now onwards always address me as Mlle Stephanopolous. There will be no exceptions, or excuses.'

Maggie knew she had no alternative. 'Yes, Mlle Stephanopolous.'

'Now telephone my mother and tell her I am on my way up.'

'Yes, Steph ... sorry Mlle Stephanopolous.'

'Don't play games with me, Maggie. It will be a contest you can only lose. I intend to interfere in everything. I shall be sharing control with my parents from whom I shall eventually take over. As Director of Personnel you are directly under me. I would hate you to be the first victim of the authority that has been given to me. Remember, you are expendable. However, so long as you recognise who I am, and where I am going, you could end up part of my own personal team. All you have to do is prove you understand where your future lies.'

Maggie felt humbled as all her strength drained out of her and she recognised a lady whose venom would be deadly. She also knew she had received an early warning of the war that might one day be fought between two women both of whom regarded themselves as being her mistress.

Two floors up Stephanie and her mother hugged and kissed and her mother said she was sorry for not having been in touch, but she wanted her daughter to have time to get used to her new senior position. Stephanie explained: 'I have been busy letting everyone in the building know there is a new Director of Personnel, and that she will be making fresh rules affecting everyone. I have already dealt with my first rebellion. I don't think there will be any more.'

While they drank coffee, she told how she had dealt with the three typists who had dared challenge her new dress code, adding 'staff throughout all nine floors have been informed that they are to stand up whenever I, or any director, walks into their department.'

Her mother was unaware of the storm that was about to blow up as she assured her daughter that she had her complete trust, but that would not stop her keeping an eye on all Stephanie did. 'You may have had your coming of age party, but you are still a teenager who is being given responsibilities beyond her years because you have my genes in your blood.'

Stephanie crashed her fine china coffee cup onto its saucer so that both splintered into several pieces. She shouted, 'You may be my mother, but you no longer control me. Remember we are both directors of a multi-million dollar corporation. If any matter is put to a vote based upon the number of shares we hold, you cannot any longer be guaranteed to have your own way if you continue to regard me as a child instead of your business colleague. I want to work with you, but not for you. My final loyalty is to myself and Stephanopolous International.'

For a moment her mother looked dumbfounded at the onslaught that had been launched, but she quickly regained her composure. She recognised that much of what she was hearing was true, but the word apologise was not in her dictionary. Instead she said simply, 'You are right. You are no longer a teenager, except in years. You have the brains and the authority of a woman twice your age. But you are still my daughter. We shouldn't fight one another.'

That was still not how Stephanie saw the situation. She was insistent her age was of no importance. What mattered were the number of shares she now possessed. She might not be in control, but she could hold the balance of power between her parents; a kind of balance of power. By offering her support to either her father or her mother, she had sufficient shares to have her way. It would be just as easy, despite their present clash of words, to side with her mother against her father, but if she opted to support Ulysses her mother would suddenly become impotent. She stood up and looked down upon her mother. 'I shall be happy to be your partner, but from now onwards please think of me as a senior shareholder. In any major dispute you could be powerless without my votes. This teenager holds the balance of power in any disagreement that may surface between my mother and my father.'

'Stephanie, darling, there are ways, believe me, in which your apparent strength can be countered. But it will be disastrous for everyone if we ever allow any clash of opinion to surface.'

Stephanie stayed furious and stormed out. She ignored the salute of the security man as she stepped out of the private lift on the ground floor, but observed everything as she walked through the open plan outer office of Personnel. She noticed that too many were talking because they had too little to do. That meant they were overstaffed. She also noticed that one of the male clerks was wearing an open-necked shirt. She told her secretary to identify him and bring him into her office.

The clerk who stood in front of her was ill at ease having been told by Dolores why Madame Stephanopolous wanted to see him. Nonetheless, he could not stop himself wondering how he might impress this quite gorgeous young woman who was both frighteningly wealthy, but also his boss who was in a filthy temper after an altercation with her mother of which he knew nothing. Surprisingly, despite her annoyance at the way he was dressed, she found him attractive. He might not be an Adonis, but he had been blessed with the features of an ancient Greek who several thousand years ago might have been a god in human form. However, today the opposite was true. He was a nobody, and she was an empress in waiting. He was not a god, and she was preparing to remind him he was a mortal of no importance. Her world of riches was light years away from his shirt with frayed cuffs. Yet he was fascinating, even desirable Nevertheless, she attacked and told him, 'I am trying to make out why I am wasting so much of my time on someone as unimportant as you are. I own a large slice of the Stephanopolous corporation, yet am allowing you to keep me from my work. Bring me my coat which is hanging in the wardrobe behind you.' It was a Burberry raincoat. He helped her put it on. She was facing him as she asked, 'Why do you risk every chance of achieving promotion? I am constantly on the look out for potential senior executives.' He replied almost without thinking who he was talking to, 'May I congratulate you on your new position of authority. I am sure you will be a great asset to your family's business. And please let me apologise for ignoring your orders.

I did not think you intended them to apply on such a warm day.'

'Mr Leopardis, you are not being paid to think. All you need remember is to carry out my instructions. That is the difference between us. I give the orders, you obey them. If I decide to come to work in a mink coat I am not showing off, but emphasising the unbridgeable gap that exists between me and the rest of the staff. However, your actions today are making me think that you might be persuaded to accept greater responsibilities. For starters would you be prepared to carry my raincoat and escort me through the outer office where you can pick up your jacket and take me to one of the bars where you and your colleagues congregate after work?'

He breathed in the expensive fragrance that had been one of her coming of age presents. 'I would never have thought, or dared, to ask for such a pleasure and honour. Now, whatever the future holds, for the rest of my life I shall remember that I once escorted the richest heiress in Europe.'

She slipped her arm through his and reminded him, 'I still have to decide what your punishment will be for disobedience. Now let's go and have a drink. I shall pay.'

'I am sorry, Madame Stephanopolous, but I could not possibly accept such an arrangement. Although you have the authority to sack me, I still like to pay for a lady whenever I am out with her.'

'Agreed,' and she smiled at him for the first time; he was also a gentleman. Every eye turned in their direction as they walked through her outer office, her arm through his. But they caused hardly a stare as they entered the almost empty bar. It was past two. Any earlier and she would have been recognised from the many photograhs that had appeared in newspapers and magazines, and minds would have wondered why someone worth millions had condescended to mix with people who she must sometimes think of as lesser mortals. What would she like to drink, he asked?

'A glass of red wine, please.'

'A cheese sandwich?'

'I would prefer, smoked salmon,' not realising the difference in price.

Fortunately for him, they did not serve smoked salmon. He settled for two glasses of wine and two cheese sandwiches.

She was already asking herself why she had not stayed in her office and ordered lunch to be sent to her from the directors' kitchen. And she was not enjoying herself after tasting the coarse red wine he had bought for them both. Was she being foolish? Or was it good that she was experiencing for the first time what life was like for those who knew nothing about the protected, luxury life that was all she had ever known? She was experiencing something that was entirely new in her carefully protected life.

As he munched his cheese sandwich, she asked, 'Tell me about yourself, Mr Leopardis.' She liked the sound of his name.

'There is very little to tell. I am a lowly paid clerk who is glad to have a job.'

She was about to suggest that she should be allowed to pay for their wine and sandwiches, but at the last moment realised that would humiliate him. Instead she asked: 'What is your ambition?'

He did not answer immediately. He was thinking how he had reacted with admiration every time he looked at a photograph of the lady sitting with him. She was like a gorgeous Hollywood film actress who waved to her fans, and then forgot them. She would probably do the same to him. Finally, he told her, 'I would like to work for you.'

'But you already do.'

'But that is as a nobody. Being here with you, I am being encouraged to be a somebody.'

'That might be arranged. Walk me back to my office.'

They left arm in arm, but once outside she asked him to help her to put on her raincoat as the temperature seemed to be dropping. They were still arm in arm when they re-entered her outer office. Her last words were, 'We will talk some more. Keep your jacket on.'

Back at her desk, she could not get him out of her mind. Was he going through the same kind of hell that she was enduring? She told Dolores to inform Mr Leopardis that Mlle Stephanopolous wanted to see him.

'Are they making your life miserable in the outer office?' she asked.

'Miserable might not be the right word, but they wanted answers to questions like, "What were you like?" "What did we talk about?" "Did you relax?" I told them you never relaxed, but seemed to spend every twenty-four hours thinking and planning the future of the corporation.'

'You have just won yourself promotion. Anyone who could answer their questions in that way, is someone who has a future within this corporation and under me. I am not sure how, but you will have a new future very soon. If you had your way, how would you make it happen?'

'I want to learn everything that is happening within your corporation, And the only way this can be achieved quickly is to be allowed to sit here in your own office and listen to you at work. Given the chance I know I will learn quickly because that is what I want.'

As she drove herself home in her new two-seater Mercedes she felt lonely. Anton Leopardis kept intruding upon her thoughts, despite her life being so remote from his. Why was she finding it impossible to drive away her memories of him? As they talked she discovered they had more in common than she thought possible; they both enjoyed swimming and listening to classical music, even the pleasures of wine, although she prayed she might never again have to endure the near vinegar, or so it had seemed to her, that he had bought for them both. They also enjoyed the history, and the tales and legends of ancient Greece. Would he be receptive to all she could provide? Until now she had enjoyed tormenting men with either her tongue or her beauty, or both, but that did not now include Mr Leopardis.

She wanted him, and not just to make love. She wanted him for himself. She had read about love at first sight, but until now she had thought it only happened in novels. Could she gently ease him into her life, and if so could they become equals?

Strange to relate, her mother had never considered that a young lady like her own daughter would ever experience the same urges as other ordinary young women. Surely she had been protected from such influences. She only met young women and young men from backgrounds at least similar to her own.

There were tears in Stephanie's eyes. All she wanted was to be with Anton. Yet despite the almost regal position she occupied, she could not order him to love her. First she would encourage him to fulfil his ambitions; he could have boardroom potential. There was also a place for him in her arms. Surely he would welcome her intrusion into his life just as he was encroaching on her world. This was for the first time the kind of interference she was not only enjoying, but learning to love. Already she realised that Anton Leopardis was the man she wanted to marry. No man had ever excited her before, and he was doing so even more when he was absent.

As she slowed down at a dangerous crossroads, she realised that her mind and body were pulling in different directions. Her mind was demanding that she stopped her foolish thoughts and started remembering the power of the purse that her mother had instilled in her, and accept that people like the clerk in her outer office could only be regarded as a human toy to amuse her until she tired of him. He was a momentary whim, no more than a passing pleasure. What could he give her that she could not give herself? He was content to buy the cheapest shirt he could find while she would not be content with anything less the most exquisite and expensive blouse that could cost her several hundred dollars. But ... and it was the biggest but she had ever known. Her mouth was aching for the taste of his lips and the wonders of the orgasm she knew he would provide. She was in conflict with herself. Again, her mind intruded with a reminder that rich women, whatever their age, never needed to worry about trivialities which was all a man like Anton really was. He would feel flattered that she even shown an interest in him. To think of him being permitted to touch and cradle her sensuous breasts, or experience the privilege of sharing her bed was little short of blasphemy. The arrows from her heart that she was shooting at him, left her wondering whether Anton might be content to be just her plaything. A moment later she was flaying herself for daring to think such a despicable thought. Hadn't she been brought up to understand that whatever she wanted she could have? Her wealth was beyond the wildest dreams of other women. If it was Anton she desired, all he might lose was his dignity. Yet, a moment later she knew that such whims were only making her false to the true Stephanie. The true difference between them was that she could be a ruthless bitch, while he would give her neverending kindness and happiness.

When she turned off the country road and touched a switch close to the steering wheel the massive, high wrought iron gates that guarded the entrance to the family estate opened, and in a moment she would leave the outside world behind. But not this time. Anton was still with her. She might be a young heiress who was now driving in a domain where she and her parents were the equivalent of the three rulers of a kingdom where entry was denied to all but a handful. She wanted Anton to be one of them. First, however, she needed to ask whether he was willing to become part of her life. And she needed to find out how he would react to what she was planning for him. Until then he would have to stand up whenever she approached. And that would be demeaning. Such a thought was abhorrent to her.

The moment she brought her car to a halt she was back in a world that Anton could not even visualise. Two members of staff were hurrying down the marble steps to greet her and carry out whatever orders she gave. 'Put my car away,' she ordered the footman, and a maid was told to take her raincoat and briefcase out of the car and up to her suite.

'Yes, madame. Is there anything else I can do for madame?'

'I shall send for you when I need you, but before you go tell cook to serve dinner in my suite in thirty minutes.'

She took herself into the family drawing room where she poured a liberal helping of her favourite homecoming vodka which she topped up with less tonic water than usual because she needed to rid her mouth of the sharp acidic taste of the wine Anton had bought. She had drunk it to help him bridge their divide.

Upstairs in her suite she decided that the only way to cheer herself up was to dress as she would if she was dining with the man she wanted to be with, and rang for a maid to come and help her dress. She rejected the first three dresses she looked at because she wanted to appear seductive, and that was achieved by a floor-length emerald green off-the-shoulder gown which both revealed, yet largely kept hidden, what would have had Anton drooling with desire, an emotion she would have encouraged by her favourite and enticing perfume that was part of her collection of toiletries from Cartier, Yardley, Bulgari and Halston. Next the maid was instructed to bring her black silk underwear and then brush and comb her jet black hair so that

198

it fell loosely around her shoulders, which Anton would one day touch as he snuggled up to her before revealing his manhood.

Fully dressed and jewelled she walked into her sitting room where a waiter had already filled her wine glass with her favourite Chambertin, and was serving her a hot homemade soup. As she ate dinner she continued to feel restless and out of sorts with herself, and everyone else. Was it because there was no one except the waiter to admire the trouble she had taken to look her most desirable? She left half her soup, picked at her excellent steak, and really only enjoyed her wine and a selection of Greek and international cheeses. To amuse herself she put on a recording of Puccini's *La Bohème*. She had seen the opera and then, as now, she found it hard to imagine how anyone could find happiness, or want to make love, in such miserable surroundings as a garret without any comforts, and unimpressive views that anyway could hardly be seen due to the uncleaned windows. Why didn't they get a maid to clean the place up, she mused? Or had they become so used to the surroundings they no longer noticed? Feeling spiteful, or more correctly miserable, she phoned the maid and told her to stay on duty until she called her to help her prepare for bed, adding, 'I have no idea when that will be because I have brought home a great deal of work from my office.'

Determined to finalise new dress instructions for the summer for the staff at headquarters, it was more than an hour before she was satisfied with what she had decided. Her notes read:

DRESS CODE FOR SUMMER

With immediate effect the following dress code will come into operation for all headquarter employees of Stephanopolous International whose rank is below that of board director and their staff.

WOMEN may wear a skirt or trousers, but not shorts, with open-necked blouses or shirts of any sensible colour. Scarves are also permitted as well as shawls. They may also come to work with legs bare, or wearing stockings, as they wish. Shoes must be worn, but not sneakers.

MEN must wear trousers at all times, but of course they can be of whatever weight they choose, and of any acceptable colour. As with the women, sneakers are not acceptable, but lightweight shoes will be permitted. Jackets should be worn when arriving at the office, but may be discarded providing they are wearing a clean shirt. A tie or scarf must be worn.

No deviations from these instructions are permitted.

Signed Stephanie Stephanopolous, Director, Stephanopolous International, Director of Personnel.

It was past midnight before she sent for the maid, and started to undress leaving her clothes on the floor for her to pick up. She was told to prepare her bed and lay out the pink silk pyjamas that matched the sheets. Her breakfast was to be delivered sharp at eight o'clock.

When it arrived punctually, as ordered, the heavy silver tray was carried by a young maid she could not recall seeing before. She asked, 'What is your name? I don't recognise you.' And learned, 'I am Sophie, madame, and I have only worked for your family for a month.'

'Do you know who I am, Sophie?'

'Oh yes, madame. You are the most beautiful lady, and one of the wealthiest in Greece.'

'Who says so, Sophie?'

'Everyone in the kitchen, madame. And the gardeners, too. They also say that, except for your mother, you are the richest lady in our country, madame.'

'How old are you, Sophie?'

'Just seventeen, madame. But I want to learn to be good at whatever I am asked to do, madame. I left school when I was thirteen because my family needed extra money. For two years I worked in a factory as a seamstress, then as a waitress in a café for two years.'

'Is your family very poor, Sophie?'

'My father was invalided out of the army with a tiny pension and all we have to live on is what I earn and what my mother makes from taking in washing.'

'How would a poor girl like you enjoy being the personal maid to the richest young woman in Greece? Before you reply, you should know that I am very selfish and intolerant. You will need to get up at six most mornings so that you can bring me my breakfast at whatever time I tell you, and remain on duty until midnight or whenever I don't need you any more. Every day you will press whatever clothes I have been wearing and quickly learn where everything is kept.'

'Please, madame. Give me a chance. I shall do anything and everything you order.'

'Let's start now. In one of my wardrobes there are three linen suits, one white, one blue and one green. Bring them to me and I shall decide which one to wear today. Before you go fill up my cup and butter me some toast, and I shall get up and enjoy my egg. I shall talk to the head housekeeper and tell her that I have appointed you my personal maid and you are not to be given any other duties.

'For the next month you will belong to me. You will live here and I shall arrange for you to be allocated your own bedroom in the staff quarters at the top of the house. During this trial period your wage will be increased by one third. At the end of four weeks, if you have satisfied me, you will be paid twice what you are currently earning and from then onwards you will devote your life to looking after me. But if I have any doubts about your ability, you will be demoted to scullery maid and your wage will be the same as you are earning now. Do you understand the opportunity I am giving you? You will be surrounded by luxuries and may occasionally accompany me on my travels. You will look after all my clothes including my furs which are kept in a separate closet. Only my jewels will not be your concern. You must never reveal to anyone, including your mother, anything you may hear me say, or confidences I may share with you. Disobedience will lead to you being dismissed. Your future from now onwards depends upon me.'

'Please, madame. For me it will be like working for a goddess. I know you must be respected. Every hour of my time I shall give to you. I promise you will not be disappointed.'

'For your sake, I hope not. I shall also go and see your mother and tell her that I have decided that from now onwards you will have your own bedroom in the Stephanopolous mansion. She will see you once a week. You will have every Wednesday off, unless I need you. She will agree with whatever I say. I shall also allow her to wash some of my clothes. What I pay her, together with your own higher wage, should enable her to buy some much needed extras. Working for me can have many advantages. But they have to be earned. Mistakes I do not tolerate.'

That morning before she drove to work she gave their housekeeper her instructions regarding Sophie's new duties and the increase in her wage while she was on trial. Before driving to her office wearing her green linen suit and a boater decorated with matching green ribbon she ordered Sophie to spend the whole day opening every drawer, cupboard and wardrobe so that after two days she would know where everything was kept. And, finally, Sophie was always to be ready to greet her when she returned home from the office.

As she turned out of the estate she felt happy with what she had decided. After all, the Director of Personnel should know how to pick her own staff, and heaven help Sophie if she proved her wrong. It was just before 9.30 am when she entered her outer office where everyone stood up, including Anton who received a special smile. When Dolores asked whether she should take her green jacket and hang it in her wardrobe, Stephanie told her she would keep it on, for the moment, but she was to put her boater away. She was then given the new Summer Dress Code and instructed to prepare sufficient copies for every department and have them delivered by one of the commissionaires.

Three weeks of continued misery failed to give her the confidence to express her feelings to Anton, partly because she feared his refusal, and partly due to the battle she continued to wage with herself. Whenever she had a moment to herself, it was spent trying to decide how to express her feelings for the man she loved. She also thought of various plots that might be necessary in the distant future when it would have to be decided whether she or her mother would be passed the baton to the presidential chair. By accident she found what could be the way to solve both problems. She asked her father whether she could spend a large part of each day with him in his office so that she could learn everything she needed to know about all aspects of the corporation. This also avoided the problem of continually having to walk past Anton and forcing him and everyone else, to stand up out of respect. Now it need only be two or three times a day. She also worked out a way to let him know how much she desired him. Her parents, of course, continued to know nothing about her feelings for someone who was among the lowest paid members of staff, not even her father in whose office she spent several hours each afternoon reading, listening and digesting everything about the empire over which she would one day rule. She yearned to tell him about the man in her life, and was confident he would understand, but worried how he would cope when it set him on a collision course with his wife who was certain to object.

It was while in her father's office that many of her ideas for the future efficiency of the family corporation were born and developed. Almost always he told her: 'I have no objections to that suggestion. Do whatever you think best. You are the future head of this international empire. You must be given your head, even if you initially make a few mistakes. That is the only way to learn.' Thus her early seeds took root and headquarters became an increasingly more efficient operation than before her arrival. One member of staff, not in her hearing, likened the changes she was initiating to coming from the same broom on which she had flown into headquarters before using it to sweep away every piece of dead wood.

Soon it would be time to set in motion the wheels that would help her win the man for whom her love had grown day by day, but first she and Dolores dealt with her daily mail, and as soon as she was left alone she decided it was time to tackle another hurdle that had been troubling her, and phoned the head of accounts, She told him: 'This is Stephanie Stephanopolous. I want to see you in my office in five minutes.' She had never met Frederick Edberger, a Swedish accountant, and thought it time he met his new boss, not least because her female intuition told her they would not get on. In that case he would have to be tamed by whatever means were necessary.

When he presented himself in her outer office he was told by Dolores that he would have to wait until the red light on the door to Mlle Stephanopolous's office turned green. Although surprised, he had no alternative. The moment the green light appeared he walked into the office of the new director and she invited him to sit down and told him, 'I thought it time we met and talked. I have twice been up to your floor, but sadly you were not at your desk. I have spent much of my time studying the efficiency of the corporation, and now I need your co-operation.

'Stephanopolous International is overstaffed and I intend to make the necessary changes to ensure that we slim down and become the streamlined organisation we should be. On too many occasions I have watched typists manicuring their nails and combing their hair because they had nothing to do, while men read magazines. I am not prepared to allow this situation to continue. My aim is to reduce staff levels in all departments, including your own, by at least ten per cent and, in some cases, by more through sensible and efficient pruning which will lead to greater productivity. The days of easy living at Stephanopolous headquarters are over now that I am the Director of Personnel. There is a new broom and she is determined to sweep the building clean, and not under the carpet. I want heads of departments to begin the pruning at once. I shall not tolerate any attempts to slow down or ignore my instructions. If I sense any kind of unwillingness to carry out my orders, I shall take the necessary action to achieve my demanded ten per cent staffing cuts myself. I shall be talking personally to all heads, but decided to pay you the compliment of being the first departmental head to hear of my decision. I expect the cut-backs to begin at the end of this month and be completed within another month. Please let me have the list of your ten per cent to be axed within forty-eight hours. To save any embarrassment, all notices of dismissal will be issued from my office. You currently have a staff of thirty-three in your department. That means I only initially require three names to fulfil my requirements. Less, and I shall feel I am being disobeyed. And that is a situation I shall not accept, from anybody.

'If that happens in any department, I shall simply add one or more additional names myself. Thank you for your co-operation, Mr Edberger.'

'I have to say...' That was as far as he got before she interrupted to make it clear that, 'Like my mother, I thought I had already made it clear that I expect to be addressed either as Madame or Mlle Stephanopolous. I hope that is now quite clear. As you were saying...'

'You may be partially right in your thinking, Mlle Stephanopolous, but you seem to be determined to use a sledge hammer, when all that is needed is a gentle hoovering to get rid of any unnecessary debris. In my own department there is no debris.'

'There will be no exceptions to what I intend, and that includes your department. Please understand that I shall not tolerate disobedience from whatever source it comes. My sole interest is the efficiency of Stephanopolous International which, within a few years, I expect to control. Please, do as I ask.'

She stared straight at him forcing him to look away and accept that the Director of Personnel was the equivalent of 'she who must be obeyed'. He started to fiddle with his tie as he accepted that unless he carried out her wishes it might soon be his name on her own list of casualities. His voice had lost a great deal of its confidence as he told her, 'Of course, I accept your demands, Madame Stephanopolous, but my problem is that I am currently preparing a draft of the company's half yearly accounts for your father and he has requested them by the end of this week. I don't think I can achieve both targets.'

'Mr Edberger, in your own best interests, tune into my wavelength. I shall expect to have your list within seventy-two hours, instead of forty-eight. Good morning.'

No sooner had he left than she telephoned through to her father, and was immediately put through to him by his own PA. 'Dad, can I come up and see you? I have something important to discuss.'

'Of course, sweetheart. I hear you are starting to make waves.'

'It is more like a storm. And not before time, as I shall explain.'

She walked straight into his lavish office, ignoring the secretaries in his own outer office. Both offices had been designed by her mother with all the chairs in bright blue leather 'to match the waters of the Aegean Sea', as she had once put it to Stephanie, who thought it ostentatious and lacking in dignity. She made a mental note that it would be all-change when she took over the presidency. She sat down facing her father and opened the last annual report at the page which detailed expenditures and salaries, and told him:

'Because I know that both you and mother are far too busy to spend time walking through the floors where much of the detailed, and necessary, work that helps us to make the profits we demand is carried out. I decided that was my job, as the Director of Personnel. I have not been impressed with what I have seen. We currently employ a staff in this building, not including those who work on these three top floors, of more than two hundred whose total salaries add up to around three million dollars annually. Far too often during my travels up and down using their lifts I have watched typists manicuring their nails or listened to them talking on the phone to their boyfriends, and not stopping even though I was in their office. Too many of the men spend too much of their time reading newspapers and magazines. I have decided to cut the staff levels in all departments by at least ten per cent, and where necessary by as much as fifteen per cent, including Personnel. My clean-up will reduce staff costs by almost half a million dollars and that, even to people like ourselves, is a considerable saving. As a result those who remain will have to work harder, and earn what they are paid. As a fellow board member I thought I should let you know my intentions in case any head of department comes crying to you and suggesting I was interfering. If they do, I should expect you to tell them that if they have any problems they must discuss them with the Director of Personnel. Perhaps you might add that you agree with what I am planning.'

She paused. 'There is one other matter. In my department, although there are several who will be sacked, there is also a clerk who is way above average. I intend to promote him to be my assistant, and eventually deputy. He is also very handsome.'

'You are the boss sweetheart in everything that affects staff. I shall not interfere.' Her thanks was to kiss him on his forehead.

'Shall I tell mother?'

'You might as well. She will learn soon enough. She has informants everywhere.'

'If you know any of their names, please let me know. They could be among the first to feel my axe.'

Back in her own office she asked Dolores to tell Mr Leopardis she wanted to see him. When he arrived she told her secretary to stay. She explained that she had come from a meeting with her father who had agreed with her plans to cut the current staff by at least ten per cent, probably more, in order to achieve greater efficiency. She was immediately appointing Mr Leopardis to be her assistant to help her with her efficiency programme. 'Have his desk moved in here without delay and in the morning arrange for an executive desk to be installed here. Finally, send this memo to accounts: "This is to let you know that I have, with immediate effect, promoted Mr Anton Leopardis to be my personal assistant. His salary is at once to be increased fourfold." To save time, sign it on my behalf and take it to accounts. One final point, Dolores. Remember, you are my personal and private secretary. Anything that happens in here is strictly private and confidential, and for your eyes and ears only. Go home early tonight once you have finished all your work.'

Once Dolores had closed the door, the red light went on.

14

Anton was about to thank Stephanie for his promotion and her generosity when she cut him short and kissed him on his lips, explaining, 'I have wanted to do that ever since you took me out to your pub and brought me a glass of wine and a sandwich. Now it is my turn and I would like to reciprocate your hospitality. I hope you will spend the night with me and we shall drive back to work together in the morning. And then, as far as I am concerned, we shall be on our way to becoming as one. Please, darling, tell me that what I want is what you want, too. I love you. Perhaps, for a short while we may have to be a little discreet, but as far as I am concerned you are the man I would like to marry ... if I am asked.'

This time it was Anton who took her in his arms and kissed her passionately. 'I have dreamed of this for as long as you have, darling, but I never even thought it could ever happen. Do you really mean that I can take the richest girl in the world to bed tonight?'

He could have burst into tears when she answered: 'Well not exactly, darling. As you are coming home with me, it will really be me who is inviting you into my bed. But once we have broken the ice, and something else, who cares. Oh, but there is one person who will object when I tell her. My mother. But don't worry. I am in love with you and nothing else matters. And I have been for something like four months. And I am supposed to be a very impatient young lady.'

She took hold of his hand and gently led him onto the settee which her mother had installed in her office during the weeks before her daughter arrived at headquarters. She must have thought, Stephanie suggested, that anyone likely to be a future President of Stephanopolous International should have a settee in her office; actually, it is very comfortable. I have stretched out on mine a couple of times – by myself. This will be a new experience. 'Shall we have an undressed rehearsal?'

She unzipped his trousers and for the first time in her life was holding a weapon she had dreamed about since her earliest teens. It became bigger at her touch, 'May I kiss it?' she asked and blushed at the same time. 'Please,' he begged. And drips from his weapon tasted like a fine wine to Stephanie. 'I love you, Anton. I have been so miserable without you, but when I am with you I am the happiest woman in the world. You will never want for anything again. All I ask is that you understand that I am chained to my destiny which means that one day I shall inherit the entire Stephanopolous empire, and you will be by my side. But when we are alone, all I possess will be yours, my body, my wealth and my love.'

Anton could hardly believe what he was hearing. She was one of the richest women in the world and he was a lowly clerk in an office where every time she entered he and all his colleagues had to stand up out of respect for her authority. Yet unless he was dreaming, she was almost going down on her knees and pleading with him to marry her. She kissed him again, and assured him: 'I want you, my darling. And not only your body, but all of you. One day I shall give you a present like no other; our child.' She kissed him again and for the first time their lips became wedded to one another. He was drowning in her passion, her perfume, her diamond ring as he sucked it and kissed her earrings. 'Please touch my bosoms,' she begged and he felt her nipples harden with desire.

Fifteen minutes later she was dressed, Dolores had telephoned for her car to be brought round to the front entrance and together they were hugging one another and walking through her outer office as a quite obvious couple. Half an hour later, she was coming to a halt at the entrance to her mansion home where Sophie and two footmen were waiting to greet her. Her maid curtsied not only to her mistress, but also to Anton and immediately gathered up the soft black baby crocodile brief case, while Stephanie asked the butler whether her parents were at home. When he informed her that they were dining in Athens that night she instructed him to inform cook that she wanted dinner for two to be served in the family dining-room at eight o'clock.

Anton stood silently beside her. Hearing her give orders did not surprise him, but the luxury that greeted him as he stepped into the overwhelming splendour of the hall with its marble columns and domed ceiling certainly did. She clasped his arm and quietly told him, 'This is my home. Oh, how I love you.' Several servants standing nearby heard what she was saying.

Up in her suite Sophie was introduced to Mr Leopardis and told that she was to obey any orders he gave, because 'he belongs to me.' And she snuggled close to Anton and corrected herself. 'What I should have told you is that I belong to him.' She hardly knew what she was saying, but if this was what it was like to be in love, she loved it. For their first tête-a-tête dinner she put on the same evening gown she had worn when she had been forced to play make-believe that Anton was with her. Dreams could come true. In a few hours time Anton, she knew, would make her a woman. As she fell into his arms she could feel that he was in heaven, too. Even Sophie, who moments earlier had been on her knees helping Stephanie put on her shoes, had tears in her eyes at her mistress's obvious happiness as Anton whispered, 'I knew you were beautiful the first time I set eyes on you, but now you are blazing with a rainbow-like glory.' And she held out her diamond decorated hand. 'You must wait until later to mess me up.'

It might have been unfair to the cook, but they could not help hurrying through the dinner she had prepared. Nevertheless, they both found it impossible to hide from the two waitresses what they were thinking, saying and wanting. When they embraced in the family dining-room there was nothing chaste about their touch. The passion of both was like a torch that would send a message to everyone who worked in the Stephanopolous home that the president in waiting was in love.

Back in her suite, Sophie was quickly sent back to her own room and told to bring them both breakfast at seven in the morning She could clear up after they left for the office. If there had been a prize, Stephanie would have won gold for the speed in which she undressed and made ready to give herself to the man she adored. A few moments of pain quickly gave way to the most sensuous moments she had ever experienced, and somehow Anton knew how to make the pleasure last before they both fell asleep exhausted. It was how they both hoped they would spend the rest of their lives. Alone with each other. All alone.

The following morning she changed plans and asked him to guide her to where he lived. It turned out to be a distant suburb of Athens that she never knew existed, and while it could not be called a slum, Stephanie hoped she never had to see it again. She urged Anton to pack every item of clothing he owned into his suitcase, plus his toiletries and any personal possessions, and bring them to the office where she would arrange the disposal of everything he did not need to keep, and afterwards would buy him what would amount to his own trousseau. By the time they arrived at headquarters the building was buzzing with rumours and gossip. It was about midday before someone dared tell Christiana, and it was about the same time that a note was delivered both to her and her father, asking to have dinner with both of them at home that evening, adding, 'there will be four of us'.

The rest of the day rushed away, but they did spend two hours shopping and when they had finished he had two expensive off the peg suits, a blazer and grey flannels, half a dozen silk shirts, socks, shoes and ties, plus slippers, a dressing gown and a raincoat. The expedition lasted until she told him, 'that will do for starters' and then revealed she was going to introduce him to her parents that evening.

They lunched at one of their two Athens hotels where she entered with that same look of authority which everyone at headquarters had by now come to respect. Certainly the other diners, mostly tourists and overseas businessmen and women, found it hard to believe that such an attractive young woman could carry herself as though she never wore anything except the most costly clothes. The only lady who had the mystery solved for her was an Italian who was lunching with a Greek businessman who told her, 'She is an heiress who has inherited millions and is obviously determined to enjoy what few others will ever possess.' His guest answered, in Italy they all have the name, Agnelli.

After she had ordered a celebration bottle of Bollinger champagne and some wild smoked salmon for a starter, Stephanie assured Anton that, 'From now onwards I shall be the only godmother you will ever need. You are part of my life. You will never want for anything, You are not only my bedmate, but my partner and my man.'

Meanwhile, the sackings had begun at the end of the month as she intended. They had started in her own department which was cut from an unnecessary forty-plus down to thirty-three. Those who were dismissed included the former head of the department, Harold Surplus, to whom she wrote: 'I am sending you this termination note because for too long you have run a department that included, in my opinion, too many men and women who did too little work and spent far too much of their time manicuring their nails, phoning their friends or reading magazines while they were supposed to be working for the corporation. I can only assume that you were too busy with your own responsibilities to notice this lack of discipline. Nevertheless, I want to thank you for all your attempts to serve the corporation to the best of your ability. The enclosed cheque is a token of our recognition of your loyalty over many years from both my father and mother, as well as myself.'

In all the other departments, most of the men and women sacked had been with the corporation less than two years, and received a more formal note personally signed by herself as Director of Personnel. Enclosed with their final pay packets were formal notes that read: 'With effect from today, as a result of necessary economies, your services are no long required by the Stephanopolous Corporation. However, in recognition of your past contributions, we are enclosing two months' salary.'

The Head of Marketing also received his come-uppance for putting less than the demanded ten per cent of names on the list he had sent her. He was informed: 'With effect from today, I am appointing your deputy, Roberto Pinakoulakis, to take over your department temporarily with instruction to let me have the names of at least three more men or women who he regards as surplus to requirements of the department which until now has been your responsibility. Your formal dismissal note, with generous compensation, is in the post.'

Within an hour news of this sacking was known throughout the twelve floors. Sensing it was their necks on which the axe might next fall if they disobeyed the demands of the young lady who they now knew was ruthless and intolerant, her reputation led to all the other department heads accepting that, in their own best interests, they had no alternative but to bow to her overwhelming power as a director of the corporation.

They all kept their jobs and Stephanie, as she had demanded, received the required numbers to be dismissed. However, she had not forgotten the name of the typist who had left the lift as soon as Stephanie had entered it to go to her own fourth floor office, thinking it would be an imposition to share the lift with one of the family which owned the corporation. When her name appeared on one of the lists of those to be dismissed, it was immediately struck out.

With the dismissal of Mr Surplus, Stephanie set about reorganising not only her own department, but all the rest. She decided to invite two women and one man who she believed were ripe and ready to take on more responsibilities to have lunch with her in her office. This was to be a final test of their potential. She needed to confirm whether the young man she had already appointed temporary head of Marketing after the sacking of his boss, was the right man to make his appointment permanent. The second was Sonia Vrettos, a lady in her early forties who she had selected as ready for greater corporate responsibility. She frequently sent Stephanie ideas for the future of the corporation. Although none had been adopted, Stephanie felt they indicated initiative. The third was Helena Konstantinides, the young woman who had led the rebellion within a few days of her taking up her appointment as Director of Personnel. She had guts and it was now time to begin shaping her future in the corporation.

As for Anton, she intended to appoint him during the next few weeks to be her deputy and he would continue to share her office so that gradually he learned everything that went on in all departments in Athens as well as their offices, factories and warehouses around the world. When she felt he knew all that was needed, she would promote him to be the next Director of Personnel which would give her the time to expand her in-depth knowledge of the corporation, but specifically the vitally important shipping division. And so it happened.

15

Some of the seeds of the change she was determined to achieve were discussed at the luncheon which took place in her office. When they were alone in the privacy of her own office Stephanie begged Anton to understand that she was two people. 'One is the disciplinarian I have to be in the office where I need to exercise control over all our staff, but from now onwards I shall transform myself, even here when we are alone, but always when we are at home. Then you will be with a lady who is as soft as silk, warm as mink, and as loving and generous as only the future Stephanie Leopardis can be.

'Now let me tell you what I am planning. My recent spring clean of excessive and unnecessarily high levels of staff throughout headquarters is complete, but it has left vacant several potential positions as heads of departments. I intend to appoint you to take my place as Director of Personnel, but not for several months. First you will be appointed as my deputy, and will continue to share my office so that gradually you will learn everything that goes on in all our departments, plus our locations around the world, all of which are controlled from this building. By then you will know almost as much as I do about the vast empire I shall eventually inherit. At that point you will be appointed Director of Personnel. This will leave me free to expand my interests, particularly in our vitally important shipping division.'

But first she had to introduce the man in her life to her parents. It would be doubly appropriate, she hinted as strongly as she could, if she could let them know that he had asked her to marry him, and she had said yes. 'You now have a new home where we can romp and play and enjoy as many repeat performances in each other's arms as we want. We may not yet be husband and wife, but to me we already are. You are mine, and I belong to you. After I have told my parents of our decision, no one will dare interfere with what we have agreed.'

214

16

In cricket parlance, Stephanie had finished playing herself into her new business role while Sophie had achieved everything that justified her selection as her personal maid. She slept in the bedroom which had been allocated to her by the head housekeeper, but spent every hour she could in her mistress's suite so that she quickly knew in which drawer, closet or wardrobe all the hundreds of items Stephanie chose to wear were kept. Once that target had been achieved, she pressed every gown, dress or suit so no matter what was chosen it would almost look as though it had never been worn. She discovered everything she needed to know to make Stephanie's life at home smooth so she could concentrate on her growing business responsibilities. Sophie learned to memorise not only where every item of clothing, from furs to slippers, was kept, but even their colours. Each evening when her mistress returned from her office the sideboard in the sitting room of her suite had been well stocked with all the drinks she liked, both hard and soft, and the silver ice bucket was filled with fresh ice and an unopened bottle of champagne. After all her clothes had been pressed she began the task of polishing her hundred or more pairs of shoes. At the end of her first three months her position had not only been confirmed and her salary increased beyond what had first been promised, but her life had become intergrated into Stephanie's. And she loved every moment of it. This was now her life's work. She even began to develop an extra sense that enabled her to know what Stephanie would want to change into when she arrived home and, once she became privy to her business diary which was kept in Stephanie's soft crocodile briefcase, she found it easy to anticipate what she would need to wear at work the following day. Put simply, like the diamonds her mistress always wore, she too was a gem.

On that first evening when Stephanie came home on the arm of Anton, Sophie had been alerted that she had entered the

estate and was downstairs ready to welcome and curtsy her
arrival. She might smile her pleasure, but never spoke unless
her mistress spoke first. She sensed she would probably want
to wear a dinner gown now that she had a guest and had a
choice of three waiting for her approval. For once, however,
she was wrong. Stephanie had already decided to wear the gown
and all the jewellery she had put on in her loneliness after her
first meeting with the man she intended to marry.

'Run me a bath,' she ordered as she wanted to feel fresh for
what lay ahead.

She began to think ahead to the luncheon she was to host
which was just one part of the changes she would introduce
even before she held the presidency. And it would all be so
much easier now that Anton had asked her to marry him, and
she had said yes. No one, not even her mother, would be allowed
to interfere with her achieving her birthright.

She talked softly, as though she did not wish anyone to hear
even though there were just the two of them in their bedroom.
'I am going to try so hard to make sure my wealth never comes
between us. You have asked me to marry you, and I have told
you I want nothing more in my private life. Nothing and no
one is ever going to stop me becoming your wife. From now
onwards we will share everything. And sharing does not have
to mean fifty-fifty. If one person contributes one per cent and
the other the remaining ninety-nine per cent, it is still sharing.
All you have to do is to think of yourself as the heir to sharing
my good fortune. I only want my money to make it easier for
you to adapt to the life we are going to share.'

Watching her staff stand up as she walked through her outer
office she thought, 'Thank goodness Anton is no longer part of
their world.' The gap was there and could not be denied or crossed.
She sincerely believed it was the way the world had been made. A
handful had to rule and take the decisions that could bring both
riches and progress, while the rest were fated to walk the routes
that others decided. The fact that the coat she was wearing cost
more than many of them would earn in two, three or more years
did not cross her mind. *Plus c'est la même chose.*

With Anton now sharing her office, she was convinced it
would only be a matter of time before he could take over many
of her responsibilities. He was on his way to sharing her burdens

and duties. She told him, 'You have climbed the first rungs of the ladder to where you are going to end up. From now onwards I shall have our lunch sent in here from the director's kitchen, and when today is done I shall drive you to your new home to meet my parents. I know it is not going to be easy for you, but with me by your side, and holding your hand, everything will happen as I intend. Trust me. From now onwards we belong to each other.'

She and Anton deliberately left a little earlier than usual and, equally deliberately, she gave him a peck on his cheek so that everyone in her outer office would know where her love and riches had landed. And before the night was out, so would her parents.

Half an hour later she drove through the gates of the family estate to her expected welcome. The door of the Mercedes was opened while Sophie gave them both a curtsy. Anton was still mesmerised by the magnificence that was Stephanie's home and which she had taken for granted for as long as she could remember. If possible he was now more impressed by the impeccable carvings and decorations on the English oak walls, and as he lowered his eyes, he felt fascination for the highly polished parquet floor with its rare Persian carpets.

Stephanie's parents were waiting for them in the family lounge where Stephanie blatantly announced, 'This is Anton Leopardis, the man I am going to marry. Please make him welcome and give us your blessing.'

Her father got up and kissed her and explained to Anton: 'This is a complete surprise to Stephanie's mother and myself. But I like to believe that anyone who can please my daughter is likely to be someone special. Have you bewitched her?'

'On the contrary, sir, it is she who has bewitched me.'

Christiana sat impassively staring at Anton and thinking what rudeness on his part to imagine he would ever be permitted to marry her daughter, but then revealed the strength of her position as she announced, 'I shall not give my blessing until I am quite certain that this is not the whim of a multi-million dollar heiress. I can well understand why you want to marry my daughter; she has everything while you have nothing, and perhaps less than that.' She was being deliberately rude and vindictive so that he would know from the outset that he had no place in their family. 'You must be brought to understand that anyone who marries my daughter will be her inferior when it comes to money, and everything else.'

Stephanie's answer was to kiss Anton on his lips and tell her parents: 'I know this is a surprise for you both. Anton and I were going to have dinner together in my suite, but why don't the four of us have dinner together so we can get to know one another better, and become used to being a larger family. Give me half an hour to change and then let's celebrate with champagne.'

She raced Anton up the stairs where she found Sophie waiting for her. 'Don't worry about curtsies,' she was told. 'I have thirty minutes to get dressed for dinner with my parents, and if I am late it will be your fault. Now come with me while I choose the dinner gown to wear and then you can give it a light press and pick out the accessories I shall need, while I take a five minute shower.' She and Anton shared the bathroom and she asked him to 'Please love me and cherish me as no one has ever done. In return, I shall spoil you. You're very special. You have a good brain; all it needs is encouraging.'

As they stepped out of the shower he kissed her breasts before she wrapped a vast towelling sheet around her nakedness. Back in her bedroom she phoned her father's valet and told him to bring one of her dad's blue ties to her suite as she had a guest who had arrived unprepared and was to dine with her parents. There was still five minutes to spare when she presented herself to Anton and asked for his approval, before joking, 'I like the tie you are wearing.' Before going downstairs to join her parents she told Sophie, 'You are not to say a word to anyone, neither the servants nor your mother that I have met the man I intend to marry. No one, except my parents, knows about Mr Leopardis except you. That's how much I trust you. Would you like to come to our wedding?'

'Oh, madame. Could I?'

'You will be our personal guest.'

Sophie was shaking as she told her mistress: 'Your secrets are mine, believe me, madame. I hope you will both be very happy.'

Sadly, it became obvious to Anton as soon as they rejoined Stephanie's parents that while her father seemed prepared to accept him as long as that was Stephanie's wish, her mother was equally determined, if not more so, to give him a hard time and oppose what her daughter had foolishly decided. Anton sensed that she did not think him good enough for Stephanie. While he was willing to accept that she had every right to feel that way until he proved her wrong, she had no right to deny him the opportunities that Stephanie had opened for him. He believed there were tens of thousands of men who were regarded as failures because no one had ever given them a chance to succeed. Women, too. And if push came to shove, Madame Stephanopolous had no rights at all. She had recently hosted a coming of age party for her daughter who was now free to make up her own mind without seeking the approval of her parents. However, because she was a loving daughter that was what she was now seeking. She had decided to be open and honest in telling them her feelings for him. As far as he was concerned only Stephanie could reject him, and by the way she was now squeezing his hand, he was certain that was not, and would never be, her intention. Surely her parents could see the esteem in which Stephanie held him, and why he was the man she intended to marry. Her mother might think that Stephanie was too young to know her own mind, or had been taken in by his manliness, and that he in turn had been seduced by her beauty, brains and wealth, especially the latter. That might be partly true, but equally was there a man anywhere who would not feel powerless to resist her combination of everything that was desirable? It was she who had enticed him into her web of golden silk. Now he had no desire to escape, and nor would she permit it.

When her mother confirmed his worst fears by openly stating that she did not think he was the person who could make her daughter happy, and would do everything possible to convince Stephanie that she was making a mistake, Anton was denied any chance to respond to the vitriolic outburst against him, because Stephanie decided it was her duty to defend not only him, but herself, from her mother's onslaught.

Stephanie released his hand and moved across to where her mother was seated on the deep high-backed satin covered chair she regarded as a kind of throne before which she should be paid homage, and told her, 'You have no right to say the things you have just uttered. You were talking of your future son-in-law. I am sure Anton must feel hurt and unwanted. Well, I want him and whether you, or anyone else, objects, I intend to marry him and will be proud to be his wife. I shall never allow anyone, not even my own parents, to humiliate the man I love. He has asked me to marry him, and I have accepted. I shall not put up with the open hostility you have expressed. You have the power to impose your authority on most people, but I, and now Anton, are not among them. I will make my own decisions and no one can stop me, not even my mother. So let me warn you that if you continue to talk to your future son-in-law – and that is what Anton will soon be whether you like it or not – with such venom as you have expressed, and continue with your refusal to accept him into our family, we shall simply fly off and marry without your blessing. What I do with my own life is for me to decide, not you. I regard your present attitude as a declaration of war not on Anton, but against me. Understand once and for all, that you cannot have me as your daughter without Anton as your son-in-law.

'I have inherited a little of your brutality towards those who oppose me, and you will find that your daughter has the strength, power and will to challenge even her mother if she continues her current viciousness. Despite all I have said, it is still my wish for all four of us to become a family which will provide new strength to Stephanopolous International. Another hope, which you have dashed this evening, is that when I came of age you would no longer regard me as a young girl, but your equal, a kind of younger version of yourself. What really hurts you is that I have not consulted you, but made my own decision. If you persist in your present attitude I shall fight you with the man I love by my side, and we shall throw your unjustified cruelty towards him back in your face. Just remember it is you who have thrown down the gauntlet, but it is I who will pick it up if you force me. I don't want to say any more as I still hope to receive your blessing for the lifetime of happiness I expect to enjoy with the man I love. All that is up for discussion is when the wedding will take place. If we don't reach agreement on that simple matter we shall simply make our own arrangements. If you want to have any say in this or any other matter that involves Anton and myself, you need to begin thinking hard about your future relationship with your daughter.'

She turned and went back to Anton and kissed him passionately. Turning to her father she told him that now that he had seen the love, respect and admiration she had for the man with whom she was now engaged, she hoped she could count upon him to give them his personal blessing, adding, 'Please don't come between me and the future I have decided for myself.'

Before her father could answer, Anton intruded into the battle of words which was raging around him. In his opinion, he hoped that one day the words that had been spoken would be consigned and forgotten as a kind of momentary hysteria. He felt it was time to make his own position clear, so that no one could be left in any doubt about his feelings towards their daughter.

'Forgive me, sir, for speaking just as you were about to answer your daughter, but I hope that what I am about to say will be acceptable to you and be welcomed by Madame Stephanopolous who, believe me, I still hope will one day allow me to call her mother, and one day, perhaps, even Christiana. She is fully entitled to have the reservations she has expressed, but it is my intention to show her by example that her first judgment was neither fair nor accurate. I love your daughter and will do everything in my power to make her happy. In addition, I intend not only to show how passionate I am about her, but to play a part in her plans to expand the reputation and profitability of Stephanopolous International, even before I am her husband. I already have your daughter's trust and shall be by her side in everything she undertakes from now onwards. Please, let us all forget everything that has been said this evening and accept, in our different ways, that a new era is dawning, and that you are not just gaining a son-in-law, but a man who will be proud to be a member of the Stephanopolous family. Let me make a promise. I hope that when Stephanie and I are married she will accept my suggestion that she becomes known, not as Madame Leopardis, but as Stephanie Stephanopolous Leopardis.'

'I would like that very much,' she told him. 'Thank you, Anton. You could not have given me a nicer wedding present.'

Although her mother remained silent, her father told Anton, 'That is a very generous gesture and I for one want to thank you for going such a long way towards convincing me that my daughter may be making a wise choice which could be to the benefit of us all. Now I suggest that we all agree to make no further comments this evening on what is a very touchy matter, and one that will only be resolved when we have all had time to think on it and avoid any hasty conclusions. Instead, let's adjourn and try to enjoy a family dinner which could easily become a regular happening, and not just a one-off occasion.'

Anton left Stephanie's side and walked over to where Madame Stephanopolous was seated. 'May I kiss you, please?' he asked. Instead of denying what she might have regarded as an insulting request, she offered him her jewelled hand, and he kissed it gently.

The waiters and waitresses who were waiting patiently in the family dining-room drew out the chairs and were surprised when the head of the household directed them to seat Anton at the end of the table opposite him with the two ladies on either side and facing one another. For several minutes there was silence while the first of two bottles of the family's favourite Chambertin was poured. The meal began with another of the family's favourite dishes, especially when the temperature began to fall, rich hot vegetable soup and just before the main course of Chateaubriand steaks was brought to the table, each hidden under its own domed silver cover which were opened in unison at a nod from Madame Stephanopolous, her husband raised his glass of the deep red nectar and proposed a toast 'to the family, old and new'. Whether reluctantly, or because it was becoming obvious that her hostility to what her daughter had decided was not achieving its aim, Stephanie's mother drank to the toast and looking at Anton told him, 'Let's see how things work out,' and gave him a smile which everyone accepted as, if not the end of hostilities, at least the calling of a truce. Stephanie got up from her chair, walked round the table and kissed her mother's cheek and assured her, 'I love you, mother, but I also love Anton. Thanks for being so understanding. How about forgetting the business for one day and going shopping together tomorrow. I want to buy a thank-you present for yourself and another for dad, and then something for Anton. After we've had lunch together I shall go to the office, collect Anton and together we shall buy my engagement ring.'

It was hard to tell whether she was seeking to provoke her mother, or was simply overflowing with happiness now that a thaw appeared to have set in. Christiana Stephanopolous, however, was thinking back to a very similar, yet in her view, very different, situation that had arisen twenty years earlier when in the space of a few days her life had been turned from being nothing more than another attractive, strong-willed, Australian eighteen-year-old, to becoming the wife of one of the wealthiest tycoons in the world; overnight the cost of anything she wanted became unimportant. Her wedding present from her husband was his ocean going yacht on which they had been married. At home in the family's mansion home and estate outside Athens, where they now were, her youthful intolerance saw nearly half the staff being dismissed within two months of her arrival, either because they were too old or because, in her opinion, they resented taking orders from an eighteen-year-old. Year by year, she took control of more of the industrial colossus her husband had built into its present dominating global position. Her husband could not deny her anything. She taught Stephanie to treat all their staff as servants, explaining 'that is all they are'.

All these thoughts were racing round Christiana's mind as she wondered whether Stephanie, now that she was independent and fabulously wealthy, was using her freedom to make a major mistake which she would regret later by marrying someone like Anton who was at the bottom of any ladder from which she could choose her husband. It had to be opposed.

As mother and daughter shopped together the following morning, Christiana wore her favourite sables while Stephanie luxuriated in the tantalising warmth of one of her two gifted full-length mink coats. They were driven to a succession of exclusive and expensive boutiques and jewellers in one of their Rolls. 'Do you realise how lucky you are?' Christiana asked her daughter.

'If you mean the money I am spending, the answer is no. It was mine from the moment I was born. But if you mean Anton, then yes, I do know how lucky I have been to fall in love when so young with the man I intend to stay with for the rest of my life. Like you have groomed me, I shall teach him, but in my own way, not yours.'

'But surely you understand that even if you find the happiness you seek, you will always rule him because of your wealth and position within the corporation of which, by comparison, he will be but a small part. It cannot be any other way. Money talks. In time he will begin to resent always having to play consort to your empress. What can he ever give you that you cannot buy for yourself?'

Stephanie retorted, 'I am starting to wonder whether you ever really loved me, or was I just a tool that would one day turn the engine of our industrial empire? Perhaps I have never known real love until now. I don't say this unkindly. After all, look how you have behaved towards Daddy almost from the day you were married. You took over his life and made it impossible for him to deny you anything. I am not blaming you. Put in that position, I might have behaved in exactly the same way. But my situation is different. I intend to share everything with Anton as soon as he makes me his wife. And I have told him so. We shall be equals. Once we are married my bank accounts will be in both our names. He won't have to depend upon me for anything.'

'Please be sensible, Stephanie. That is not the way to handle your money. At least wait until you have been married for three or four years before taking such a drastic step. Men, just as much as women, are acquisitive and selfish. Please make sure that he never forgets that everything he has is solely due to you. And don't you forget that in life there can only be one top dog. It is you who must sit on the throne of all you possess and inherit. He can never be more than your loving consort. He can never take decisions. That will always be your responsibility. Accept this and I shall be content, if not happy.'

With those words she succeeded in raising the first doubts in Stephanie's mind. 'Thank you for your advice. I cannot promise to take it, but I am grateful for your warning.' She only half meant what she was saying. She might delay for several months the opening of her first joint banking accounts with Anton, but she was also having her first doubts whether she should ever pass over to him joint ownership of all the vast sums she was due to inherit over the next seven years. He might have to be content with sharing only a small part of her millions. After all, men as well as women, had roving eyes, and her riches could be a near-irresistible magnet. She was not having any second thoughts about marrying Anton, simply remembering the mammoth difference between her enormous wealth and his lack of anything. It might be sensible to draw up a legal document making it impossible for him to make any legal claim to any of her wealth, except an agreed and legally recognised sum. Her mother had made her realise that a woman in her privileged position had to protect not only herself, but any children she might have. What she really wanted was to make it near impossible for him ever to escape her golden web, or ever want to.

Which was why at the end of her shopping expedition and lunch with her mother, she ordered the Rolls to drop her at their corporation's headquarters, but instead of going to her own office where Anton would be waiting, she headed straight to the out-of-bounds top floor where her father had his suite of offices.

'Daddy, I have just come from lunch and shopping with mother, and she has indicated that while not ecstatic about my marriage, there will be no further objections. Now it is your turn to give me your blessing for my marriage. Tell me, who earns the highest salary after what the three of us are able to draw annually?'

He did not know, but buzzed his own senior secretary to bring him the file he required. After studying it he told his daughter: 'Last year, with bonuses, our International Shipping Manager, who is responsible for all sales of our tankers and container ships, took home more than a hundred and seventy thousand dollars. Why do you want to know?'

'Daddy, you are either getting old, or you are playing games with me. I am not prepared for the man who will soon be my husband, and your son-in-law, to remain on his present, miserable wage. I intend to promote him to the position of Deputy Director of Personnel at a salary of fifty thousand dollars which I want you to authorise. In due course he will take over my present position and then we can decide what his salary should be. At the same I shall start to devote more of my time to helping you run our family empire. Will you do that for me?'

'Of course, darling But I have something more important to tell you. Sometime in the not too distant future I intend to hand over to you my reins of power. But not until I believe you are ready, perhaps when you are twenty-five, perhaps younger. When that day dawns I shall pass to my daughter the position of president of the world's largest privately owned global corporation. Your mother may not like it, so I prefer that what I am saying remains, for the moment, between the two of us. Meanwhile I shall authorise my secretaries to show you any confidential files that you ask to see. Learn as much as you can, but don't rush. Digest and try to remember everything, including any special arrangements I have agreed with some of our associates in the Middle and Far East and Asia. Such generosity has helped us become the huge global empire that within a few years will be yours. You must honour all my agreements and, in time, make similar arrangements yourself. To quote a military analogy, I want to see you move up the ranks from being the equivalent of a captain or major, which is where you are now, until you have the knowledge and experience that I shall regard as comparable with the rank of general, perhaps even a field marshal. By the time you move into this office everyone will be aware who you are, what you stand for, and how ruthless you can be when you believe your actions are in the best interests of our corporation.'

He buzzed for his senior secretary and PA. 'I want you to take a memo and send it to Accounts. "This is to authorise the appointment of Mr Anton Leopardis as Deputy Director of Personnel under Madame Stephanie Stephanopolous the current director, at an initial annual salary of fifty thousand dollars. The appointment to become effective at the beginning of the month following receipt of this instruction." Sign it for me.' He went on: 'I also want you to make available to my daughter any confidential file she asks to see. I want her to know as much about the corporation as I do. But none of the files are to be removed from this office.'

Left alone he explained to Stephanie that for the first couple of years he would like her to concentrate upon two divisions. 'The most important is shipping where our biggest profits are made and, probably, always will be. I will arrange a meeting between the two of us and Carl Ellungsen who has served this company so well in arranging record orders both for our tankers and our growing fleet of container ships. I want the two of you to work closely together, but for the moment learn from him, and try not to interfere. That should not be on your agenda until you assume the presidency. Sometime before then, I shall pension off my brother and you will be appointed the director of our shipping division. This reminds me, while you are still Director of Personnel I would like you to find a job for your cousin Dimitrios. I appreciate that he may not be the brightest of young men, but he is family and deserves consideration.'

Stephanie interrupted: 'I will do as you ask, but I shall not hesitate to dismiss him if he does not measure up to what I demand. And, let me add, I would do the same to Anton if I had any doubts about whether he would make an efficient Director of Personnel, although I am sure he will. Perhaps I will offer Dimitrios an overseas position, and if he refuses then we shall both have tried our best to be helpful.' Her father assured her that whatever she decided would have his full backing.

'The other area where I want you to take an ever-increasing interest is in Asia where we currently have three very profitable shoe-making factories making low quality, but well designed, shoes which are selling well in eastern Europe and the USSR as well as China and much of South America. One plant is in China and the other two elsewhere in Asia. China runs itself because it is under the rigorous control of the Communist government which receives one third of our net profits. In return the several hundred women who work at the modern machines we have installed, work twelve-hour shifts with twenty-four hours off. They are all paid a basic wage with bonuses when they exceed their daily quotas. We run the plant, but the workers are controlled by the local Communist party which guarantees no strikes; production is continuous throughout the year. It is similar at the other two factories in Asia where the minister for trade is paid a bonus based upon the level of production we stipulate. All who work at the two plants are controlled by a local trade unionist who literally has the power of life and death over our five hundred workers. He is well paid by us, and always in dollars, to look after himself as well as the best interests of our corporation. In return it is his job to ensure that productivity matches the levels achieved in China where everyone is brought up to obey every order given by the local representatives of the Communist government in Beijing. Three years ago they fell far behind their rivals and I decided to shut down one of the two factories with the loss of three hundred jobs, but gave an assurance to the trade unionist that he would continue to receive his usual payments. A year later I installed new, modern equipment and reopened the shutdown plant, but with only half the work force getting their jobs back. Today, because productivity is higher thanks to the new machinery, those at work take home more than they earned earlier. And our profits are now at record levels. Under you, I am sure they will rise still higher. I think you should meet our trade union friend when you are ready. Let me know when you intend to go and I will cable details of your arrival. Finally, we have two plants in China close to Shanghai; one makes lengths of cotton which are made into dresses, while the other manufactures equivalent garments, including blouses, in silk. All sell well in China and throughout South America. There is room, I think, for expansion into the Balkans and eastern Europe, but that I shall leave you to decide.

'Never forget that capitalism is a cauldron of competiveness. For every Stephanopolous International there are thousands of little known businesses which are scalded when times get tough, and never recover from their burns. They have sweated in vain, and sometimes we sweep what remains into our net and begin selling to their one-time customers. At the level at which we operate there are only a handful around the world which provide any realistic competition in all the industries where we operate. Occasionally there are mergers, but that word is a fiction. At the end of the day only one of the two firms can be in charge. Happily when we are involved it is always ourselves. There is a never-ending cycle of boom and bust, when the years of plenty are followed by years of recession. Both are inevitable. You cannot go on producing without finally over-producing. That is when markets collapse. Thousands are laid off, others are forced to work a shorter week, for less wages. At the other end of the scale others, like ourselves, continue to thrive, although with lower profits for a few years. As the recession bites deeper, companies are forced to accept our bargain basement prices for their business. When you sit in this presidential chair it will be your responsibility to anticipate the recession before it happens and take steps to cushion us from its worst effects. Seek advice by all means, but the final decisions have to be yours. Business is brutal, and big business is a jungle where only the ruthless survive.

'From now onwards I suggest we both have an all-day meeting together every two weeks, say on alternate Fridays, so that you are kept constantly abreast of what is happening in our worlds of shipping, fashion, banking, hotels, as well as shoes and textiles, and wherever else you think there are new opportunities. Think of the millions we have in reserve as like the fire power of an army. Few can resist us if we decide to go to war.'

He ended their meeting by telling his daughter, 'Between the two of us, I think you may be making a wise choice in the man you intend to marry. Keep an eye on his business potential, and so shall I. So far he impresses me.'

A week later she hosted the luncheon in her own office that she had twice postponed, and to which she invited Anton, of course, plus Sonia Vrettos, Roberto Pinakoulakis and Helena Konstantinides.

A waiter from the director's kitchen handed round a glass of a light sparkling wine that tasted like a good, but not great, champagne, cost two thirds less than the overpriced original. As Stephanie told Anton, 'they won't know the difference.'

When they sat down to lunch Stephanie explained, 'I have almost completed the clearing out of those members of staff who were deadwood and surplus to our requirements, including the aptly named Mr Surplus. Currently there are two vacancies for a head of department with a third likely within a few months. Mr Leopardis has already been appointed, with the approval of the president, to be my Deputy Director of Personnel. If not tomorrow, there is a strong likelihood that I shall appoint Roberto to head up the marketing department, although it is likely that what is now called Marketing and Advertising will be broken up into publicity, which will include Publicity, Public Relations and Promotions, and Advertising and Marketing. If that means an extra department I shall supervise its staff levels, and unless Roberto has any suggestions as to who might head up advertising, we shall advertise the vacancy. As for the oldest among us, Sonia Vrettos, she is likely to be appointed head of the Administration Department whose previous head I sacked for incompetence. Sonia has struck me as an enthusiast for whatever she undertakes, and also for the corporation as a whole, but is also very intolerant of any signs of slackness or inefficiency. Finally, Helena. She is the youngest of my guests, but with a great deal of potential. She is not afraid to speak her mind, and there are not many who dare do that to my face. I intend to recruit her as Assistant Director of Personnel with opportunities for further promotion. Let's eat while we talk. As I have ordered steaks I suggest we drink a Beaujolais.'

Roberto agreed with Mlle Stephanopolous's idea for the break up of the Marketing Department, but with her permission he would prefer to discuss in private his views on who should stay, who should be replaced and who might be a good choice to take responsibility for Marketing and Advertising. He also had some ideas for future Public Relations.

'Have a word with Dolores on your way out and find when I have a spare hour sometime during the next two or three days.'

Sonia next informed her host that she had been recruited into Administration for a few months a year ago, and long before Mlle Stephanopolous began her clear out. 'It was clear to me at the time that there were far too many with too little work. Within a month of being appointed I shall inform you whether the situation is the same, or has improved thanks to your recent pruning.'

'Just remember, Sonia, I am not yet giving you the right to hire and fire without first discussing with me and receiving my permission.'

Helena had nothing to say except to thank Mlle Stephanopolous for keeping her promise. 'I shall not let you down.'

Before she brought the luncheon to a close Stephanie, as always, had the last word: 'Let me make it clear that no final decisions have been made around this table. The various promotions will be confirmed to you in writing when I have made my final decision, but until there is an official announcement say nothing to anyone. Good afternoon.'

Dolores arranged her hour-long meeting with Roberto for three the following afternoon. Anton remained with her when he arrived. As at the lunch Roberto had dressed neatly and in a way that would not be out of place wherever he went, including if it meant accompanying Stephanie to a meeting where publicity and a promotion would be on the agenda. She invited him to explain what he had in mind.

'For the past two years, Mlle Stephanopolous, I have been employed in the corporation's publicity department drafting press releases highlighting profits, sales, acquisitions and senior appointments. I had learned how to write good editorial copy when at the age of seventeen I was offered a job on a small weekly newspaper. Since then I have tried to use everything I was taught for the benefit of your family's business. But I believe there is far more to be done. However, when I made suggestions to the head of my department, I was warned not to rock the boat. I for one was not sorry when you decided to do just that and your purges cut a swathe through the total number employed in the Advertising Department. Some spent too much time polishing their nails and combing their hair, or ringing boyfriends instead of concentrating on their typewriters. I don't suppose you enjoyed what you did, but many throughout the building supported your decisions.'

Stephanie raised her hand as a signal for him to stop. 'I can assure you that sacking men and women who were cheating me and the best interests of my family, gave me a great deal of pleasure. And it will happen again in the future, believe me. Now tell me what you would do if you were the permanent head of our Advertising, Marketing and Publicity department.'

Roberto was determined to take full advantage of the opportunity to speak his mind and thoughts. 'As a former journalist I believe we have wasted many opportunities to let the world know of our successes, for example the growth of your fleets of tankers and container ships, as well as our leadership in the world of luxury hotels and the way you have achieved a position close to dominance in the world's popularly priced shoe market. And the best way to achieve this has not been recognised. Yet it has worldwide possibilities. And you are the key. Your rise to fame and recognition as possibly the youngest woman in the world to sit on the board of a global corporation is a worldwide story. Women are news, especially when they are wealthy and photogenic. And if she dresses like a dream we have someone who will make headlines for Stephanopolous International. And if we include your mother and the countess we almost have a global empire run by women. And that is news, too.'

With natural femininity and a surfeit of confidence in her own ability, Stephanie enjoyed what she was hearing, yet was annoyed that it had not been recognised earlier, although she could take the credit for discovering Roberto. What he might lack in top level experience, he made up with enthusiasm, and her support. She was no snake on the ground. On the contrary she not only walked tall, but like a female mother elephant she would crush anyone who stood in her way. 'Have you anything more you wished to tell me?'

'I think it must be left to you to decide whether to set up a separate Advertising and Marketing department, or employ an outside agency, perhaps two agencies with one responsible for corporate affairs and shipping and the other concentrating on the sales of our products. What needs to be remembered is that we are involved with such a wide range of goods that the kind of advertising required to convince senior executives of the need for new tankers and container ships is quite different from selling popularly priced women's shoes. With the former we would be targeting a few thousand chief executive officers or corporate chairmen, but with shoes we are seeking the attention of a potential audience of millions.'

'Thank you, Roberto. You have given me much to think about. Carry on as the head of your department until I have made up my mind how best to use your talent.'

17

An hour later she was driving home in her sleek silver two-seater Mercedes with Anton by her side when she ended the silence by suggesting: 'Having listened to Roberto we both have some serious thinking ahead of us. It is obvious that the future look of the corporation will be very different from what it is today, while I begin to steer it towards what I want it to be when I finally take over from my father. Start thinking with me, darling. Together we can be a very formidable team. Please kiss me.' She had meant on her lips, but she had to be content with his lips landing on her gloved hand. She was driving.

Twenty minutes later they were home and Anton was still impressed by the Persian carpets and their hand-crafted designs that were as unique as they were perfect. All that concerned Stephanie was to scamper up to her suite and enjoy the new wonderland that belonged to her and Anton. Until a few days ago she had only Sophie to pamper her and react to her every whim. Now there was a man who excited her and gave her something that was even more remarkable than the pear-shaped and square diamonds that decorated her fingers. She pouted her lips and her eyes sparkled with words she did not need to speak, but suggested that she was more important and desirable than what he had since admired, while he was handsome in a way that fascinated her. His physiognomy was compelling and his grey-blue eyes indicated both softness and resolution. She was convinced he would be a shrewd business colleague. Her only doubt was whether he could be as ruthless as she had been brought up to be. But one of them was probably sufficient.

They bounded up the stairs to her suite where Sophie was standing by the open door just in case her mistress suddenly had second thoughts and needed her. She curtsied again, and once more to Anton and then disappeared as it became obvious she was not required. Stephanie fell into Anton's arms and her hands felt for the zip of his trousers and touched the rock

233

hardness of his manhood. 'Darling, your future is in my hands.' And smiled at her own rather bad joke, but forgave herself because at that moment she was a woman in love, and the heiress who within a few years would control the livelihood of thousands of men and women she would never meet or know, but whose decisions might decide whether they worked or starved. Nearer home hundreds of men and women twice her age, were powerless when in her presence. Yet with Anton she was the one who pleaded for him to quench her thirst with his own juice.

His trousers fell to the floor, and she fell onto her knees and took what she wanted more than anything in the world into her mouth and caressed it with her tongue while allowing her lipstick to leave its mark of love. To him her skin seemed to glow like sunshine reflecting itself on the white marble of ancient Greece as she reacted to his touch and gave herself to him. Soon she drifted into a slumber of contentment while he stayed in a sea of warm delight inside her. Later when they were both content to be lying together she suggested: 'Why don't we drive to Sunion and play at being ordinary tourists watching the sun set on a Greece that was once god-like and still today captivates the modern world?'

It turned out not to be her finest idea. With Sophie's help she chose a pair of white shorts, white socks and tennis shoes and a short-sleeved silk shirt plus a pink cashmere sweater. She decided to carry her white mink jacket as it might be cool by the sea when the sun was extinguished. Sophie was told to put clean sheets on the bed ready for when they returned and to tell cook she would need dinner for two in her suite. An extra splash of her favourite perfume and she was ready for the drive to one of the highlights of any visit to Athens. Yet she found herself hurrying because she was already thinking of the pleasure to be enjoyed when they were back in bed.

Sunion was crowded with coaches and cars, but she parked where it said 'No parking'. 'Don't worry,' she told Anton, 'I have displayed my personal gold card and no one will dispute where I have left my car. Money, as you have still to find out, has many privileges.' They walked hand in hand through the crowds; some standing, others just waiting for nature's nightly and wondrous natural performance. In the twilight no one

234

seemed to recognise her, although several looked with admiration, and surprise, that someone so young, albeit beautiful, could be carrying such a magnificent white fur over her arm. They sat on the ground and she cuddled close to him as the marble columns became a kaleidescope of changing colours.

A moment later it all turned sour. She had hardly finished telling of some of the magnificent presents she had been given at her coming-out birthday party when she began to feel cold and slipped into her white fur jacket as the cicadas played a lively serenade in the nearby pines. Nearby a woman now recognised her and seemed to shout, 'Look who's here! That's the rich bitch who has just inherited millions!' Stephanie urged Anton, 'Let's go home before someone else recognises me, and that will spoil a wonderful evening.' But the news had spread. Someone shouted, 'Why don't we grab her fur? She won't miss it.' But Anton put his arms round her shoulders for protection and told her, 'Get in the car. I will drive us home.' Even as they drove away someone gave vent to their spleen by banging on the rear of the car, and Anton could only hope she had not heard the words they shouted.

Arriving home she handed Sophie her fur to take upstairs while they went into the family drawing room where they poured themselves goblets of fine cognac with an added touch of water to develop the flavour. They touched glasses and drank 'To us' and sat down and created their own warmth until the cognac began to travel through their bodies and bring a glow back to Stephanie's cheeks: 'I am sorry darling, but you will have to get used to people, men as well as women, staring at me. Between the two of us, I actually enjoy it, but not at such close quarters What woman does not like to be admired, although in my case it is mostly envy.'

Anton assured her he would always protect her from anyone's unwanted attention. 'For your information, I was a pretty good boxer at school and college, and from now onwards if anyone should touch, or seek to assault you, they will end with a broken jaw.'

'Thank you. I knew you would, even before you told me. You are almost a member of the Stephanopolous clan who will have my love, as well as the comforts I can provide. You have to admit there is much to be said for being able to buy whatever you want, rather than being forced to stare through a shop window before walking away.' And then added: 'Don't forget, I inherited all my money without having to work for it. Now the same thing is happening to you. That surely makes us equals?'

Upstairs Sophie was dutifully waiting for her mistress happy in her own privilege of being able to live surrounded by such luxuries, even though none of it would ever be hers. Stephanie instructed her to phone cook and tell her Mlle Stephanie was ready to be served dinner, and disappeared into the bathroom, threw off everything she had been wearing and Sophie was ready to help her slip into her black frilly underwear that she could not remember ever seeing her wear, plus a near see-through silk nightgown, before being despatched back to her own room again. Shortly afterwards her place was taken by two waiters who laid out two place settings and two halves of grapefruit which had been cut into perfect segments. Stephanie informed them that after they had poured the wine they could leave and she would serve the rest of the meal, adding they were not to be disturbed. Stephanie was increasingly happy that Anton had discovered her hidden femininity and, when they were alone she could throw off her imperious cloak and be her true self. Secretly she enjoyed both halves equally. She could tantalise by showing what could be seen, but not touched, while later revealing all, but only to one man. While at business she achieved the same effect by wearing a different business suits with matching high-heeled shoes, and her diamonds that created a look of imperious, but natural, insolence. Supremacy had been inbred into her as a child, but was forgotten when she was at home and alone with Anton.

Their meal finished, she threw off her robe and revealed her black frilly tantalisers, and quipped, 'At times like this I remember the saying of the American columnist, Dorothy Parker, that brevity is the soul of lingerie.' As she revealed still more of her provocation, Anton nipped her neck, kissed her tummy and stroked her navel. They were at the beginning of a long night of luxurious pleasure. Both were glad, but said nothing, while Sophie with her growing intuition let them lie in until eight o'clock before bringing their breakfast. It was only when she drew back the curtain to allow in the sunlight that either moved. 'Good morning, madame, Sir. I hope you did not mind me

236

letting you have a lie in?' It was after ten before they arrived at the office.

Even though she had not said a word to Anton, her first task was to dial the number that connected her directly with her father. 'Dad, it's Stephanie. Could I bring Anton up to see you? It won't take longer than ten minutes.' She turned to Anton. 'Dad will see us now, but will throw us out in ten minutes as he has an even more important meeting in fifteen.'

They swept through her outer office and hardly gave anyone a chance to stand before they disappeared into a lift that took them to the ground floor where they transferred to an elevator that whisked them only to the top three floors. Now even her father's secretaries stood up as she arrived and were told she had an appointment with her father. Stephanie had decided, and again she had not told Anton, that she wanted her dad to explain what had been agreed for both herself and Anton.

Ulysses Stephanopolous asked them both to sit down, but he directed all his attention on his future son-in-law. 'Anton, I can sum up quickly what Stephanie and I have agreed. I want you to know there will be no opposition from me to your marriage providing Stephanie does not change her mind. If she does, and I don't think she will, we will face that hurdle when we come to it. Assuming nothing changes, Stephanie has agreed that with effect from the first of next month your salary will be increased tenfold in accordance with your new position as Deputy Director of Personnel. I am sure you will be worth it, but I need to add three words: you must be. And that leads directly to Stephanie herself. I believe she is the lady who has what it takes to move into my chair not later than seven years from now, and perhaps sooner. That is why I would like you to be ready and able to step into her shoes as Director of Personnel within six months, and certainly in not more than nine months. She will decide when you are ready, and then she will begin sitting side by side with me and concentrating upon every aspect of the powerful empire over which she will rule. And now I must ask you both to leave as I do not wish to keep my next visitors waiting. One thing more, Anton: Congratulations.'

Neither said a word until they were back in their office and then it was Anton who broke the silence, but instead of thanking

Stephanie for his promotion which he was sure she had made possible, he told her, 'Your father is an exceptional man. He runs this empire by never wasting a single moment. And is happy in the knowledge that his daughter is a young lady with all the qualifications that are required to take over from him when the time comes, as it surely will.'

'Assuming you are both right, that same young lady has other matters on her mind at this moment that are just as important. Us. I would like to become Mrs Leopardis on my nineteenth birthday. And, if possible, I would prefer a quiet civil wedding with just immediate family and a few friends, probably not more than thirty people. Believe me when I tell you that, with the exception of my father there is no one who matters more to me than you. Which is why I am asking whether you are happy that we should be married on my nineteenth birthday. Let's face it, for all practical purposes we are already living together as man and wife. We sleep together, you share my home, and soon you will be earning a salary that means you are no longer dependent upon me for everything. What is more, when in six or nine months time and you are ready to take over from me as the Director of Personnel, your salary will be doubled and, with one exception, you will become the highest paid member of our staff anywhere in the world. Finally, I intend to arrange for my parents to place an announcement in Greek newspapers and, perhaps, *The Times* and *Daily Telegraph* in London announcing our engagement. In a comparatively short while we shall be man and wife. I hope that is what you want, too?'

Anton could not resist making a joke and asking, 'Do I have any choice?'

'Now I know why I love you so much. You will always let me have my own way.'

She buzzed Maggie to check whether her mother was in, but she wasn't. 'Leave a message asking her to ring me.' Instead she phoned her dad and invaded his working day for the second time in an hour. She told him what she and Anton had decided for their wedding. He did not reply directly to her request, but suggested a foursome dinner the following evening. One of his secretaries would let her know where and when.

Stephanie reported the arrangement to Anton and asked: 'Will you allow me to buy my engagement ring if I promise we shall share the price?' This would mean flying to Paris. Anton agreed, knowing that whatever her gem cost, at least ninety-nine per cent of the price, probably ninety-nine-point-nine-nine per cent, Stephanie would pay, and without giving the price a second thought.

Stephanie told him that her mother would be furious when she heard about their wedding plans from her husband, but she was still prepared to bet she would join the three of them for dinner on the morrow. 'By the way, Dad has now also agreed that as soon as we are married he will at once make you the highest paid member of the company except for himself, my mother and me. From then onwards you will be part of the family.'

On the following day they knew they would have to leave early if they were to be ready to meet her parents at seven for the family foursome dinner, but Stephanie insisted there were still many questions she wanted answering about the tanker *SI 7* which would be the largest vessel of its kind in the world when launched. 'Why is it almost two weeks behind schedule? Why haven't I been sent the photographs I demanded; which seems to suggest that some people would prefer me not to know how badly behind everything is? Some heads are going to roll. I have always known that my uncle is not up to the job of supposedly being in charge of the shipping division. The quicker I can persuade my father to pension him off the happier I shall be. And that reminds me I need to talk to his son about a job. Finding a slot for him may make it easier to ease out his father.'

When she phoned Carl Ellungsen, Head of Shipping, he was not at his desk, and his secretary told her he was down at the shipyard and did not want to be disturbed by anyone. 'Well, I am not anyone. I am Mlle Stephanopolous. If I have not heard from him within the next thirty minutes, you will be sacked in the morning. You may be his secretary, but you work for me.'

She slammed down the phone. Turning to Anton she told him in a voice that was no longer shrieking, but was almost purring with a threatening kind of pleasure: 'I fear that Mr Ellungsen is getting a little big headed. He is beginning to believe that he is indispensable and we could not do without him. He obviously has not heard about the man in my life. I will introduce you both tomorrow. I want you to concentrate upon our shipping division, and learn everything that has happened, and is happening. Sometime soon, once I have persuaded my father to pension off his brother, this department that is vital for our future profits, could become our joint responsibility.'

Twenty minutes later her phone rang. It was Carl Ellungsen. 'I believe you wanted to talk to me,' he began. 'Be in my office at ten o'clock tomorrow morning.' And she put the receiver down.

They carried on working until five before driving home. As they arrived the footman handed her a note from her father. 'Your mother will be joining us for dinner. I had thought of going to a taverna, but she wants to eat at our favourite restaurant in Pireaus. I have ordered the Rolls for seven o'clock.'

She handed the typewritten note to Anton. He was smiling as he admitted: 'I always knew you were brilliant as well as beautiful, but I did not realise just how easy it is for you to foretell the future. How were you so sure?'

'Mother does not like to be kept out of anything, especially her daughter's wedding. She will meddle, but do not worry, we shall win the war, even though we let her think she has won a few battles; watch how I handle her tonight.' As she had expected, and told Anton, her mother would be wearing her ankle-length sable coat. This would be an evening when she would insist upon performing her interpretation of the Empress Catherine the Great of Russian and wear furs that were forbidden to anyone except herself and her daughters who were grand-duchesses. Stephanie and Anton were first in the hall, followed five minutes later by her parents.

There was an obvious coolness in the way her mother offered her cheek to be kissed by Stephanie and her gloved hand to be pecked by Anton, whereas her father responded to his daughter's kiss with a warm hug, and a more manly hug for Anton. Once in the back of the Rolls with the two couples sitting facing one another, Stephanie reminded everyone that this was meant to be a family celebration, and went on: 'As far as Anton and myself are concerned we withdraw anything we said to my mother when she first met my future husband, but with one condition, my mother does the same. I remain her loving daughter and I want her to be my loving mother at my wedding to Anton.' Her smile was not an indication of surrender, but was intended to indicate an end to hostilities between them all.

Her mother's reply was hard to interpret. It could have been a veiled withdrawal of the sentiments she had previously expressed, or could be an indication that her earlier demands could be amended. She told the couple, although her eyes were kept on her daughter: 'I know it would be damaging to the family if I were absent from your wedding, so all I ask is that you are married in church.'

Before she could continue, Stephanie held up her own gloved hand and uttered one word, 'Agreed', and then added, 'but I would like it to take place in our own village church adjoining the estate. We could still have our own private celebrations with family and close friends, but I would like the villagers to have their own party to celebrate our marriage as soon as possible after the wedding. It would be nice if my parents joined us, at least for part of the time.'

This brought her father into the exchange of views and ideas. 'I regard that as a splendid idea. I will be happy to pay for whatever it costs, as well as all other expenses.' It was his way of letting everyone know that his daughter's wedding to Anton now had his full blessing.

Before they reached Pireaus and the Michelin-starred restaurant, the ice had been broken. Madame Stephanopolous showed no objection when Anton took hold of her arm and together they followed Stephanie and her father, who were holding hands, into the restaurant that was nearly full, yet did not seem crowded. They were as always seated at the best table. It was secluded and away from any draughts, while providing sufficient lighting to read the menu. Their parents were seated with their backs to the wall so that Christiana could see almost everyone, as well as being able to call the waiters whenever she demanded attention. The young couple held hands. As the restaurant overlooked the waterfront, fish was its speciality. They each began with a dozen oysters which Ulysses insisted should be opened at their table. He and Christiana followed with sole off the bone while Stephanie ordered squid stuffed with herbs plus rice, and Anton chose *soupies*, which is better known as cuttlefish, with French fries. For dessert they tucked into plates of baklava and fresh fruit. The wine was two bottles of a grand cru Chablis. As expected Christiana sought to dominate the conversation and set the pace by asking Anton, 'How many of your own family would you like us to invite to the wedding. Are your parents alive?'

'Yes they are and they live in the north of the country in the shadows of Mount Athos. Of course I would like them to be invited, but I doubt if they will come. My father is an invalid and my mother stays home to look after him. If they go anywhere it is always locally.'

'That will not be a problem. We will arrange for a taxi to take them to the nearest airport. I shall arrange two return business class tickets for them, but I think it would be polite if you sent them. A car will meet them upon arrival in Athens and they can stay with us for two or three days, or as long as they like. They will never be alone while they are travelling, and will be treated like VIP guests in church, at the celebrations and throughout their stay.'

'This is most generous of you, Mother,' said Anton as he leaned across and took the hand of his future mother-in-law. 'Please don't think I am trying to pour cold water on what you have suggested, but I fear they will be overwhelmed by the hospitality you will lavish upon them.'

Madame Stephanopolous accepted his hand and even squeezed it in recognition of his forthcoming status. 'I understand your concern, but trust me; all will be well. I have faced such situations on many occasions since I married Ulysses. Even some of his family are in awe of our wealth, but endure it. Your mother will get used to us, and she and your father will love Stephanie. I shall personally take care of your parents. Everyone is beguiled by wealth, and much more so when they are Greek. They will have their own large double bedroom, but because they might be embarrassed, they won't be allocated their own personal maid, but I shall arrange for one of our friendliest members of staff to look after them, discreetly. Just let me have their address and I will write letting them know how happy Stephanie's parents are with the decision of our daughter to want to marry their son.' His reply was to blow her a kiss. In reply she pouted her lips and blew one to him.

The mood was set for the evening, and Anton understood

what Stephanie had meant when she told him that her mother would be allowed to win some battles, but they would be victorious in the war.

Stephanie went to bed happy and contented, thanks to a combination of good sense, plus a realisation that family unity had to take precedence over any personal wishes. When you were part of a family that was in the public eye, accord was essential. Neither side had been made to feel victorious, and nobody was defeated. Most important, a mother had not lost a daughter, and now openly accepted that she was gaining a son-in-law who she was beginning to like more each time they met.

It was a quite different Stephanie who woke up next morning. She had welcomed the outcome of last night's family party in Pireaus, but now her mind was taut like hard steel and ready to fight and win another battle, this time against the Swede, Carl Ellungsen. She told Anton as they drove to work: 'I shall try to be as polite as possible, but he has to understand that there will be a new regime within a few years when I assume control of Stephanopolous International. Listen carefully to everything that is said, and be prepared to join in if I ask.' As they drove slowly through the morning traffic, she thanked him for making her mother realise what a fine son-in-law she was gaining.

'Now, with you by my side, and everyone happy, I can concentrate, together with my father, upon planning the future of our empire. Somehow, before the end of another year has passed I shall find a way to secure you a place on our Board of Directors, even if it is only with one share. Perhaps you could take over the single share of my uncle once he retires. Dad will agree, and by that time Mother may find it hard to refuse anything to her one and only son-in-law.'

They were in her office fifteen minutes before their visitor was due, and he, realising he might have a difficult time ahead, arrived a few minutes earlier than requested. Stephanie, hoping to avoid conflict, did not keep him waiting, and when he was shown into her office she told her secretary she was sure Mr Ellungsen would welcome a cup of strong coffee. 'Bring in three cups and biscuits,' she ordered.

To everyone's surprise there was no clash of interests. He apologised for not sending the documents she had requested, and she accepted that it was inevitable there could be delays when building the largest vessel of its kind. What mattered was the final result. She introduced Carl to Anton and said that she wanted them to spend time together as she wanted the three of them to work as a team to ensure the continued success of the shipping division. She made no reference to her planned pensioning off of her uncle, nor her intention to take over his position as president of the shipping division with Anton as vice-president. That could wait. For the moment what mattered was that Anton and Carl developed a good working relationship. Finally, it was arranged that Anton would spend three full days at their shipyard finding out and learning as much as Carl could teach him. Stephanie simply told Carl that as she took control of more of the family empire his position was safe and secure for as far ahead as she could plan. He had nothing to fear from Anton who was simply her deputy and possible successor as the Director of Personnel. As her deputy he needed to know about every department of the corporation.

After he left, Stephanie informed her secretary that she and Mr Leopardis would be going to Paris the following Monday and she was to book the smaller of the corporation's two aircraft for their flight. She was also to reserve them a suite at the Ritz Hotel and request the head concierge to make an appointment for Madame Stephanopolous at Cartier for ten o'clock the morning after their arrival, She told Anton, as if to break the ice, that when a Stephanopolous bought diamonds they judged them by weight and cut, plus a very high refractive power. They were not the diamonds you saw in a jeweller's shop window. 'I want a diamond that will be as individual as myself and pear-shaped. You will love it nearly as much as you love me.'

Anton drove them home and on the way she asked him to remind her when they arrived at the office next day to order him his own Mercedes which would be like her own, but he could choose his own colour. He tried to suggest that she had bought him sufficient already and with one hand showed her the ruby and diamond cufflinks she had given him. She was so happy she was in a mood for jokes and asked, 'What else can you wear when you are driving a young lady in a mink coat and you are driving a unique Mercedes that is the only one of its kind?' He called her darling, and she blew him a kiss.

When they reached home Sophie was there with her curtsy, and was told to bring to their suite a bottle of her favourite vodka with tonic water, and a bottle of their best malt whisky and some water for Mr Leopardis. And a bucket of ice. They had much to celebrate.

When Sophie returned carrying all that had been ordered on a heavy silver tray it was too heavy to risk another curtsy. Stephanie did not either notice or care. She simply instructed Sophie to go to her room and wait until she was called.

As Stephanie poured the drinks she looked lovingly into Anton's eyes and added, 'I may have staff who obey my every order, but I am happy to pour drinks for the man I adore. I am like a chrysalis which can only become a beautiful butterfly if someone brings sunshine into her life with a love that is honest and sincere. This is what you have done. The love of my parents is a duty love, but yours is something far purer. Please love me again.'

At such moments she was his girl and he was her man, like a million other couples. But were they like a million other couples? The others had to live in bedsits or tiny two bedroom houses with no individuality and would never wear anything more valuable than costume jewellery, while she often went to bed still wearing diamonds sometimes worth hundreds of thousands of dollars. At home they were surrounded by staff who came running at the snap of her fingers. At the office, and around the world, she was a princess who knew that it was only a matter of time before she became an empress. Even Anton who was the love of her life, had to obey any business order she gave. How could they ever be like other couples? Neither did it matter so long as they all found happiness. She revealed, 'I have an assurgent life sign that means that I shall climb my own Everests. I want you to be my Sherpa Tensing and stand with me on the summits we shall reach together.'

He knew she had molten metal in her veins and nothing would ever stop her from reaching her goal of expanding the empire she would inherit to far beyond its present size and power. Anyone who stood in her path would be swept aside ... and he would always be there to back her every move. Not only did she have knockout looks, she could land a knockout punch too.

Stephanie looked at the clock and reminded him, 'It is now ten o'clock, and I am hungry. Shall we have some supper sent up, talk some more, and then make love again?'

As they lay in bed finalising plans for Paris where she knew she would find the gem she wanted to wear as her engagement ring for the rest of her life, she promised, 'It will be worthy of you, darling. If you agree, I would like Marianne to join us. Until I found you, she was the only person I would trust with my innermost secrets, and I am sure she will always be on our side. She and I have already started to make plans for the future, but now all my intentions will first be shared with you, despite her already being a member of our board.'

Less than a week later the three of them checked into the Ritz Hotel on the Place Vendome where Stephanie and Anton settled into a suite while the Countess von Rugerstein had a large double room on the same floor. Next morning Stephanie and Anton spent more than two hours at Cartier and the following evening the three of them dined at *Le Tour d'Argent* where they shared a perfectly prepared duck complemented by two bottles of a Château Neuf du Pape, 1955.

As the wine began to weave its magic, the countess leaned across and touched the rare blue-white, pear shaped thirty carat solitaire diamond that Stephanie had bought and was wearing for the first time. She moved her left hand so that the ring was close to Marianne's face. 'Do you like it?'

Her reply was what you could expect from a lady who was now the fourth most powerful man or woman at Stephanopolous International. 'I may not be a professional when it comes to judging diamonds, except by its price, but I would suggest this is a very serious gem. It is not a question of liking it, as appreciating it. I cannot believe there is another young lady anywhere in the world who would have the grace or confidence to wear such a ring without having two armed guards in close attendance. But you wear it with absolute ease as though it was there when you were born. How did Cartier know what you wanted?'

'They knew I was a Stephanopolous.' Stephanie told how they were escorted to a sumptuously furnished salon with thick pink curtains, but no windows. They were two or three floors down for complete security. She made it clear that she was not interested in diamonds of less than twenty-five carats. Her preference was pear-shaped, but she would consider square-cut. Having been brought up by her mother to understand fine diamonds, she was able to explain that she should only be shown diamonds with a high refractive power that would show off the gem's extraordinary brilliance. The hint was taken. Fifteen minutes later she was gazing at a tray of eight superb diamonds, four square-cut and four pear-shaped. Only three possessed the brilliance she was seeking. But she did not ask for the price of any of the threesome as she did not wish to be influenced as she had already made up her mind. She whispered to Anton her choice and he told her that had been his choice, too. It was massive and pear-shaped and had originally been worn by one of the last Russian grand duchesses and was now being sold as part of the estate of an American heiress, It weighed thirty carats. They measured her ring size and that afternoon it was delivered to her at the Ritz Hotel. She had estimated that it might cost her half a million dollars, but nearly jumped with joy when told their lowest possible price was three hundred and fifty thousand dollars. Her business instincts told her to make an offer, but decided to be content to have saved one hundred and fifty thousand dollars on what she was prepared to pay. With the sale agreed the Cartier director who had been admiring the diamonds she was wearing asked what fascinated her about diamonds when she could afford emeralds of the same weight and cut which were mostly more valuable. She replied, 'I have always been fascinated by the clearness and brightness that shines through those diamonds that have been cut by master craftsmen. When I first placed the gem I had chosen for my engagemet ring in the palm of my hand the touch was cold, yet it blazed like fire. What a combination.'

Now she looked at Marianne across the table at *Le Tour d'Argent* and explained: 'That is how I am now able to show you a mix of fire and ice that was once enjoyed by a Romanov grand duchess. Finally, I insisted on the ring being polished in diamond dust and delivered to the hotel by four o'clock, and then arranged payment.'

'You are a very lucky young lady,' the countess suggested, 'but not because of your wonderful new diamond which will outshine anything I am ever likely to see, but because you have found yourself the most wonderful man who is making everything happen that you could possibly want, deserve and desire. I am so happy for you both.'

In response, Stephanie suggested that Anton asked for their bill and they went back to their hotel and drank some more coffee and cognac in their suite where she would reveal some of her thinking for the corporation, even before she took over from her father hopefully before seven years had passed. She confirmed, 'You are my two loyal comrades as I prepare to win my future, and will be there when I become the equivalent of an empress. When that happens I shall encourage my mother to leave the board and spend her life travelling the world with my father, and looking after him. But how they spend their time will be for them to decide.'

Marianne found herself being reminded that the young lady who was talking was not only clever, but cunning, too, and had been brought up to stamp on anyone who got in her way. Her fortune was so enormous, that even in her private life she could drown people who dared make a splash in waters she regarded as her own. That morning Stephanie had shown her power and wealth, and that she was prepared to spend nearly half a million dollars on a single diamond with hardly a second thought. How many other old or young women could do that?

Back in her suite at the Ritz, Stephanie took a sip of cognac and reminded her two closest friends: 'In ten years time I shall still only be thirty, but by then Stephanopolous International will be considerably stronger than it is today, and with still more influence globally. By then I shall have given birth to a child and I shall hope to groom him or her for the position that I shall occupy shortly. To achieve my goals I have an agenda that is one hundred per cent flexible. We live in a fast-changing world. Nothing is written in tablets of stone. After all, my father took us into China; I might establish our identity in India which, after all, is the largest democracy in the world with resources that are still largely untapped. Yesterday the Greeks built glorious buildings so that their generations would be remembered. Just remember that Stephanopolous International is controlled by a family who has some link to the blood of the ancient Greeks, but we believe in permanent power.

'In my empire one fact will remain. Our core business will

248

always be centred around shipping and transportation. For starters, within the next six to twelve months I shall persuade my father to pension off his brother who is currently the near useless president of our shipping division. I shall take over from him and Anton will become its Deputy Director as well as being Director of Personnel. For the two of you there will always be positions of responsibility. That is how much trust I have in you both. By the time I occupy my father's throne, Anton should be ready to take over from me as the Director of Shipping, and one of two women on our staff at HQ may be ready to assume the role of Director of Personnel. There will be new leaders of most departments. I have made it clear to Carl Ellungsen, who has been a great success as the chief salesman of our tankers and container ships, that provided he understands that my word is law his future will be secure. Finally I can reveal, but only to the two of you, that my father anticipates that I shall be ready to take over before I am twenty-five.'

It was after Anton had refilled their glasses that she dropped her next bombshell. 'While as far ahead as I can visualise, the bulk of the world's trade will be carried out by ships of ever-increasing size, I also believe that the world will take to the skies. However, it is not my intention to create our own airline, fascinating though the prospect might be. I shall leave that risk to governments or consortiums of airlines. However my forecast is that top industrial tycoons, heads of state, and those men and women around the world who have money to burn because they are celebrities, successful sportsmen and women, heiresses like myself, and women who have married and divorced multi-millionaires and been awarded a massive slice of their wealth by the courts, will want to show off what they can now afford. All will fall out of love with flying aboard commercial airliners as they become increasingly overcrowded as well as unreliable timekeepers. Highly paid directors and senior executives who always fly First at their company's expense will begin demanding that they fly aboard their company's private aircraft in order to increase their own efficiency by avoiding delays and arriving on time for their business appointments. As a result, there will be a growing demand for private short and long haul planes that can fly non-stop to their destination and land at smaller airports far nearer to where they want to be than most international terminals. I want a Stephanopolous-owned company to be building them. It will be Anton's responsibility to identify a handful of technicians and designers as well as the companies we should have in our sights. After he has identified them, Marianne and I will conduct the negotiations. To the former we shall offer a near free hand to develop the type of private aircraft they have long dreamed about. They will be as contented as schoolboys eating ice cream. In most takeovers it is not the company, but its talent that is most important.'

After Marianne had kissed them both goodnight and left them, Stephanie indicated she was tired and wanted to have a good night's sleep. Ten minutes later she was breathing deeply and steadily. Fortunately a little went a long way with her and she could start again where she had left off hours ago. It was as though her own words had been recorded. Anton, in contrast, had the ability to be instantly wide-awake irrespective of the hour. His immediate liveliness meant they could soon be making love or talking business. The big difference was that while his thoughts were completely focused on now, hers were centred upon today, tomorrow, and the day after.

Back in her office in Athens one of her first tasks was to arrange a meeting with her father. 'Dad,' she explained, 'I have not been idle since our last meeting which set me the task of being ready to take over your responsibilities before I am twenty-five, and being handed your baton at the same time.' She quickly summarised what she had explained to Marianne and Anton, and went on: 'Our shipping, tanker and container ship interests, although not unsuccessful, are too important to be left to someone of the calibre of Uncle Boris. I want you to pension him off with seventy-five per cent of his present salary, and appoint me to take over his responsibilities. I would like the title "President, Shipping Division".'

'Do you really think you are ready for such a task? Although I accept that Boris contributes little, is that because he is not given any real responsibilities? But he is my brother and I shall protect him from the obvious venom of my own daughter. Leave it to me to inform him that sometime within the next twelve months I intend to replace him with yourself, but that he will continue to receive his present salary in the form of a pension. And don't forget I want you to find a job for his son, Demetrios and you have my permission to bully him as much as you like. Meanwhile, spend the next six months learning as much as you can about shipping and containerisation, and tell Mr Ellungsen, our highly-paid Scandinavian salesman, that I want him to be your teacher.

'Believe me, when I tell him that is what I want, it will be sufficient.'

Feeling annoyed she had not won all she wanted, she also had to listen to Anton suggesting her father was right. 'We both know you are an ambitious young lady who is determined to get her own way, and believe me, darling, it will all happen before you are twenty-five. Just make sure that whatever you plan has been prepared beforehand. I shall always be here to undertake whatever else is necessary.'

'You are probably right, but I am not in a mood to admit it.'

She told her secretary to get Carl Ellungsen on the phone, only to be told that he was out of the country on a sales mission to Turkey and Egypt. He would not be back until the following Monday. 'Tell his office that Stephanie Stephanopolous expects to see him in her office next Monday morning at nine-thirty sharp. Meanwhile get my cousin Dimitrios on the phone and tell him I want to see him at the same time tomorrow morning.'

It was now Thursday and she remained irritable for the rest of the day and was only half pleased when Anton suggested that Carl would welcome having someone stronger than her uncle as his boss. 'He'd better,' she snapped back.

She buzzed for her secretary. 'Take down this memo and tell reception I want it delivered today. "Dear Mr Ellungsen, So sorry you were out when I telephoned today as I wanted to let you know, in confidence, what is being planned for the shipping division. Please be in my office at nine-thirty next Monday morning. What I have to tell you should not take more than twenty minutes."'

Carl Ellungsen arrived punctually for his appointment, but she was still irritable at not having convinced her father that it was time to pension off his brother. Her guest was shown into her office and explained that he had been away on a not unprofitable trip for Stephanopolous International.

She at once asked: 'Tell me more about your trip.'

'In Ankara,' he informed her, 'I finalised a deal for us to build a one hundred thousand tonne container ship for the Turkish government, and I gave a promise that it would be delivered within two years, but in Cairo, although it was my third visit, the government officials continued to prevaricate over the cost of hiring for two years one of our largest tankers to transport oil from Saudi Arabia, with the option for a third year. They want a reduction of forty per cent in the third year. I assured them I would use my influence, such as it is, in Athens, to seek some kind of reduction, but made no promises. My recommendation to your father will be to offer the Egyptians a five per cent discount on the main order, plus a further ten per cent if they took up their third year option.'

'Would you like me to use my influence upstairs?' she asked.

'It could only be helpful, of that I am certain.'

'Now you can see how easy I am to work with,' Stephanie smiled. 'Will you join me for a coffee?' When he accepted he was again surprised when it was bought in on a silver tray by her secretary. 'If you take milk and sugar, please help yourself. I prefer mine black and strong,' she told him, 'and so does Mr Leopardis.'

She carried on: 'I like to think that as we get to know one another I shall find you to be the kind of expert lieutenant I shall need. Let me explain. My father and I have agreed, and what follows is in strict confidence, that within the next year I shall take over as president of our shipbuilding, tanker and containership division. My uncle is to be retired. That means that in say six to nine months, perhaps sooner, I shall become your boss. How does the idea appeal?'

'It will be a new experience, but one that I shall happily accept. Beauty, brains and confidence is a rare combination.'

'I am beginning to understand why you are such a successful salesman. I would like to accompany you on one of your forthcoming overseas sales visits, and meet some of our customers before I take over responsibility for the entire Stephanopolous empire.

'Let me go on. I want to receive on the first of each month a report of your activities during the previous four weeks, and when we next meet our discussions will be minuted by my secretary. Mr Leopardis, as my deputy, will join us. Am I making myself clear?'

He leaned forward and looked up at this vision of feminine power, and things to come, while she looked down on him from her raised desk. 'I understand perfectly your growing authority within the corporation, and where my own best interests lie. Be assured I shall seek to be your most loyal servant.'

'Sadly I have a complaint. Why is the building of tanker *S17* so far behind schedule?'

'I did not know it was. You must understand that when you are building the largest tanker in the world you are moving into unchartered waters. You can only hope that what was suitable when building smaller vessels will hold good when you go where no one has been before. You cannot be sure, and in the case of tanker *S17* we discovered that the propellers did not provide the thrust required for such a massive tanker. At first it seemed all that was needed was an adjustment to the angle and positioning of the blades. Our technicians were wrong. The adjustments they suggested made little difference. I then ordered new propellers of a different design and strength which had to be tested and constructed to meet whatever weather conditions the tanker might face. All this took six weeks, but the new props have been delivered and fitted. We are four weeks behind schedule, but not behind budget. As the date of its launch has never been announced it will be near impossible for anyone outside ourselves; and the Finnish yard where it has been built, to be aware of any delay. And if there were to be a leak, I don't think anyone would mind or care. Successful final trials, which will begin in a few weeks time, are all that will interest any potential buyers or users. What is more, we shall learn from our mistakes and the next tanker we build, even if it were larger than *S17*, will profit from the errors made during the past weeks.'

'Thank you for your explanation. As a result I want both myself and Mr Leopardis to be on board for her trials. How long do you expect to be at sea?'

'At least four days, and not more than seven. Four days if everything goes according to plan, but several more if problems arise. However, I have to tell you that your request raises a problem which I am not sure I can resolve. There are only a limited number of cabins. They are all small singles and they have been allocated to the senior officers who will be on board when she sails, plus representatives from the yard that has built the vessel, plus officials who hopefully give us the all-clear. With difficulty I might be able to squeeze in yourself or Mr Leopardis, but not both. One other point, Madame Stephanopolous; it will not be a comfortable ride. We shall head for the South Atlantic in order to seek out the roughest conditions that will test a tanker of her size to the limit. I think it would be wise for Mr Leopardis to be on board.'

'Thank you for your advice. I shall let you know my decision, once I have receive a copy of your last report which was not delivered, as I demanded. Make sure it is on my desk by tomorrow.'

In bed that night she and Anton cuddled, but also fondled two glasses of her favourite cognac, and she admitted, 'I always feel more randy and wide awake as these juices start to circulate inside me, where I hope you will soon be.' He was. As she lay delighting in the pleasure he had provided she informed him that it would be best if he went on the trials. As soon as this was settled, she asked: 'Once we are married where shall we live? We could stay here in the family home; we could build our own residence; or buy an estate a short distance from Athens; or we could find a sufficiently large apartment close to the centre of the capital. As for our honeymoon, I would like to follow the example my parents set and have it aboard the oldest of their two yachts. It may not be as sleek or as fast as its younger sister, but it has more class, and I like it best. We shall have it all to ourselves with a crew of twenty to look after the honeymooners. What do you think?'

'First, where to live. Providing it is not here, I shall be content. It should be our home. As whatever is decided will be bought or built with your money, unless you are prepared to live in a two-room bachelor apartment, which I do not recommend except as a possible overflow for your constantly growing wardrobe, I shall agree with whatever is your decision. And a honeymoon aboard the family yacht is something I have never in my wildest dreams even considered.'

A few days later Stephanie phoned Carl Ellungsen and invited him to join her for an evening drink in the rooftop bar of their hotel on Constitution Square. When she and Anton arrived their guest was already waiting for them at a table overlooking the Accropolis, an ouzo in front of him. Carl rose as he saw

Stephanie enter the bar on the arm of Anton. 'You remember Mr Leopardis,' Stephanie said as she shook hands with her guest. 'I don't think I mentioned in my office that he will assume the role of Vice-President once I assume control as president of the shipping division. Before then I shall have changed my name to Madame Stephanie Stephanopolous Leopardis. We are to be married shortly. My parents have given their approval. I hope you will be free to come to our wedding, subject to any business commitments.' Stephanie noticed a look of surprise on Carl's face. 'You look amazed,' she mocked. 'Don't you think I am good enough for him?'

'Perish such a thought. Mr Leopardis, you are a very lucky man. You have won a unique young lady. My warmest and sincerest congratulations to you both.'

Stephanie's reply was to signal to a waitress to bring them a bottle of vintage Bollinger and three glasses. After the champagne had been poured, Carl proposed a toast to their future happiness. Turning to Anton, she reminded him: 'Didn't I tell you that Mr Ellungsen had all the attributes of a successful salesman? He knows when to say the right words at the right time.' Turning to Carl, she told him, 'I have agreed for Mr Leopardis to come with you on the tanker trials.'

A moment later she asked, 'Which are our biggest customers?'

'Without doubt, Saudi Arabia, and elsewhere in the Middle East, plus Russia and the United States. Together they account for more than eighty per cent of our orders and have done so for the last seven or eight years. With Egypt I am not so successful. That country's bureaucrats believe they are still powerful, and try to forget that tiny Israel has already spanked them twice in two wars. Nevertheless, I don't want to lose their business. The Middle East is a very volatile area and could easily erupt into another war overnight. When that happens the need for tankers and container ships will rocket. And we shall be able to name our own prices. So, with your permission, I shall continue to negotiate.'

To himself he was thinking that it was just as well she had decided not to come on the *S17* trials. Even in a sou'wester she would tantalise every man on board and in a sweater and slacks before they hit the roughest waters they would all, including himself, find it difficult to concentrate on why they were at sea.

She might not be quite the goddess of Greek legends, but her head of jet black hair and her firm breasts and desirable ruby red lips made her a target for any man, including himself. Fortunately he was aware that she was like a wasp with a sting that could be deadly. She might still be a teenager, but she had the kind of majesty that enabled her to wear magnificent jewels that would overwhelm far older women.

With her highly developed femininity she sensed what he was thinking, and deliberately gave him one of her flirtatious smiles, although there was a note of authority in her voice as she told him, 'If you are prepared to move ahead several months to the time when I assume the presidency of our shipping division, I will now give you permission to inform the Egyptians that you have discussed their contract with the future president of Stephanopolous International, an attractive multi-millionairess member of the founding family, and she has authorised you to agree to their request for a reduction. Our final quoted price will be reduced by ten per cent for each of the first two years of hire and by a further fifteen per cent for a third year. My strategy will be jam today, whenever possible. However, if I have a choice I prefer to keep our present customers before seeking new clients. Put another way, like you, I am looking ahead to the future when, as you rightly forecast, there could be another explosion in the volatile Middle East. Then countries could come begging for our tankers. That is when we make our killings. And because of our mammoth investments with several major banks we are guaranteed most favourable rates of interest on any loans we request. They know we can always withdraw our investments. Business for me is not a game, but a deadly serious occupation. The gloves I wear cover hands that can be as hard as iron, although as soft as silk when Anton is holding them. My attitude can be ice-cold.'

'Thank you, madame. Your business acumen amazes me. I am looking forward to working under you.'

A moment later her thoughts had drifted on and he was instructed to 'Make sure that Mr Leopardis is properly briefed and kitted out for the tanker trials.'

Back at headquarters next day she instructed her secretary to tell Miss Konstantinidis who was still working in her outer office that Mlle Stephanopolous wanted to see her.

Unlike most staff who were ordered into her office Helena was only kept standing until Dolores had closed the door behind her. 'Sit down, Helena,' Stephanie ordered. This was followed by the normal silence whenever she was dealing with staff below heads of departments. Helena grew more nervous as she remembered the first time she had been called to where she was now seated, and been reduced to tears and the threat of dismissal. Once again she was starting to feel like a sacrificial lamb. Without any warning Mlle Stephanopolous asked in a voice that could only be described as social, 'How do you like your work, Helena?'

'I like it very much, madame.'

'I don't believe you. Stop being afraid of me. Tell me the truth.'

Helena was sensible enough to realise that this time she need not tremble. 'I like my work, but feel I could handle a more responsible job, but I daren't take a chance of resigning and looking for work elsewhere. Jobs like mine, which is reasonably well paid, are hard to find. Why, if I may ask, do you ask, Mlle Stephanopolous?' As soon as the words were out of her mouth she knew she risked being lashed by her boss's tongue for daring to ask questions.

'Have you forgotten how brutal I can be to those who think they are my equal? But I can sometimes reveal to those I admire how much I respect their ability to express themselves in front of me. And that is why you are here. So let me ask you another question. How do you get on with the rest of the men and women in the outer office?'

'Well enough, but none of them are close friends, simply colleagues.'

'Good. Another question. Would you like to work directly under me?'

'Oh, please, madame. I will do anything you command.'

'Could you fire one of your colleagues, and not think twice about it?'

'I could, but only if I had your authority, madame.'

'You have my authority, Helena. Tomorrow you will be appointed my personal deputy with full responsibility for ensuring maximum efficiency in the outer office. You will allocate additional work to those you think can handle a heavier workload. And those unable to cope with the work you give them will be reported to me with your recommendation. With effect from tomorrow your salary will be increased by twenty-five per cent. I shall review the situation in three months' time. As you know I began the weeding out process throughout headquarters as soon as I was appointed a director. Now I want you to finish the job for me, at any rate in Personnel. But remember, if I am not satisfied at the end of three months, your life will become impossible in the outer office if you have to return to being just another typist or clerk. Satisfy me, and you salary will go up by another twenty-five per cent, and the sky could then be the limit. Think of everyone in the outer office except yourself as being potentially expendable if they fail to satisfy the high standards you will set.'

She buzzed for Dolores. 'Prepare sufficient copies of the following memo and place one on every desk in the outer office before you leave this evening, but only after everyone else has gone home. Date it tomorrow.'

Staff Announcement. With effect from today Miss Helena Konstantinidis is appointed as my personal deputy for ensuring maximum efficiency in the Personnel department. Any order she gives is to be regarded as an order from myself, and will be obeyed without question. Any refusal will lead to instant dismissal. Her new title is Personal Assistant to the Director of Personnel.

(signed) Stephanie Stephanopolous

Next she dictated a brief memo to Accounts authorising her salary increase.

She confided to her new assistant: 'To make your task easier, I shall come into the outer office from time to time and talk to you in full view of everyone. Your task is to tame them to accept you as their immediate boss. You will always have my support. What begins tomorrow need not be the end of your climb up the ladder.'

Helena Konstantinides and Sonia Vrettos were part of her agenda to create a team of young executives who, during the coming years, would form the backbone of her personal team of women, and men, who were prepared to dedicate their working lives to ensuring that her corporation's turnover, profitability and efficiency increased on average by at least five per cent annually, once she assumed the presidency. Whether her cousin, Dimitrios Stephanopolous, son of her uncle Boris, could be moulded to become part of that vanguard she was doubtful, but her father had asked her to find him a job and give him a chance. She felt duty bound to carry out his request. Then it would be up to Dimitrios. If after a few months he disappointed, she had her father's permission to sack him, or send him out of sight and overseas. She had no doubt that was what would finally happen.

She told Dimitrios: 'After much pleading from your parents, I have found you a job. I am not sure you are worth it, but what I do know is that I have a file containing nearly one hundred letters from young men and women of your age who would give anything to have the opportunity I am giving you. But one thing I need to make clear. Your name may be Stephanopolous, but you will receive no special privileges. These are confined to my mother, father and myself. To me you will be just another employee. You will work in the Publicity and Marketing departments which I have now merged, and work directly under Mr Pinakoulakis who I am grooming to accept more responsibility. You will obey whatever orders he gives, even if it is to make the coffee. Your salary will be exactly what I would pay anyone else who wants a job, but has no experience. Your parents may be horrified when you tell them what you are to be paid, but tell them from me it is a take it or leave it situation. You will arrive for work at nine next Monday morning and report to Mr Pinakoulakis.

'My office is not an ever-open door, so don't think you can come running to me because we are related. People are only allowed here when I send for them. I am taking a gamble with you. However, to show you I am not the tyrant you probably think I am, let me tell you how to impress me. Send me ideas. I may not accept them, but they will give me an indication of your potential. You are on three months' trial. Spend them thinking how you can play a part in the future success of our family corporation. Impress me and prove that you have Stephanopolous blood in your veins; and then, who knows?'

'I really am grateful to you, Stephanie, although I am a little disappointed at the salary you are willing to pay me.'

'Find somewhere that will pay you more, and I will wish you every success. Obviously, you did not understand me when I told you that no one here has any privileges except my parents and myself. While you are in this building you will always, like everyone else, call me Madame or Mlle Stephanopolous. And never again, Stephanie. Report for work next Monday morning. And good luck.'

She had also arranged for Anton and herself to have dinner at home with her parents the following night, but before then they both went to see the vicar of her local church, who recognised her at once when she rang the bell of his vicarage. Ten minutes later she had booked for her wedding to take place on the first Saturday in May which was four months away and just before her nineteenth birthday. Anton she knew was happy with the date, and that she wanted a homely wedding. He agreed he would wear a morning suit.

She spent more than an hour getting ready for dinner. He was in and out of the bathroom while Sophie fussed around her mistress who kept changing her mind about what to wear. Finally, she selected a black silk ankle-length, high necked gown which was relieved from looking too funereal by a single diamond brooch, and her thirty carat engagement ring which her mother would be seeing for the first time.

When she saw it, she reacted, 'It is what I would expect any daughter of mine to wear on her engagement finger.' Stephanie knew she meant it.

Stephanie let her know that, 'Anton and I bought it together in Paris, and that it was once worn by a grand duchess, a daughter of the last Czar of Russia.'

They drank champagne while Stephanie broke the ice by explaining that they had not made up their minds where they wanted to live after they were married, but it had to be in their own home. For the luncheon after the wedding she and Anton would like to celebrate the occasion with around fifty friends and relations of which they would choose half and her parents the other half. Whenever the same people appeared on both lists, her parents could add another couple to their personal list. She went on, 'After we are married we would like to honeymoon alone aboard the yacht on which you both sailed on your own honeymoon, and where Count and Countess

Rugerstein spent their honeymoon, too And, finally, we would like you to make the formal announcement in the press within the next forty-eight hours. Is there anything I have forgotten, Anton?'

'Only the most important point. You wanted to assure your mother and father that we both love one another very much, and that we saw the vicar of your local church this afternoon and agreed a date for the ceremony on the first Saturday in May.'

She took his hand and kissed it before adding: 'Within a reasonable period of time we look forward to presenting you both with your first grandchild.'

It was not her mother who followed, but her father. He rose to his feet in order to receive everyone's attention. He was well known for his ability to get his own way either by forceful aggression or by compromise, whichever tactic he decided would be most effective. This evening he was determined upon compromise. Much as he admired his daughter, he did not wish to appear to be siding with her against his wife, although he accepted it was her wedding. And within a few years she would control Stephanopolous International and everyone who was part of the corporation, and that would include her mother. She would also become the head of the Stephanopolous family. Yet he continued to seek harmony. As a result he talked about her becoming the head of their empire, 'one day'. And because her parents would, of course, happily pay for the wedding, he hoped she would give way to some of their foibles if ever there was a difference in preference. To himself he accepted that he was partly to blame for his wife's aggressiveness to others, especially those who could never answer back. He had always given way to her caprices, even allowing her an ever-increasing influence in the running of Stephanopolous International, although never to the point where she might be in a position to mount a *putsch*. Now in a voice that was both calm yet authoritative, he told Stephanie: 'All your mother and I want is your happiness. You will never stop being our much-loved child. Let us go and enjoy another family dinner together with a glass or two of fine wine. The combination should help us find the compromises we all now need, and I hope want.' The four of them sat down at the carved mahogany table which was now covered with a crisp white linen tablecloth, plus an assortment of glasses that would match their choice whether for champagne, wine or water. While they ate all talk was confined to business which was far over the heads of the waiters and waitresses. It was not until they had been served their coffee and chosen either a cognac, malt whisky or an apricot brandy, that the butler was told they would pour their own drinks and that all staff, except those on night duty, could retire until tomorrow.

Ulysses assured the three members of the family: 'This is now the time for goodwill and compromise, not for disagreements or confrontations. I want all of us to show our love for each other. We have already agreed to the church wedding and the date. All that remains are the details and the honeymoon. In my fair and reasonable proposals there will be no winners or losers, just family. Stephanie would like just fifty to be invited and we would be happier with at least two hundred. Let us compromise with one hundred and twenty that is seventy more than the bride would like and eighty less than would please her mother. I love both my wife and daughter equally.'

He stretched out a hand and poured a liberal dose of a single malt whisky from a cut glass decanter, and offered the same to Anton who accepted as an indication that he would try to support whatever Ulysses proposed providing Stephanie gave her nod of agreement.

Ulysses Stephanopolous did not have the pomposity of his wife, but still wanted his daughter's wedding to be an occasions that reflected the family's position within the Greek community. He went on: 'Fortunately the bride is a young lady, and although only nineteen has the intelligence and wisdom seldom possessed by people of thirty. For this reason I know she will permit me to host a luncheon or dinner after the wedding ceremony which will take place in the ballroom of our home and be attended by one hundred and twenty guests, and perhaps a handful more. I know that neither my wife or my daughter will show any pettiness about the final figure. What matters is that it is the happiest of days. And I like the idea of a separate party for the villagers who are our tenants, and will happily bear the cost of that hospitality as well.

'As for their honeymoon, I believe Christiana will allow them the pleasure of sailing aboard the same yacht where we spent our first weeks together as husband and wife. If she feels I am demanding too big a concession, then to soothe her feelings, I will offer them the use of the family's new and larger private yacht, but my wish is that Christiana, who can be the most generous of ladies, will give the young couple what they want. Back to the guests, the lists will be divided as near as possible on a fifty-fifty basis with myself acting as arbiter if one is ever needed, which I doubt. But no royalty this time. I want Stephanie to be the queen when every eye will be upon her as she stands for photographs beside her equally fabulous mother who I still love as much as upon the day I asked her to be my wife.' He mopped his brow and took a second sip of his whisky before adding: 'That is how I want us to celebrate a joyous occasion, and the beginning of something beautiful and fruitful. I cannot wait until Stephanie presents us with our first grandchild.' He looked around the table for a reaction to his declaration, but the only positive sign came from Anton who raised his glass to his father-in-law to be and gave him the thumbs up sign. Neither of the two women gave any indication of what they were thinking; it was as though neither was prepared to make the first move in case it was regarded as surrender. Deep down Stephanie was willing to accept all her father had suggested in order to avoid a private family row over what her father had called 'a matter of details' which could so easily become a public squabble in the media. She wondered whether if she accepted all he had proposed it might encourage her mother to do likewise. She was trying to decide who she loved more, Anton or her father. Her father's blood was in her veins, but Anton's love was what would provide her with the support for all she intended to achieve.

Her mother's feelings were different and continued to be unexpressed. She accepted that all her husband had said had been like the wisdom of Solomon. In his own way he had met her wishes without offending her dignity. Suddenly she surprised herself, and everyone else, by declaring: 'I am happy to accept all you have said, Ulysses. Don't let us squabble over minor matters and, of course, they may have my yacht for their honeymoon. And I hope that Stephanie will allow me, as her mother, to help choose her trousseau, and listen to my thoughts on where she should live with Anton after their wedding. You both have my blessing.'

It may not have been the wisdom of Solomon, more the way

a modern, multi-millionaire tycoon had of getting what he wanted by making it clear there was no other route to take. The result was kisses all round.

18

Her father had given Stephanie the first five of the next seven years to prepare for taking over his reins of power whenever he decided to step down, either because of ill-health or because he thought it time to pass on the responsibilities that were growing all the time. He was beginning to believe he was no longer the right person for the task. It was a cocktail of the traumatic, celebratory and the inevitable. The traumas were mostly between Stephanie and her mother who accepted, but did not agree, with her daughter taking control of the family corporation while still only in her mid-twenties. She thought that honour should be hers until she in turn decided to hand over to Stephanie. But her husband had made the decision and it had been agreed by the board of directors. She abstained, but it was recorded in the official minutes of the meeting that no one opposed the election of Stephanie Stephanopolous Leopardis as the next president of Stephenapolous International. The celebrations came not only at the wedding, but as a result of how Stephanie, as she was eased into the presidential office, faced and overcame every challenge. She won new contracts, expanded their overseas factories and developed a feminine ability to open doors while still the princess in waiting. And there would be joy in everyone's heart when she and Anton presented her parents with a grandchild who they would name Cleopatra, which would be quickly abbreviated to Chloe, if it was a daughter and Ulysses if it were a son. The reason for the choice was that Stephanie was convinced a daughter would develop the same ruthless and vicious streak that was part of the history handed down of the Egyptian queen. The new princess would be baptised in Athens cathedral which would delight both her mother and grandmother.

Inevitably there were setbacks and sackings for those who lost the trust of Stephanie, or stood in her way, while those like Anton, Marianne, Carl, Roberto and Helena in different ways fulfilled her expectations. She wanted her husband to be elected to the Board, but decided his elevation should wait until her own reign began, and it would then be automatically agreed.

Sonia Vrettos, too, had risen steadily up the ladder of responsibility by carrying out every order she was given, but finally floundered by refusing to sack her personal secretary, who was also her lesbian partner. Only she should be allowed to sack her own secretary, she told Stephanie in a confidential memo. The result was a brief phone call instructing her to come at once to Stephanie's office which was now on the eleventh floor together with her desk that was still on its elevated stage. When at last she looked up she told Sonia, 'I have read your letter explaining why you feel unable to sack your own secretary as I ordered. That is not a problem. With effect from this moment you are both sacked and I am appointing Helena Konstantinides to take over all your responsibilities. Collect your things, clear your desk and do not enter these headquarters again. Good afternoon.'

It was quite the opposite with Roberto. He had kept his promises to make her a celebrity among business editors around the world and, thanks to her combination of beauty, brains and wealth, also a constant subject for features in glossy magazines in every continent whose writers loved to encourage their readers to salivate as they revealed the number of pairs of shoes in Stephanie's wardrobe, the latest diamonds she had added to her collection and the number of furs she owned.

As Stephanie had foretold, Roberto had boosted the reputation of Stephanopolous International through his spicily written press releases announcing increasing half yearly profits, mergers and takeovers. In some she was described as 'A Woman in a Billion', and in others as an industrial princess who regularly worked a fourteen-hour day 'while still finding time to be nominated as one of the ten best dressed women in the world.'

There had been surprises, too. Dimitrios had been an un-expected success under the guidance and instruction of Roberto who now regarded him him as his immediate deputy with a flair for marketing. As a result his salary after just two years with the corporation had risen five fold. At headquarters he was now permitted to call Stephanie by her first name, providing they were not with clients or other members of staff. Then she had to be Madame Stephanopolous.

266

Meanwhile, Anton had proved a good husband at home and an excellent and wise partner at the office, plus a wonderful father to their daughter. He had learned the wisdom of letting her have her way, although many believed Stephanie was working longer hours than ever following the arrival of Cleopatra in order to make sure her daughter inherited a still larger trust fund than her mother when she was eighteen.

All this was after the marriage had been celebrated in her village church that was overcrowded with invited guests, family and the press. Most of the villagers had to be content to listen to the service and the vows which were broadcast to those standing outside under a warm May sun. Stephanie's decision not to be married in Athens cathedral made headlines, and a new opportunity for the press to ask questions. How had she met her husband? Had he bought the engagement ring? What would she wear for her wedding? Where would they spend their honeymoon? Where would they live? And others. Fortunately, Roberto seemed to know when to ride to her rescue like a modern Sir Galahad. This resulted in him being brought into her small circle of men and women she trusted, including her father, Anton, Marianne and an Arab prince who she had met and who now accompanied her whenever she wanted to meet Middle Eastern and Asian political leaders who either ruled their countries or had control over their oil millions and needed tankers. She described her close friendship with Prince Hussein as the man who 'has the key to open normally locked doors. He is worth millions of dollars to us by making sure that whenever possible we receive priority over competitors.'

Inevitably, Anton became aware of this relationship because he took charge when she travelled to meetings in different Pacific, Asian and Middle East countries with the Arab prince as her constant companion, and her security. He had to accept that it was not his place to interfere with anything his wife undertook that was in the best interests of Stephanopolous International. Nevertheless, he could not help wondering whether the prince was coming between him and his wife, despite her hurrying into his arms and then their bed as soon as she returned home. As they lay together she assured him that there was nothing between herself and Prince Hussein. 'He will never be allowed to marry me, even if that was in his mind, which it isn't, and anyway I would never convert to Islam. But I do love you. And if you want to remove a stumbling block, I don't love him. I may admire the respect in which he is held wherever we go. He asks for nothing except my company, and I simply try to express my thanks for all the business he is pointing in our direction. However, I do the selling. Those I am targeting are always surprised, even amazed, at the competence of a mere woman who also has control over a giant corporation, which is renowned the world over, and whose profits are increasing. Did you know that our global empire has larger financial resources than several of the smaller Islamic states? Finally, I enjoy the prince's company and he has become an essential part of my inner circle of advisers. But you, Anton, are my husband, and the father of our child. Whatever I do is only in the best interests of our corporation.'

She decided to keep him guessing whether she had slept with the prince, but simply decided to tell him that she had read that in most western countries twenty-five per cent of women and more than fifty per cent of men were unfaithful before they were forty. The figures were believed to be far higher elsewhere in the world, although all the figures were believed to be underestimates. If she gave her body to the prince it was as her thank-you present for the millions of dollars in orders he had won for Stephanopolous International. Rich men were attracted to beautiful girls or young women, and could trap them into fur-lined nets that were decorated with other fabulous gifts. While Stephanie had a body which she occasionally gave to Prince Hussein because he deserved to know how appreciative she was, he would never own her. Women who were lured into the lives of wealthy businessmen seldom shared marriage vows. Their mink coats and jewels were like handcuffs from which they seldom wanted to escape. Every woman, rich or poor, prayed to be admired.

What caused another problem for Stephanie and Anton was finding a home that came up to Stephanie's exacting standards. Until then her money had been all she needed to obtain whatever she wanted. Now several Athenian estate agents felt her whip-like tongue for failing to find a home that compared with the family home and estate where she had lived all her life. She told Anton: 'I am not prepared to lower my demands, and it has to be where we want to live. We will need a minimum of six, and preferably eight, bedrooms with ensuite bathrooms, plus a large dining and separate drawing room, nursery and a large book-lined study. Anything less is not for me, or you.' It was more than six months after their marriage and they were dining in her suite at the mansion where they continued to live and love when she suddenly interrupted herself, as she often did, and exclaimed: 'Now I know why I married you, Anton. As well as being madly in love with you, you are a genius. We have spent weeks and months looking for a home without finding what we are seeking. Yet until this minute I had forgotten the solution which you suggested months ago. Why don't we build our own home? I am going to ask my father to allow me to build my own slightly smaller mansion home on our estate but as far away as is practical from where we are living now.'

It was to take more than a year to build her dream home which, except for calling it Leopardis House, was a modern incarnation of where she had lived all her life. It was almost eighteen months after building began before they hosted their first party for around fifty guests. For the occasion she annexed half a dozen of her parents' staff for a couple of days to help with the preparations and serving. The most frequent compliment she received was, 'We knew that eventually you would have a home that was worthy of you, Stephanie.' Certainly it showed off her flair for style, and the kind of lavishness that only a vast amount of money could provide. The end product showed she knew how to dazzle, but with sophistication.

Their own eighteen square metre master bedroom was dominated by a large, genuine Jacobean four-poster with thick damask curtains that kept out every chink of light even when they made love on the sunniest day. There was a second bedroom for Anton if she was unwell, or he offended her. Such punishments seldom lasted more than a single night. Neither could do without the other for longer. Adjoining was a spacious sitting room where all the mahogany furniture had been hand lacquered in shining black. The rest of the suite included two marble bathrooms and wardrobes and closets galore of which eighty-five per cent were annexed by Stephanie for her own clothes, but Anton was content with his fifteen per cent, and accepted such a division as fair.

Every morning when the pair came downstairs for breakfast

before driving to the office, the first delight that greeted them was the pink marble tiled floor of the Great Hall which was illustrated with scenes of the victories of Alexander the Great. Stephanie had instructed her housekeeper that everything in the hall had by that time to be polished and cleaned by two of their parlour maids who always gave a curtsy to the heiress and her husband. The only words spoken were to tell their cook that they were ready to be served breakfast. Meanwhile, Stephanie's wandering eyes checked that all the small tables shone with brightness while her fingers checked for any dust on the life-size sculptured marble heads of Greek heroes including Aristotle and Alexander, the goddess Athena, plus Homer, Sophocles and Euripides – but not Helen of Troy, whose presence could well have offended Athena. The spacious lounge was home for comfortable armchairs, sofas for two or as many as six, all covered with an expensive design of soft satin. The walls were as bare as they probably would have been in ancient times. A six-foot-long air-conditioned passage separated the dining-room from the kitchen whose modern German equipment might have seemed ostentatious to some, but to the majority who were privileged to be shown the expensive fittings and highly polished work surfaces, it was a housewife's dream.

The white marble staircase curved its way from the hall to a first floor, half of which was occupied by their private bedroom suite. In addition, there were four double bedrooms with ensuite bathrooms for guests, plus an extra door that was marked private and led to the third floor where there were six more bedrooms for their live-in staff; the three largest for the housekeeper, cook and Sophie, each with its own bathroom, plus three more twin-bedded rooms with two bathrooms which the six maids shared. The rest of the space was taken up by a nursery suite which included a large main bedroom, playroom and a separate, smaller bedroom for nanny.

The final part of any tour was down a steep, well-lit stairway that secretly led off from the hall. At the bottom they were faced with a choice of two doors. One took them into an air-conditioned cellar whose walls were filled with vintages from the extensive wine collection that Ulysses maintained, including champagne and fine French, German and Italian vintages from which Stephanie had been given cases of Montrachet, Chamberton,

Petrus and Pomerol, as well as Grand Crus Chablis and a couple of cases of single Chablis. Finally, there were a couple of racks of less expensive red and white wines for the staff who were allowed to drink at dinner twice a week on Wednesday and Sunday, but were not to sit down until they had finished serving Stephanie and Anton, and any guests. The second door led to a small cinema with just ten bright red cushioned armchairs where the family and their guests, or staff when they were away, could watch Hollywood films that had been sent to the Leopardis couple before general release as a kind of continuing wedding present because of her family's friendship with several Hollywood moguls. Behind the screen was a games room for table tennis, plus an array of keep-fit equipment.

It was her exceptional business ability, plus family contacts, that now saw her sending her husband and Carl Ellungsen on a mission to Britain to test the water for a possible takeover of one of the largest shipbuilding yards on the Clyde in Glasgow. Confidential information had reached her indicating the company was prepared to consider any reasonable takeover bid.

Two days before Anton and the corporation's top salesman flew to Britain she gave them a second assignment which was to assess the possibility of taking over a leading manufacturer of small light aircraft which she believed could bring rising profits to the family empire. She missed Anton immensely when he was away, and they talked on the phone each evening. When he was due home she arranged for one of the family chauffeurs to drive to the airport and meet the couple. On Anton's arrival home she told him she had ordered cook to prepare a hot supper for them both as she had not had dinner and was certain the food on the plane would have been near inedible. She cuddled into his welcoming arms and suggested that they just enjoy each other until they had been served and then he could tell her about his visit to London and Scotland. As he sipped his wine and cut into the golden brown of the breadcrumbs that covered his freshly caught plaice, he leaned down and took from under his chair a neatly-wrapped Harrods parcel which, when Stephanie opened it, revealed a colourful Gucci one yard square scarf. She blew him a kiss and thanked him for spoiling her, adding she would do the same to him later on. Without seeming to change gear she asked about his visit.

271

'I think your intuition may once again prove to have been tuned to perfection. Fred Ellungsen and I quickly discovered that the founder of a company making small private aircraft for businessmen and celebrities had died suddenly and the firm was now without a pilot, or rudderless if you prefer. His widow is seeking a buyer and the business is currently being run by its three directors who seem competent, but out of their depth. Two banks have turned down their requests for loans to enable them to buy the business as too big a risk, and with too little collateral. For the last two years the company has been making a loss.'

He paused to enjoy another mouthful of his plaice before going on: 'I met their spokesmen and let him know that we might be able to assist them, providing they stood aside while Stephanopolous International made its own bid, but without any publicity. If successful their jobs and most of the rest of the staff could be secure for at least one year, but we would almost certainly recruit additional executives. I have arranged a second meeting, hopefully with yourself, on a date to be agreed. They gave an assurance there would be no further bids from themselves and hopefully not from outsiders either. They believe that being part of Stephanopolous would guarantee their security and new prosperity. I told them my wife, who was a director of the main Board, wielded immense financial power and no final decision would be allowed to take place without her authority. They have been softened up for your kill. I believe the company could be the base from which the expansion you have in mind could begin. However, I am convinced new blood will be needed. Scotland, by the way, was a waste of time.'

Stephanie decided not to rush into unknown waters. Instead she and the corporation's financial advisers spent the following six weeks investigating the current financial status of the company on which she had provisionally set her sights. Meanwhile, she began direct and personal negotiations with the widow. By this time Stephanie knew what the company was worth, and that it was on a nosedive towards bankruptcy. Rival manufacturers seemed not to be interested because its collapse would mean one less competitor. This lack of foresight allowed Stephanie to slip easily under the guard of the widow, and make a killing. Through her legal team she put in a bid that bore no relation to the potential worth of the company, and explained to the widow in a personal letter that the offer from Stephanopolous International was the best she could expect because news had got around that two British banks had refused a loan. However, if she agreed the amount they were prepared to pay, that sum would be placed in her personal bank account within seven days of the contract being signed. The vast resources at the disposal of Stephanopolous International could be her lifeline to a contented future. She scribbled in ink at the foot of her letter which she marked private and confidential: 'I am trying to help you. Please don't force me to show my steel-like claws which would leave you with nothing.' Seventy-two hours later she received a cable from the widow's solicitors in London indicating that on their advice the widow had agreed to accept the offer from Stephanopolous International and confirmation was in the post. As she put it to Anton who knew nothing of her written words, 'I did not even have to bully her. Her solicitors did the job for me.'

Two months later she with Anton flew in one of her corporation's private jets and landed on the short runway at the headquarters of the company she had acquired and taxied towards the hangar where a small amount of production was still carried on. They were taken on a tour of the offices and the hangar and workshops before they and the three former directors retired to a small boardroom where Stephanie quickly reminded them: 'You must understand that we are now the owners of this company. We shall decide future policy, and you will obey any instructions that are given by myself or my husband. I am assuming the position of president of the new company which will be known as The Stephanopolous Aircraft Company. My husband becomes chief executive.

'I have not been impressed by what I have been shown. There will have to be changes. Even to my unprofessional eye everything seems to have passed its sell-by date. My family has become a five hundred million dollar corporation because it has never been satisfied with anything except the finest equipment and the best brains. That is what we shall install here. Nevertheless, I am willing to confirm my husband's provisional offer to guarantee each of you your jobs at your present salaries for the next year, providing you carry out all instructions that we give, and all other employees sign a two year no-strikes contract. I shall terminate the contract of anyone who refuses to carry out a single order. Think of me either as the angel who has saved your jobs, or the Amazon who crushes anyone who gets in her way.'

She took a sip from the glass of water someone had placed on the table in front of her and went on to announce: 'My first decision is to appoint Mr Greenhalgh as managing director with the personal responsibility for beginning the turn-around in the company's fortunes. He will supervise the carrying out of our orders. Meanwhile each of your employees will receive a letter guaranteeing them continuing employment for the next two years providing they sign our no-strike agreement, and accept a wage freeze. But to the three of you, I want to make it clear that you have only one year to begin turning this business round after we scrap all current production and begin planning the designs for a new series of aircraft which fly longer distances than your present planes, and have more luxurious interiors. What I have in mind you will see when I show you the interior of my own private plane that is on your runway. One final word. I have a reputation of being ruthless. I am also impatient. Are there any questions?' There were none. Already they were in awe of everything about her from her raging black hair, her steely eyes that bore through people, and the way she smiled when she threatened. How could they know that she was only afraid of being afraid? She was no acolyte; more the equivalent of an archbishop.

It took rather longer than one year to begin the turnaround she had demanded, but she decided not to rock the boat – yet. Nevertheless, a few months after the meeting she and Anton agreed that changes were necessary. Without anyone being informed, Mr Greenhalgh had his salary increased for his loyalty together with the senior trade unionist for his help in persuading the entire workforce to sign the no-strike clause. Nevertheless, the younger of the three former directors had become a thorn in Stephanie's side by frequently querying her orders. She also learned that he had disagreed with the takeover. She terminated the services of John Greenaway, paid him three months in advance and cancelled his contract. Meanwhile Anton was searching for the best man in the industry who was both a trained engineer and an aircraft designer. Stephanie's instructions were straightforward: 'I don't care if we have to pay him more than Mr Greenhalgh's increased salary, but find him. We need new blood. Without it we may find that we have wasted millions of dollars, and that I will not allow to happen.' Happily she had increasing confidence in her husband.

Her confidence proved justified. He spent so much time in the UK that although they only saw each other at weekends, he met, while in London, the chief executive of a successful head-hunting partnership who had warned him that finding the expert he was seeking could take months. What Anton did not know was that he said the same to every new client, yet his firm had a near hundred per cent record of finding the man, or woman, each client was seeking.

From the day Fred Baldwin joined The Stephanopolous Aircraft Company, it was all-change as Anton put in motion every request Fred made. He even persuaded him to tempt one of his colleagues, with still more technical know-how than he possessed, to make the same move. Within two months designs for two new aircraft were on the drawing board and plans were in motion for tooling up. All signs of the old fleet disappeared and there was a new spring in the steps of all the assembly and technical staff. Almost overnight morale improved as the workforce understood they were at the start of a new beginning. Three months later the new long and short haul aircraft moved off the drawing board and into the new hangar that Stephanie had authorised. As day followed day the two planes came nearer to reality. The increased range, plus better fuel consumption was being achieved by lowering the weight of the planes and furnishing them with lighter Scandinavian designed seats and other furniture. Yet it was not until he had been with the company for more than seven months that Fred Baldwin met Stephanie. She had too much on her plate involving the more established divisions of the corporation, and had been forced to leave the new aircraft division to Anton. She had challenged him to find someone like Fred Baldwin and his discovery had been like hitting a hole in one. When she and Anton were dining together, she announced: 'I think it time I met this boy wonder.' A week later she flew to London leaving Anton to hold the fort in Athens. And moved into a suite at the Savoy and booked a double room for their new protégé. As they shared a glass of champagne in the bar before dining in the Grill Room, she told him, 'I think we shall get on because you understand which side your bread is buttered; recognise that you have my complete confidence, and also because you and I are as different as fish and fowl, which means we shall have nothing to quarrel about. Just keep my husband and myself informed of everything you are planning and you have nothing to fear.' His response was to give her the assurances she was seeking, adding, 'I respect you, Madame Stephanopolous, because of the power you wield, but also because you have given me almost carte blanche to carry out changes which I believe I can achieve. But please remember that once both aircraft are on the production line, they will need to be marketed. That is a task for someone else.'

'You have my permission to call me Stephanie,' she told him before asking whether he had any more ideas, 'that will make me a still richer woman than I already am.'

His answer was to assure her that while he understood that one could never stand still, nevertheless he and his colleague, Herman, who was an even better technician than himself, were currently concentrating all their time and energy on the two planes. But he promised not to forget the day after tomorrow.

It was not until they were enjoying their dinner that he disclosed, 'For the last three months I have been working in my own time on designs for a new aircraft which will have a fuel capacity sufficient to take eight passengers in still better First Class comfort across the Atlantic from any capital in western Europe, including Athens. I have shown my designs to Herman who thinks they are full of potential, but Mr Greenhalgh thinks they are impracticable because of the expense involved in constructing and testing yet another untried aircraft which could be in competition with the aircraft currently on our production line. I felt it unwise to persist in my disagreement until I had the pleasure of meeting you and telling you of my ideas. After all, he is my boss.'

'Wrong. I am your boss, Fred. And when not I, my husband. Mr Greenhalgh will do whatever we tell him. Or we shall need a new managing director. Have no more fears. You will have your own way. Tomorrow I shall cable your mythical boss with a copy to you that will give you my permission to proceed with your plans for a still better private transatlantic aircraft.

'Now enough about business. Tell me more about yourself.' She gazed at him with more than casual interest. He told her: 'First, I am thirty-four and your devoted servant. I am married and have an eight-year-old son. We live in a semi-detached house in Streatham, like thousands of other middle-class families. We cannot afford to be extravagant, but we are comfortable and contented. My wife's parents named her Helen, and hoped she would grow up to be as attractive as your ancestor. Until today I thought she had succeeded. Now I have met a lady who is not just beautiful, but as electrifying as I presume Helen must have been. In addition, you are immensely wealthy and wear clothes that breathe elegance and were not purchased in the high street, plus jewels that I once thought were only worn by royalty. Add to all that, you possess a brain that is as sharp as a razor blade. How you are able to control the lives and future of hundreds, perhaps thousands, of men and women around the world is something which, until recently, I never imagined could be undertaken by a woman. Is there a secret?'

'There are two. First, I am a Stephanopolous which means I was born with the right genes to be a successful businesswoman. Second, I encourage staff to fear me. As a result every order I give is carried out without question. Loving me, I leave to my husband, although that does not mean that I am always a one-man girl. Life is too short to miss opportunities that will help our corporation which is, perhaps, another reason for my business success. Would you like to come to my suite for a night cap so I can learn more about you?'

'Forgive me, Stephanie, but I am feeling tired, perhaps because the wines you chose for dinner were so delicious I may have drunk more than my fair share.'

'Shouldn't you have added that you are also a married man?' she asked with just the faintest of smiles, or were they smirks, on her lips.

'I am sorry. I foolishly forgot that my hostess is a woman who says what she thinks. But please believe me, I really am feeling tired, and until this evening I had never thought of being with another woman except my wife.' Now he was worried; she was a woman who did not like to be thwarted, she might make him pay for what she could regard as a personal slight. He touched her hand and admitted, 'You are very beautiful, Stephanie.'

'But not as beautiful as Helen,' she mocked.

Because he had disappointed her, Stephanie cut short her visit, checked out of the hotel early the following morning and headed back to Athens. Fred would remain in her sights because she admired his ability and enthusiasm and, still more important, he was valuable to Stephanopolous International. And she was first a businesswoman.

When he rang her room he was surprised to be told she had checked out. He began to wonder whether his loyalty to his wife had damaged their future. He decided that if another chance was offered it might be suicidal to reject a lady who was svelte, curvy, gorgeous and thought nothing of spending thousands of dollars on a single dress. She was also his boss, and he now remembered her final words and wondered whether they had been a warning. 'And don't you dare forget me.'

19

Fred found it easy to obey her, but impossible to forget her. He was like a puppy with a new bone as he supervised every move towards the completion of his new flying babies. His wife was glad to hear that his new project was going well, but could not help noticing that when he arrived home on a couple of Friday nights he had not been carrying her usual bunch of flowers. It never occurred to her that another woman might be the cause. Once his excuse was that the florist at his London station had sold out of her favourite red roses, and a second time he admitted he had had to rush to catch his train, and apologised. She knew nothing about his evening with his millionaire boss except that she was 'a very dynamic woman'. Certainly his salary had risen by more than twenty-five per cent since he joined the Greek owned company, and that meant they could afford a few of the luxuries that could only be afforded by a family whose breadwinner was earning a salary in excess of fifty thousand pounds.

Meanwhile, Stephanie was more than a little surprised he had not written. Surely, she asked herself, he did not expect her to write first? But a surprise incident forced her to forget about Fred and focus her entire business mind on the target on which it had been focused since she joined the Board. It began with her father asking her to come to his office. There he told her that the time had come for his successor to present herself to the world as one of its most successful businesswomen. He wanted her to represent the Stephanopolous corporation at an international forum being held in London to discuss the deteriorating world economic situation. Three hundred of the world's top businessmen, financiers and industrialists had been invited; she would be one of the few women delegates. It was time she was seen in person instead of simply being read about in newspapers, magazines and financial columns and diaries. All thoughts of light aircraft and the man who had designed them were wiped from her mind. Although she could not know it, the curtain was about to go up on a new act which would dictate her future both as a businesswoman, and a princess.

Attending the London forum was to prove a global step towards being handed the baton which her father had promised to pass to her when she was twenty-five, or sooner. She was now twenty-three. She told Anton the news and he was thrilled for her. But problems arose as soon as her office tried to book her the kind of accommodation she demanded and expected. Every suite at Claridges had been booked weeks ago and it was the same at the Grosvenor House Hotel in Park Lane where the three day forum was being held. Disaster was avoided when they had a suite cancellation at the Dorchester which could also offer a back room for her maid.

The International Monetary Fund, which was hosting the event in co-operation with the British government, arranged for a fleet of Daimler limousines to ferry delegates and wives from their various London hotels to Park Lane for the opening evening reception at Grosvenor House. Stephanie shared one of them with a Hiram J. Blackwell, a Texan oil multi-millionaire and his wife, Kathleen, who wore a long sable cloak draped over her shoulders which rather outclassed Stephanie's mink jacket, although none of her diamonds outshone Stephanie's thirty carat pear-shaped diamond engagement ring. As the three were driven from the Dorchester by what seemed like a short, but circuitous, route Stephanie introduced herself as Stephanie Stephanopolous Leopardis and Mrs Blackwell responded, 'Now I know why you are wearing a ring that could only be on the finger of one of the richest women in the world. As you are here without your husband I will make it my duty to ensure you have an escort worthy of who you are.' In reply Stephanie joked that her visit to London had meant deciding between bringing her husband, or her maid. 'Guess who won?' she asked before adding, 'But she is not sharing my suite, just keeping it warm while I'm working.'

That was how she met Prince Hussein.

Mrs Blackwell suggested that she never left her sables in a public coatroom, and it might be wise for 'Miss Stephanopolous', as she insisted upon calling Stephanie, to do the same with her fur. She and her husband went ahead at the reception line where arrivals were greeted by Prince Philip, representing the Queen. Stephanie noticed that the Texan lady curtsied and decided to do the same after the master of ceremonies had announced in a clear, booming voice, 'Mrs Stephanie Stephanopolous Leopardis, Vice-President, Stephanopolous International.' Scores of heads turned in her direction for their first look at this new global industrial princess. There was even a twinkle in the Prince's eye. Waiting for Stephanie as she moved into the main reception area where she was immediately offered a glass of champagne, was the leach-like wife of the Texan oil magnate who was determined that nobody should snatch this gorgeous young lady, who she was already regarding as a grand-daughter, unless she agreed. Her eyes searched the room for a prince from one of the oil-rich Middle East states who she knew was attending the forum. He would make the ideal escort for Miss Stephanopolous. As soon as she spotted her prey she took Stephanie's arm and guided her towards the only man she regarded as worthy of escorting an heiress to a multi-million dollar fortune.

'Prince Hussein,' she said taking hold of the arm of the man whose oil wealth was even greater than her husband's, despite them living on a twenty-thousand acre estate in the heart of Texas; the prince was an heir to an entire oil-rich country. She told him: 'I want you to meet and take care of a young lady whose wealth puts her in the same league as ourselves, Stephanie Stephanopolous. The Prince bowed and kissed the outstretched gloved hand of the Greek multi-millionairess who was more beautiful than any in his own harem in the desert kingdom over which his family had ruled for three generations.

Left alone with her he snapped his fingers and signalled to a waiter to bring them fresh champagne even though Stephanie had hardly had time sip the glass she had been offered upon arrival. Holding both their glasses, he guided her to where the buffet would soon be served. Experience had shown him that when it came to food the rich had the same appalling manners as the poor and hungry and wanted to grab whatever was going ahead of anyone else. He found a table for two well away from the piled-high food. Momentarily he left her and, with the magical powers of two ten-pound notes, encouraged the head waiter to order two of his waiters to fill two plates with an assortment of all that was best from the buffet and take them to the table where the prince was sitting with, perhaps, the richest heiress in the world. The prince also ordered a bottle of Meursault, a *grand vin de Bourgonne*.

There was a smug look on both their faces as other tycoons and millionaires began hurrying towards the piled-high buffet table where they and their wives took on the roles of a large herd of cattle elbowing its way to be among the first to be milked. 'That scene is a mini-version of what is wrong with the world,' Stephanie suggested. 'We are all greedy. We think only of ourselves no matter how many poor sods suffer to make us rich. The debate tomorrow should be interesting, but we'll all be wasting our time. Pious words will be spoken, but action will be nil until economic circumstances force some to change course, and then for many it will be too little, too late. The difference between you and me and most of the others who are here this evening is that we can afford to wait before snapping up some business that is facing extinction. The only effect on corporations like our own is that our profits may drop a few blips.' She stopped as she so often did, and changed the subject. 'By the way, I cannot go on calling you prince. My name is Stephanie. What should I call you?'

'My name is Hussein. And you fascinate me, and remind me of my sister. But not in beauty. She is only in love with herself and her control over our millions of citizens is the result of being my father's only daughter. Otherwise it is a kingdom ruled by men. Her lack of many feminine qualities has not commended her to any of her eligible suitors, and because of her immense wealth she does not need them. She is fourth in line to our throne behind myself who is third, and two elder brothers. Together with our father who is king, the five of us control all the wealth of our country which has been estimated to possess the fourth largest reserves of oil. We also own an emerald mine in India of which my sister is president and I am vice-president. I would guess she has the largest collection of fine emeralds in the world. She regards them like lucky charms. Once a year all the finest gems that have been mined, cut and polished are sent to her for approval. She will probably keep a couple for herself and authorise the sale of the rest on the world market where they command higher prices than the finest diamonds. As president she keeps forty per cent of the annual profits, which total millions of dollars while as her deputy

I am allocated fifty per cent of what remains, and our father and two brothers share the remainder. She has at least two emerald necklaces.'

'Is she not married?' Stephanie asked

'No. My very unattractive sister appears to be content with a harem of half a dozen young males.'

Stephanie's response was: 'I am more interested in you than your sister. Do you have a harem?'

'Of course, but none of them has your beauty or your intelligence. They have only one use. As for my wealth, every barrel of oil we produce and sell is divided between my father, his three sons and his daughter. There are no requirements under our laws for us to produce any figures concerning profits or production, although we do provide figures in respect of barrels produced to the body that seeks to control the oil industry worldwide.'

'With that kind of pedigree why has no woman attracted you into her bed?'

'In our country, Stephanie, it is the men, or their parents, who decide who both men and women should marry. However, as third in line to the throne, my father leaves me free to live as a I like, but has chosen the brides for my two elder brothers. Now they both have children so the likelihood of me ever inheriting the throne is remote. When I look at you, I am sad for two reasons; first because you are already married, and second, our laws forbids me to wed any woman who does not practice our own religious beliefs. You are very beautiful.'

'I think my diamonds are blinding you.'

Stephanie hesitated as she sought what to say next. Instead, she kissed him on his cheek and told him: 'You are a very attractive man. Would you like to help me?'

'Would it mean seeing more of you?' he asked, hoping that her answer might be the key for what he was hoping.

'Of course you would see more of me. Perhaps much more.'

Next morning at the first session they sat together and were both equally bored listening to worthless speeches given by a lot of so-called specialists who knew as well as they did, that nothing they said would lead to any effective action being taken to prevent hundreds of thousands around the world losing their jobs if the threatened recession became a major reality. As

Stephanie put it: 'They will be the sacrificial lambs. Those over forty will probably never work again. All this comes easy to me because from an early age I knew that one day I would inherit the entire Stephanopolous empire and become an empress. That was quite a spur. But now I would like your help. And am prepared to pay for it.'

They spent the next two days together, becoming more concerned with what they were hearing from one another, than from the platform. Finally, he asked: 'What can I do to help you, Stephanie?'

'I am attracted to you, Hussein, and I know you would like to come to bed with me. But you must understand that, before anything else, I am the vice-president of the largest privately owned corporation in the world. If I am to give you my body it can only be in payment for the help you have given to me as a businesswoman.'

'I ask again, how can I help?'

'I am assuming that a man in your position has considerable influence with the heads of state and rulers of most, if not all, Islamic countries, and others, too. I need you to introduce me to them. Why? Because I want to tell them about our fleet of tankers and container ships which can transport their oil or other exports faster than other vessels. We recently built and launched the largest tanker ever built, and it was immediately hired by the Saudis. In addition, Stephanopolous International, is becoming a major player in the world of armaments thanks to our ownership of a piece of mechanism that increases the effective efficiency of any tank to which it is fitted, plus our new powerful and lethal automatic small arms with a very high rate of fire, and near pin-point accuracy up to two hundred metres. And the larger the number ordered, the lower the price of each weapon. We have already received contracts for more than one million weapons from half a dozen states and two revolutionary armies in Africa. With your influence I want to double our small arms sales within six months. I would like to begin in the Far East where I am flying in a few weeks. I would like you to come with me. We already have a ministerial contact thanks to my father, but I prefer to deal directly with the president, or the head of state.'

'If you will accept a young general who is now vice-president,

I may be able to help. Many of the Islamic states are finding it hard to pay for the large shipments of oil we have delivered to them now that their own economies are showing signs of recession. They owe us tens of millions of dollars, and my vice-presidential contact will find it hard to withstand your own sales charm if it is backed by the influence of Prince Hussein.'

That night everyone was invited to a final banquet and ball in the Great Room at the Grosvenor House. When the prince arrived to escort Stephanie he was wearing a dinner jacket with a bright red sash across his chest on which was emblazoned his country's insignia in diamonds and rubies that encircled the largest emerald Stephanie could ever recall seeing. Although she wore her own diamond necklace, a diamond bracelet on each wrist, matching drop earrings and her pear-shaped, Cartier engagement ring and a second square-cut diamond, she still looked longingly at the prince's decoration.

Before they left her suite he took a jewel box from his pocket and to Stephanie's surprise presented her with an enormous square-cut emerald ring which she guessed could weigh twenty carats. She protested she could not accept such a present from someone she hardly knew. He replied, 'That is a situation entirely of your own making. But as I can be very generous to those I admire, and who deserve to be spoiled, accept it just to please me.' And she did.

She and the prince danced the night away, but he still had to be content with touching her breasts, squeezing her hand, kissing her and once more becoming intoxicated by her perfume. It was almost two in the morning when she returned to her suite. The prince was permitted one final, more passionate, kiss on her lips before: 'I shall cable you with details of the date of my flight and where I shall be staying. I am looking forward to our reunion ... and perhaps our union.'

20

Back in her office what first caught her eye was a thick file marked 'For the attention of Madame Stephanopolous Leopardis.' On top was a telegram from Fred Baldwin, 'Work on new planes almost complete and ready this year's air show Farnborough. Have taken liberty of booking stand for sales discussions with potential buyers, hope you approve. Suggest you hold press conference on first or second day. May I have permission to book room? Fred Baldwin.'

She had told Anton about her meeting with Prince Hussein and how he had agreed to introduce her to some of the heads of Islamic states in Asia and the Middle East, all of whom might be interested in their tankers or container ships and their weapons. She did not add that he was coming with her to Asia. On company business, she did not need her husband's approval. She also dictated a report to her father and admitted that the forum had mostly been a waste of time, although she met some interesting contacts who might sometime in the future prove helpful to the corporation. She also telephoned Marianne and explained there had been a change of plan. For confidential reasons they would not be travelling to Indonesia together. She would now be flying on the same flight but two days after Stephanie's departure. Her office would change her flight bookings and she could collect her new ticket at the airport. They would be staying at the same hotel. Finally she sent a cable to Fred Baldwin; 'Proceed with Farnborough plans. Confirm full details myself and PR head, Roberto Pinakoulakis – Stephanie Stephanopolous Leopardis.'

Ten days later Stephanie met the Prince in the first class lounge of British Airways and this time he was wearing full arab regalia. She did not ask permission, but simply told the uniformed receptionist that her personal maid was flying with her and they were meeting Prince Hussein in the lounge, and she could see that he had already arrived. His bodyguard got up as soon as Stephanie approached and she did not see him again until they disembarked at their destination. Sophie sat down in his place. Once on board she disappeared into the back of the aircraft while Stephanie and the prince were cosseted in First where, during the flight, she drank vodka while he stayed with champagne and they shared the wines that were served with a light lunch and four course dinner, plus his comment, 'Very nice, but not quite up to the vintages served on Air France.'

He told her he had arranged for his suite to be next to her own. He had also arranged for her to be received by the vice-president in the palace at noon the day after their arrival. 'I told him you were my personal friend and the most beautiful girl I had ever seen, but also the toughest businesswoman either of them were likely to encounter.' Her thank-you was a squeezed hand.

They were both tired when they landed at their destination, but all four were hurried through customs and immigration thanks to the prince's diplomatic status. A bullet-proof stretch Mercedes with an armed guard in the front took them to their hotel where after checking in all they wanted was to catch up on the sleep they had lost during the flight but first Sophie had to unpack Stephanie's two cases and hang up her clothes.

Next morning she and the prince had breakfast together in his suite and she wore one of the several silk dresses she had brought with her. She was determined to make an impression on the vice-president. Her dress had style and class, but revealed nothing except its obvious expense, plus a spectacular diamond brooch which she complemented with a diamond bracelet and her diamond engagement ring, plus the prince's emerald. Round her neck was a simple rope of pearls. As they ate breakfast, the prince explained, 'The country gained its independence from the Netherlands in 1949. It is one of the world's poorest countries. Following a recent and bloody military coup it is now governed by the army and there are the first signs of prosperity. Many of the ministers in the former government of Sukarno were executed including, I believe, your father's then influential contact. There is a parliament but for the moment its purpose is to rubber-stamp whatever bills the president and the army sends them. There is considerably more freedom than before,

287

but it is wise not to express criticism. The army is all-powerful and the president and vice-president who you will meet this morning, have both risen from its ranks. You are quite safe so long as you are under my protection.'

They were driven to the presidential palace in a Rolls Royce which had been sent by the vice-president with the inevitable armed guards which this time consisted of two men in military uniform. She admitted, 'I am used to being treated as a VIP, but not until now like royalty. Thank you.'

'That is how you will always be treated and respected whenever we are together, unless we wish to travel incognito.'

They were kept waiting for only a few minutes in a marble floored ante-room where the prince alerted her to curtsy when she met the vice-president, while he would bow. In fact it was the vice-president who stood up when he saw the impeccably-dressed Stephanie being escorted into his extravagantly furnished office. 'Welcome to my country, madame, and of course, your highness.' He indicated his guests to sit down in two deep armchairs upholstered in fine embroidered silk. Their host sat opposite. 'I have been reading about your family's major investments in our country. We are most grateful. If there is any way I can assist you during your visit with Prince Hussein, or at any other time, you have only to ask. Consider yourself under my personal protection.'

Stephanie explained that until now all her family's investment in his country had been made by her father who had great faith in the future of the country. However, because of ill-health he would soon vacate his position as President of Stephanopolous International and she would be voted by the board of directors to take his place. As a result, all future investments would be her responsibility. 'My sincere wish is to receive your full support and co-operation.'

The longer he looked at her, the more he thought what a pity Madame Stephanie was under Prince Hussein's protection and not available to be taken to his bed. Stephanie guessed what he was wishing, and went on: 'My father dealt directly with a minister who I understand has since died. Even if that were not the situation, I would have hoped to deal directly with the president or his immediate deputy. You, so Prince Hussein has informed me, are the gentleman to be contacted to ensure that everything I have in mind for our future co-operation is expedited via your personal powers and support. The beneficiaries will be your country and my empire.

'One of my first plans is to open a new factory on a site adjoining our present operation a few miles from the capital. This will concentrate solely on producing the finest and most expensive ladies' shoes for which there is a growing demand from wealthy fashion-conscious women in every continent. Only they can afford to forget the drabness and monotony of the last two decades. I am determined to produce the most exquisitively designed shoes made from the finest and softest leather mixed with the rarest and costliest animal and snakeskins. Price will not be a factor, only quality will count, which is why I would welcome having, if possible, a supply of your own rare leopard skins which will enable me to publicise the part your country has played in meeting the desires of some of the most influential and wealthiest women in the world. Perhaps the president's wife would accept one of the first pairs of shoes to come off our assembly line which, with your support, will take place in less than a year from now.'

'With my support let us target for your production to commence in nine months time. It will not be a problem, I assure you. Our government's aim is industrialisation. While I am grateful for your offer, the president's wife is dangerously ill and only occasionally leaves her home where she daily receives the finest medical attention. However, I would be pleased to accept your generosity on behalf of another lady who I hope you will meet while you are here.'

'Mr Vice-President, you and I are on the same wavelength. Your aim is industrialisation. Mine, like my father's, is to take advantage of your cheap labour which, with your co-operation, will work long hours in the best interests of their country whose government has found them work. That is one of the reasons I am here and willing to invest new millions in your country. In the years ahead I believe many more industrialists will follow in our footsteps, but I would welcome your assurance that Stephanopolous International will always be given priority over any potential rivals. I shall be happy to see that your friend, who I look forward to meeting, receives a gift that will help confirm her place as the nation's leading lady and companion of the vice-president.

'I would, however, like to take up just a little more of your time. There are some other business matters I would like to discuss with you so that we may extend our growing commercial co-operation. First, I need to meet the trade union leader who has been working closely until now with my father, but will from now onwards be responsible to me and the Countess von Rugerstein who is my immediate deputy, and who is also in charge of our expanding armaments division, the Stephanopolous Armaments Corporation. She has outstripped, by a wide margin, the targets I set her. Thanks to her, orders for our new automatic small arms weapon have passed the one million mark in little more than one year. I have taken the liberty of having a model of the gun together with ammunition delivered to my hotel via your own customs, and would like to have it demonstrated to yourself and your army colleagues before I fly home with the prince. Once you and your experts have seen it in action, I am confident you will recognise its devastating firepower. With it in your armoury, you will not only be able to control every extremist minority, but destroy it. Its technical superiority and price advantage, over all its rivals throughout Asia and the Middle East, had been recognised by six national armies and two guerrilla groups in Africa. And my price drops by almost half for orders of half a million rifles. An order for that amount was placed by a North African state and was paid for in full before final delivery. In addition, we operate what is the second largest fleet of tankers and container ships in the world and have recently launched the largest and fastest tanker afloat. Working directly with me, or the countess, will ensure that your country receives our best possible terms for everything you purchase from the Stephanopolous family, especially when you buy, or hire, one of our tankers or container ships to transport your own exports.

'When would it be convenient for me to meet the trade unionist who will be responsible for controlling the workforce that will produce the kind of shoes that will make your friend the envy of every other woman in your country? Perhaps sometime tomorrow, if possible, so that I can explain to him that the easy-going days when my father was his contact are over, and that from now onwards he will receive his orders from me who is in direct contact with the vice-president, if you will permit.

And, finally, when would it be convenient for me to supervise a demonstration of our fast firing new automatic rifle?'

The vice-president stood up as though indicating that the audience was at an end. Because he was fascinated by the confidence with which this Greek multi-millionairess went about her business, he went on, 'Why don't you and the prince dine with me and my friend here at the palace this evening? Meanwhile I shall command your father's trade union friend to be at your hotel at ten tomorrow morning, if that is convenient. Please let me know if he does not measure up to your own high standards. I shall warn him that he is to obey every command you give him as though it were an order from me. Any failure will be regarded as an affront to the reputation of our country and will not be tolerated. Until eight o'clock.' He kissed her hand.

Over lunch, the prince told Stephanie that she had made an undoubted impression upon the vice-president. Her answer was to smile and hold his hand. He sounded like a poet as he described the country as 'a girdle of emeralds entwining the equator.' The emeralds, he explained, were the islands of Java, Sumatra, Borneo and the Celebes whose soils were fertile with rich green vegetation. There were around fifty active volcanoes of which the best known was Krakatau that frequently erupted. On the western isles were elephants, tigers, cloud leopards, rhinoceros and orang-utans, but all were threatened with extinction as millions of acres of rainforest were being cut down to make way for palm oil plantations. Palm oil could become the country's major export as it was in increasing demand throughout the world where it was used in the manufacture of beauty products, biscuits, soaps, detergents and margarine. There is extensive poverty everywhere which means cheap labour, while a tiny elite owns or controls all the nation's resources. He went on, 'I am looking forward to meeting his friend at dinner, who by the way is European. Rumours abound about her, but few know anything for certain. The government-controlled media never publish her photo nor that of any members of the government, nor write about her. There have been several unsuccessful assassination attempts on the present ministers. All have failed, but according to diplomatic bags an estimated two thousand suspects have disappeared and are unlikely to be seen again. Perhaps you will be able to solve some of the mystery about his friend this evening. She is said to have her own retinue of maids, and has an armed escort behind and in front of the car in which she travels.'

Stephanie was intrigued and determined to be the best dressed of the two that evening. She was only half-successful.

When the four met at the palace the vice-president's arm was around the waist of a ravishingly beautiful lady who he introduced as 'my friend, Greta'. She walked and moved gracefully in a way that commanded attention and admiration. Her dull, grey-coloured shift dress could only have been chosen so as not to provide any distraction from her provocative display of jewels. Her perfectly coiffured blonde hair fell on a necklace of diamonds and there were diamond bracelets and rings even round her ankles and toes. Stephanie had never before thought you could display too many diamonds. No wonder Greta was guarded wherever she went.

At dinner they were served by a team of eight petite Malay maids all in matching white uniforms and wearing purest white gloves. And it was Greta who gave them orders in a voice that was cold and commanding, although she never contributed to the conversation around the table. The vice-president told Stephanie that he had ordered the trade union official to present himself at her suite at ten the following morning, and to obey all her orders. In addition, he had arranged for the colonel of his personal bodyguard and member of his unit to attend at the palace at eleven o'clock a day later to test her new automatic weapon that seemed to have attracted some considerable interest worldwide. She thanked him for honouring her with so much of his authority. After dinner Greta escorted Stephanie into an adjoining salon while the men remained at the table and smoked Churchillian size Cuban cigars. The ladies drank more of the wine they had been served during the meal. Stephanie congratulated Greta on the royal ease with which she carried off wearing such magnificent jewellery, and added, 'Please tell me about yourself. Where were you born?'

'In Budapest, but more than that I am forbidden to tell you. However, I will tell you that when the Nazis occupied Hungary my mother was selected to service the general who was in charge of the occupation and we lived in the Hotel Gellert so that she was available whenever he called for her. I was only a child but I had my own nanny. When the Russians came we were smuggled out of Hungary and into Austria. I was too young to remember how it happened but we ended up in Jakarta. Here my mother again earned a lot of money selling her talents to please. I have inherited her skills. And now I live in luxury with the vice-president. Don't question me further. It might be dangerous, for me. I would love to show you where I live, but I am forbidden to invite guests because of security. Please don't tell the general what I have told you. If he asks, tell him we talked about fashion and men.'

Next morning precisely at ten the trade union leader was shown into Stephanie's hotel suite where she and the prince were waiting for him. He was nervous having received a personal warning from the vice-president that Stephanie was one of the most powerful businesswomen in the world and had a reputation for being ruthless with those who disobeyed her. Stephanie deliberately kept him standing when he entered her suite; she was convinced that for several years he had fleeced her father, and now it could be revenge time. He might be feared by the members of his union who were forced to be members if they wanted to work, and had their union fees deducted from their wages. They worked long hours six days a week mostly in a constant tropical heat. Now he had been warned over the telephone by the vice-president that his safety could not be guaranteed if he let his country down by not carrying out every order he was given by the young princess.

Stephanie asked the prince whether he wanted her to identify him to the shop steward. 'Best leave him in ignorance that I can speak his language as well as English until you have finished with him. Then, if necessary, I shall deliver a kind of *coup de grâce*.' Meanwhile, their victim continued standing, his head bowed. It was as though he had been forbidden to look at her royal face. Now in a voice that was rasping as well as regal she commanded him to look up and listen to what she had to tell him.

'Until now you have always been looked after by my father. He is about to retire and from now onwards I shall be all powerful as the head of my family's global empire in which you are a tiny cog. I believe you have cheated my father. Those days are over. No one cheats me. From now onwards you will receive no further payment from me until you prove by results that you are worth what we pay you. I am not interested in what steps you have to take, but from tomorrow I want every production target I set to be met on every shift. I shall not listen to excuses. It will be up to you to make certain that I receive the production levels I insist upon. With immediate effect, targets are to be increased by ten per cent. I do not care whether each worker reaches the target so long as it is reached by the entire shift. How you deal with anyone who lets the side down is up to you. I am arranging to have your output checked every month at my Asian headquarters where all production is sent and packed for shipment to customers in different parts of the world. If at the end of the first month your workers have given me what I demand, your dollar payments will be resumed. Any slowdown will always lead to the amount you receive being reduced. Any questions?'

There was silence. She had placed a noose round his neck which the vice-president would have no hesitation in pulling tight if required. He was forced to speak when she asked: 'How many are working at each of the two shoe-making plants that are your responsibility?' He hesitated, not because he did not know, but because his mouth was dry from fear.

'Pour yourself some water, and then sit down,' she ordered. He knew the old era was at an end as again she asked: 'How many?'

He still hesitated, but slowly told her: 'At the largest of the two plants there are four hundred and twenty workers who work twelve hour shifts each with two hundred and ten workers. Friday is for maintenance work. When they resume work those who previously worked at night, now work days. It is the same at the smaller factory which is doing identical work but with just one hundred and eighty workers with ninety on the day and night shifts, both of twelve hours with Friday maintenance, madame.'

'Thank you. That sums up stage one, Now I shall explain stages two and three. Within the next month the vice-president will authorise the building of a new modern plant on an adjoining site. While this work is being completed in nine months you will select your sixty best workers from the current two plants. But they are to be told nothing about my future plans for them. Shortly after completion of the new building, the most modern equipment for making the best and costliest ladies shoes in the world will be delivered and installed. Once this machinery is in place and operational you will transfer the sixty workers to their new location. By then two Philippinos will have flown in from Manila. They are experts in designing and making some of the world's most expensive shoes, including many for the much publicised collection belonging to Madame Marcos, the wife of the Philippines' president. They will be responsible for training and production for at least the first four months after the factory becomes operational. One of the first pairs to come off the production line at the new plant will be presented to the lady who is acting as your country's First Lady. When all your workers have passed the rigorous tests they will be set, we shall deliver supplies of the finest, softest and most expensive leather, plus selected animal and snakeskins. The vice-president has promised me a supply of the rare cloudy leopard skins. At first we shall concentrate upon court shoes, sling-backs, and high heeled sandals. An entire range is currently being designed for my approval by the Philippinos. The vice-president has guaranteed that the new plant will be ready to begin full production in not more than nine months. If that deadline is not met, you will be held responsible. Do I make myself clear? With such costly materials mistakes will not be tolerated. Each worker on every twelve-hour shift will be required to make three perfect pairs which will be stamped with an "S" for Stephanopolous shoes, but only when they have been meticulously examined by the two Philippinos. Providing your workers each produce a minimum of three pairs per shift they will be paid double what they were paid at the old plants where mass production was the aim. For every extra pair approved their wage will be increased by twenty per cent. Each shift will be allowed only one rejected pair per shift. Any more will see wages slashed by twenty five per cent. Making sure this does not happen is up to you. Succeed and your bonus will be bigger than before. Failure will lead to me informing the vice-president that I am considering transferring all production to our factory in China where production has never failed to meet targets thanks to every shift being supervised by members of the local communist party. As I am investing several million dollars in the new plant, you can imagine the reactions of the vice-president if your inefficiency forces me to consider transferring production to China.'

She turned to the prince and asked whether he had anything to say 'to this man'.

Prince Hussein stared at him for a few moments before adding, 'For your sake I hope you have clearly understood everything this very powerful lady has told you. Not only does she wield immense power, but she has the protection of both the president as well as the vice-president of your country. You don't need to know who I am, but I control one third of the world's oil supply and this young lady also has my protection. You have, I am told, done well until now. But now you are being entrusted with new responsibilities. Think of the ladies who will buy Madame Stephanopolous's shoes as vipers. They are vicious, intolerant and dress to express their high status in the world. As one of them told me, "What you wear is what you are. It is up to you to ensure that every pair of shoes that leaves the new factory is more than just perfect, but perfection."'

The trade unionist was used to being bullied by men of power, wealth and influence, but being whipped by a woman's tongue was a new experience. It left him bemused and scared. It was like entering unknown territory. To make him still further bewildered, she stood up until she was standing over him: 'Let me make the position between us absolutely clear. I do not worry. That is something I inflict upon people like yourself and those who work under you, and have to carry out my commands. Do my bidding and obey every order you receive from me or my colleague, the Countess von Rugerstein, who is now in overall charge of my shoe division, and all will be well. What you have to worry about are the consequences for your own future if a single one of the objectives I have outlined is not met and I threaten to withdraw our millions of investments. Whether you have a future depends solely upon me and whether my profits grow month by month.'

Once Stephanie and the prince were alone she confided: 'I am not sure I can rely upon him. But I intend to find out. My deputy, the Countess von Rugerstein, flies in late tonight. I shall let her take charge of the sales pitch for the new automatic weapon tomorrow, and the next day I would like to hire a car for the three of us to drive down and see our shoe factories for ourselves. Marianne will from then onwards take over responsibility for our shoe division, but always under my personal supervision. As a schoolgirl at the family breakfast table I listened to my parents discussing plans that would make millions for our family business and I learned that we lived in a world where the many slaved down mines, worked long hours in hot, fume-ridden factories, or hours hitting the keys of a typewriter while a tiny handful of us own the factories and the mines and the offices and pay ourselves salaries, or dividends, that dwarf into insignificance what the rest earn. Women like your sister and myself can wear emeralds and diamonds that cost ten times more than the millions of unknown women will earn in a lifetime. Yet more millions of women in the western world are fascinated to read about how celebrities like myself can afford to dress. We have our Rolls, Mercedes and Ferraris as well as private planes, while they take buses and fly in cattle class. And in poorer parts of the world there are still more women who scrabble frenetically to live out their lives sweating in sun baked fields, drinking and fornicating to produce children they cannot afford to clothe or feed let alone educate. Coming back to my new line of shoes I am reminded of a saying that English women are elegant, Americans glamorous, but only French, Italian and South American women understand chic. But wherever they live they will be the target for our new range of expensive shoes that will be far beyond the purses of high street shoppers.'

With Sophie sent back to her hotel bedroom, Stephanie flashed the 'do not enter' sign and locked the door of her suite. She confessed as she fell into his arms: 'The more I am with you, the more I want to be part of you. We are two of a kind, yet can never be one. You would never be permitted to marry a non-Moslem, while I love my husband although that need not stop us being the business lovers I promised. If such a thought pleases your highness, we could get into bed where I hope you will find my body more than just acceptable. If you agree, and Marianne persuades the army brass to buy our arms tomorrow, you will then be in line to receive the first instalment of what I talked about when we met in London. What happens now will just be doing what comes naturally. What a wonderful friendship we shall have. And, if you don't know it already, sex in the morning can be much better than late at night when both are hungry, yet tired.'

The hour that followed was ecstasy of a sublime kind. His sexual conquest of her was an act of pure desire, never hurried, but full of passion uncontrolled. For the first time in her adult life, Stephanie was not in control, and she had never felt happier as she responded with the wildness of a tigress being tamed without being whipped. As they lay side by side she asked, 'Do we have to wait until tomorrow before we have a second bite of a very juicy cherry?' Being together for the first time was hedonism and luxury, sensuality and glamour, between two people who had everything that life could offer, and now had each other. Together they were both winners. They showered in each other's arms, and playfully she thought, who wants Sophie when I have Hussein to dry me. Back in bed they slept, not through exhaustion, but contentment. Even when they awakened, lying together in their nakedness was all they needed. The fact that they had slept through lunch did not matter. They had fed one another, 'I don't think I have ever been so happy,' she purred like a kitten which had stolen the milk. 'You are the only man I have ever allowed to be in control when in bed with me. When I first saw Anton he was a clerk in my outer office, but for me it was love at first sight. Yet I spent a couple of months making sure that my feelings were not another whim of a wealthy young woman. They weren't. While there have been many men who have dreamed of the pleasure of touching me once they saw my unbelievably fine legs, Anton was not one of them. He knew that he might lose his job if he ever allowed his eyes to wander whenever I walked through the office where he worked. I am not one of those women who kiss broken dreams better. Today, no matter how much he is paid, the financial gap between us can never be bridged. But I still love him for himself, even though I now have my own prince charming.'

They had an early dinner to make up for their lost lunch, but were back in the hotel to welcome the countess when she arrived. In the restaurant where they ate they nestled close to each other and cut their food so they could eat with a fork and keep one hand free to excite the other with their touch. The prince admitted he did not know what he would do without her, and confirmed that if the countess impressed him with her presentation and demonstration of the weapon which the vice-president had asked to see demonstrated, he would immediately place an order on behalf of his own government which might also serve as an an encouragement to the army officers to follow his example. As Head of Security he had the authority, but only if it had the fire power to quell any threat to the ruling family or any insurrection. But he had to be impressed, or he would be criticised by his family when he returned home. After ordering the weapons, he planned to discuss with his brothers whether it was not time to think about placing an order for a new, larger and faster tanker to deliver their oil exports. He was wondering out loud if her husband could be persuaded to accept a *ménage à trois?*

Stephanie kissed his cheek and in return asked him to kiss the emerald ring he had given her, and mused that there seemed no limit to the problems a young empress might be called upon to solve. And resolved not to answer his enquiry; she was not sure what to say.

The Countess von Rugerstein had checked into Room 241 when they arrived back at their hotel and Stephanie suggested that if she was not too tired she should come to her suite and share a night cap, explaining 'I have much to tell you.'

Sophie poured drinks for the three and was then, as was becoming a habit, sent back to her own room to await any call from Stephanie.

Stephanie joked that she had once regarded Marianne as her older sister but now, although like herself she was also a member of the corporation's board, and her unofficial deputy, all she needed to do was obey every order she gave her, while everyone else throughout the Stephanopolous corporation had to carry out any instructions her one-time-sister gave. All the time she was speaking Stephanie was holding the prince's hand so as to alert the countess that there was a relationship between them.

Marianne was given a full report on the meeting that morning with the trade unionist who was in charge of the workforce at the two local factories that produced the popularly priced shoes that had captured over thirty-five per cent of the high street markets in eastern Europe, South America, Poland, Hungary, Moscow and St Petersburg. He was fully aware that there was now a new regime, and in future he would take his orders from either herself or Stephanie who confirmed: 'From now onwards, Marianne, you are the director in charge of all shoe production and sales, but under my direction. Within the next nine months we shall open a new plant adjoining the two current factories which will continue producing our low priced shoes while the new plant will concentrate exclusively on the production of our new luxury range. All three will come under your control. Only designing will not be your responsibility. I have hired a car to take the three of us on a twenty-five mile drive to where our two factories are in full production and where the new plant is to be built. I shall be responsible for all designs for the luxury range in co-operation with a Mr Chow, a Philippino, and his assistant, who for the moment work in Manila, but will later move here to train sixty of our best workers in the techniques needed to make luxury shoes without a single flaw when using the very finest materials.' She made no mention that the vice-president had agreed to let her have some of the finest quality snakeskins which breed on two or three of the more than one thousand islands that made up Indonesia. 'He has also promised me some of the skins of the rare cloud leopards, but I am thinking of having them for myself for one of the rarest fur coats in the world.

'When we arrive at the factory I shall introduce you to the trade unionist and I want you to confirm that in future all his special cash bonuses will only be authorised once you have personally checked all his production against our profitability. Finally, I have arranged for you to meet the vice-president at the royal palace the day after tomorrow at eleven o'clock to make a sales pitch to him and some of his senior army officers for our top selling, fast firing automatic weapon. A sample for you to demonstrate is under my bed. I suggest we all need to get a good night's rest and meet for breakfast here at nine-thirty.'

When Marianne had left them, Stephanie told the prince: 'Don't worry about her. She will do exactly as she is told. She is not paid a salary but receives a tax free bonus of between two and three hundred thousand dollars annually. No sensible woman walks away from that kind of money.' She made no mention of the plan to buy her husband's successful business empire and make Marianne joint chairman, unless by that time she wanted to take complete control. How she ran Stephanopolous was not the prince's concern. All he had to concentrate upon was herself.

21

Once again a car was sent to drive them to the palace where there was immediate concern when the heavy parcel Marianne was carrying was identified as a powerful gun. It was not until they received permission to allow them to enter the palace that those guarding the president and vice-president released the three of them and their weapons and escorted them into the palace itself where they were welcomed by the vice-president who stood up as the three of them entered his reception salon. Three high-ranking officers also rose to their feet while six ranking soldiers came to attention. Stephanie introduced the Countess von Rugerstein, her deputy. No time was wasted before Stephanie raised her eyebrows as a signal to Marianne that the spotlight was now on her.

'Mr Vice-President, officers of your country's armed forces, the weapon which I am cradling in my arms has proved a revelation to all to whom it has been demonstrated. It not only has the highest fire-power of any weapon in its category, but can be one hundred per cent accurate, and foolproof, on any target within a range of fifty metres and will still be scoring bullseyes at one hundred and fifty metres. It is lightweight and we supply live and training ammunition with every order. Stephanopolous International Armaments, of which I am Chief Executive and where my friend, Madame Leopardis is President, has sold more than one million weapons during the past year. In fact we have not so far given a demonstration without taking an order. We guarantee commencing deliveries within three months of receiving the agreed down payment of fifty per cent of the total costs.' She went on to explain the price of each weapon for a minimum order of one thousand, with reductions of five and seven-and-a-half per cent for orders of ten and twenty thousand weapons, while a sale of fifty thousand guaranteed a reduction of fifteen per cent. 'The secret of its rapid firing and accuracy was digital equipment for which Stephanopolous

Armaments held a worldwide patent. She or Madame Leopardis would be happy to answer any questions, and she would hand over her weapon with a supply of blank ammunition so that the accuracy of her words could be tested, and she hoped confirmed.

The officers led the way through long corridors with an armed guard at every corner, down a wide carpeted staircase, and out into the grounds until they were several hundred metres from the palace into an area marked 'Off Limits'. Here targets had been set up at fifty, one hundred and one hundred and fifty metres. Marianne loaded her weapon and handed it to one of the officers who immediately handed it to his superior. Without any noticeable command one of the soldiers stepped forward, saluted and moved into a position fifty metres from the first target which was twelve inches square. He first took up a standing firing position and next went down on one knee and fired off another couple of three second automatic bursts. Nothing was left of the cardboard targets. There was an identical result at one hundred metres and at one hundred and fifty metres the target was no longer recognisable. The targets were replaced and an officer followed. The results were the same.

To everyone's surprise, Prince Hussein asked permission to personally test the weapon. He had trained at the RAF college at Cranwell and had won his wings. He, too, shattered the first target, skipped at fifty metres, and tore apart his objective at one hundred and fifty metres. As he handed the weapon back to the senior officer he told the vice-president that irrespective of the verdict of his army colleagues, he would be placing an order on behalf of his own government. 'Very impressive,' was his verdict, as the group walked back to the palace. The non-commissioned sergeant who had fired the first test rounds was convinced that either lady in the party would win any beauty contest they entered, including Miss World, while never forgetting that the slightest look of interest in their direction by him or any in his platoon would be rigorously punished. Instead they presented arms to the vice-president, who himself was a senior general in the country's army, and were dismissed back to their own guardroom where they could freely express their views on the ladies who had so won their admiration, if that was the right word.

Back in the reception salon where coffee was served the prince explained that he had been impressed, not only by the weapon's firepower and accuracy, but also by its lightness. It was purpose-built for continuous automatic fire thanks to its minimal recoil. Any rebel group could be eliminated within minutes. He then revealed that his order would be for fifty thousand weapons for his five thousand strong army whose duties were solely concerned with defence, at the price indicated by the Countess von Rugerstein, but he would seek an option for an additional fifty thousand.

The vice-president stood up and announced; 'Madame Stephanopolous Leopadis will understand that in a country such as ours I am unable to make such an instant decision like his highness. But I shall consult with my army colleagues and let you have our decision within the next forty-eight hours. I believe we were impressed. Probably all that we shall need to discuss is our own total requirement.' What he did not reveal was that their own equipment was out of date.

Stephanie was surprised at the ease with which the prince could spend more than two million dollars without a moment's hesitation, or consulting with his family. Had her own generosity been an influence? As they drove back to the hotel, still with their armed escort, she told him and the countess that she would show her appreciation for this morning's sales pitch and its results, by taking them both to lunch in the hotel's restaurant. Looking directly at the prince she confirmed that he would have to wait until after lunch before giving him the present she had promised. By now Marianne had broken the code they were using. This was confirmed at lunch when Stephanie proposed a toast, 'To my two friends who both know how to please me.' A short time later she explained to the prince, 'Now you can understand why I am happy to pay this woman an immense amount of money for as long as she continues to perform as she did this morning.'

They walked Marianne back to her room having agreed to meet in the main bar at seven that evening, and this time the two of them headed for the prince's suite where they found his own bodyguard on duty. He was immediately dismissed and told to continue his guard duty outside in the corridor. Knowing from experience what was about to happen he requested permission to take a chair with him.

Going to bed with Stephanie the prince now knew was much more than 'being a morsel for a king' as Voltaire, France's best known writer, courtier and lover in the eighteenth century, described Madame de Pompadour whose reign in the royal bed at the court at Versailles lasted for more than twenty years thanks to her powers of seduction, plus much else. Now it was the prince who was being seduced, not by the vast wealth and industrial power of this modern Grecian goddess, but because he was willing to abase himself at her feet in order to remain in her favour. Until now he had paid or ordered women to sleep with him, since no Arabian princess, whether twelve or sixteen, had ever been chosen to be his bride in order to create a political alliance. Now he could concentrate all his attention on this reborn Aphrodite who could do whatever she liked, except have two husbands. However, she had even solved that problem by believing that extra-marital passion needed to be accommodated within a marriage in certain circumstances. As for him, he was convinced she was giving him her body because that was what she desired, and not as any kind of payment. They had much in common as was confirmed by her sensuousness as soon as he touched her. He thought she would explode before he was ready, but if anything her control was at least as great as his so that his entry and firing was timed to create her own orgasm.

The following morning the three of them took the car she had hired for the twenty-five mile journey to the industrial estate which still consisted of only her two factories, but would soon have a new, more modern sister plant concentrating on the production of ladies' luxury footwear. This isolation was due to Stephanie's father having insisted upon including in the original contract a clause that no other factories would be permitted to be built at any time within sixty kilometres of their plants, unless they were part of Stephanopolous International. This was in order to ensure that the men and women who worked for them would never have any alternative local employment.

Their journey was delayed by long troop convoys heading for manoeuvres around the port of Tandjungpriok, and the narrowness of the road. However, the few chances of overtaking gave them time to admire the continuous stretches of vegetation, mostly rice fields but also crops of maize, tapioca, soya beans, kapok, but few tall trees which confirmed, as the prince had told Stephanie, that many rain forests were being cut down to make way for palm oil production.

Finally they reached the village whose livelihood depended entirely upon the millions of dollars the Stephanopolous family had invested, and the inhabitants' ability to learn the skills that enabled them to become tiny cogs in a gigantic human wheel that constantly reached the targets that had to be met. Nothing better emphasised the vast ocean that separated the owners of the wheel from the cogs than the arrival of the two godmothers in the form of Stephanie Stephanopolous and Marianne Countess von Rugerstein. The way they dressed, the confident way they walked and their undoubted beauty made them appear like women from another planet that was closer to heaven than anything the villagers would ever know. To the godmothers the rest were little more than human pawns who could be moved from one job of work to another whether or not they liked it. They simply had to obey every order given by the local trade union leader who controlled every moment of their working lives, but now he, too, was in the power of these two goddesses whose words had whip-lash force. Mariannne found it hard to accept she was part of the same species. Stephanie quickly disillusioned her. 'Except for the colour of their skins they are no different from the four maids who look after you throughout every twenty-four hours. The slightest mistake, or act of disobedience, and you could shatter their world. Stop being so sentimental.'

The village was larger than Stephanie expected, and she began to believe what she had read that Java was one of the most thickly populated areas in the world. Most of the dwellings were made of bamboo, long overcrowded hovels separated from their neighbours by the thinnest of walls. A tiny handful of shops were made of timber with living accommodation above for the owners and their families, mostly Chinese. The only brick building was the local headquarters of the powerful trade union to which everyone had to belong if they wanted work, and where they were now taken for refreshing cold drinks. They met the trade unionist's wife and eldest daughter; but not his younger children who were at school in Jakarta. By comparison with the bamboo shebangs of the majority of villagers, his home was luxurious. He even had two servants who worked alternate shifts so that one of them was always on duty to look after the family of seven who ate and dressed better than anyone else in the village, except the Chinese. How the rest survived their poverty did not concern Stephanie who regarded them as the responsibility of the government and the union. She told her host for the day, 'It is amazing what American dollars can buy when your union gives you a position of power over the lives of one thousand men, women and children. Just never forget what I explained to you in Jakarta. As far as you are concerned I am more powerful that your own trade union bosses. Serve me and you will be rewarded, and in dollars. Let me, or the countess, down and you will end up in a hovel like the rest of the villagers, and working at one of our machines, or worse.' Marianne heard what she was saying, and realised that it was the way she would have to behave, too. The locals were no different from everyone else; give them a centimetre and they would try to take a kilometre. Soon, there might be new jobs once the new advanced machinery enabled a higher production to be possible.

All three were provided with sunshades to protect them from the fierce midday sun as they walked the two hundred yards to the site of the two factories. The noise in the larger plant was near deafening as scores of pairs of shoes were machine sewn into patterns printed on designs in front of each worker. On completion the shoes were placed on moving conveyer belts, marked with their own number and transported to the section where they were first inspected by one of the foremen whose salary was twice that of the rest of the workforce. He signed them as perfect once he had inspected each shoe and passed it on to the packers who placed each satisfactory pair, not into boxes but into self-sealing bags on which were printed on both sides 'Stephanopolous For Quality'.

Except for the fact that most men worked bare-chested in the excessive heat it was difficult for strangers to be certain which worker was a man and who a woman because both wore long skirts, or sarongs. Many were husband and wife teams who had requested permission to work on the same day or night shifts. All were continually under the watchful eye of three trade unionists whose salaries were the same as the inspectors. Their task was to make sure that no one stopped working at full stretch throughout their shift, and that none took more than the allotted breaks of twenty minutes every four hours. What surprised Marianne was that no one seemed to perspire despite the temperature being a couple of degrees higher inside than outside in the sun, yet perspiration was pouring off her own forehead and from under her armpits. Stephanie explained that the villagers were accustomed to the excessive temperatures from childhood and heat was part of their everyday lives. 'It is because of this that they can work the twelve-hour shifts that enable us to produce shoes around the clock and undercut our competitors without sacrificing quality.' Secretly she was deciding whether it might not be better to install the new equipment when it arrived in the largest of the present plants and transfer the best of machinery in the existing plants to the new factory. This would achieve the best for both worlds. The new plant would have efficient machinery and the best workers, while the more popularly priced shoes would be produced in a far greater quantities and thus, achieve greater profits for the company and more dollars in commisson for the trade unionist. Those using the new equipment would, of course, have their targets raised by possibly twenty per cent. She would satisfy the selfish caprice of the tens of thousands of women who were rich, super-rich or mega-rich, and did not know, or want to know, that there was another world light years away from their own. What mattered to them was being noticed, envied and recognised for their wealth which separated them from the rest of society. Stephanie would let Marianne and the trade unionist know of any change of plan when she made her final decision.

None of them troubled to go down onto the factory floors, but watched the work in progress from a balcony behind which was an office where a team of clerks worked producing detailed lists showing levels of shoe production on every shift, and whether the totals matched the targets. On normal days a supervisor would stand on the balcony where he could keep an eye on every piece of machinery and ensure that it was being used to maximum capacity. Then it was time to return to the union's branch office in the village where to everyone's surprise they found that the wife of the union official had cooked them a lunch of freshly caught fish and cooked rice which they washed down with ice cold coconut juice. While eating they enjoyed a performance of Javanese dancing by the wife's two eldest daughters, wearing gorgeous garments, who gyrated with exceptional grace to the rhythm of drums and gongs.

As soon as they ended their performance to much applause they disappeared together with their mother without taking a bow. Meanwhile the trade unionist and four of his six supervisors entered the room. At once Marianne rose and addressed them under the watchful eye of Stephanie and the prince whose eyes never seemed wander from his bedmate. Marianne knew what she was expected to say. 'First, I want to thank you for your welcome and your hospitality which far exceeded our expectations. It is, I hope, typical of the kind of efficient production we can expect from now onwards.

'Yesterday the head trade unionist in the village, under direct orders from your country's vice-president, presented himself to Madame Stephanopolous in her hotel suite in Jakarta where he received details of our new production targets which were the same as the Chinese are already meeting. He is now aware that in future all orders will be given either by Madame Stephanopolous or myself whose title is the Countess von Rugerstein, and Madame's deputy. Any failures on his part, or as a result of bad supervision by his deputies, would result in punishment as authorised by the vice-president of your own government. That is an indication of the importance he attaches to the millions of dollars which Madame Stephanopolous, who will shortly became the empress of her family's vast global empire, has invested in your country and elsewhere in China and the Philippines. Myself, as well as each of you, are at risk if we fail to carry out her orders. She can be merciless with any one who interferes with her plans to make her empire still more profitable and successful. This policy enables her to provide employment for several thousand men and women around the world, including six hundred in this village. I can reveal, as proof of her confidence in everyone who works for her in this village that within the next nine months, again with the support of the country's vice-president, she will install new modern equipment which will enable selected workers to earn still higher wages. She is also to build a third factory. One final point. From now onwards she has made me responsible for the three factories and all production in this village and elsewhere at our other plants throughout Asia. As a result you are all now responsible directly to myself. I have a reputation for not tolerating any slackness from those under my control. Anyone, including yourselves and every worker on the factory floors who fails to live up to my own exacting standards will lose their jobs. All our targets must be met during every shift. Failures we do not tolerate. Your futures are now in my hands. If you ever think you can challenge me, just remember that both Madame Stephanopolous and myself have the ear of the vice-president who we met yesterday in the royal palace. He is determined that our empire shall prosper and continue investing in your country. I don't want you to think that what I am saying is simply a warning. It is more than that. The vice-president has asked us to keep him informed of any insubordination, or failure to meet the targets we set. He has promised that his response will be immediate.

'I shall end by letting you know that I was not impressed by what I saw in your office at the main plant this morning. I do not believe that anyone there has the experience to produce the kind of accurate statistics that will be acceptable to me in the future. I suggest you ask headquarters to transfer one or two trained accountants here for three or four days each month. I shall personally go through all the figures you submit with the eyes of an eagle, and if they are unsatisfactory you will feel the sharpness of my claws. If any monthly figures indicate that production has fallen you will receive a warning that any further failures will result in me recommending to Madame Stephanopolous that she should consider closing all factories in this village and transferring its production and machinery to either China or the Philippines. It is my intention to return here shortly to begin making plans for the opening of a third plant which I anticipate will be attended by your country's first lady.'

As she sat down, Stephanie stood up. Her first words left them in no doubt about the stranglehold she had over the lives of everyone in their village. 'I am used to people standing up when I enter a room, or when I stand up.'

Every one of her audience felt like schoolboys who had been found out, and got to their feet. 'Thank you,' and her voice was as barbed as it was sarcastic. For a few more moments she stared at them one by one so that they began to feel like offenders in the dock awaiting sentence. Finally, she continued:

'I was very disappointed by what I saw in the plants I visited this morning. I was under the impression that everyone worked continuously throughout their shifts except for the two twenty-minute breaks. But I saw several standing idly by their machines, and none received any kind of warning from the so-called supervisors. I realised at once that my targets were too easy. And were being reached without anyone having to work full out. With effect from the beginning of next months all targets will be increased. That is not all. My future investments in this village include the immediate provision of the most modern shoemaking machinery in the world. Originally I had planned to install the new equipment in the new and third factory. Instead, the best sixty workers selected from the two present centres of output will be trained and transferred to the new factory where they will take with them the machines they are currently using. When the up-to-date equipment arrives it will be located in the two present factories. But because of the speed at which they can produce shoes the targets of all those nominated to work them will be increased by twenty per cent. I want no more laxity from you or any of the hundreds under your control.' Looking directly at the senior shop steward she told him: 'You will receive written confirmation of all that I have just announced. All you have to do is see that my orders are carried out.'

It was a quicker drive back to the capital.

On arrival back at their hotel Stephanie was informed by reception that the royal palace had twice telephoned because the vice-president wished to speak to her, and would she telephone him as soon as she returned. Knowing that he knew the Islamic mind better than herself, she consulted the prince. He suggested that he should be permitted to make the return phone call. He would simply tell the vice-president that she was feeling unwell, but he did not think it was serious, just too much sun and over-tiredness. He believed his own order had probably forced the vice-president into a difficult position where face-saving demanded that he place an order equal to the prince's. However that would present a problem because of the parlous financial situation in his country. He was sure the army and police wanted the new weapon.

Stephanie excused herself by saying she needed to go into the bathroom. In fact, she needed to think. The prince had placed her in an embarrassing position. She was more than happy to have him on her side because of his knowledge of the Middle and Far East, plus his contacts in the Muslim world, which were invaluable, but she could not accept him usurping her own powers in front of a subordinate.

While Marianne was left alone with the prince she took the brief opportunity to explain that she did not think Stephanie was too happy with his suggestion. Talking in little more than a whisper she pointed out: 'I have known Stephanie far longer than yourself and can read her like a book. I know when it is wise to accept whatever orders she gives me, and when she will welcome my suggestions. I don't know what has been agreed between the two of you, and it is none of my business, however, I do know that she is unhappy with what you suggested. As far as I am concerned I welcome any help you can give me to win more orders for our automatic weapon, but she is probably thinking that you are seeking to push her to one side and take over some of her undoubted power. Please tread carefully; she needs you.'

When Stephanie rejoined them she quickly told the prince she did not agree with what he had proposed. She also decided it was the time to inform Marianne about Prince Hussein's business relationship with her boss. But first she confirmed to the prince how happy she always was to have him by her side. 'I know your offer of help can win us millions of dollars in orders. However, you must always allow me to be in charge of the affairs of Stephanopolous International.'

'Of course.' The prince, who had rather more experience than herself in diplomacy, knew that an early show of aggression was often a near guarantee of defeat. An ability to accept compromise, at least at first, was more likely to lead to final success. Stephanie had to become accustomed to Muslim men who initially would find it near impossible to accept that women, no matter how beautiful and wealthy, were their equals. They could never openly agree to being defeated by a woman, even one who wielded great powers. It could be suicidal for her to adopt the attitude of She Who Must be Obeyed. He did not express these thoughts, and instead told her: 'I accept all you say, mine was only a suggestion. My intention was made because I believe that it would be best from all our points of view if the vice-president was not forced to lose face. What do you suggest we should do?'

'By all means ring the palace and say I am a little under the weather, but let him know that I shall be better after a good night's sleep and could the three of us meet him at ten tomorrow morning. If possible I would like to try to fly home on the night flight to London tomorrow evening, but this can only happen when we know what the vice-president has decided.'

The prince said nothing, did as he was bid, although he remained convinced that the vice-president would want to talk to him in private before conveying his decision to Stephanie.

That was what happened. Saving face was an essential factor in Islam.

When the three of them drove into the palace grounds they were quickly ushered into the same salon where Marianne had made her presentation. The vice-president was wearing a well-cut western suit although it did not have the touch of Savile Row, probably Italy or even, perhaps, Hong Kong. He was accompanied by the officer who had supervised the test firing. Immediately the two ladies had sat down he asked them to forgive his rudeness, but he needed to talk to the prince on a private matter, but General Kalimantan would remain with them.

In the privacy of his own office, which once a week was swept for bugs, he informed Prince Hussein that, while the army certainly wanted him to place a substantial order for the automatic weapons, their immediate requirements were for only half what the prince had indicated he would be ordering. The prince assured him that the last thing he wanted was to place the vice-president in an embarrassing position. They spent the next twenty minutes seeking an acceptable compromise that would satisfy everyone. Sadly for the vice-president, he knew that in such circumstances the prince held all the aces and might enjoy playing them because he wanted to please Stephanie. Finally, he issued his conditions, but in such a way that it looked and felt like a concession. He said, sounding like a judge summing up, 'Mr Vice-President, here is my solution to our problem

313

which I urge you to accept. I cannot remember the exact sum, but I know you are overdue with the payment for our last delivery of oil by several million dollars. What I am prepared to authorise is a delay of a further six months before your full payment needs to be made. In return you must give me a written guarantee that payment will be made on or before the date due. We will not be able to make any further oil deliveries until the present debt is cleared. However, the amount you will be saved in the immediate future will enable you to confirm to Madame Stephanopolous, without ever mentioning this discussion, that you have decided to match my order for fifty thousand weapons for which an advance payment of fifty per cent will be required before the first delivery is made. I presume both our orders will come in batches of ten or twenty thousand guns. In this way you will be seen to have negotiated a good deal for your own country in respect of oil deliveries. You may not be regarded as a hero, but certainly someone who can negotiate an acceptable deal. You have not lost face as you have won a six month moratorium in respect of your oil payments. And you will now be able to accept the conditions outlined by the countess regarding your first payment.'

'This is very generous of you, Prince Hussein. When in the future we want to improve our own commercial fleet I can assure you I shall talk first to Madame Stephanopolous who I am sure will offer my country the best possible terms.'

They were both smiling when they rejoined the ladies. The vice-president announced to the two ladies: 'I am pleased to inform you that my government will be placing an order for fifty thousand weapons, the same as the prince has already announced on behalf of his own government. In our private discussion we agreed that whenever the Stephanopolous armaments division makes a delivery to one of us, the other will receive an equivalent number of weapons. Neither will expect to have any advantage over the other. We accept that a fifty per cent deposit must be made before the first delivery. We would like to receive our deliveries in five batches each of ten thousand weapons. I suggest, a gap of three months between each delivery.'

The countess stood up and thanked both the vice-president and the general for their decision. She would do all she could to meet their delivery requirements, but before sending a final confirmation she would need to check with the factory how advanced current deliveries were. 'Try not to press us too hard in respect of your first two consignments. And, of course, each government will receive the agreed reduction in the price of their weapons based upon a total delivery of fifty thousand. There are no restrictions in respect of where or how the weapons can be used.'

Not a word was said during the drive back to their hotel, except when Stephanie asked whether the prince would be able to fly back to London with her that evening. She did not know whether he was joking when in reply he told her, 'I only make one condition, Stephanie; that we sit side by side and you use my shoulder as a pillow. What a pity they don't offer beds in First Class.'

For the first time Marianne understood the expression, 'three's a crowd'.

Back at the hotel Stephanie arranged for the concierge to check whether there were three seats available in First Class on the night flight to Heathrow two of which should be side by side, and he should let them know at what time they would need to leave for the airport. The prince intruded to explain they would also require two seats in economy, but not necessarily together. Stephanie ordered a bottle of vintage champagne with three glasses to be sent to her suite as a celebration on a successful morning, while Sophie was told, 'The holiday is over. We are flying home tonight. You have plenty of time, but start packing everything I bought with me except for the outfits I travelled in.' Sophie discreetly closed the bedroom door behind her.

On the flight home, Stephanie, Marianne and the prince were the only three seated in the front of the aircraft, and by identifying herself as part of the prince's party, Marianne persuaded the chief steward to allow her secretary, as she described Sophie, to sit in First because she needed to give her urgent dictation. In truth, she saw no reason why she should be the only one sitting alone. Sophie was even permitted to enjoy her dinner up-front, but no wine. Stephanie spent most of the flight cuddling close to the prince, or dozing. It was only when they were an hour out of Heathrow that she noticed Sophie was sitting in the gangway seat next to the countess.

315

But she said nothing. She was feeling too content. When they started their descent Sophie returned to her seat in economy and Stephanie took her place next to Marianne and told her: 'As my one-time sister, you will be the only person to know that the prince and I have agreed an arrangement. We shall make a good team, and as a result some of our rivals will not receive some of the orders they expected. Instead they will be made out to Stephanopolous International thanks to the prince's influence with heads of state and rulers of many Islamic nations. He has the key that will open doors and thanks to his connections it will not always be necessary to rub palms. But I shall always seek his permission to give personal gifts. And talking of gifts, how do you like my new emerald? It is a present from the prince. His family own an emerald mine in India. I have promised to wear it whenever we are together, but not in front of Anton who I love as much as on the day we married.

'Nor shall I forget my promise about your own earnings which will be expressed when we work out the bonuses to be paid at the end of the present financial year. Thanks to your successes for the armaments division and elsewhere I imagine it will now not be less than half a million dollars, and possibly considerably more. Aren't you glad I once regarded you as my elder sister?'

She suggested that Marianne should go back to Indonesia in three months' time to check on production and inspect progress on the third factory, and then back again three months later to begin finalising arrangements for the opening and deciding the date, perhaps in co-operation with the vice-president. Invited guests and the press should watch the first pairs of luxury shoes costing up to two hundred and fifty dollars a pair coming off the production line. She might, just might, attend herself. She would send Marianne some ideas for her to consider. 'Keep me informed about everything,' and, as though anticipating what Marianne was about to say, suggested she should take her husband with her on all future visits. 'That part of the world should not be visited alone and without an escort, never by a woman as attractive as you are, and wearing dresses like you can afford.'

As they began their final descent into Heathrow she returned to her seat and was holding Prince Hussein's hand as they touched down. The prince decided to stay in London while

316

Marianne took a Lufthansa flight to Munich. Sophie was given the rare privilege of sitting in Business Class next to her mistress who spent the entire flight to Athens drafting memos she would dictate to her secretaries for sending to the heads of departments and regions now under her direct control, instructing them to let her have within the next forty-eight hours detailed information of what had been happening while she was away expanding the corporation's business interests in Asia. Page after page of notes were filled as Sophie watched in amazement that anyone could have such a lively mind to cope with so many responsibilities without seeming to have any second thoughts about anything. Jet lag was one problem Stephanie did not have to solve.

22

The Acropolis stood out like the finest jewel in Athen's crown, rather like Stephanie's pear-shaped diamond engagement ring, as Sophie could not resist telling her: 'You are a wonderful woman, madame. Not only do you dress like a queen, but I now appreciate just how hard you must work when in your office. Thank you for allowing me to take care of you.' Probably because she, too, was at last beginning to feel a little tired herself, Stephanie had temporarily forgotten that she seldom talked to her maid except to give her orders. Now she answered, 'Thank you, Sophie.' And let her into a secret. 'You are now the highest paid servant among my personal staff.'

Once the limousine that had met them at the airport passed through the estate gates it was back to the old routine. As they went up the marble front steps there was the usual staff welcome. Sophie was to start unpacking and leave everything out that needed either washing or pressing. She was also to lay out a clean pair of pyjamas for both Mr Leopardis and herself, but before that she was to tell the cook to serve her and her husband a light meal of two boiled eggs, plenty of toast and some hot coffee in the dining-room in thirty minutes.

Anton had let his wife close her eyes throughout the drive from the airport, and it was not until they began to enjoy their eggs and toast that he asked how her trip had gone. She told him, 'I had my way in almost everything. We shall open a new shoe factory within twelve months, and the best of the present staff of more than six hundred will be trained to make the most expensive shoes in the world which will be promoted and publicised to those thousands of women in every continent who insist upon following every fashion trend that is dictated by publications like *Vogue* and *Harpers*. Two senior Philippino experts who know exactly what this specialist market demands, will begin retraining the sixty best of our existing workers to a far higher standard of workmanship once the new plant is ready and the necessary machinery is transferred from the existing factories. Many of those who remain making the popularly-priced shoes are being warned by their union that they must increase production to make up for output that will be lost when their colleagues move into the new plant. But my higher targets will be reachable because they will have the benefits of working at the most modern and efficient shoe making equipment. And they will earn more. But if they let me down the first person to suffer will be senior trade union representative, and then the workers under him.

'The Arab prince, Prince Hussein, who I met at the London Forum has agreed to open doors for us, and during this visit alone, thanks to his influence, we received orders worth millions of dollars for our new, and very destructive, automatic weapon. He has promised to introduce me to other heads of state and decision makers in the Islamic world. I will tell you more after I have caught up with the backlog that has accumulated while I have been away.'

As she finished her second round of toast and was half way through her second cup of black coffee she told Anton: 'Marianne has been informed that I want her to take charge and officiate at the VIP opening of the new plant. I find the weather out there too debilitating. She now knows that under me every penny she is paid has to be earned. She may not have my Midas touch, but she is very competent sales lady and organiser.'

Anton interrupted: 'Rumours have begun circulating around headquarters that your father is planning to make an announcement in the near future of his intention to relinquish the presidency, but will remain on the board with a role still to be decided. Obviously there has been a leak, whether deliberately or not I do not know, because two newspapers yesterday carried front page stories wondering who will step into his shoes. Will it be his heiress daughter or his Australian-born wife of Greek parents who has been by his side helping to run the Stephanopolous empire for the last twenty-five years, and is not yet fifty? One newspaper suggested that Ulysses might be planning to bring in someone from outside the family, while its rival publication suggested that the battle for the succession was only between his wife and his daughter. I'll be surprised if there isn't a message from your father awaiting you when you reach your office.'

'I think it time I went to bed. My travels and work have finally caught up with me.'

Next morning she had hardly set foot inside headquarters before everyone knew that the next president of the corporation was back from her overseas travels and in the building. Everyone who saw her immediately stood up as an act of respect while Dolores took her coat and hung it in her personal closet. On her desk was a file marked, 'Matters requiring the attention of Madame Stephanie Stephanopolous Leopardis', and on top a typewritten note informing her that her father wished to see her urgently. She scanned through all the other messages and correspondence in case there was anything that required her priority attention. There was a long telegram from Fred Baldwin informing her that the new transatlantic private jet was ready to be introduced to the aviation world at Farnborough in three months' time. He ended his message with a request for a meeting, but although she was delighted with his news her reply would tell him he would have to wait until she had time. Her own notes reminded her she should give priority to a meeting with her head of PR about the new shoe factory but that, like Farnborough and everything else was put on hold until she had talked with her father. She checked her make-up and ordered Dolores to notify his outer office that she was on her way. She entered her father's outer office with its sofa and two matching armchairs for visitors, as well as two large desks for his confidential secretary, Mrs Kronion, and Josefina her deputy, both of whom stood up and gently curtsied. Stephanie sensed they both knew she would be the next president of the Stephanopolous corporation and, equally important, their new boss, if she decided to retain them once she assumed control of the private monolith whose worldwide interests were owned by a single family and estimated to be worth more than five hundred million dollars, although no one knew for certain as the shares were not quoted on any stock exchange. The two secretaries accepted that she was a unique young lady who had been groomed to rule. Her mother lacked her daughter's intelligence or ability to make immediate decisions based upon an uncanny awareness of what was required. Stephanie could often sense dangers before they arose, and primed herself with solutions before they were needed. As the senior secretary said to her colleague as Stephanie disappeared into her father's office, 'She even walks as though she is aware of her superior position compared with the rest of us. We will never be really close to her. She is about to inherit her destiny and I think the female of the species will prove more venomous than the male. I remember hearing her father tell a visitor that there were three kinds of would-be entrepreneurs. Those who missed the opportunities, those who could not see them, and those who foresaw them and took action. His daughter is one of the latter.'

Stephanie walked round her father's emperor-size desk with its black leather blotter, three gold fountain pens, plus a single thick notepad on which he had written two words, 'Empress Stephanie.' She kissed him on his cheek and told him, 'Good to see you looking so fit and well, dad.'

'Looks, unfortunately, can be deceptive,' he told her, but added with a smile on his face. 'I had not seen a doctor once during the last ten years, yet I have had three meetings with heart specialists during the last two months. When I flew to London for an appointment with the top heart specialist in Harley Street, everyone imagined I had flown there on a business trip, and ditto when it was recommended I should get a second opinion from an equally eminent specialist at a clinic in Montreux on Lake Geneva. Sadly, Switzerland and Britain were in complete accord. Only your mother knows the full verdict which means that my old heart is no longer working well. Both the experts agreed there is a heart block, but happily rated mine as the least severe form which means that the delay between the contractions of what are called the atria and the ventricles are only slightly longer than normal. But still worrying. When similar tests were carried out a month later the delays had lengthened. I have been warned to ease up on all my responsibilities. Fortunately for me I have the most beautiful angel waiting in the wings to take over many, and eventually all my duties.'

He invited her to come and sit on his lap. 'What I intend to do,' he went on as he held her hand tighter than she could ever remember and fixed his gaze on the radiance of her large pear-shaped diamond ring which encouraged him to come straight with the news he had to tell her, if she didn't already know. 'Your ring, as much as anything else, confirms to me that you have every right to be the next person to sit at this desk.

Everything about you convinces me that I shall be making a wise change when I move aside and announce your succession. I shall stay by your side in an advisory capacity for as long as you need me, but this will be your office and you will have full charge of our entire family business which, as you now know, is larger than any other private corporation in the world.

'Here is what I suggest, but it is for you as the new president of our corporation to say yes or no to what I am proposing. An announcement in the form of statement will be made not by me, but by the company secretary, and sent to the Greek and international media to the effect that from this date, Mr Ulysses Stephanopolous has resigned due to ill-health as president of Stephanopolous International. His daughter, Stephanie Stephanopolous Leopardis, has been unanimously elected by the board of directors as the new president with immediate effect. A press conference is being called.

'There are no objections from your mother. I have told her about my medical condition and she agrees that I should step down and that you should take my place, while she devotes herself both to looking after me and helping you in any way she can while continuing with her business duties for the corporation which she has undertaken with considerable efficiency for many years. In future this office will be your office, not mine, although I shall come whenever you ask me. You will occupy this office suite and inherit my two personal secretaries, Mrs Kronion, who is the senior of the two, and Josefina Philips who is equally efficient and competent. Both have been with me for several years and are aware of everything about the corporation except the most confidential information. Both are fully conversant in both Greek and English, and are completely trustworthy. Whether you keep your own two secretaries is for you, and you alone, to decide, while I am offering you my continuous services as a consultant, and your father, for the next six months.

'Just remember that it is when everything is running smoothly that most people make their biggest mistakes. When events go awry you will be criticised for being too young for such a global responsibility. I don't think you are. One final point. From now onwards anything you say or do will be newsworthy and the spotlight of publicity will always be directed towards you and no one else. You need to discuss your future public relations very carefully with Roberto Pinakoulakis who I think has exceptional talent for the job, and has already prepared the press release announcing your appointment. Nevertheless, I wonder whether, perhaps, we need a new man to be responsible for advertising and marketing worldwide. I am sorry, but from now onwards your life will be very different, and very public. Don't be ashamed to ask for, and take, advice. You will be headlined as the wealthiest businesswoman in the world, and be a target for every crank. I suggest you employ a team of professional, and armed, bodyguards so that you are protected twenty-four hours a day. You are an obvious target for kidnappers. You already have a high profile, but from the time of our announcement you are potential front page news. Your dad, on the contrary, has always sought to keep a low profile and contented himself with seeing our family bank balances increase year by year so that his daughter can now wear the largest diamond I personally can ever recall seeing on any woman's finger. I have called a board meeting to confirm your appointment for ten tomorrow morning. This will be followed two days later by a press conference at noon which will be held in the ballroom of our hotel in Constitution Square. The board meeting will also be asked to confirm a new allocation of the shares in the company so that you will control fifty-five per cent, you mother and I will each own twenty per cent, your Uncle Boris with one share and the countess with two. It is up to you to decide about the holder of the remaining two. Does that arrangement meet with your approval, Madame President?'

As she went to get off his knee he immediately vacated his seat and asked his daughter to take his place, adding, 'This is where you now belong.' Her reply was to admit: 'Although I have been waiting and hoping for this call for several years, ever since you told me that you hoped I would be able to take over the reins of power on my twenty-fifth birthday which is still a year away, now that the moment has arrived, I am overwhelmed by my responsibilities and my power to make decisions that could effect the lives of thousands around the world. For the first time, I feel a little scared, but please don't ever breathe a word to anyone that I said so. That has to be our secret.'

Slowly she accepted that this was her rightful place and began to savour what was hers by right. She could do exactly as she decided. For all practical purposes she was already the president of Stephanopolous International. While she relished the moment, her father went to the door of his one-time office and asked his two secretaries to come in. 'Meet your new boss,' he informed them. 'As you know, I have called a board meeting for ten o'clock tomorrow, but as far as you are concerned the only orders you are to take from now onwards are from Madame Stephanie Stephanopolous Leopardis, and only occasionally from me, and even then only with her consent.' The senior of the two secretaries walked round the desk and kissed her new boss on her cheek and said, 'Our warmest congratulations, Madame.' Stephanie decided that for once she would allow such presumption, but the next time they met after her official appointment she would let them both know how she was to be addressed at all times. They needed to realise that her regime would be far stricter and more disciplined than her father's had been.

Back in her own office she immediately informed Anton and his response made her once again realise that he was the man she would always want by her side whether in business or in her bed, even if she occasionally roamed on behalf of the corporation. He told her: 'You are going to enjoy your new role. And I will be wherever you want me to be. Did you know that when you pout your lips one never knows whether you are teasing your target into believing you like them more than a little, or are deliberately bewitching them so that from then onwards they are powerless before an empress, which is what you now are? Believe it or not, you are now pouting your lips and looking still lovelier, and I should be humbling myself before you.'

However, there was no pout when she told her own secretary that from now onwards she would be the third secretary to the new president of the corporation whose authority would be confirmed at a board meeting the following day, but until then her seniority had to remain strictly confidential, and was for Dolores's ears only. She went on: 'You will remain at your present desk and I shall move upstairs and occupy the presidential office where I am inheriting my father's two senior secretaries and you will work under them until, and if, I decide if any changes

324

are necessary. Now leave me alone with my husband, but when I press the green button that will be my instruction for you to ring for Roberto to come to my office, here.'

Anton took her in his arms and hugged her tightly and kissed her lips. 'I am so proud of you, darling. This is what you deserve and I know the future of the family empire could not be in better hands.'

He was a little surprised when she told him that she hoped he would be just as happy when he heard two items of information. 'Firstly there is to be a board meeting tomorrow morning at which my appointment will be proposed and passed, I presume. After this I shall move a resolution proposing that you be elected a member of the board, after which I shall propose that you receive two shares, the same as Marianne.'

She hesitated before continuing 'I told my mother before we married that, unlike her and my father, I would never have secrets from my husband. For this reason I want you to hear from myself that while I have been away with Prince Hussein I have been sleeping with him and will probably go on doing so. However, I am not in love with him. I remain in love only with you. I have told the prince my relationship with him is purely because it benefits Stephanopolous International. He has already proved his value, and there is a strong possibility that he will soon authorise the purchase of a new oil tanker which could be worth hundreds of millions of dollars. In the interests of the corporation I am not prepared to risk losing him, at least not for the moment. Please believe me, I love you as much as I have always done. But I need to know that you understand my position. Please tell me you love me as much as I love you.'

'I love you, darling. I shall never allow anything to come between us. My task is simple. To love you as I have done even before we were married, and to be by your side whenever you need me.' He meant every word, although deep inside him he wished it had not been necessary to say them.

Although he had been informed in confidence what was to happen on her return, Roberto maintained a position of ignorance until she confirmed her new title. He kissed his congratulations and it was immediately back to business. She commanded him to prepare a new press release of her appointment to be issued to all those attending the press conference, plus an updated biographical release. She also told him of the two mammoth orders she had won during her trip to the Far East, one from an Asian government and one from one of the world's largest suppliers of oil who could shortly be placing an order for the world's largest tanker. 'I would like to see your drafts before I go home this evening. Bring them to me to me in the president's office which is where I shall be found from now onwards.' She added: 'During the next weeks and months there will be many changes within the corporation. There is much that I have to discuss with you, and as I shall increasingly be in the public eye my security and my public relations will take on a new importance. My father and I have agreed this morning that your own brief is far too wide. Sometime soon your sole responsibilities will be to concentrate on my own and the corporation's international public relations, and overall publicity and promotions. A new executive with equal status will be appointed to handle advertising and marketing worldwide. Finally I think it essential that you appoint or recruit someone with the necessary qualifications to act as your deputy to look after my interests when you are unavailable. Keep me informed of what you plan. Let me know if you think my cousin, Dimitros, could be a candidate.'

Before he left he was also instructed to contact Fred Baldwin and together plan whatever needed to be done before Farnborough and during the event. As soon as he left she told her secretary that she was going up to her new office where she would work in future. She was to follow in ten minutes. And bring her fur coat. She would introduce Dolores to her new senior secretarial colleagues.

Roberto took his two draft press releases to her in the presidential office early that afternoon. He had been working on the wording unofficially for the last twenty-four hours since being informed in confidence of her coming status. It began: 'Stephanie Stephanopolous Leopardis was this week (December 18) confirmed by the company's board of directors as the new president and chief executive of Stephanopolous International, probably the largest privately owned corporation in the world. This followed a decision by her father, Ulysses Stephanopolous, to stand down on medical advice. He has a serious heart condition and has been advised to rest, etc.

'Introducing his twenty-four-year-old daughter, after he had confirmed his own resignation, he described her as a *wunderkind* who had, almost from birth, been groomed to the position she was now inheriting. He explained: "For the last seven years she has been trained to know as much about our global activities as I do myself. She is fully competent and conversant with everything she needs to know about our fleets of tankers, container ships as well as aviation, hotels, property, shoes, fashion, textiles and finance, everything for which she is now responsible. Originally her succession was planned for her twenty-fifth birthday, but because of my own ill-health, and because she is ready, it has been brought forward by a year. She recently celebrated her twenty-fourth birthday. As a loving father I shall be by her side whenever she needs my assistance, but I doubt whether it will be very often. As of now she is in full command of the corporation following the unanimous confirmation of her appointment by the board of directors yesterday."'

She accepted his draft, but was to add something along these lines: 'The new twenty-four-year-old tycoon, who has recently been acclaimed as one of the ten best-dressed businesswomen in the world, recently returned from a visit to Asia which resulted in confirmed orders for more than ten million dollars for what is now her empire.'

Prints were to be available at the press conference, while her first hour of her first full day in the presidential office was taken up with photographs of her sitting in the presidential chair, dictating, taking phone calls and showing her unbelievable legs. Roberto knew that in her new exalted position she would become the equivalent of a queen bee, with a very powerful sting. She told him: 'You and I have much to discuss in addition to my own personal image, including Farnborough where we will showcase our two new private aircraft, one able to fly across the Atlantic non-stop from any capital in western Europe, as well as the launch of a new range of shoes aimed solely at the upper echelons of society in all parts of the world or, if you like, the readers of *Vogue* and *Harpers* and other colourful fashion publications. The countess will have overall charge, and report only to me. I shall arrange a meeting between the three of us as soon as my schedule allows.'

23

Stephanie revelled in her move into the presidential office within hours of being told of her elevation, and was still there with Anton at nine that evening. All her secretaries had been sent home hours earlier. Now it was her husband who suggested, 'It is time we did the same, darling. Your father has sent his Rolls Royce to bring you home where I believe he will be opening a bottle of champagne for just the three of us and your mother to celebrate your succession. And then I shall take you to bed for a more personal celebration. Now, more than ever, I realise I am married to a most exceptional, wonderful and beautiful lady. I cannot say that I am happy knowing that my wife is deliberately sleeping with another man, but I can also understand why it may occasionally be necessary in the best interests of her empire. Nevertheless, I hope you will also understand that I would prefer not to meet the prince unless you decide it is absolutely necessary and unavoidable.'

'Thank you darling. I fully accept everything you say. But for the moment you have no alternative but to accept the current situation. When you are dealing every day, as I shall be, with business worth millions and millions of dollars, and the jobs of thousands of men and women, the normal rules of marital behaviour cannot always apply. I promise to be as discreet as possible. And I know the prince will also exercise maximum discretion if we ever have to appear in public. The prince is fully aware that according to his religion, and his position in direct line to the throne, there is not the slightest chance of our marrying unless I declared publicly my willingness to become a Muslim. And that I shall not do, not even for Stephanopolous International. I insist that you trust me. I love you as much as I ever did, but my life has been changing for the last several months, and if you love me, your approach to my new life and responsibilities has to change, too. Please, don't let the interests of Stephanopolous International come between us; after all, it was the corporation which brought us together.'

Anton was brought face to face with the same problem that had faced every consort throughout history. Being married to an empress, with all its advantages, also meant accepting that he had to live as she commanded.

The white Rolls was parked immediately outside what was now her own empire state building. The night duty security guard saluted and a uniformed chauffeur helped her into the limousine followed by her husband. As they drove off, she asked the chauffeur whether the intercom was on or off. 'It is on, madame,' and was immediately warned that it is always to be turned off whenever she was in the car, adding, 'Whenever I want it switched on I shall do so myself. Is that understood?'

Not for the first time, Stephanie kept her parents waiting in the family sitting room while she and Anton prepared for the private family celebration. This occasion marked the beginning of a new order that in different ways would affect them all, and everyone around them. Their staff were now her staff and they needed to understand that from now onwards it was she who was the head of the Stephanopolous dynasty, and it was her orders they had finally to obey. It was not so much the end of an era, more the start of a new reign. Nor was it only within the Stephanopolous empire that changes would take place. The mid-1960s saw the start of economic growth; money was being spent more freely throughout the western world, and occasionally elsewhere, especially in Japan. An increasing number of women were beginning to take up new challenges that previously would only have been open to men, although you could still count on your fingers the handful who had crashed through the glass ceiling that had hitherto been a near unconquerable barrier through which they could look, but not go. Wages were at last on a rising curve, although there were few signs of any equality between men and women who did the same work. To Stephanie this also meant she was the new head of the Stephanopolous household, a fact confirmed when her father asked whether he and her mother had her permission to sit down.

'Of course,' she told them and at the same time motioned Anton to do the same. She continued to stand. She remembered that until then her father always remained standing until everyone else was seated. She walked towards her mother and kissed her and explained that as far as she was concerned anything that had been said between them in the past was now history, or as she put it, 'I am wiping the slate clean. I want you to know how grateful I am for making this transition so easy by giving your generous approval of my elevation to power and dominance. As far as I am concerned it was you who helped mould me into the woman I have become.'

Her authority had to be recognised. There could be no exceptions. Her father rose from his chair and filled four glasses from a bottle of vintage champagne which had been opened a short while earlier. Perhaps even that privilege should now be passed to her husband, but that was for her and Anton to decide. Her father proposed a toast: 'To the success and happiness of the new head of the Stephanopolous family and empire; I am sure it is in safe hands.' All clinked glasses with each other and Stephanie responded: 'It means a great deal to me to know that I shall have the full support of the three people who mean more to me than anyone else. But I feel it would unwise of me not to make it clear that while I welcome this support, the authority which will be given to me at tomorrow's board meeting means that I have absolute power to make whatever changes I think necessary to ensure the continued prosperity of ourselves as individuals and the corporation which we own.'

Her father responded: 'That I am sure is fully understood by us all because we have complete trust in your undoubted abilities. However, there is one matter which has not been mentioned. Your mother and I both hope you will allow us to continue living here in our main home for as long as we are both alive. In the event of my death, and because of my age I have to presume that I am likely to die long before your mother, then it will be a matter for you to decide where she should live. I am certain you will take good care of her.'

Stephanie answered: 'The only reason I did not mention this situation was because I imagined everyone understood that I had not thought of throwing my own parents out of their home. No, everything will remain as it is while you are both alive. If mother is left a widow then Anton and I and our family will move into this house and make it our home. My wish would be that mother will move into my own home and regard it, as they say in England, as her dower house. My intention, together with Anton, is to spend our time ensuring that Stephanopolous International grows and becomes still more powerful and respected than it already is. However, I intend to take possession of the white family Rolls as my own. It is the kind of limousine people will expect the president of our global empire to travel in. You and mother will still have a Rolls to share as you deserve, and there are also two Mercedes saloons for you to use providing they are not required by myself or Anton.' She did not ask for her parent's agreement. It was no longer necessary.

The following two days were the busiest Stephanie had known as events forced her to realise the near intolerable pressures that were now on her slim shoulders. Each morning at six Sophie brought breakfast in bed for herself and Anton and laid out whichever outfit she had selected the night before and were suitable for the different meetings her secretaries had entered into the same office diary that had previously belonged to her father, but was really the diary of whoever was president. Stephanie quickly accepted that anything less than a twelve-hour day would be a rarity, but that was nothing new although previously it had been her choice, now it was her duty.

Meanwhile, she insisted upon her parents driving with her and Anton to headquarters in what was now her own white Rolls on the morning when she would officially become the corporation's president. They sat round the large mahogany boardroom table with all the directors present, athough only five of the eleven had voting rights; herself, her father and mother, her uncle Boris and Marianne. On a proposal moved by her father and seconded by her mother, Stephanie was unanimously elected the corporation's president. Her father had begun the meeting by telling the directors that what was happening that morning had been agreed five years earlier when he had told his daughter, Stephanie, that he hoped that by the time she was twenty-five, or earlier, after completing several years of rigorous training and induction into the works of every division of the corporation, she would be ready to sit in the presidential chair. Although that birthday was still a year away, she was now ready and fully prepared to take his place. All was minuted, and he immediately vacated his chair and invited

Stephanie to take over as only the third president in the history of the corporation.

Stephanie told the board it was not her intention to call regular meetings, but, instead, would appoint her own inner cabinet of five, at the most, six, whose decisions would be put to the board for approval. Its minutes would be circulated. She had not yet decided who would be asked to serve in her cabinet, but her father would be one of them. Before the meeting ended she moved her first resolution as president which was to vote her husband onto the board with two corporation shares. There was no opposition.

With that she brought the meeting to a close, and returned to her office where her first task was to dictate a letter to her Uncle Boris: 'I am writing to you as one of my first tasks as president of Stephanopolous International. Several months ago, while still the empress-in-waiting, my father and I agreed that you should remain in charge of our shipping division until I took over the presidency. With immediate effect I am appointing Mr Anton Leopardis as the new head of our shipping division. I am, however, authorising that your pension in retirement should remain at the same level as your final salary, and this will be paid to you monthly until your death. Please vacate your office within the next forty-eight hours. As a result of this change you will no longer be a member of my board of directors. Your voting rights as the holder of a single share are now null and void. However your one share has a value of several million dollars and if you decide to sell, I shall be happy to make you an offer. However, please be assured that none of these steps are being taken out of vindictiveness, but solely in the future best interests of the family corporation. Let me put on record my warm appreciation of your loyalty to the corporation over many years. With warm regards to you and Aunt Olga. Signed, Stephanie Stephanopolous Leopardis, President.

'Send blind copies to Carl Ellungsen, Accounts and Personnel. Bring me the copies for signature as soon as they are ready. Meanwhile, please have two cold luncheons sent to the president's office at one o'clock. I shall go through my morning correspondence and give you and Miss Philips further dictation after lunch. Make sure that you and Miss Philips are never at lunch at the same time. Now I have private matters to discuss with my husband.'

She turned on the red light which would ensure that no one could walk into her office until she switched the light to green, and even then not unless she gave permission. She turned to Anton: 'I intend to stamp my authority on the corporation within the next few days. I cannot do this without you. During the next few weeks I shall need your constant support and co-operation. It is for this reason that I want you to take charge of our shipping division, while continuing in your present role as Director of Personnel. My intention is to appoint Helena Konstantinides to become Assistant Director of Personnel until we both feel that she is able to take over all your duties. If, after three or four months she does not fulfil our expectations, we shall have to review other options. I shall have a talk with Helena as soon as I can spare the time. Strange as it may seem, I am impressed by reports I am hearing about the enthusiasm being shown by my cousin, Dimitrios.

My personal first hurdle will be tomorrow when I meet the world media. I would like you by my side especially as you are now a member of the Board with two shares which makes you the fourth largest shareholder. Marianne also has two. Although they are not quoted on any stock exchange they are regarded as having an estimated value of five million dollars each, based upon the $500 million, which is the estimated and minimum current worth of the corporation. I am giving you, as you deserve, a present of ten million dollars. I told you I was a good catch. And so were you.'

The largest hall in either of their two hotels in Athens was crowded with media from Greece, Europe, America, Britain, and Japan and five international news agencies. Photographers and TV camera crews seemed everywhere, but were marshalled into some form of order by Roberto. After Ulysses had introduced his daughter as the logical choice to take over from himself, it was Stephanie's turn.

Stephanie slipped out of her mink jacket to reveal a low-cut little black dress which was relieved by a glowing white three row pearl necklace and an impressive diamond brooch, plus her empress size engagement ring, and admitted: 'If you were to ask me my aims as the new president it would simply be to increase and extend our worldwide sales and the reputation of the family corporation which my father has achieved. This will

333

begin in a few months time when we introduce to the aviation world two new private jet aircraft, the largest of which will be able to fly businessmen and women, or anyone else, non-stop from any capital in western Europe to the United States in complete luxury. And this, I can add, is only the start of our ventures into the skies which is where much of tomorrow's travel will take place. Already one of the most influential Arab princes in the Middle East has indicated to me that he is considering placing an order for two of the long distance planes and three of the short haul version. Nor is that the only indication of the kind of family business I shall seek to develop. On a recent visit to the Far East my deputy and myself won orders worth just short of ten million dollars for the Stephanopolous Armaments Division. I also intend to follow in my mother's footsteps, and try to be the good samaritan either on my own, or through our Stephanopolous Foundation which supports under-privileged children in many parts of the world.'

As she sat down everyone in her audience whether reporter, columnist, city editor or photographer was aware that here was not only a lady who was gorgeous, wealthy and talented, but also a story that would run and run. She took questions and caused a ripple of laughter when she answered one journalist who asked whether she had any personal hates. She smiled and told him, 'They are not for men as good looking as yourself but sadly, I have to add that I am happily married.' And she blew her husband a kiss. She went on: 'As for hates, I hate being kept waiting, and I hate inefficiency.'

Next a representative from Reuters asked whether she did not think she was too young to run a family business with an estimated value of five hundred million dollars? She answered: 'That is a question which I believe should be put to the board of directors who yesterday were kind enough to elect me unanimously as the corporation's president. Anyway, ask me what the business is worth in twelve or eighteen months time, and that will be my answer.'

The last question was asked by a woman journalist: 'My congratulations on the magnificence of your mink jacket. How many more furs like that could you have worn today?' Stephanie again proved she could handle questions that were meant to embarrass, by replying, 'At least a couple, I must admit. Like every woman, I enjoy being admired.'

The end of the press conference was not the end of her stint. It was followed by four television interviews and four more radio recordings. She was continually being photographed, and it was almost four in the afternoon when Roberto called a halt to further media attention by pointing out that Madame Stepanopolous Leopardis had been talking for more than four hours. There had been no time for lunch, although she did share a cup of coffee and a slice of fruit cake with one of the TV crews. It was around six o'clock when Anton quipped, 'I think it time for lunch.' The two of them dined in the hotel's rooftop restaurant and even there the media followed. A Japanese television crew were to follow her everywhere for the next two days, including Sophie bringing her breakfast in bed at 6.30 am. The commentator estimated she worked an eighty-hour week, compared with an average of seventy hours by her Asian workers.

Even at weekends, because of the corporation's growing activities in the southern hemisphere including South America, Australia and southern Africa, the flow of letters, telexes, cables, and increasingly computer messages that flooded into her office, meant that one of her three secretaries worked one weekend in three. This duty included being in the office each Saturday from eleven in the morning until four in the afternoon and on Sunday from ten in the morning until she drove to the president's private residence with everything that had arrived since Friday evening where she dictated notes or replies which were to be ready for her signature on Monday. So great were the pressures on her young shoulders that Sophie had once been forced to remind her how long it had been since she had been to her hairdresser. Stephanie's response was to phone Marcel and tell him: 'I am far too busy running this empire to come to the salon even for a wash and set. If you want to keep my custom I need you to come to my office at nine o'clock every Friday morning for one hour to make sure that I keep up the appearance that is essential for the new president of Stephanopolous International, who has been nominated as one of the ten best-dressed women in the world.' Marcel recognised it would be unwise to argue and lose his most prestigious client. He knew she had a reputation of being hard to please, and if he was her personal hairdresser, it had to mean that he was as good as his own publicity with her name among his clients confirmed.

Shortly after becoming president, Stephanie appointed Anton as her immediate deputy in place of Marianne, but not vice-president and he moved permanently into the president's office which meant that Helena was now in day-to-day charge of personnel. Stephanie issued a press release announcing his new position and his appointment as a director of Stephanopolous International as well as becoming head of the corporation's shipping division. Next she dictated a memo to Helena Konstaninides, informing her: 'Due to a reshuffle in the responsibilities of senior executives, and the appointment of Anton Leopardis as my immediate deputy, and a member of the board of directors, I am now appointing you Deputy Director of Personnel. I shall rely upon you to run the department with full control over everyone except those working on the top three floors. You have powers to both hire and fire. Make sure you keep Mr Leopardis informed of all decisions. I shall be issuing an announcement of your appointment. For the time being your salary will remains unchanged, but it will be considerably increased at the end of three months if Mr Leopardis is satisfied with the way you are running the department. Stephanie Stephanopolous, President.'

Despite the amount of paperwork that snowballed onto her desk like an unceasing avalanche she decided the only way to filter the load was for Anton to read everything and only pass to her what he knew she needed to see, or anything about which he was not sure. The correspondence covered everything that was happening throughout her empire whether in the form of reports, sales figures, statistics or requests for guidance. At first she walked through every department once a month, often accompanied by Helena Konstantanides in order to emphasise the authority of the new deputy director of Personnel, and also to gauge the quantity and quality of the work being carried out at head office, but after two months she passed the task to Anton with Helena instructed to submit to Mr Leopardis her assessments on each department and whether they were understaffed or overstaffed. Helena enjoyed her authority and within a week of being appointed sacked two typists who had suggested she had sucked up to Madame

Stephanopolous. Helena quickly showed herself to be an important cog in the fast-changing wheel that Stephanie was turning as she sought to see more women promoted to positions of responsibility. Her Board now had three women shareholders with voting rights, but only two men, her father and Anton who could vote on any resolutions. The exception was the long standing financial director whose views were always listened to with respect.

Despite all the pressures, Stephanie never forgot her femininity, and every few months tried to find time to fly aboard one of the corporation's private aircraft, either with Anton or Marianne, or the prince when he was in Europe, for two days' shopping and fun in London, Paris, Milan or occasionally Geneva where appointments were a made in advance for her to visit whichever couturier she thought might have something suitable to add to her constantly growing wardrobe. It was rare when she did not return to Athens without at least one new outfit, plus gifts for her secretaries. Nor was Sophie, who always travelled with Madame Leopardis, forgotten.

It was not until more than three months after becoming president that Stephanie decided who should be members of her inner cabinet. It initially consisted of her father, Anton, Marianne, Fred Baldwin and the president of one of the leading Swiss banking corporations where Stephanopolous International had invested in the region of forty million dollars and, in return, paid low interest rates when they decided to request a temporary loan. It was almost like borrowing their own money except that their investment earned a high rate of interest. The latter appointment had surprised her father who expected their own director of finance to be invited. When he queried her decision she joked: 'It is my decision, but your fault. You always taught me that money talks. That is the reason for my decision.'

She began the first meeting of her cabinet, with Mrs Kronion present to take minutes, by assuring those present that it was her intention to keep them informed, whenever practicable, of all major issues, but added: 'Whatever you are told must be treated as strictly confidential as you will be the only men and women privy to my plans. In carrying them to fruition I shall welcome your thoughts, advice and comments.'

She reported that she was seeking to recruit a new head of advertising and marketing so that Roberto Pinakoulakis would have more time to concentrate on her own and the corporation's public relations, publicity and promotions which were of increasing importance globally as international competition hotted up. She also gave the first details of the planned opening of her new plant in Asia which would be making the highest quality ladies' shoes for the growing worldwide market of women who insisted upon nothing but the best, adding, 'I know what they want because I am one of them.' She made no reference to the targets she had insisted must be met by her Asian workforce, but did reveal that she had initiated a painstaking search for hidden corporate talent among the company's male and female staff at headquarters with a view to promotions and possible overseas assignments. She also read out a report from Carl Ellungsen indicating that the demand for tankers was increasing as the world's economy expanded, and recommended they should consider concentrating production on tankers of no more than one hundred thousand tonnes, rather than the larger vessels weighing in excess of two hundred thousand tonnes. Her response had been to tell him she was 'not convinced', and not to take any action until he received her decision. Did any of the cabinet have any views? Herr Schulmann, the president of a Swiss bank, informed her: 'I have always made it a rule to accept the advice of those experts who know more than I do about their own specialist subject.' As a good tactician, Stephanie thanked him for his contribution which she would bear in mind when making her final decision.

Roberto reported on the success of her first press conference and suggested that their president was already recognised and respected as one of the world's industrial leaders. Stephanie announced that she had asked the corporation's finance director to send her quarterly figures showing turnover and profits from each division rather than every six months.

Back in her office she asked Anton for his thoughts on her intentions regarding the next annual bonuses. She passed him a scribbled note which indicated that, providing net profits had not fallen at the end of the current financial year which seemed unlikely, bonuses should be:

Herself – $2,500,000;
Father – $1,000,000;
Mother – $750,000;
Marianne – $500,000;
Anton – $250,000;
and the director of finance and other heads of departments
– $1,000,000 divided equally
Total $6,000,000.

She explained she had worked on the basis of contributions each would have made. She added: 'By the end of next year I shall slash the sums awarded to both my parents whose positions will become little more than sinecures, while you will be contributing so much more than either of them and will be rewarded accordingly. I have been alerted that the possibility of a kidnap attempt has probably increased by one thousand per cent since my election and subsequent publicity. As a result I am setting aside an annual sum of two hundred and fifty thousand dollars for my personal and our daughter, Cleopatra's, safety. This will cover wages for a security team of at least six, possibly more, with at least one on duty throughout every twenty-four hours, plus the bullet-proofing of the white Rolls and one of the Mercedes limousines.'

On the way home in the Rolls, she suggested that 'After you have given me my long overdue share of your love, I shall talk to Carl and tell him I accept his suggestion regarding the tonnage of future tankers because profits are more important than publicity, but the smaller tankers should, when possible, be built in our own yards in Greece. This will please Herr Schulmann and encourage him to give further independent advice.'

Before the next meeting of her cabinet she invited Mr Anthony Mortlock, a British legal expert who spoke perfect Greek and headed up the Athens office that handled much of the corporation's legal and international affairs, to join her group. She was certain he would alert her of any legal problems before they made headlines. Her timing was good because Anton had not been able to attend that meeting or the one that followed because, first, he was at sea on the delayed final trials of the largest oil tanker in the world, during which he spent more time being seasick in his Lilliputian cabin than on deck, and afterwards had flown, as president of the shipping division, together with Carl to Tokyo where they finalised negotiations with the Japanese for a medium sized tanker and a larger container ship, both to be hired for two years with options for a third year.

During the trials his seasickness began soon after they set sail from Helsinki and were buffeted by squally conditions in the North Sea. It was much worse when the tanker reached the South Atlantic where the unnamed vessel was thrown around like a cork as the new propellers battled against near hurricane winds and currents, as well as sky-scraping waves for more than twenty-four hours. By this time, however, Anton had been saved from further purgatory by one of the Finnish shipbuilders who came to his cabin carrying a small plastic pail containing a supply of Icelandic yoghurt which he promised would keep Anton free from further seasickness provided he ate nothing else until they were back in calmer waters. As Anton reported to Stephanie, 'I would not recommend it as food to be enjoyed, but as a medicine it is a lifesaver. By the second day I even began enjoying it as a meal.' While he was confined to his bunk the representatives of the international authority which provided full authorisation for the tanker to be used in every kind of weather conditions were reaching their conclusions.

On his return Stephanie had two items at the top of her agenda – the launch of the mega-size tanker, and plans for the Farnborough Air Show. After the media had reported her comments on the new aircraft at her first press conference, enquiries had been received from half a dozen potential clients, three of them from the Middle East, two from Europe and one from New Zealand. Stephanie decided she would fly into Farnborough from Athens with Anton and Sophie aboard the first of the new short haul planes. While it was on the ground it was next to its slightly larger brother that had flown in the previous day and could fly non-stop from Europe to New York. Both aircraft were open for inspection throughout the duration of the show by all visitors and the media.

She intended that Stephanopolous International would order one of the short haul aircraft for use by the president and her deputy. Both models, she was convinced, would prove magnetic showpieces. She decided that it was important for Prince Hussein to be her guest at the show where she was certain she could urge him to confirm his order for three short haul planes and two which could fly the Atlantic, and also encourage other potential buyers from the Middle East to follow his example. As soon as he accepted her invitation, she told Anton that she wanted him to meet the prince, adding, 'You are my husband, and he knows it, but he is a close friend and I shall need his help at the show All I ask is that you behave like the fourth highest shareholder in the corporation, darling. Your interests in our family corporation are second only to my own and my parents'.'

The next item on her agenda was the planning of the launch of their new multi-tonnage tanker whose name Stephanie had decided would be *Ulysses*, after her father who would also be asked to launch the vessel now that it had successfully completed its trials. Every member of the Stephanopolous family would be invited to the launch and the luncheon afterwards, including Uncle Boris who had been put out to grass, Aunt Olga and their son, Dimitrios, plus her favourite aunt and her family in the north of Greece who had written thanking her for the extra business that had resulted from Stephanie agreeing to let photographs of her wearing their swimsuits be published in advertisements and editorials. They would be asked to bring Anton's elderly parents to the launch as they had met them briefly at the wedding. But the vast majority of guests would be the workers who helped build the monster tanker in Finland and those who had fitted it out at their own yard near Piraeus where it dwarfed everything in sight as it waited to be electronically launched like a baby entering its own watery world having been given a clean bill of health by the world's seagoing doctors. At Roberto's suggestion, at each place where the workforce would sit there would be an envelope and letter which Stephanie would sign personally, and would read; 'My personal thanks for all your help in making today's ceremony possible. If you were one of those who has left your personal mark on the tanker let me tell you that I and my colleagues are actively at work seeking to ensure your future employment by Stephanopolous International. Signed, Stephanie Stephanopolous Leopardis, President.'

Meanwhile her inner cabinet heard a report from the Countess von Rugerstein in her capacity as chief executive of Stephanopolous Armaments Division on the sales successes achieved. Profits were now six or seven times higher than when they took over a company in Britain. She suggested that 'considering we are minnows in an armaments pool of piranha, I think we are entitled to feel proud of what has been achieved, but not complacent.' She also revealed that a secret piece of tank equipment on which the company's considerable profits had originally depended, and had been exclusive to the British government, was now being sold to other countries, subject to an undertaking that all new customers would either be members of the Atlantic Alliance, or recognised allies. Since then sales have grown by more than fifty per cent. She added: 'This in turn has helped open doors for the sale of our new high powered automatic lightweight rifle which is produced at our new factory in Bavaria, West Germany. Sales of the automatic weapon have passed the one million mark, and plans are in hand to increase production.'

This was followed by Fred Baldwin, the designer of the two new aircraft, announcing that there were potential orders for nine aircraft and discussions for five more were being negotiated.

When this was repeated at a meeting of the inner cabinet, the Swiss banker intervened to congratulate Stephanie on her foresight and ability to recruit people who could make her aviation visions become reality, but warned there was only a limited market for long haul privately-owned jets which was mainly in the US where requirements were almost entirely serviced by American aircraft manufacturers. 'It is like a closed shop.' He went on: 'By all means sell as many of your present long hauls as possible, but you should concentrate upon luxury short haul aircraft produced at prices that successful chief executives, and others, throughout Europe will find hard to refuse. I may be able to supply you with the names of several potential purchasers in Switzerland, Austria and Sweden. And, of course, our special banking facilities will be at your disposal at interest rates that are only available to those few corporations and individuals who have invested many millions of dollars with us.'

These were the kind of thoughts Stephanie had hoped to hear expressed by those who sat on her inner cabinet. As the meeting ended Stephanie quietly indicated to Roberto and Anton to stay behind with her secretary who would take notes of what they discussed and add them to the official minutes. Roberto was instructed to prepare a costing for an advertising campaign for their aircraft plus copy for two alternative adverts that aimed at the same restricted target audience. He was then dismissed together with her secretary. Left alone Anton was invited to come and sit beside her. She told him, 'I want to say two things. First, you impress me more every time we talk of business. You never say too much, but when you do speak it is because you have a worthwhile contribution to make. I need you so badly, and I love you so much. My mother is away; let's go to her apartment,' and she guided his hand to her breasts so that he would know how much she wanted him and told him, 'To the world I am an aggressive female tycoon without mercy on those who oppose me, but you never forget that I am also a young lady whose needs must be satisfied, but in a very different way.'

Even in the apartment there was no escape from the switchboard which sought her out because the head of her shipping department was insisting upon speaking to the president. Carl told her: 'I wanted to tell you that the last plate has been riveted into place aboard your new two hundred thousand tonne tanker, and I need your instructions regarding its name and when you would be free for the launch. By the way, it is already chartered for the first two and a half years at a fee that already covers half the construction costs. And there is interest from others who want to hire the facilities she offers. Soon it should all be profits.'

She told him, 'She is to be named *Ulysses* after my father who will carrry out the launch ceremony. As I shall be busy with aircraft for the next two weeks including being away from the office for three days at the Farnborough air show. How about the fourth Thursday of next month?' He would be responsible for ensuring a successful occasion including an invitation to the Greek prime minister and all members of her inner cabinet, her family and Prince Hussein plus, as already agreed, everyone who had helped build the ship in Finland and those who had fitted her out in Greece. She added: 'I also think it would be good public relations to invite those who have already hired the tanker and those who are considering doing so. Let me have your finalised timetable within three days.'

She confirmed Roberto's final plans including his suggestion that instead of making a formal speech, she should walk around the tables where the workforce would be sitting and greet them individually. She scribbled, 'I shall also make a speech. Let me have a draft of what you think I should say within the next forty-eight hours. And don't forget to provide seats for the media at the luncheon and the launch.'

As always her mind was working weeks ahead. She also reminded Roberto to contact Fred Baldwin and meet with him in order to draft factual and technical press releases in respect of the two aircraft at Farnborough, including the names of all confirmed buyers and others who were considering placing orders.

The British press and the specialist international media had a field day photographing one of the world's richest women talking happily with the team of workers who had helped her corporation build what was currently the world's largest tanker. It began when she rose from her seat at the luncheon and announced, 'Now I would like to meet all those who have made this day possible, and helped build this oceangoing masterpiece.'

Each of them felt the softness of her fine leather glove as she shook their hands and occasionally allowed a few of the boldest to kiss her gloved hand and enjoy the merest whiff of her perfume that was syrupy and magical beyond anything they had experienced. When she came to the senior shop steward she put her arms around him, kissed him on his cheek which immediately flushed with Finnish embarrassment and allowed him a once in a lifetime feel of a fur that cost more than he would ever be able to afford despite the bitterly cold winter weather the Finns received from the Arctic Circle. As she returned to her seat the shop steward led the singing of the Finnish version of 'For she's a jolly good fellow'. So magnetic was the speech she made that before the luncheon ended, the chief executive of one of the two corporations which had indicated they were considering chartering the tanker came over and told Stephanie that he had been so impressed by the way she conducted the launch and the luncheon that he had been convinced that Stephanopolous International was the kind of company with which he could do business. He would be writing to her colleague Carl Ellungsen, confirming their charter for a period of one year, with the option to continue for another six months.

By the time she returned home the shop steward and his colleagues were not even a memory as she dictated a short two line memo to Roberto: 'You are a genius. Thanks for the part you played in making today's launch such a success – Stephanie Stephanopolous Leopardis, President.' A similar message was sent to Carl Ellungsen. To her father she declared, 'Thanks for making it a perfect launch, and the ease with which you scored a hole in one as the champagne bottle smashed against the side of the tanker which is named after you. You are the perfect dad. Love you so much.'

Although Farnborough proved a success, it was nearly a disaster. She had sent Roberto to England five days ahead of her arrival with sufficient suitcases to ensure at least three changes for each day. She hired a helicopter to fly her and Anton to and from the show and Claridges. The press release announcing the time and place of her press conference described her as 'The new 25-year-old president of Stephanopolous International, a privately owned global industrial giant that has been valued at five hundred million dollars. Probably the most successful businesswoman in the world.'

Prince Hussein had given her permission to announce that that he was planning to order five of her new aircraft. In addition, she revealed that the designer of the aircraft and herself were currently in discussions for the sale of a further thirteen aircraft which she told the media 'I hope will prove my lucky number.' The following day one daily newspaper headlined its report, 'At twenty-five this millionairess is flying high,' and an international news agency began its own story which was circulated around the world: 'Stephanopolous International, which started life as a small shipping company at the beginning of the century, and is now estimated to be worth more than five hundred million dollars, flew into the skies at Farnborough yesterday when its twenty-five-year-old millionairess president announced sales figures during her first year in the aviation industry as totalling more than seventy-five million dollars...'

The number of journalists who swarmed into her press conference was only matched by those attending a press call by the Douglas corporation which nonetheless lagged far behind her in the editorial space given to the *wunderkind*, as well as the time allocated to her on TV and radio. As always her natural beauty captivated photographers and their picture editors who could not get enough of her wearing a white wool suit with a contrasting black mink collar and cuff, plus a black matching fur hat which served as her crown. She knew how to smile for the cameras ... and pout her lips.

It was on the final day that storm clouds appeared on her horizon. A fabulously wealthy Arab sheikh had flown in aboard his own personal 747 surrounded by a dozen security men and accompanied by two eighteen-year-olds from his harem and four equally attractive stewardesses who were also aware that their services might be required in other ways than at table. But when he saw the overpowering sexuality of Stephanie in her photographs in the newspaper he decided that it was her he wanted to purchase at Farnborough, whatever the cost. However, when he sent one of his security team to the Stephanopolous stand with an invitation for her to come to his 747 where he wished to discuss placing an order for her new aircraft, he was informed that Madame Stephanopolous only discussed business on her corporation's own stand; and she was due to fly back to Athens in two hours time.

Twenty minutes later the sheikh arrived surrounded by four security guards and demanded to see Madame Stephanopolous at once as he too was scheduled to take off on his own flight home to the Middle East in two hours. One of the two model girls Roberto had hired as glamorous hostesses during the show were warned by the sheikh that he did not like being kept waiting. Stephanie deliberately kept him kicking his heels before sending Fred Baldwin to escort the sheikh into the lounge which was furnished with several armchairs and other soft seated chairs, tables and a well-stocked cocktail cabinet. The walls were decorated with blow-up photographs of the new aircraft and shots of her tankers and container ships. Two of his guards were left outside and two accompanied him inside where Stephanie offered him her hand and directed him to the empty chair nearest to where she was seated. He immediately confirmed that he expected to discuss his requirements only with Madame Stephanopolous. Stephanie ignored what he was suggesting and introduced her husband, Prince Hussein 'a close personal friend', and Fred Baldwin, the designer of their new aircraft. She was determined to maintain her status, especially in front of this sheikh who was pompous, rude, and probably vicious. However, she was also in a good humour as further orders had been confirmed since her press conference. She asked Sheikh Abdullah, which was the name on his card, whether he would like a drink. He rejected her invitation, and she toasted his good health and thanked him for his interest in her aircraft while explaining that they now had confirmed orders for more than twenty aircraft including a booking for five from Prince Hussein. The sheikh responded that he could be interested in at least six more. She invited him to see the two planes, which were parked side by side a few hundred yards away, and said she would be happy to show them to him personally. She requested her husband and the prince to accompany her. 'Do you never go anywhere without a bodyguard?' goaded the sheikh.

She decided to encourage his obvious vanity: 'When I inherited my family's vast business empire I decided that I and my daughter needed round-the-clock protection. Shall we all go? I have two golf carts outside and as there are only six of us that will be sufficient. She deliberately sat next to the sheikh with her husband in front next to the driver, plus one of her bodyguards hanging on to the outside. The prince and Fred Baldwin followed and others of the sheikh's guards travelled behind in their own cart.

'Please accept me as being of royal blood,' she suggested, tongue-in-cheek, to her guest. 'Now that many people in the West think of me as the empress of my family's vast industrial empire. But let's stop talking about me and instead concentrate on the business that brought you here.'

Together they inspected both planes leaving Fred, her husband and the prince on the tarmac. Before they descended from the second plane she was informing him of the price of each long-haul aircraft, when he gripped her arm, and told her, 'Let me lay down my terms. I am prepared to give you a written order for ten aircraft, all long haul with the first to be delivered within four months and the other nine within twelve months. I shall also take an option for another five, all short haul. For all fifteen aircraft I shall expect a twenty per cent discount. In addition, within one year I am prepared to place a separate order for your tanker of two hundred thousand tons providing you can guarantee delivery within two years. At some other time I shall also discuss your weaponry. There is one other condition. You will fly to my country with the official contract for the ten aircraft and the option for five more. You will have no male companions not even your guards. But maids are permitted.'

Stephanie sat down. It did not often happen, but she felt sick, and a little afraid. She looked up at the sheikh who was standing over her. He reminded her of a slave driver reincarnated from ancient Egypt. All that was missing was a whip. She stood up. 'I am sorry, Sheikh Abdullah, but I am unable to accept your terms. I am calling off our negotiations. If you want our aircraft, our tanker and our military equipment they can only be discussed once you have accepted the business terms normal in all civilised nations. It is not that I do not trust you, but simply that you seem to have forgotten that I am a married woman. The only concession I am prepared to authorise is a ten per cent reduction in the price of my long haul aircraft in return for a written order for fifteen planes. The price of our tanker is not negotiable, but I will allow you the same varying reductions in the price of our automatic, high velocity weapons that are available to all our clients. I look forward to receiving your written orders. Finally, I would be prepared to meet you in Paris for the signing of these contracts, but I shall not be alone. I shall confirm my terms in writing within the next three days. If I have not received your acceptance, plus the first advance payment within seven days I shall assume that you are unable to accept our terms. I sincerely hope this does not happen. Finally I wish you a safe flight home to your own country.'

She walked down the steps of the long haul aircraft with her head high, but feeling as though her legs might give way. She told Anton: 'Let's drive back to our stand with Roberto and Fred, then collect Sophie and fly home to Athens as soon as we get clearance. Fred and the girls can clear up and close the stand. But before then I shall need a very large cognac.' Turning to the prince she suggested: 'Why don't you fly with us and spend a few days with us in Athens?'

'That is very kind of you Mme Stephanopolous, but I think I can be of more help to you by waiting and having a long talk with the sheikh. I think he needs to be reminded that you are my friend.'

While she flew home with Anton, Roberto and Sophie, the prince and the sheikh were sitting in the lounge of the Stephanopolous stand after Fred had provided them with refreshments and left them to talk privately. They were both drinking malts and enjoying Churchillian size cigars, provided by Abdullah. The conversation was dominated by the prince who was doing his best to make the sheikh understand that, although he ruled a wealthy oil rich kingdom, he could not rule Stephanie Stephanopolous. And for two reasons. Firstly, she was happily married and, secondly, she was a close friend of his and he would not allow her to be hurt or embarrassed, or threatened. 'I am simply asking you,' he sought to explain, 'to treat her with respect in any business dealings you may have with her. In my estimation she is a brilliant businesswoman, and with the two of us that is all she will ever be.' He had decided that it was none of the sheikh's business that on occasions Stephanie gave him wonderful rewards for helping expand her global empire. He went on: 'I will use whatever influence I have to encourage her to give you the same kind of concession prices she gives to any of my orders. Have you placed any orders with her at Farnborough?'

The sheikh was beginning to become irritated by the prince's attitude. His own kingdom might be small by comparison with the size of the state over which the prince's family ruled, but both had vast reserves of oil, and were impregnable as far as the rest of the world was concerned. Also, it was widely known in the Arab world that the power behind Hussein's throne was not himself or his two brothers, but his vicious, dominating sister. In fact she was the only exception he made regarding his attitude to women. He told the prince: 'To me, your Stephanie is just another woman and I will treat her as such.'

The prince, who was much the better diplomat, responded: 'You are absolutely right as far as your own kingdom is concerned. But not in Europe. Just as she might have no alternative but to bow to your demands if she were to travel to your country, so you must respect the position she holds in Europe and elsewhere in the world. When in London, Athens or anywhere else, you could be damaging your own best interests if you treated one of the fifty wealthiest women in the world with the same disdain as you regard all who have been privileged to be taken into your bed. And because I regard you as a friend, as well as fellow Muslim, I will let you into a couple of secrets I have learned since my friendship with Stephanie began long before she became the empress of her empire. Like her father before her, Stephanie is using her massive reserves of millions of dollars to undercut any rivals, even large corporations.

'The secret behind her power is that almost every share in her business is owned by her family, and the majority by herself, plus a couple of favoured friends of whom I am not one. Nor are they traded on any stock exchange. Hers is the largest privately-owned corporation in the world. Its shares do not go up and down because they are not traded, but each has an estimated value of five million dollars. And she personally owns more than fifty per cent of them, which makes her unchallengeable. Basically she is self-centred and wields immense industrial authority. She is ambitious, adores valuable possessions, but cannot be bought. And has one thing in common with both of us. She expects others to obey her.

'Finally, I am prepared to tell you that I have placed, or am planning to place, some very large orders with Stephanopolous International. For starters her fast-firing automatic weapon, which I have personally tested, is the best value armament of its kind, and devastatingly destructive on any target. When my country receives its delivery of the first fifty thousand I am ordering, our security will double overnight. I would urge you to consider buying as many of the weapons as you need. However, you may have a problem. The lady who has achieved most of the million plus sales is a German countess and I doubt if either she or Stephanie is likely to offer a demonstration in your own country of the amazing rate of fire and accuracy of their weapon. When I fired at targets of fifty, one hundred and one hundred and fifty metres, there was nothing left of any of the targets after a couple of short three second bursts. A human body would have been cut into shreds. There is more you should know. Her corporation has recently launched the largest oil tanker at sea, and also owns what is probably the world's second largest fleet of tankers. I am about to sign a contract for them to build for my country a carbon copy of the new giant with ten per cent off the normal price. I regard that as a coup. Delivery is between two and two and a half years. Feel free to request the same terms if you place a similar order. Or, of course, you could hire the big one although I am informed that before it was in the water it was already hired out for the next two and a half years, I think, by the Saudis. They also have smaller tankers for hire.'

The sheikh had listened intently to every word the prince spoke, but in his eyes Stephanie remained nothing more than a fascinating woman who foolishly regarded herself as forbidden fruit. This was a new experience for him, and he found it hard to accept. Since the age of thirteen he had commanded girls older than himself to satisfy his growing manhood while at sixteen he had the power to sign death warrants. He assumed the throne at the age of eighteen and was now rumoured to have the largest harem in the Middle East. Aboard his 747 the only passengers were women he intended to enjoy either in the air or on the ground. But now he was being forced to accept that Madame Stephanopolous would never provide him with a moment's pleasure. Although this annoyed him, he might be forced to accept that her corporation was manufacturing weapons, tankers, container ships and aircraft that his country needed, especially if she agreed to the same concession prices she allowed Prince Hussein.

She was surprised when she received his order for twelve of her new aircraft, six long and six short haul planes a week later, plus a trial order for fifty thousand of her automatic weapons, providing one of his officers was able to test their efficiency on their firing range in Bavaria. Her long haul aircraft would carry some of his bodyguards and servants when he travelled overseas. The six short haul aircraft were to be the foundation of his new airline which would make regular flights to all parts of the Middle East for those sheikhs and other businessmen who did not want to travel in planes with men and women whose status was below their own. When he explained his plans to the eight ministers who made up his government he joked, 'Who needs a personal bodyguard at thirty-five thousand feet? Just a couple of female bodies.'

24

Back home with her husband, Stephanie puzzled over how much she should tell Anton about the sheikh, his demands, and how she had extricated herself from them. As they dined alone she confided, 'I always knew I had the ability to become a successful businesswoman. Long before I became president I began planning how to use my name, my inheritance and my power to increase our wealth. Since then I have become increasingly aware that one of my biggest assets is my body, but I can assure you it will only be on offer on very rare occasions. The sheikh demanded it, but he was rebuffed and that nearly cost us hundreds of thousands of dollars until the intervention of Prince Hussein. Earlier I had made it clear to the sheikh that he must think of me as a businesswoman, and nothing more, if we were to do business together.'

Anton told her: 'I always knew you would be irresistible to other men. However, as your husband and now your immediate deputy I accept, albeit with some regret, that your first love has to be the future of the Stephanopolous empire, and that there may be occasions when what is at stake are orders worth millions of dollars which would guarantee the jobs of hundreds of men and women. In such circumstances I shall understand. All I ask is to be told when this has had to happen.'

There was an undoubted throb in her voice as she resumed: 'Now that you have met the prince you must realise that any relationship I have with him does not involve anything except a kind of thank-you present for his part in helping us win new orders, sometimes in the face of severe competition.' Anton whispered: 'You are still my empress, and I am your husband, and I think you have been overworking and need a holiday. If you must go to the office only stay until lunch time. I shall stay home and make arrangements for your private aircraft to be ready from five this evening to fly us to your private island where we'll stay until Monday morning together with Chloe and her nanny and Sophie. Hopefully we'll have nothing to do except lie in the sun and play with our daughter. Sophie will pack a couple of suitcases for you with relaxing clothes, but also a couple of evening dresses for you to change into if that is your mood. It would also be helpful if one of your secretaries would phone the villa on the island and alert them of our arrival so that everything is ready when we touch down.'

Before Stephanie left for her office, she told Sophie: 'Pack the kind of clothes I'll need for two and a half days of informality and as near to a couple of days of peace and quiet as I am ever likely to know. And as you will be coming with myself, Mr Leopardis, Chloe and her nanny, don't forget to pack a case for yourself. I shall be home early this afternoon.'

At the office her first task was to tell her secretaries of her plans and ask them to alert the staff on their island home of her impending arrival, adding, 'But I still want one of you to be on duty throughout the weekend.'

She dictated a cable to Sheikh Abdullah confirming the terms on which his order for a mix of twelve short and long haul aircraft would be accepted, with an open option for a further five short haul planes, all at a ten per cent discount on the standard price. She also restated her terms for payments, in advance of deliveries. She then added: 'Due to business pressure unable meet you Paris. Instead will send contract for signature special delivery.' She stopped when she saw a quizzical look on the face of her senior secretary when she mentioned meeting the sheikh in Paris, and her voice was as sharp as a tree-cutting axe as she looked straight at Mrs Kronion and reminded her: 'You are my senior personal private secretary which is why I am dictating this delicate cable to you and no one else. But remember, you will only hold this senior position as long as I know I can trust you implicitly. One mistake is one too many for a person in your position.' Her secretary quickly confirmed, 'I fully understand, madame.' But Stephanie remained uncertain.

Twenty minutes later a perfectly typed copy of what she had dictated was on her desk. She signed it and renewed her warnings: 'Make certain no one else has sight of this message. I hope you are beginning to understand how different life is when there is a woman at the head of this multi-million dollar enterprise. Every order we receive is seldom worth less than a six figure sum, and in such circumstances nothing, and no one, will be allowed to stand in my way of winning a signed contract. I need to be absolutely certain that I have your loyalty and obedience and that nothing you hear in this office will ever be revealed in any form to any third party.'

Mrs Kronion was beginning to worry about her future, and knew she would never find such a well-paid job. 'Madame, all I can say is that your father, for whom I worked for almost ten years, thought I was worth what I was paid. I don't believe I ever let him down. He trusted me. I hope very quickly to prove to you that I shall always be as loyal to you as I was to your father. Please trust me.'

'Thank you, Mrs Kronion.' However, she was still not as sure as her words might suggest.

Forty-eight hours passed before a cable was received from Sheikh Abdullah. It was not a direct reply to her own cable, but it seemed as though it had been dictated as a result of his conversation with the prince. It confirmed his acceptance of her terms, and added that he was also interested in placing an order for her high velocity automatic weapon, and discussing a possible order for a new tanker of the same dimensions as the monster tanker she had recently launched. Such orders needed to be discussed in detail He was prepared to fly to London. When?

She showed the cable to Anton whose response accepted that Prince Hussein's power and influence appeared to have had a sobering influence on the sheikh whose orders, if confirmed, could be worth hundreds of millions of dollars to Stephanopolous International.

Mrs Kronion was given further dictation. 'This is to Sheikh Abdullah:

Your cable received. Will do all possible to meet requests. Will begin construction your first aircraft immediately receive agreed advance payment. Suggest meeting at Bayerischerhof Hotel Munich where I shall also stay for two nights and arrange demonstration of automatic weapon produced locally. Suggest 30/31 this month with first meeting fifteen-thirty 30th followed by demo. You will be my guest for dinner that evening. Please make your own bookings as do not

354

know how many will be with you. On 31st we can hopefully finalise orders for both weapons and tanker? In case you not know, Prince Hussein has ordered fifty thousand weapons, plus option. Also planning to order tanker. Grateful your urgent confirmation Munich.

She turned to Anton: 'I want you to come with me and play host. I shall also take Sophie.' And to Mrs Kronion: 'Book the presidential suite for Mr Leopardis and myself with, if possible, an adjoining room for Sophie. Also book double bedrooms for Carl Ellungsen and Roberto and a double room for two members of my security team. When making these bookings emphasise that they are all provisional, but will be confirmed or cancelled within seven days.' Next she dictated a memo to Carl Ellungsen:

Possibility of receiving orders for two more largest tanker. Please check estimated delivery times, and whether both could be constructed at same time, and if not how soon after construction of first tanker could construction of second commence? And when start. Request info 48 hours. Shall need you to join me on visit to Munich. Keep 29/30/31 free.

She telephoned Fred Baldwin and invited him to dinner in Athens the following weekend to discuss the thirty-plus orders received since Farnborough, and how they should be handled. This was followed by a phone call to Marianne confirming that she would be needed in Munich for meeting and providing a demonstration to Sheikh Abdullah, and she could stay at her castle, but attend all meetings at the Bayerischerhof Hotel.

Despite the continuous pressures, all five of them still had their weekend of relaxation on their island home where Chloe never wanted to stop playing with her parents until finally she was tired and all she wanted was her bed and the care of her nanny. And for once both Sophie and Chloe's nanny dined with Stephanie and Anton under the stars each evening but the husband and wife had their cognac and coffee alone in the lounge of the hilltop villa, and Anton wished he had a glass ball into which he could look and see where she would be leading them in ten, even five years time. Stephanie's happiest moment had been when Chloe told her, 'You are so beautiful, Mummy.' And Mummy replied, 'I take after you, darling.'

Despite their different temperaments, both Stephanie and Anton were completely aware of the part Sophie had played in easing the path for the future president, and more than ever now that she had reached the peak of her own Everest. Sophie, her adoring and personal maid, who seemed able to anticipate all her mistress's whims and needs, while selecting the correct clothes, jewellery and toiletries that were necessary for her appointments the following day and after office hours if they were not being driven home until later in the evening. She saved Stephanie uncountable hours which she was able to devote to her office, meetings and social events. Nothing was ever too much trouble for Sophie. She was a walking description of the word 'treasure'. Hearing this, and agreeing with it, Stephanie let Anton into a secret. 'A couple of months ago, as my personal thank you, I had the home of her parents in the village on the outskirts of our estate completely repainted inside and out and largely refurnished. I told them their daughter was paying for it out of her wages, with just a little help from me.'

Anton knew that men and women everywhere were in awe of his wife. Yet she surprised him once more by telling him that he was playing the role of Sophocles in her life by showing her the way to combine wisdom with power. 'I love you, Anton,' and she smiled her love.

The timing of Chloe's birth had been like a gift from the gods. Ulysses had lived just long enough to hold his granddaughter in his arms, but ten days later he had a mammoth heart attack and was gone before any medical help could reach him. It was hard to imagine that any more people could have lined the streets of Athens for the funeral of a businessman. As his daughter put it in the oration she gave in the cathedral of Athens: 'He lived and ruled like a benevolent emperor, and is being laid to rest with the honours worthy of his achievements.'

Now Stephanie vowed never to forgot that as the president of the family business, and head of the Stephanopolous clan, she had to follow where he left off, and it was her task to perpetuate the glory of their name for future generations. This she was already achieving, and by training Chloe to accept her destiny, she would be securing everyone's future.

Christiana, now a widow and a dowager was expected to find a new life for herself, or travel the world in her yacht whose crew and staff were never allow to forget who she was and the power her millions gave her. What remained difficult for her to accept was that it was now her daughter, and not herself, who was all-powerful. It was also her daughter, not her, who was increasingly recognised as 'one of the ten best dressed women in the world', in the biggest selling popular newspapers, while on the business and financial pages she was lauded as 'the *wunderkind* of industry who dressed better than most Hollywood stars'. Invitations poured in for Stephanie to attend dinners, receptions, first nights, but only a handful were accepted. Mostly she was driven straight home from her office with Anton, where her first task was to have an hour's romp with Chloe who was far more important than any reception or first night. The rest of Stephanie's time was spent running her empire. As empress, she worked from an office where she had installed a small boardroom table to help balance the feminine look she had demanded and achieved with flowers plus oil paintings that reflected the sunshine for which Greece was famous, as well as armchairs covered in light apple green satin. Here day after day executives from her divisions attended meetings to plan the future or to find answers to whatever had gone wrong. Inevitably this sometimes meant sackings, but also promotions.

As the corporation's president she had annexed her mother's apartment and used it for moments of quiet, hoped-for escape from the telephone, or the chance to be alone with Anton. Here they often ate the light lunch sent up from the director's kitchen. But whatever she was doing, wherever she went, she was never less than dressed to perfection, and lavishly. To every one of the two hundred plus who worked at headquarters, except her secretaries, she was an enigma. She ruled their lives from afar, as though she was living on another planet. She sincerely believed she would be wasting her time to worry about individuals in her employ; that was a responsibility she passed to people like Helena Konstantinides. A note from Helena suggesting that someone had potential for possible promotion would lead to an interview with the president, and if they impressed her they would within a few weeks receive a memo, personally signed by Madame Stephanie Stephanopolous

Leopardis, informing them where their future lay, and in what capacity. Refusal was never an option. They were being given an opportunity which they had to grasp, wherever it took them.

25

Ten years to the day after Stephanie had been elected a member of the board of directors of the empire over which she now ruled, she hosted a meeting of her inner cabinet and, the same afternoon, a full board meeting. She informed both meetings that, just after she had taken over as president, she was asked by Reuters did she not think she was too young to assume such responsibilities for an empire worth five hundred million dollars. 'I answered that I would prefer to give him my answer sometime in the future when it would be fair to judge me. Today, I am happy to reveal figures that justify the confidence my father placed in me. A few days ago I received an estimated valuation of the present resources of our corporation. They now exceed not five, but six hundred million dollars.'

The next hurdle was to bring to an end the two years' moratorium she had placed on herself as a gesture to her mother. Now it was time for Stephanie and her own family to take possession of the mansion home which had legally been hers after the death of her father. Stephanie Stephanopolous Leopardis was now determined that her daughter Cleopatra should spend the rest of her childhood in the mansion she would one day inherit. Whatever the consequences in her relationship with her mother, Stephanie intended to take possession of not only the mansion but everything else that was now hers by right and law, unless she gave permission for it to be used or occupied by someone else. It was now time to keep the promise she had made to both her parents that when, and if, her father passed away first, she would permit her mother to get over the shock of being alone for two years before claiming what belonged to Stephanie, including all their homes and estates, the next door village with its shops and cottages, the Cyclades island they owned in the Aegean, as well as their cars … everything except her mother's personal possessions, and her secret hideaway in the woods.

Stephanie hoped the inevitable change could be agreed without trauma. To counter the blow, she would offer her mother the only slightly smaller mansion that she and Anton had built and occupied since their marriage. This meant she would still be living on the three hundred hectare estate where she had lived since marrying Ulysses. To make the upheaval as easy as possible Stephanie would offer to move out of her present home and take possession of the penthouse apartment which her mother thought of as her own, but in fact was owned by Stephanopolous International, which also owned the entire block of nineteen expensive apartments within walking distance of both the royal palace and their HQ. She would stay there for one month, which would give her mother plenty of time to make a leisurely move from one mansion to the other.

The crunch came after an innocuous dinner between herself, Anton, her mother and Byron, her aide, in the mansion that was still Christiana's home. The four had adjourned to the library where coffee and cognac were served and the servants dismissed before Stephanie fired the first salvo that would bring her mother's unofficial reign to its inevitable end, and signal the beginning of her daughter's succession to the throne and everything she rightly inherited. What was unknown was how much blood might flow before the white flag of surrender was finally raised by the older of the two women. From that evening onwards many of the jewels that Christiana had thought were her own because they had been presented to her by her late husband in the early days of their marriage, but were in fact part of the Stephanopolous estate and owned by its president and head of the family, were reclaimed by Stephanie. She insisted however that her mother, who was not yet fifty, was entitled to the respect that was still her due now she had reached dowager status.

Christiana was still sitting in the same tall, high backed armchair that she had regarded as her throne from the very first day she had arrived in Athens from Australia two weeks after her marriage. Overnight she became the empress of an empire with the right to wear priceless black pearls, emeralds, diamonds and rubies. She thought it could never end, until her daughter said in a voice that was commanding and imperious, 'Out of the love I have for you, I have delayed for more than two years my decision to take possession and occupy this mansion.

360

That day has now dawned. You have one month, or a little longer if you really need it, to arrange your move from this home into the mansion which I and Anton occupy a quarter of a mile away. You will still live on the Stephanopolous estate; we shall still be neighbours. I have already taken over your white Rolls Royce which was never yours, but belonged to the corporation, but you may continue to use Ulysses's black Rolls unless I require it on behalf of the firm. I also want you to hand over to me within the next ten days every piece of jewellery that you inherited from the first wife of Ulysses. They were all family heirlooms given into the possession of the lady who bore the prestigious title of Madame Stephanopolous and châtelaine of this mansion and our many other homes and residences. In due time I shall pass them to your granddaughter.

'If you decide to challenge my authority in these or any other matters, you will force me to withdraw my offer of my own home, and I shall instruct my solicitor to forward you a copy of my late father's will in which all this is made clear. As he sensibly put it: "I have made adequate provision for my wife to continue to enjoy the lifestyle she has known since our marriage".'

'What you are suggesting is scandalous.'

'This is how it is going to be, mother. You should be grateful that I have delayed asking for what is rightfully mine for so long. Let me make it clear, there is no debate. You either do as I ask, or face the consequences. Do as I ask and you will find me the same loving daughter I have always tried to be. And to show you how loving and caring I am, you still have a Rolls which you can regard largely as your own, and the corporation will continue paying the chauffeur's wages. But he will be in my employ, not yours.'

Before leaving she confirmed that she would arrange for her solicitors to send written confirmation of all the changes she was making as the president of Stephanopolous International, and thus, automatically the head of the Stephanopolous family. 'The letter will itemise all properties which, understandably, you regarded as your own although in fact they belonged either to the family or the corporation. All you have to do is to sign the document which will accompany the letter, and return all the itemised pieces of jewellery to my solicitors.'

When the letter arrived Christiana could not believe what she was reading. Not only was she being forced to vacate the mansion and staff that she had controlled for more than two decades, she no longer owned her penthouse apartment in the heart of Athens, her apartment at headquarters, their private Greek island, or their villa in Northern Greece in the shadows of the holy mountain of Mount Athos as well as the villa in Monte Carlo. She was also losing the fleet of cars, limousines and run-abouts, unless sanctioned by the new president, with the exception of the corporation's black Rolls. Even the horses in the stables could not be ridden without her daughter's consent. No property of any kind was permitted to be removed from any of the family homes without written permission from Madame Stephanie Stephanopolous Leopardis. The letter stipulated that from the date she took up occupation in her new mansion home within the grounds of the family estate, its maintenance would be her personal responsibility, but the said Madame Stephanopolous Leopardis would be happy to give her permission for any reasonable number of staff, up to a total of eight, to leave their employ at her present home and be relocated to her new mansion; all other staff would now be in the employ of Madame Stephanie Leopardis together with her own present staff who would take up residence 'in your former home'. No reference was made to her hideaway which had been purchased with her own money. Finally the letter ended, 'We have been asked by the president of the corporation to remind you that you are obligated to hand over all jewellery that previously belonged to the first wife of Ulysses Stephanopolous, as each item is the property of the Stephanopolous estate, as listed on the attached sheet. Each piece should be itemised and delivered to our offices within the next ten days from the date of this letter.'

Christiana could not believe that her only daughter was taking such decisions, while she was forgetting that she had inherited fifty million dollars in her late husband's will, and was still the owner of shares in Stephanopolous International worth an estimated one hundred and seventy-five million-plus dollars and would continue living in a luxury mansion on the family's estate. All she understood was that she would now have a staff of not more than eight when she had become used to at least twenty-five. To her it seemed she was being robbed by her own daughter.

26

The relationship between mother and daughter became almost non-existent. They conferred through their legal representatives, but all the aces were in one hand. While Christiana thought her daughter was being deliberately cruel, Stephanie knew that her mother would finally have to submit, and it was nothing more than foolishness to prolong the agony, yet could not forget that she was still her mother; the lady who had brought her up to understand that what finally mattered was having the strength to command and rule. Some kind of blunt implement kept hammering into her brain that this time the target was her mother, and not some foolish typist. Almost as an act of penance she decided to employ a third chauffeur so that Christiana would always have a driver for her Rolls. She sent a handwritten note to her mother confirming this decision and also let her know she could visit the family's island in the Aegean whenever she liked, 'But please phone my secretary to make sure it is not being used for corporate entertaining.' Blood was proving thicker than water.

However, she was back in her role of president when she drove her own two-seater Mercedes into the forest a few kilometres from their estate before pulling up outside the pub that was Christiana's hideaway from prying eyes. Her target was not her mother, but Mrs Castralia, the woman who ran the pub with her husband and took care of her mother whenever she visited. She did not need to introduce herself as she was immediately recognised from the number of times her photographs appeared in newspapers and on Greek TV – especially the television news.

'I want to talk to you in private. Give me the key to my mother's apartment.' The pub's landlady asked her to follow her, only to be told by Stephanie, 'I asked you to hand me the key. Tell your husband to stay here and look after any customers.'

'I meant no disobedience, Madame,' she assured Stephanie.

363

'For your sake, I hope not. Just get it into your head that from now onwards I am your mistress, not my mother.'

'Yes, madame.' And she wondered whether a poisoned dart was about to tear into her. Nor did she have more than a moment to find out.

'I am aware that my mother owns this pub, but the Stephanopolous corporation owns the land on which it has been built. I could have it pulled down if I needed the land for a new development, or if I didn't. But I have no such intention. Nothing is going to change providing you understand that you are now working first for me, not my mother.'

Stephanie sat down on what she felt certain was her mother's favourite armchair. The landlady was left standing.

'Your duties will largely be unchanged. You will continue to accept any instructions my mother gives you But you will never, under any circumstances, let her know of my visit. If I ever believe there has been a leak you will be dismissed without a reference. But obey my simple instructions and you probably have a job for the rest of your life. All you have to do is to let me know by phone or by letter whenever my mother pays a visit whether alone, or with a companion. I shall want to know his name. For your own sake, don't try to mislead me. In my position I have ways of finding out if I am being cheated. Don't risk it.' As she left she could see that Mrs Castralia was trembling, and her words had hit home.

Back in her Mercedes, she knew that her mission had been in the best interests of the corporation of which her mother was the second largest shareholder. Christiana was now a widow, and a very wealthy one, which meant she could become a target for young and older men on the make. Every widow was in that situation, but someone as wealthy as her mother might easily become an endangered victim of a deliberate smooth-talker. That might spell danger for the corporation as Christiana knew at least some of the plans for the corporation's future. She might become a target for blackmailers. That was a risk Stephanie was not prepared to take. Provided Byron remained her aide and constant companion, she would not interfere. He was on the firm's payroll and she could deal with him if it ever became necessary. However, if a new face was suddenly brought to the inn, she wanted to know. Her mother's love life did not

364

interest her, but if there was someone unknown to the president of the corporation, her daughter would need to be concerned and certainly interested. An accidental revelation of a company secret was what she feared most. Such a leak to any source would be a problem too many.

Nevertheless, there were some security matters that she did not even discuss with Anton, but which needed her attention now that she had settled into a daily routine for running the corporation. When she demanded the code to open her father's wall safe behind her desk Mrs Kronion wrote it out for her because she was aware that refusal would lead to instant dismissal. Her worry was that Mr Ulysses had once mentioned, as he put some sheets of notepaper into his safe, that they were very personal documents, and the secretary of the late president was fearful that personal, private and confidential papers might might now be read by the new president, who was his daughter. Stephanie, of course, had no idea what she might find, and was certainly not looking for any particular document or information; as far as she was concerned her interest lay solely in the right to know everything by whoever was president of the corporation. However, as she knew that all the official, and confidential letters and documents were stored in the large Chubb safe in Mrs Kronion's office, she was intrigued why her father had needed a second safe behind the desk in his own office.

When Stephanie inserted the code to the wall safe her first discovery provided her with details of some never-discussed financial arrangement with contacts around the world, and some letters from women with whom her father had enjoyed himself, thanking him for his generosity, usually jewellery or a mink coat or jacket. But there were also half a dozen scribbled notes from her mother warning her husband that if he did not respond positively to what she was requesting he would be denied her bed until he changed his mind.

As she read and reread them, her daughter began realising that while she was making these and other threats her mother must have been receiving not far short of two million dollars in bonuses annually. Stephanie was furious. But nothing annoyed her more than the last letter. In it Christiana had threatened to sue for divorce in the United States where they both had a business residence, and would claim fifty per cent of his stake

365

in Stephanopolous International and a further fifty per cent of all his other assets unless she was elected to the board of the family's corporation, and given complete control of all their business divisions covering textiles and the world of fashion, including all plants involved in the production of cotton and silk fabrics for dresses and blouses as well as shoes. She had been given all she demanded. Her father must have recognised that if she carried out her threat and won a divorce, she would win control of the corporation. And that might lead to the Stephanopolous empire becoming a target for predators.

Learning this, Stephane carried out an exhaustive investigation into the state of the division which her mother controlled. She read through her reports on visits to their plants and factories in China and elsewhere in Asia, and the distribution chain she had built up in South America. Inevitably she was impressed by the growth in sales her mother had achieved, as well as the techniques she had adopted to produce higher profits year by year. A few quick calculations told Stephanie that her mother was producing nearly ten per cent of the corporation's total profits. Members of local political parties in the Far East and elsewhere, whether left or right wing, were in her pay, but only when they used their authority to guarantee high levels of production, sales and easy distribution facilities. The pockets of less powerful trade unionists on factory floors were given crisp dollar notes, but only when the workers under their control met the high targets she personally set. Christiana made it clear to everyone who received her kick-backs that whether the factory was making cheap or high quality textiles, dresses, blouses, skirts or shoes, production costs had to be kept low. Her motto was 'make 'em cheap, sell them dear'. In a way it was the same tactic that she used on her aide, Byron, which was 'treat him mean, and make him keen'. Yet her high level of profits was achieved without any specialist assistance. She simply had her way by making threats, and occasionally carrying them out.

As she continued her probe, it seemed that her mother's two secretaries spent much of their time sending cables, letters and postcards to Christiana's overseas 'family' who were mostly executives, salesmen and their wives, plus a few of her biggest customers. Most were critical, so why the postcards? All was revealed in one of Christiana's reports to Ulysses. It revealed a once a year visit to the countries in South America where they had warehouses to which all textile and fashion productions were sent, stored and then distributed. This centralisation kept overheads at a low level. The warehouses were also the headquarters for her managers, each responsible for sales in a single country, and under them were teams of salesmen. In addition, the Stephanopolous name and reputation had enabled her to negotiate concession rents, while threatening to withdraw her multi-million dollar investments in any country that hindered her expansionist aims. Everyone seemed to be in her pocket which was probably why her managers received monthly wages that, on average, were one-third of the rates paid for equivalent jobs in western Europe, together with her salesmen's, whose earning were solely on a commission, plus bonuses when they exceeded her targets.

Christiana's once a year visits to South America always included Brazil, Chile, Argentina and Ecuador, where the highest sales took place, but increasingly included Bolivia and Peru where she was planning to establish a warehouse from which the increasing levels of production and sales would be distributed. Wherever her mother went, her technique was basically the same. First, the managers and salesmen were called to a meeting where she lashed them with her tongue for not reaching her targets, a situation she warned would not be allowed to continue. Sacking would be inevitable for those who let her down again. Such meetings were followed by a buffet lunch to which their wives, mothers and girlfriends were invited, but the men were not allowed to sit with them. This enabled Christiana to talk to the women out of hearing of their men folk. She warned them that any of their men who, for a second year running, failed to meet the targets she set would have to be sacked. It was in their hands to avoid the threatened dismissals. It was their responsibility to encourage, and if necessary force, their men to work longer hours. If their pressure succeeded there were bonuses to be won. Women being women were fascinated and intrigued by the diamonds she wore, but never envious because they were brought up to accept that such wealth was not meant for women like themselves. Occasionally her gems inevitably came within touching distance, which was why there were always two guards with truncheons on either side of her with instructions to disable any hand that dared reach out to touch her or her jewels. Whoever tried ended with a damaged wrist, plus confirmation that she not only held the aces, but the kings, queens and jacks as well. The following day the man in their life would be dismissed. Word quickly spread that she was all-powerful. However, the others began receiving postcards. There were two kinds. A handful congratulated them on how well their men were doing as a result of their influence, and enclosed a present of twenty dollars ... 'to be spent making yourselves more desirable'. But periodically there were final warnings to 'use your feminine wiles a little harder, or my axe will have to fall'. Less than five per cent needed to be dismissed, and they were quickly replaced.

Yet Stephanie remained puzzled. During all the many confidential meetings she had with her father as she prepared to take over the presidency, he had never once mentioned his wife's successes, or the contribution she regularly made towards the corporation's profits. It was impossible to believe that he regarded such a money-making division as some kind of toy to keep his wife amused and occupied, while he strayed into younger beds. Why his secrecy? Now she could never ask him. She probed Mrs Kronion as to whether her father had specifically instructed her not to include details of the textile division when he went through the final figures for the year's trading. 'No, madame. He simply asked for the divisions he wished to see.'

'Didn't such a constant omission of the textile division surprise you?'

'No, madame. He told me what he required and that was all I brought him.'

'You had better remember that when I ask for figures or facts about our divisions, that will mean all divisions. See if you can trace my mother, and tell her that her daughter would like to see her in the president's office.'

It was situations like this that caused Stephanie to worry about Mrs Kronion, and whether she was being paid more than she was worth. Nevertheless she was sufficiently perceptive to guess that if Christiana was in the building she would be in the office of the director of personnel which was now occupied by Helena Konstantinides who would not dare dispute anything the former vice-president said, or more correctly, demanded. She guessed right. 'Madame, I have a message for you. Your daughter would like to see you in the president's office, when you have time.'

'Did she really say that, Mrs Kronion?'

'Yes, madame. Her exact words. But I think it is urgent.'

Five minutes later Madame Stephanopolous was in the new-look presidential suite. Stephanie got up from her desk, kissed her mother and told her, 'I think it time we talked about the future of the corporation ... and your part in it. Let us sit in the armchairs.'

Stephanie told her that she had read all the interesting reports she had sent to her father during the last several years when he was still president. Whether deliberately, or by accident, her father had never mentioned the successes Christiana had achieved. She had only found out when she opened the division's files which were kept in the corporation's confidential safe. Could she think of any reason for what seemed like deliberate secrecy?

Christiana hesitated, 'I don't know, but I can guess. While I don't like speaking unkindly of the dead, suffice to say that your father and I lived a lie for several years. But I had him over a barrel and he dared not deny me anything. I had warned him that if he didn't do as I asked I would seek a divorce in the US and claim half his interest in the Stephanopolous empire, as well as half of all his other assets. I don't think I would ever have carried out my threat as it could have had deadly consequences for Stephanopolous International, but he could not take such a risk. Perhaps he hated me for the successes I was chalking up.'

Stephanie was so happy they were alone. She kissed her mother, and admitted: 'I owe you an apology. I just did not know how much you have been contributing to the profitability of our corporation. Not far short of ten per cent of our annual profits are due to you and the textile division. Please forgive me. Nor did I know how far apart you and dad had grown. Perhaps I was not really interested. It was your life, just as Anton and I are living ours. Can I borrow your ideas about postcards and your twenty dollar incentive award for wives? It is brilliant. And now, something equally important. Would you accept a verbal invitation to join the small inner cabinet I have formed to forge the path ahead for the corporation? On the board itself we have too many experts, but not enough visionaries ... like me and you.'

'Thank you, darling. Let me know the time, date and place, and I'll be there.'

'Come and have dinner tonight with Anton and myself.'

'Only if I can bring Byron.'

It was a happy evening as everyone forgot the recent family disagreements, mistakes and what had been written and spoken. After dinner they adjourned to the main lounge for brandies or other tummy settling drinks. At Stephanie's suggestion they talked about everything except Stephanopolous International. And no one clashed. When it was getting late she suggested it was time to adjourn, but hoped there would be many more such occasions. Her mother expressed the wish to see her granddaughter before she left. Stephanie's reply was to make it clear that it did not matter if they woke her nanny, but they must try not to wake Chloe. The two of them took off their shoes and tiptoed up the stairs to the nursery suite while the two night duty maids curtsied as they passed. Christiana could not resist giving her grandchild a kiss on her forehead. She stirred, smiled, and went back to sleep.

Halfway down the stairs, Christiana stopped and whispered to Stephanie: 'I learned soon after I married your father that he was a very generous man, but secretive about personal matters, although seldom about the business. I knew everything that was happening at headquarters, or thought I did, but it was not until the last moment that I learned of his decision to pass the presidency to you in preference to myself. However I knew more about his private life than he imagined. As his affairs became more frequent they also seemed to be more open. With his kind of wealth he could have almost any woman he wanted whether mannequins, actresses, singers, foreign women with titles, as well as celebrities. There were that many. They all thought they were onto a good thing. And they were. But so was I. I accepted there was little I could do about his wanderings if I wanted to remain the wife of one of the wealthiest men in the world. Every time I discovered another affair he bought me an expensive piece of jewellery as compensation But the finest of them all was the diamond collar that had belonged to the last Czarina of Russia. It cost him two million dollars at an auction in Geneva. That, and most of my collection of personal jewellery, I shall leave to Cleopatra; what a lovely name.'

Stephanie's response was to thank her mother for revealing at least some of her secrets, adding, 'I think we have opened a new chapter in both our lives. As president I can now pick your brains for the benefit of our global empire, but you must never openly oppose any decisions I make. That I do not accept from anyone, and in the circumstances I have to include my mother. However, now that we understand one another, and I hope we do, together with Anton we shall form what might be described as an inner family cabinet of three.

'Anton and I remain immensely happy because he understands that at the office and anywhere we go on business, although he is now a senior executive and a member of the Board, I am the president of the corporation. He is a sounding board for my ideas for future expansion. I think I love him more today than when we married. Now that you and I are alone, let's sit down on the stairs. Tell me about you and Byron.'

'He is a great comfort to me, but he is never permitted to forget who I am, or what he is. He shares my bed, but is like a dog on a lead. He does what he is told. He is a stop-gap in my life. Some day I hope to meet someone who will truly take the place of your father. After all, I am still in my forties, fabulously wealthy, and quite an attractive woman, although I say so myself. Byron is expendable, but I think you as president should make use of his undoubted business talents elsewhere in the Stephanopolous empire when I unlock his handcuffs.'

She sounded like the perfect misanthrope to Stephanie who was herself distrustful of everyone until they proved themselves. If anything, her mother was the more vindictive of the two. Stephanie often debated with herself how, if humans were also animals, they had managed to separate themselves from the beasts whose brains mostly reacted only to inplanted urges. Beasts only enjoyed sex during the mating season. For the rest of the year they were just brutes. Yet she was prepared to admit she had much of the beast inside herself. She, too, knew how to inflict punishment on those who stepped out of line, and enjoy it. When she was subjecting a man to a verbal onslaught that aimed at destroying his confidence as well as his manhood, the physical pleasure of her bullying occasionally led to an orgasm. Her personal debate usually ended with her being forced to accept that the only difference between humans and the beasts was that we had found ways to live in far larger communities while they mostly had packs and prides, but in all it was the few who ruled, and the many who lived out their lives subservient and afraid of tomorrow.

Stephanie accepted that there was unlikely ever to be any close rapport between the two. In the case of herself and her mother they were too much alike; her mother resented the power her daughter now wielded, even over her, and the simple fact that she had no authority, unless it was granted by her daughter. For the moment Stephanie contented herself with telling her mother, 'As the largest shareholder at Stephanopolous International after myself, I shall always listen to what you have to say, but I will make all the decisions, and you will obey them.' That was the moment when Christiana knew that she was subservient to her own daughter, just as Stephanie would one day be forced to accept the authority of Cleopatra, the little mite whose forehead she had recently kissed.

To complete the undermining of her mother's confidence, Stephanie told her before they rejoined Anton and Byron, 'I have decided to divide the textile division into two halves. You will control all of South America and Eastern Europe, which is currently the most successful of the two parts, while Marianne will take charge of all production, most of which is carried out in China and elsewhere in Asia. Both of you will report directly to me. I will arrange new offices for yourself, Byron and your two secretaries at headquarters. That means you will move out of Personnel where I understand you have been making life difficult for Helena Konstantinides who is already running the department to my complete satisfaction. I expect to appoint her Director of Personnel in the near future.'

Christiana accepted, because she had no alternative, that there was no going back. The past could not be recalled, and the future was unpredictable. Her days of dominance were ended, except in South America. Perhaps she should go there more often. There she ruled as she done for so many years in Athens. She remained convinced that the more she continued to raise the profits of the corporation, the more her contribution would be recognised and appreciated. Nevertheless, she found it hard to dispel the feeling that her daughter regarded her as little more than another employee. And in Christiana's vocabulary that was almost a derogatory word.

As always Sophie was waiting for her mistress in the main

bedroom after she and Anton had waved goodbye to their guests. Stephanie, almost automatically, accepted the garments Sophie had hung outside her wardrobes for her to wear for her office appointments next day. It was an uncanny relationship of complete trust that had grown between them since that morning ten years ago when she had dictatorially appointed a slip of girl one year younger than herself to be her personal maid. Today it was Sophie who made it possible for her to combine being wife, mother and business tycoon.

As she cuddled Anton, she reminded him that tomorrow morning they had a meeting with a team from the hotel group which five years earlier had been awarded a ten-year contract to manage the most successful of the two five-star luxury hotels they owned in the centre of Athens. Tomorrow they had to renegotiate the terms for the second five years. She intended to insist that Stephanopolous International should in future receive a five per cent increase in their portion of the profits the management group earned from the hotel, plus an increased rental charge of ten per cent for the next five years. She also revealed that her mother's relationship with Byron was nothing more than a convenience. She also explained, 'I intend to keep my mother firmly under my thumb. She resents being powerless, but that is how she will remain. She has achieved amazing results for our textile division and, as a result, I have invited her to join my inner cabinet. Finally, I shall take her with us to Munich when we meet Sheikh Abdullah. I am sure she will want to seduce him. Nothing gives her more pleasure than slipping a noose round a man's neck while slowly tightening it until he is completely under her control, like Byron. The sheikh could provide her first failure, or maybe not.'

She pressed a button by her side three times which was an alert that she wanted to see her housekeeper. Tamara arrived immediately, curtsied and was told to ring her chauffeur and tell him to bring the Rolls to the front door in fifteen minutes.

To Anton she said: 'It is a lovely evening and I think it time we had a walk round the village where we were married. It is more than six months since we were there at Christmas distributing presents.' She went upstairs where Sophie re-combed and brushed her hair, and slipped her arms into the sleeves of a fur bolero to protect her from any cooling evening breezes.

They stepped out of the Rolls on the edge of the village after telling her chauffeur to bring the Rolls into the centre in twenty minutes and park by the communal green. Word quickly spread that Madame Stephanopolous Leopardis and her husband were walking in the village. Women curtsied and men bowed. She stopped to talk to some of the older among them who all thought of her as the equivalent of royalty, a benevolent empress who almost always tried to accept, through her steward, their requests for improvements to their properties. Nor did she forget to increase their rents. As she gave a final goodbye wave to the villagers who were now surrounding the Rolls, she told her chauffeur to drive slowly and whispered to Anton, 'I hope they appreciate that it is only a young couple like ourselves who would spend time coming to see them. I am sure that neither my father nor his father before him ever even thought about them except at Christmas. For my mother, they don't really exist. They are just people who pay us their rents, nothing more. However, I remember the saying I often heard when I was being brought up by nannies, that if you wanted to get a job done, ask a busy man or woman. Like us. We're busy, but we still find time for them.' She squeezed his hand.

Once out of sight of any prying eyes, she rested her head on Anton's shoulder and whispered: 'One last secret before we go home and make love. I love being treated like an empress by people who are more than twice my age, but there is nothing more wonderful than knowing that the man who means everything to me will soon be showing how much I mean to him.'

And to her chauffeur she added: 'Can we go a little faster, please?'